To Bob Parker,

A great player &
coach. Best wishes
for a great
season

DEATH BY DROWNING

DEATH BY DROWNING

By

GARY W. EVANS

Death by Drowning

Copyright ©2017 by Gary W. Evans

ISBN: 978-1-68102-399-1
Library of Congress: 2017933726

Printed in the United States of America

DEATH BY
DROWNING

CHAPTER 1

"Goddamnit!"

La Crosse County Sheriff's Deputy Charlie Berzinski had been dreaming of a tall stack of pancakes. He was thinking a visit to Ma's Diner on the south side might wash away the November gloom.

Now that dream was shot and already forgotten.

The call had just come in to the 911 operator. A fisherman found a body entangled in the Mississippi brush off La Crosse's far south side. The operator routed the call to Charlie. Suddenly, this quiet Saturday morning had become anything but.

Charlie was a hulk of a man. At six-five he weighed nearly 300 pounds, and his temperament made him someone most people on the wrong side of the law tried to avoid. His home life wasn't particularly happy and it carried over to his work. More than one lawbreaker had suffered his wrath.

On this morning it was his desk that had taken the brunt of it, and the vibrations, whether from his hand or his exclamation, echoed through the department. His colleagues up and down the hall shuddered and kept their heads down. Charlie was a great guy—a teddy bear sort of man. But when he was on a case, he was anything but warm and fuzzy.

Everyone was glad when he picked up the phone, muttering to himself. "Yeah, Al? We got another floater."

"You're kidding, right?" answered Detective Al Rouse of the La Crosse Police Department. Most Saturdays, Charlie and Al had breakfast together since the two offices were only blocks away, and Al too had been dreaming of a Ma's meal. "Tell me you're kidding."

"That's what a caller said. If it's true, I'll tell you this assignment ain't for shit," responded Charlie.

Rouse, much smaller than Charlie at five-ten and 180 pounds, was handsome in a rough-cut sort of way. He had a smile that charmed suspects into confessing before they knew what they were doing. Intellectuals liked him, too, because his strong analytical skills made him one of the most successful detectives in the state. Plenty of police departments in larger cities had tried to lure him their way, but Al was a La Crosse boy and always would be.

"You're right," said Al. "I didn't take this job to fish floaters out of the river. And I sure as heck didn't take this job to stall out on a case that just keeps getting colder." Al had a reputation for bringing cases to a quick close, and he had neither the time nor the patience for one that offered no clues. "I was starting to think we might make it to Thanksgiving this year."

"Me too, but it is what it is. I'll hook up the boat and be there in half an hour."

Al and Charlie had met 10 years earlier when they investigated the drowning of a college student. Although as different as day and night, they had become fast friends. Al's analytical mind and Charlie's knowledge of the county made for quite a combination.

"I'll be ready." His call finished, Al prepared to leave the office. He thought back across the preceding years and the chain of drownings. Every fall, he and Charlie had been called to recover a body. Each time it had been a young man who had come to La Crosse for a college education that'd lead to a career and a family. But alcohol had snuffed them out. That was the coroner's ruling, anyway. Al and Charlie had their doubts. It just seemed too coincidental.

Before rising from his chair, Al opened a cabinet near his desk and pulled out a thick file—*too damn thick*, he thought. It contained the case records of the drowning victims.

He flipped through the stack of papers. Shawn Sorensen was the first, a junior at the University of Wisconsin-La Crosse. Sorensen had been working toward a dual degree in chemistry and chemical engineering. He died in October 1997.

Tad Schwartz was the second, a senior football player at UWL who was more than three-quarters of the way to his physical education degree. He died in November, three days after playing in the final football game of the 1998 season.

Jerry Przytarski became the third, vanishing from a bar in downtown La Crosse in November 1999. He hadn't been found for more than two weeks. He was in the final semester of his freshman year at Viterbo University. He was an aspiring theater major.

Tedd Duncan drowned in October 2000. He had just started his sophomore year at UWL.

There were more, but what was the use of reading through them all? They were all the same, and nothing had changed.

Al stood, still looking at the open file on his desk. He called the report desk to ask if there were any fresh missing persons reports. None.

Detective Log | Name: Allan Rouse | Badge: 786
La Crosse Drownings

Date	Name	Home Address	City	LaCrosse Address	Next of Kin	Status
10/10/97	Shawn V. Sorensen	4680 148th St.	Appleton, WI	475 Vine	Joseph Sorensen, Marge, Kopton	Open
11/24/98	Tad Schwarz	None	Cochrane, WI	755 14th St. N.	James and Emma Schwarz	Open
10/14/99	Jerry Przytarski	487 Main St.	Lodi, WI	226 Hillview Ave.	David and Helen Przytarski	Open
10/19/00	Tedd Duncan	11246 S. 75th St.	Chicago, IL	1760 Cass St.	Ted and Omni Duncan	Open
05/11/01	Jeremy Schultz	4860 5th St.	Winona, MN	Home	Olaf and Gerta Schultz	Open
11/01/02	Trevor Justin	N. 1st St.	Fountain City, WI	508 19th St. N.	Jeremy Justin, Nola Portolma	Open
09/12/03	Sam Dunlap	402 West Ave.	Omro, WI	403 22nd St. S.	Wayne and Wanda Dunlap	Open
10/21/04	Todd Hammer-meister	7880 Lincoln St.	Woodbury, MN	661 Ferry St.	Philip and Cynda Hammermeister	Open
09/24/05	Duane Rick	103 Wilson St.	Whitehall, WI	880 Adams St.	Duane and Ellen Rick	Open
10/05/06	Garth Thomas	4931 University Ave.	Madison, WI	447 10th St. N.	Ernest and Karen Thomas	Open
11/04/07	Phillip Hintzle	668 Badger St.	La Crosse	Same	Alyssa Hintzle	Open
10/17/08	Abraham Shapiro	208 Lamplighter Lane	Brookfield, WI	519 State St.	Sydney and Marta Shapiro	
09/18/09	Dustin Darst	661 Peckapa St.	Fond du Lac, WI	49 Badger St.	Lonnie and Yvonne Darst	Open
10/23/10	Jon Schneider	4240 W. Mil-burn Ave.	Mount Prospect, IL	2880 Grant Ct.	Larry and Selena Schneider	Open

CHAPTER 2

After a quick stop at the vending machine for sodas and snacks, Al stepped outside to wait for Charlie. It wasn't two minutes before the black sheriff's SUV slid smoothly to the curb. Hitched behind it was the familiar, broad flat-bottom boat.

Visibility was limited by the fog that bathed downtown La Crosse in a surreal glow. Al shivered as he got into the truck. The damp cold seemed to creep into his bones.

"Mornin'," offered Al as he dropped into the seat beside Charlie, dumping the sodas and snacks on the seat between them before closing the door.

"We gotta stop meeting like this, buddy," said Charlie. "This is happening way too often. In fact, it's become such a habit that I gave Rick a call."

"Figured you would," said Al. Rick was the La Crosse County Coroner, a pathologist at the Gundersen Clinic. "I'm catching on, partner. You'll notice I brought three sodas and snacks for more than just the two of us."

Charlie studied his friend for a moment., "I wonder what this one'll be like. Another kid, do you think? A duck hunter, maybe, lost in the fog? Or a Hmong immigrant after some early morning fish?"

Al thought for a moment. "I'm betting on another kid. I'm thinking that if it is, this is happening way too often for it to be simply one accident after another."

"You got it," said Charlie, slipping the Suburban into gear and pulling from the curb. As they drove through downtown La Crosse, each was lost in his own thoughts. The silence was heavy as they neared Gundersen. "Al, if this is another kid, we have to make sure the body is processed with a fine-tooth comb. The sheriff and chief will go for it being another accident, if that's Rick's ruling. It's just the easiest thing for them to do. If we want to conduct a thorough investigation, it's going to be tough. We'll need more than a hunch to take a good look. The sheriff and the chief won't want any trouble over a simple accident. They don't want any of this scaring the residents and the college students."

"That's the truth," agreed Al.

Rick was waiting on the curb in front of Lutheran Hospital, across the street from the new clinic building. "Hi, guys. Another drowning?"

"We'll know soon enough," said Charlie.

"If it is," said Rick, "it's going to be challenged if I rule it accidental."

"We agree," said Al. "In fact, we were thinking that if this is another kid, Charlie and I would like to work with you as you process the body."

It was a touchy subject. Rick was a kindly man but very fussy about his work. He had a sterling reputation for thoroughness and effectiveness over the years he had been the head of pathology at Gundersen-Lutheran. He had gotten the job at age 25, and many people thought he was too young. He quickly proved them wrong. Now, at age 39, his job was his life. A tall, handsome man with black wavy hair, no one could figure out why he had never married. Many questioned whether he was gay, but those questions were erased by the attractive women he dated. His dates were often gorgeous—stunningly so. If they got more than one date, they were extremely special.

"Ah, you don't trust me. You think I missed something?"

"No way," said Charlie. "But Al and I will want to spend some time on this one before the goddamn sheriff and chief climb all over our asses."

"Do you really have problems with us helping, Rick?" asked Al.

"None at all. In fact, it probably would be good for the three of us to see the same things at the same time. Maybe you will spot something that I overlooked in the past."

Charlie executed a U-turn and headed for the boat launch ramp just off 7th St.

Al and Rick got out of the car as Charlie positioned it to back the boat into the water. They retrieved life jackets from the back of the vehicle and inventoried items already in the boat. There were four poles of various types that could be used in retrievals out of normal reach. There also were short grippers, gloves, and an ominous looking lump: the body bag.

"All set?" asked Charlie.

Al gave him the okay sign.

As Charlie backed the car down the ramp, Rick and Al were already grasping lines, one on either side of the bow. Charlie stopped when the rear tires of the trailer were nearly submerged, hopped out and gave the boat a shove. It slid smoothly off the trailer, aided by well-oiled rollers.

Minutes later, the Suburban was parked. Rick and Al were already set to go. Charlie hopped in, hit the starter, and the new outboard, a four-stroke 30-horsepower Mercury, burped to life. Al cast off and jumped into the boat as Charlie backed it smoothly from the dock.

"We're going to head out to the channel, then turn south for about two and a half miles," explained Charlie. "When we're about opposite Shelby Road, there's a large island ahead where the river turns west. On the city side of the island, there's a slough. That's where they saw the body.

"I know the spot," said Al.

As the boat turned into the wind and in spite of moving downstream, it took all the power the outboard could muster to move them ahead. There was a stiff southeast wind blowing, and it churned the Mississippi into a highway of whitecaps. As Charlie fought the wheel while pushing the throttle so far forward it threatened to break, silence enveloped the boat.

No one was anxious to see the body.

CHAPTER 3

As they reached the slough, Charlie slowed the boat, turned into the narrow ribbon of water, and, one eye on the depth finder and the other on the shore, scanned the water. The boat inched along, fallen trees acting as natural barriers. The water depth fell sharply and Charlie turned the boat toward the Wisconsin shore. The boat crept along.

"There!" Al cried suddenly, pointing to a fallen tree, deadfall, that held a piece of plaid cloth. Something resembling a hand sliced through the air above the tree.

Charlie maneuvered the boat in the direction of the deadfall, and as the men drew closer they could see an unwelcomed sight. A body was jammed into the tree. They inched as close as they could get. Charlie suggested Al use the modified tree claw, a long pole with a collapsible four-prong end, to see if he could move the body away from the tree's grasp.

Once, twice, and then a third time, Al worked the pole into position, each time failing to dislodge the body from the tree. Rick grabbed the pike pole while Charlie moved the boat slightly toward the Wisconsin side of the river. He told Al he would attempt to push the body away from the tree where the grabber would be more effective. The first attempt failed, but all three could see that this was going to complete the job. Charlie worked the boat closer to the trunk of the tree. Rick waved for him to stop, moved the pole into position and pushed as hard as he could. The only thing that moved was the boat. Charlie increased the power of the motor to assist Rick in dislodging the body. That did it. Rick gave the body enough of a push to move it just enough for Al to get a better grip with his grabber. As Rick pushed and Al pulled, Charlie backed the boat slowly away from the tree. The body came free and Al steadily moved it to the side of the boat.

"Goddamnit," Charlie cursed quietly. His words captured the thoughts of all three. It was indeed the body of a young man. He was dressed in a plaid shirt and jeans. His eyes were closed and the body seemed perfectly at ease, drifting beside the boat while held in place by Al. Charlie grasped the man's shoulders, Rick took the feet, and, on the count of three, they heaved, rolling the body into the boat.

All three members of the retrieval squad slumped into their seats. Together they gazed at the face of a man just coming into adulthood. Such unfulfilled potential.

"Charlie swore again, slamming his hand on the control pedestal. "This stinks!"

The men sat there quietly, almost reverently, for more than five minutes.

"I guess we'd better get him back to the hospital," Rick finally muttered softly. He hated this part—the identification process, contacting the family and trying to arrange peacefully and sensitively for an autopsy that would, with any luck, reveal something that would provide the answers to the parents' guaranteed questions.

"The part I hate most," said Al, "is never having any answers for the parents."

"It's terrible," said Charlie, almost whispering. He grew more animated, hitting the control pedestal again. "This is fuckin' crap!"

Charlie muttered one expletive after another as he steered the boat away from the body's resting place and turned back toward the 7th Street landing.

All three were sobered by the knowledge that they would have to deliver a message that unsuspecting parents never wanted to hear. The parents who, filled with hope and pride, had sent their son to school to build the foundation for a bright future. It should have worked that way. The body in the bottom of the boat, being placed in the body bag by Al and Rick, had once been a handsome young man of, if the blonde hair meant anything, Nordic heritage. A lifeless face dashed away all hopes for his success. One night out on the town snuffed out a life of promise.

"I'm gettin' sick of this," said Charlie, loud enough to be heard over the roar of the motor as he steered the boat toward La Crosse and the landing. "And I'm even madder about the folks who wouldn't know a mystery if it bit them in the ass, thinkin' we're a bunch of bozos because we have all these drownings labeled accidental!"

"Charlie," said Rick with a laugh, "if the shoe fits…"

"Piss off!" was Charlie's quick retort. It seemed fitting that as the boat was steered out of the slough, rain began to fall. The rain drops were not big, but a steady drizzle from clouds that nearly touched the water. A murky day by all measures, the mood of which matched that of the three men who'd now completed their day's mission.

CHAPTER 4

As Charlie turned the boat back toward the marina, Rick peered ahead. The moment he saw the landing, he grimaced, then shouted, "Oh, no!"

Looking ahead, Charlie and Al understood. There was a crowd at the landing: men and women huddled under umbrellas. Behind the people were the telltale, colorful vehicles that signaled the press's arrival. As they drew closer to the shore, they could identify vehicles from all three of the local television stations as well as six radio stations, including the student-operated station from the University of Wisconsin-La Crosse. Sulking at the edge of the crowd was the gaunt figure of Harry Blanchard, the crime reporter for the *La Crosse Tribune*.

Harry was often characterized by Charlie as "a hemorrhoid's hemorrhoid…a colossal pain in the ass."

Now, with no time to prepare for a news conference or for the barrage of questions they knew was coming, it was quickly agreed that Al should field the anxious crowd's questions. Rick would stay with the boat while Charlie retrieved the truck and trailer as quickly as possible.

"Ya know," offered Charlie, the boat now just far enough from shore for his comments not to reach the crowd, "if you let me handle those assholes, this fiasco would be over in seconds."

"But Charlie, if we let you handle 'those assholes,' as you call them, we'd have an even bigger problem," said Rick. "And so would you!"

As gravel crunched against the bottom of the boat, Al stepped near the dock while holding the bow line. He offered Rick a hand as Charlie silenced the motor, lifted it from the water and tidied things up. Al and Rick stepped onto the dock's worn, wooden surface. They walked shoulder to shoulder with their heads up and jaws set. Charlie continued on while Al stopped to address the crowd.

"You're up early!" Al shouted to Blanchard. "I'm gonna have to find out who it is that keeps you so well informed. I'll quickly tell you what I know, but questions are going to have to wait until later when we know more. We have work to do."

"Is it another kid?" asked Blanchard.

"Yeah," Al responded grimly.

"If it is, we're going to need some answers, Al. This would be number 15 that we know about. We don't know a thing about what *really* caused their deaths," said Marge Mallory. "This is way beyond a number that can simply be explained away as an unusual string of coincidences."

The group quieted as Al held up his hand.

"It is another young man. We haven't even had a chance to check for missing persons reports or to process the information on the body. So we don't have a name for you and we won't until we have positive I.D. and next of kin have been informed. You all know the drill. And, before you ask, I won't speculate about when we'll have more information. We're taking the body to Gundersen. We'll first try our best to identify the victim, contact next of kin, and, hopefully, get clearance from the family for an autopsy."

"How long will all that take?" demanded Mallory.

"I really can't say exactly but 24 to 48 hours seems a reasonable guess."

As the reporters fidgeted, the detective turned back to the landing. The trailer was in place. Charlie and Rick wrestled the boat into position. Al surveyed the crowd and realized the community needed more information. Everyone's worry shone in their eyes. He turned again to the small crowd, held up his hand, and spoke.

"At 9:30 this morning, a call came into the 911 center. It was a fisherman reporting that he and his companion had noticed a body hung up on a deadfall in a slough about 2 ½ miles south of the 7th Street landing. If the slough has a name, I don't know it, but the location is roughly due west of where Markle Road intersects with North Richard Drive, near an island. We found the body without difficulty about 10:45, then came straight back here to be with all of you since we can't bear to be apart from you for too long."

The attempt at humor fell on deaf ears. Al continued. "As of the time I left the office, no missing person reports had been received." He paused briefly and then continued with a somber tone. "This is the 15th young victim in a series of drownings that have been occurring since 1997. It is also the 11th time Deputy Charlie, Rick and I have made the retrieval. We are not happy about that, obviously, and we have some of the same questions you do. Now, if you'll pardon me, all three of us want to get our official duties underway. None of these tasks is pleasant. There is a family out there who's gonna get some tragic news very soon. I am certain that if you were one of those poor man's parents, you'd not want to be kept waiting. When we know something, we will call the customary news conference and give you the information we discover.

Al gave a brief nod and moved quickly toward the waiting truck and trailer. As he hopped onto the running board, he hoped, fervently, that if there were any connections between these drowning cases, this body would reveal the answers.

"Please, God," he thought, "let us find what we missed in the 14 previous cases."

As he got into the car, Charlie told the news.

"I've made calls to the P.D. and Sheriff's office to tell them we've got another one. No missing-persons calls received. They know we are heading for Gundersen to begin processing the body. They are shittin' bricks over there. They want answers…and quick."

CHAPTER 5

As reporters in La Crosse were preparing their first broadcasts about the death, Julie Sonoma fought to keep her new Ford Fiesta on the road as she drove from La Crosse toward her home in Illinois. The radio played some syrupy pop song but Julie didn't hear it; it was only background noise. The roaring southeast wind whipped at her car, sweeping tendrils of snow across the road as icy crystals of moisture pelted the windshield.

She wished she was back home in the comfort of her suburban Chicago apartment, but she had given up her weekend and taken a vacation day from work to attend a reunion of her University of Wisconsin-La Crosse physician assistants' class. On this murky morning, she wished she had passed on what had turned out to be a disappointing time. She kicked herself mentally for making the trip and leaving her son with friends. Julie was startled back to reality by the strident tone—a newsbreak. The reporter on WIZM-La Crosse was breathlessly relaying a, "just into the newsroom" message that the body of a young man had been pulled from the Mississippi River at La Crosse.

"The victim is believed to be a man of college age," said the reporter. This could be the 15th such drowning in as many years. Stay tuned to WIZM for more details."

Julie knows the story well. It was personal for her. The first victim had been her first and only lover. She had come apart at the news of his death and it was only through superhuman effort and loving therapists that she eventually moved on.

But now, hearing the news, Julie began to tremble to the point that she had trouble steering the car. Irrational as it might be, she had never forgiven Shawn's roommate and his friends for taking her love out and—in her mind—getting him drunk. Julie greeted each report of another drowning with the fervent hope that the victim was someone who led youth astray and failed to watch out for them.

"Please tell me," she said out loud to her empty car as her trembling increased, "that this is another bad guy…one of the party organizers." It would be nice to hear that this was one of those people she knew as encouragers—the corrupters who egged on their young friends. *They were the problem*, she thought, *and they needed to be eradicated…stamped out! Annihilated!*

Her anger had reached a frightening peak—it scared her. She steered the Fiesta to the shoulder of the road, turned off the engine and stared at a landscape she didn't see.

Julie had not always been this jaded. She started college at 18, leaving her middle-class parents and small river town in West Central Wisconsin. She had been an extraordinary student, graduating at the top of her class at age 25 after taking more than a year off to heal after Shawn's death. She was smart, kind, and considerate; a beautiful young woman who had little time for the pursuits more suited for people her age. She dated but not seriously. She enjoyed parties but attended most of them alone and always left early. There were very few boys in her high school who had not, in those quiet moments alone, thought about Julie and what they might like to do to her. No one had dared to try anything.

She was one of those people who commanded respect. She seemed to relate better to her teachers than her classmates. In spite of her friendly relationships with older individuals, no one accused her of unfair advantages. She studied hard, helped her friends, and enjoyed good friendships with almost everyone at her school. Still, there was an aloofness about her…a seriousness, too, that caused the men she dated to be on their best behavior when she was around.

Many lusted after her but no one sought to take advantage of her. While the boys in her class talked frequently about the progress they made with girlfriends, Julie was never the topic of that kind of conversation. She was a dark-haired, dark-eyed goddess set on a pedestal; someone whose friendship was sought but never with evil intentions.

For one thing, she was much too serious. She arrived at school early, driving her dad's beautifully restored 1957 Chevy hardtop from her home to the school three miles outside the town. When school ended, she was quickly on the road to her father's drugstore where she worked as his aide and watched over the popular soda fountain.

It was in that same drugstore that Julie's interest in medicine began. From the age of 10, she had spent every available moment with her doting father, riddling him with questions about the various medicines he mixed and dispensed. She wanted to know what kinds of cures were achieved and what kinds of reactions could be expected. She liked it best when the medicines were compounded behind the counter of the store, and she hated it when the era of pre-mixed drugs came, noting that this took the art out of pharmacy and turned pharmacists into robotic dispensers of pills and solutions.

Her father still did compounding. In the small town where they lived, a physician visited only once a week. The clinic was otherwise left to the supervision of nurse practitioners and physician assistants, depending upon the current availability of health care providers. Her father dispensed medicines when he felt people needed them. Never once had he run afoul of the law or physician anger for this practice.

As Julie entered high school, the clinic was served by P.A. Janet Walters. Even though Janet was 20 years older than Julie, they formed a solid friendship. Janet, a plain and serious young woman, seemed much older than her years, and she enjoyed the company of this beautiful girl who expressed a desire to follow in her footsteps.

Soon, Julie was working at the clinic, as well as spending time in the drugstore with her father. She demonstrated an aptitude seldom found in a person her age. That aptitude would land her a coveted spot in the UWL program that annually turned down five times more applicants than it accepted. Janet's glowing recommendation and status as one of the program's finest were key factors, too.

Janet also helped her land a job at Richardson's Pharmacy on the south side, the only La Crosse pharmacy that still did some compounding, even before school began.

She arrived in La Crosse with the intent of excelling in her studies, working at the pharmacy to reduce her student loans, graduating with honors, and serving people in a small town dependent upon folks like her to oversee their health care.

For two years, that's just what she did. She was, of course, pursued by men but she rarely accepted. When she did, the ground rules were quickly understood. Dates led only to social friendships. If those who approached her had their sights set on greater accomplishments, they were quickly sent packing.

As she began her junior year, she began to notice with more and more interest the young man with the charming smile and blond, wavy hair. He was in three of her classes and whether by magic or fate, she found herself either sitting next to or near him in every class they shared. His blue eyes were the most piercing she had ever seen, and she fell in love with them before she did with him.

They began to talk and became friends. When Shawn proposed they walk to the Bodega for an ice cream soda, she accepted. They had a marvelous time. They found they liked the same things, shared the same dreams and worried about the same issues.

Soon, they were inseparable. When Shawn on a Friday night proposed that Julie stay over at his apartment, she accepted without hesitation. They walked first to her apartment where Julie picked up some clothes (she had to work the next day at Richardson's) and retrieved her car. She then drove them to the charming, near-campus Victorian restoration in which Shawn rented the spacious upstairs apartment.

He lived there with only one roommate, something that amazed her because she figured the apartment must command a hefty rent. When she had asked him about it, he brushed aside her questions of affordability. Aside from his apartment, though, there was nothing to suggest that he was anything but an ordinary college student struggling to pay tuition and living expenses.

That night in October was magical. They made love hungrily, a flurry of activity that ended quickly and left them breathless. After a few minutes, they went again, this time with the sweetness, the gentleness and tenderness that only young, new love can offer.

When the orgasm rolled over her, it was like nothing she had experienced. The feeling of fulfillment that replaced the tidal wave of emotions left her exhausted but totally in love, consumed by the feelings that pervaded her body. The love collected in the "v" created by her thighs, preparing her for yet another foray into the world of sexual mysticism.

For the rest of the night, they played with abandon, pausing only to restore their breath before embarking on another journey to somewhere previously unexplored. As the light of dawn filtered through the windows, Julie was spent but not tired. Her body throbbed with a sweet ache that made her simply want to wrap her legs around him and never let him go.

She would never forget that night of first love.

Soon after Shawn's death, however, the feelings of love were replaced by bitterness and the all-consuming fire of revenge. So, when the radio sounded news of the 15th such death, she was pleased. No, more than pleased—ecstatic. *Good*, she thought. *One more gone!*

Her Shawn had been the first. He was a well-known and popular man on campus and his death was much lamented. No one, though, grieved more severely than Julie Sonoma. Her world was crushed. Although she and Shawn had been an item for only six weeks, she had fallen hard. He had felt the same. Promises had already been exchanged between them of a future life together.

They had been so in love. Those few sweet nights they had spent together led to a new life, a, now, 14-year-old boy, Brody, who was being raised by his mother without the benefit of a father figure. Brody who, although he never knew his father, each day reminded Julie in look and action of the beautiful young man his father had been.

Although Julie was doing well, raising a child on her own while trying to earn a living had taken its toll on her physically and mentally. She found out after his death that Shawn came from one of the richest families in Appleton, Wisconsin. While Julie could have sought aid from Shawn's parents, it was not something she could bring herself to do. His parents were unaware of their grandson. She was now a respected physician's assistant, working for the Kahn Clinic in Arlington Heights, Illinois. Female patients loved the beautiful, soft-spoken, sad-eyed 40-year-old woman with remarkable compassion, not knowing the events 14 years before that had changed her life and molded a woman who, beneath the surface, seethed with anger over what might have been. Male patients were startled by her beauty but put off by an aura that seemed almost antimagnetic.

While Julie was respected and popular, she seemed destined to a life alone. As Brody grew toward adulthood, the fact that her "Little Man" was a spitting image of his father did little to ease the anger created by the loss of her one true love.

As the string of drowning deaths multiplied, each death provided her with moments of joy. She hoped fervently that each of those young men was one of those who led others astray.

The deaths also stabbed at her heart. While each death appeased her lust for revenge, she also knew how terrible their families must feel.

Even though Julie constantly fought mental demons, she always performed her job competently. Her patients invariably wondered why this attractive and intelligent woman with the soft heart and healing hands seemed so sad…angry, even. Julie *was* angry, trapped and haunted by the pain of her loss, and she was certain there was no one alive who could measure up to Shawn.

Now, as the sleet pelted down, Julie shook her head to clear it of memories so she could resume her trip home. Tentatively, she slipped the Fiesta back onto the concrete surface of Highway 90-94 north of the Wisconsin Dells. Her foot pressed steadily downward on the accelerator, and the little car responded nimbly, seeming to sense her need for home and comfort.

CHAPTER 6

As the Fiesta headed south, activity began at the Gundersen pathology lab. Coats discarded, Al, Charlie and Rick contemplated the black polyethylene and polyester bag lying on the gurney, its contents waiting to be transferred to the operating table. Moments later, Rick flicked on the latest and greatest Burton AIM LED procedure lights and looked at his friends. "Would you guys mind if we said a little prayer?"

"Go for it, doc," replied Charlie. "Lead us." Al nodded and all three men bowed their heads.

"Dear God, we approach you, asking you to guide our hands and focus our eyes that we might find whatever secrets this body might be hiding. Give us wisdom to look where we have not looked in the past and to see what we have not seen. In the name of your son, Jesus, Father, Amen."

"Amen," chorused Al and Charlie.

"Okay," said Rick, "let's get at it."

The three gently lifted the body from the bag and placed it on the table. At that moment, the lab door opened. An attractive woman with an angelic face entered the room.

"Al, Charlie, meet Dr. Patricia Grebin. Pat, that's Al Rouse, chief detective with the La Crosse P.D. That's La Crosse County Chief Deputy Sheriff Charlie Berzinski," said Rick, pointing to his companions.

"Good morning, gentlemen," said Pat, extending her hand. "It's a pleasure to meet the two people I have heard so much about. To be honest, I hoped we'd meet under much better circumstances. Rick told me all about this string of drowning deaths that seem impossible to label as a coincidence."

"Good morning, Dr. Grebin," chorused the two lawmen.

"Please, call me Pat. Let's dispense with the formalities. The comment put the lawmen at ease.

"Great. I'm Al."

"And call me Charlie, mam."

Without the relaxed atmosphere, the lawmen may well have been intimidated by the presence of the attractive and tall blond lady. Pat Grebin stood five foot ten, and she wore a pair of towering, spiked heels. She was intelligent as she was attractive, but her manners also bespoke a soft and superior bedside manner.

"I have told Pat about all 14 cases to date," said Rick, "with particular emphasis on the ten we have examined. I am hoping that her keen mind will be just what we need to determine if there is something nefarious here or whether it really is a terrible series of coincidental drownings."

Moving to the table, Al motioned to Charlie to help him. They rolled the body on its stomach so Al could probe the back pockets of the jeans to look for a billfold or other materials that might help with identification.

The left pocket produced a clean but soaked handkerchief. The right pocket yielded a billfold. As Al pulled contents from the soaked leather, Charlie, by now too familiar with the routine, activated the microphone hanging from the cord above the table to begin a description of the inventory.

"Three five-dollar bills," reported Charlie. "One 20 and six ones. A driver's license: Wisconsin. Issued to a Rolf Evenson of Durand, Wisconsin. Born March 10, 1993." Pictures also surfaced. A credit card was issued to Rolf Evenson. The wallet also contained some pieces of paper, matted together by river water which Charlie set aside to dry.

A plastic card with next-of-kin information and people to be notified in the case of an emergency: *Lars and Goldene Evenson, 308 North Fourth Street, Durand, Wisconsin 54736.* The card contained a phone number: *715-672-5921.*

"Shit!" exclaimed Charlie. Realizing what he had just said, Charlie turned to Pat. "Apologies, ma'am, but what a Thanksgiving gift the Evensons are going to have. Another goddamn tragedy."

Pat replied. "I doubt, Charlie, that you could say anything to rival the things I hear—and utter—in my operating room!"

"Thanks, ma'am," replied Charlie, gratefully.

The inventory continued. The front pockets contained the keys to a Ford Taurus, 79 cents in change and a slip of paper that appeared to contain phone numbers. They also set these items aside to dry.

"Perhaps I should go call the Pepin County Sheriff's Office. Maybe someone there knows this guy well enough to provide a description. If they do, maybe they'll know other things that will be helpful," suggested Charlie.

"Good idea," said Al. "I'll watch the docs work. Maybe they'll come up with something helpful."

As Charlie stepped from the room, the doctors began to strip soggy clothes from the body. Once it was nude, the doctors started a methodical search. Rick started at the feet while Pat started at the head. As they worked, each talked into a small, handheld microphone. For the first few minutes, there was nothing. Pat stopped suddenly and tapped her colleague's arm. "Rick, take a look, will you?"

As Rick joined her, Pat used a bone awl to point at a small red dot, nearly obscured by blood vessels at the entrance to the canal of the left ear. "Does that look like a needle mark?" she asked.

"Hmmm, could be, I suppose. Could be a lot of other things, too. Note it for the record and we'll take a closer look at it later."

"Okay."

The external inspection continued. Aside from some minor contusions, no doubt caused by collisions with objects in the river, nothing else of interest surfaced. Only the one question existed.

"That's it for this phase, I guess," said Rick. "Hopefully Charlie has gotten somewhere. If he has, we can make the contacts and then maybe begin the rest of the work.

"Is Charlie...the right person?" asked Pat, timidly. "He just seems awfully gruff."

Al and Rick smiled.

"He's a teddy bear, Pat. His language is rough as a stevedore's but when it comes to the delicate matter of handling tragedies, he's wonderful," said Rick.

"He really is a dichotomy, doc," said Al. "His language makes him seem a fire-breathing dragon. His work with victims makes him seem like Mother Teresa."

"I'll reserve judgment on the Mother Teresa thing. It's hard to believe he could be that gentle," offered Pat, cracking a smile.

"I'm not sure how gentle Mother Teresa is," said Rick. "But once you see Charlie work, you'll be amazed."

Then, without a word, Rick and Al turned and walked to the door. As the two men waved for Pat to go ahead, the three left the lab.

"Nice to know that chivalry isn't dead," she murmured as the three walked down the corridor. "What now?"

"We wait," said Rick. "Waiting has become standard practice. How about we wander down to the physicians' lounge…maybe get something to eat. Join us?"

"I guess I will," she said slowly and turned toward them. "You know, I'm haunted by that mark inside the ear. I'm almost afraid to believe it could be something because I know how starved you are for something—anything—that would bring some answers, but…" She trailed off.

"Pat, honestly, we don't hold out much hope of finding something," said Rick quietly. "Ten times I have come up with nothing. Teams before us got that same result four times. Because of the number of deaths—15 now—everyone wants an answer that points to something more logical than accident and coincidence. No one wants that more than I do."

"Except maybe me," chimed Al, thinking about the ridicule he and Charlie had taken when one after another of the bodies were labeled accidental.

Pat considered the looks on the faces of the two men. "Please, both of you, I am not in any way thinking that I have more skills than you, Rick. And Al, your police work is legendary; I have heard the stories. I just want to shed some light on this if I can. Why always young men? Why no women? Why each year about this time? It's just too…too…predictable, don't you think?"

"Yup," agreed Al. "We think these could be homicides but there's never been any evidence."

He paused and stared into space for a moment. Al focused his thoughts and spoke. "If these deaths are murders, we're dealing with one of the largest serial killing sprees ever. As a professional cop, it's hard for me, given the intervals, to imagine a killer who could wait so long between killings. And what could have triggered a string that's lasted…what… 12 years?"

"Fourteen," Rick corrected.

"I'm with you," said Pat. "This is La Crosse, not New York or L.A. Murders don't happen here. When they do, it's usually a domestic dispute, right? And the killer is quickly arrested."

"You're right," said Al. "I can't remember the last homicide that didn't quickly lead to closure. And as you say, it's usually a domestic…like that one in West Salem a year or two ago, when a son in need of money killed his mom and dad. Murder sprees *don't* happen here…except maybe they do."

"Why don't we take this to the lounge? I worry about people hearing things they shouldn't," suggested Rick. The bustle of the hallway traffic worried him.

"Good advice," murmured Al. Pat nodded as the three began their trip to the lounge in the new hospital. It was the most advanced in health care design, according to many. It certainly was brighter and more inviting than many similar facilities. For the three people entering the lounge, the area seemed as dark as the weather outside. Little optimism existed in these three, triggered by fear that this time would be the same as the last.

A quick trip through the cafeteria line produced coffee for all, a sweet roll for Al and a bowl of fruit for Rick. Pat passed on the food and then secured a table in the far corner of the room where quiet conversation could take place, far away from other occupants.

CHAPTER 7

While colleagues streamed in and out, Rick and Pat limited interactions to waves. It seemed as if everyone knew what was going on and kept their distance.

"They know," said Rick, looking at Al. "Every time you come in here with me, they know…another drowning…another victim…another mystery."

He paused for a moment. "Yeah, I'm a bad omen. I wonder what's taking Charlie? Has it ever taken this long?"

"Every time," said Rick, smiling. "And we have this conversation every time, too. Relax, Al, he'll be here…and with more bad news I suspect."

As if on cue, Charlie entered, looked around, spotted his colleagues and stomped to the table.

"What's up?" asked Al. "What do we know? Is it the Durand kid? What did the Pepin County folks say? Have the folks been told?"

"Whoa," snapped Charlie, holding up his hand. "You're gonna have to wait, Al. I have to get some of that coffee…and somethin' to eat, too. But I am as certain as I can be that our vic is young Evenson. I'm hopin' a call to UWL will finish off the identification."

"Then we'll inform the parents and get to work," offered Al hopefully.

"Is that really necessary?" asked Pat. "Parental permission, I mean."

"No, it's not," answered Al, "but we've always done it this way. It seems the right thing to do. Parents oughta decide whether their son's body should be torn apart."

"What if they say no?" she persisted.

"No one ever has," said Charlie. "Not sure what we'd do in that case. Hopefully, they won't. Be back in a minute."

"A minute my aunt Fannie," said Al, smiling. "Pat, you've never seen Charlie eat. His appetite is legendary!"

Silence enveloped the trio. Charlie returned with a tray heaped with breakfast food—eggs, bacon, sausage, four slices of toast, a bowl of fruit and two tubs of yogurt.

"Dieting, I see," said Rick with a grin.

"I'm a growin' boy! Besides, this goddamn call came in and I didn't have time for breakfast. Speakin' of that, Rick, you gotta do something about this food. Where the hell's the pancakes? There's no waffles. I like bacon soft and squirming. This shit is harder than rock. I really wanted to go to Ma's."

He dropped the tray to the table with a thump. Charlie tried to stuff his girth into the space between the table and the back of the booth.

"Goddamnit! They make these damn booths for midgets and health nuts. Rick, you gotta do somethin' about it! No one gives a shit about guys like me. Shit, recovering bodies on an empty stomach is shitty!"

"Are you done? At least you've injected a little comic relief into the day," said Al, a deadpan look on his face. Trying to dispel laughter, Rick and Pat lost it, loud laughter breaking out and turning heads throughout the room.

"Oops," said Rick. "We'd better cool it."

"Cool it, hell. I'd just give 'em the finger and move on," said Charlie, tucking a napkin into the collar of his shirt.

"Charlie, you look like an overgrown version of Harry Potter," said Pat, grasping the spirit of the conversation. "Is it really all for you? Or did you bring it for us, too?"

"Pat," said Charlie gravely and with formality, "I will be happy to share a little of this food with you, but if you think I'm sharin' with these two clowns, forget it. Bad as it is, I need some nourishment."

"Yup, you're just wasting away," chided Rick.

Turning to his food and beginning to shovel it into his mouth like a fireman stoking a boiler, Charlie mumbled, "Don' led m'eatin' get in way."

"God, Charlie, just eat," admonished Al. "You sound like a pig. Pat is going to think all lawmen are slobs."

Charlie stopped chewing and looked dourly at his companions. "Slobs, my ass. Now how about lettin' me eat."

Undeterred by his colleagues' remarks, Charlie, through mouthfuls of food, told them he had talked to a friend at the Pepin County Sheriff's

Office who knew the Evensons. He confirmed that Rolf, the oldest of three boys, was about six foot two and 200 pounds with blond hair.

Slowing his chewing, Charlie spoke. "He was quite a high school athlete. The kid played football, basketball, and baseball in high school. All-conference in all three. He went to UWL to play baseball. He's been a great second baseman for two years…all-conference as a sophomore. Goddamnit, a waste!"

"That means Coach Zorn is going to be pretty disappointed when he gets the news," said Al, referring to the Eagles' long-time, crusty baseball coach who was something of a legend in the Wisconsin Intercollegiate Athletic Conference.

"The death's gonna be hard on him," agreed Charlie. "But if we find out this one was out drinkin' with his buddies, it's gonna kill him. Can you imagine…"

The statement hung there. Al and Charlie were focused on the reaction the news would have on the longtime coach, a friend to both of them. The doctors conversed quietly about how they would tackle the autopsy.

The room grew eerily quiet as if everyone knew something was about to happen. Everyone jumped as the shrill ring of a phone broke the silence. Charlie grabbed his phone, answered it, and listened for what seemed an interminable time.

As the communication continued, Charlie's face softened. A small smile hit his lips. "Thank God!" he said and ended the call.

"The sheriff's talked to Pepin County again. He also talked to the dean of students over at UWL. We have the name of Rolf's roommate. There's a phone number, too. They're calling now. Assuming Rolf is missing, the Pepin County crew's gonna visit the Evensons. That's when all hell breaks loose," predicted Charlie, pointing to his colleagues.

"I expect the family will visit to identify," said Rick as if he were thinking out loud. "When that's done, we will have to be ready to talk to them. Pat would be the best. She meets people well. I have seen her handle some p-r-e-t-t-y delicate cases. She does it with ease and compassion."

"So now we wait," said Al. "I've got lots to do at the office. I think I'll take off and get some of it done."

"I'm drivin'," pointed out Charlie. "I'll drop you off and stop by the office to get somethin' done, too. I'll let you all know when I hear anything."

CHAPTER 8

After the two men left, Rick gestured for Pat to join him at a nearby lounge area. The two sat down.

"Pat, let me apologize for pushing you to the front of the communication chain. Fact is, you are the best to handle the conversation. Charlie will likely bring the Evensons in. If you break the ice, much as I dislike it, I'll conduct the official part of the visit," said Rick.

He continued. Take it from me. You never know what the reaction will be. I've had people faint, others scream and carry on for an hour; others who were silent and stoic, communicating through nods and gestures. No matter how many times I've done it, these visits are hard. You want to be positive but once they've seen the face of a loved one, they don't hear a single word. You just have to help in whatever way you can."

He stopped and chuckled sadly. "It's why I left the surgery department. I had a hard time telling loved ones I'd lost one of their family members. Where do I wind up? Pathology…where that's all I do," muttered Rick.

"I don't *relish* the task," agreed Pat, "but I've been there often enough myself. The duty to tell family members they lost a loved one is ugly. There's no way to say it that softens the message. A week ago, I worked on a 10-year-old who'd been hit by a car. The result was predetermined, but I still did everything I could. He died moments after I opened him up. It was awful."

"We'll do the best we can. If what you found proves to be something, maybe we'll have something at last to explain these deaths. The opportunity to provide the families with some closure on the 'why' would be helpful all 15 of them," said Rick.

"Well, back to work," said Pat, getting up from her chair.

"Yup, back to work," said Rick. "I'll be in touch."

CHAPTER 9

As things unfolded in La Crosse, a very sleepy Julie was arriving at her home in Arlington Heights.

Three thirty already, she thought, glancing at the clock. She'd told her best friend Peggy, who had agreed to watch over Brody, that she'd be back by 4 p.m. at the latest. Now she had only a half hour to get to Peggy's. Even on a Saturday afternoon, it was going to be touch and go.

Brody would be very ready to get home, she knew, even though he loved to visit Peggy and her kids, Lauren and Jake. He would be anxious to spend a few hours beating her in Call of Duty 4, his latest video game. Hopefully, she'd be able to stay awake.

Peggy Russell was a wonderful friend. The two women had much in common. Like Julie, Peggy was a P.A. at the Kahn Clinic. She was raising her two children alone. Her husband Matt had been killed in a shooting accident while hunting deer in Wisconsin. Peggy was a beautiful young lady. At 42 she was Julie's physical opposite. She was short—barely over five feet—but her body was sensational, voluptuous. Peggy's breasts drew stares wherever she went. Once Julie asked her if the stares bothered her, and Peggy told her looks were free—she didn't mind. Like Julie, she was from Wisconsin. She grew up in the Fond du Lac area and attended the University of Wisconsin at Madison. She was a big-town girl and loved Chicago. She was up for any excuse to go downtown. Julie was formally articulate but Peggy was not. Slang was her idiom. Julie was organized and neat. Peggy was casual. Her house was frequently a mess but she didn't seem to care. Julie was an adequate cook. Peggy excelled in the kitchen.

The two women did not meet until a year after Julie began working in Chicago, but they quickly became fast friends. Peggy was a few years older, but the two women were soul mates. They shared almost everything.

Even though no one knew or suspected it, they now shared more than just friendship.

Neither woman was interested in finding another man. Both women had been flexible in their attractions throughout their lives to both men and women, but they had fallen hard for men. Those men were their true loves. Peggy figured she had married the only man she would ever love. Julie was so taken by her intense love for Shawn only to have him ripped from her that she had never thought of a relationship with another man. On that fateful day in 1997, she vowed that her heart would never surrender its feelings, nor would the memories she cherished of Shawn be erased by another man.

Young and vibrant, both of them had developed feelings. Julie was haunted by desires of the need for physical relief. They came suddenly and without warning on those nights when Brody was away, and a glass or two of wine created a melancholy spell. Peggy would openly confess at times that she was "horny as a jackrabbit." She couldn't bring herself to a relationship with a man, fearing total disappointment after having been with Matt.

She and Peggy had talked openly about their feelings and how neither could bear the thought of contact with a man. They also agreed that neither was interested in mechanical means of release. Both had tried it, disliked it and quickly rid their homes of the devices they had hoped would provide relief.

On the night they discussed bedroom toys while enjoying several glasses of wine together, Brody and Jake were playing with Jake's X-box in the rec room of Peggy's house while Lauren taunted them about her superiority.

As the night wore on, both women suddenly realized they had more than enough to drink. When Julie expressed concern about driving, Peggy quickly suggested that she and Brody stay over.

"You know we have plenty of room. Brody is quite at home here and Jake loves the companionship, especially since it makes the odds against Lauren 2-to-1. To be honest, it would be great to have someone to share breakfast with on a Sunday morning."

Confirming she was in no shape to drive and really didn't want to take a cab, Julie agreed. When the plan was announced to the kids, the boys were overjoyed. Although Lauren protested, it appeared only to be for show.

Popcorn and pop followed for the kids. Julie and Peggy had more wine. It was well after 11 when they finally got the kids off to bed and were able to start cleaning up. Julie couldn't remember the last time she had laughed so much; it was just such a light, good-hearted evening. And there was the tipsiness…that probably contributed, too.

They giggled at almost everything and wobbled more than a little when walking When Peggy suggested they bunk together, it seemed like the most natural thing in the world. Wearing a cotton nightgown supplied by her hostess, her teeth brushed and face washed, Julie jumped into bed. Peggy joined her and they continued to talk about the trials of single parenthood, the constant budget battle that affected both and the lack of physical attention that bothered them.

It seemed normal when Peggy's hand brushed her face. As startling as it was when her hostess leaned over to brush her lips while saying good night, the kiss became more urgent, and four hands began to wander. Before either seemed to realize what was happening, the caresses became more erotic and lips explored other places while hands crept beneath nightgowns and found places both hot and wet.

When they came at the same time, the intensity of their relief was something neither had experienced for a very long time. There was no shame attached to the wonderful feelings that emanated throughout their bodies, and they soon fell asleep in each other's arms.

It was rather amazing, Julie thought later, that no feelings of remorse greeted her the next morning. There was no need to discuss what had happened or to ask if it might happen again.

Although both women felt they had their one great love, they grew closer and closer. The physical attraction spiked frequently, too. Peggy and Julie began to plan regular nights together, even as the joy they shared, they believed, was as best friends and would never replace the love they had for the men who entered their lives and vanished from them too soon.

These were the thoughts that ran through Julie's mind as she quickly dressed and left the house to pick up her son.

***

Peggy lived only a mile away in the same northwestern Chicago suburb as Julie. On this Saturday afternoon, traffic was nonexistent and she covered the distance in record time.

"Hi, girlfriend," Peggy greeted her at the door, brushing her cheek with a kiss. "Did ya have a good time at your reunion?"

"Kind of, I guess. The best part about it was that it was quick. It's always been fun to visit, but this time was different. It was a college class reunion, and, to be honest, I had a lousy time. I had nothing in common with any of those people while I was in college. I wonder what I was thinking. I guess I thought it might be different now. There's no way I could go back there to live. I guess I'm a big-city girl now."

"Well, I s'pose both big and little have their advantages," speculated Peggy, "but for me, bigger is better."

"I agree There's just so much to see and do here. Best of all, no one pokes their nose into your business. No one cares," said Julie. "On one hand that's great, but on the other there's something tragic about it. People ought to care about each other, but here they couldn't care less!"

"When Shawn died, I'd had it up to here," lamented Julie, drawing her hand up to her chin. "I was always the good little girl of whom much was expected and only the best was tolerated. It's why I never dated much in high school."

The statement hung there, an awkward silence enveloping the room as each of the women thought about the tragic circumstances that robbed them of people they loved.

"Did you have a good night?" Julie asked, breaking the silence.

"We did. Brody's such a sweet kid. He and Jake get along like brothers. Now if I could do somethin' with the catty teenager that Lauren's become, life would be really good. Ya know, Julie, I just love Brody. What a wonderful young man he's becoming."

"He's become the man of the house," said Julie with a smile. "He tries to do everything someone much older would do. He's become a pretty darn good handyman."

"Well, he's welcome here anytime," said Peggy. "And so's his mommy."

"I've been thinking about that a lot. I wonder," said Julie cautiously, "if we're really determined to raise the kids on our own, would it be good to think of getting a place together?"

"Oh, my, girlfriend. I've thought of nothin' else for the past month," said Peggy, a wide smile lighting her face. "I was afraid to ask 'cause I thought you'd hate the idea. But together we could afford a pretty nice place. And the kids would love it. Even Lauren, since we could look for a place with a room large enough to give her the privacy she wants."

"How about," Julie offered, "we watch the ads all week for places that look interesting? All the real estate ads are on the net now, maybe we could each take a couple of sites. I might even pick up a free newspaper or two.

We each could spend some time online looking for things we like. Maybe next weekend we could do a little house hunting."

"Great idea. This just became a great day! I wanted so bad to ask you. I'm really glad you brought it up."

"I think it would be nice to be together every day," Julie said. "But we should make certain we each have enough room and our own space. I'm almost afraid to get too excited about it for fear it won't work out. It will, won't it, Peggy?"

"All we have to do is make it happen, girlfriend," answered Peggy. "Givin' how we feel, I can't see anything stoppin' us."

"Great! Now, even though I'm dragging from a late night and would love nothing more than a nap, I doubt that I could sleep.

"I don't imagine Brody will allow that, either. Unless he and Jake stayed up all night with their video games."

"I think the boys got some sleep," said Peggy. "I went to bed about 11:30, and when I peeked in on them, they were sound asleep. Now Lauren, that's a whole other story. She was still talkin' to her friends at 1 a.m. I sometimes think the cellphone's the worst invention of all time."

"Fortunately, Brody hasn't reached that point yet. In fact, he hasn't even mentioned having a phone. Lucky me. Speaking of Brody, I'd better get going. Thanks again for keeping an eye on him. Now that we've got our new plan, I'll probably spend the afternoon with the online ads, seeing what I can find."

"Hi, mom," called Brody as he hurried down the steps.

"Hi, buddy!" It had been honey until three months ago when Brody pointed out that "honey" was a little infantile and even embarrassing. They had settled on "buddy."

"Set to go?" she asked. "We should be getting along so Peggy and Jake can do things they have to do."

When Brody turned and disappeared up the steps, Julie embraced Peggy. "I can't tell you how happy and excited I am. I am so thankful to have you as my girlfriend. And now we are going to be roommates, too," said Julie.

"Same," said Peggy. "I plan to talk to the kids today to see what their reaction will be."

"Oh, wow," said Julie, a frown crossing her face. "What if they don't like the idea?"

"I doubt they will object. But if they do, we'll work it out with them. It's too good an idea to give up."

With that, Peggy embraced Julie and kissed her tenderly on the lips. The kiss ended just as the boys reappeared, Brody lugging a sleeping bag and a backpack.

"Thanks again, Peggy," repeated Julie.

"Don't mention it. If nothing else, Brody keeps Lauren and Jake from having as many fights!" she joked.

"I'll call you tomorrow," promised Julie. "Maybe even tonight, depending on what I find."

"Call me regardless," urged Peggy. "Maybe I'll have news from my chat."

As the door closed, Julie put her arm around Brody and propelled him toward the car.

"What's up mom?" he asked.

"I have something to talk to you about," she said. "But let's wait until we get home."

A few minutes later, inside their apartment and sitting at the kitchen table, Brody couldn't wait.

"What's up, mom?" he asked excitedly. "Are we moving? Did you get a new job? Do you have a boyfriend? What?"

Julie laughed. "Honey—oops—I mean buddy; I don't have a new job. I surely don't have a boyfriend. But…we might be moving."

"Oh, wow," Brody replied, looking crestfallen. "You mean we're leaving Arlington Heights? Will I be changing schools?" The frown deepened.

"No, we're not leaving Arlington Heights and you'll be at the same school. Peggy and I are talking about having our two families live together."

Now happy, Brody exclaimed, "Mom! That's the best news of all! Jake and I are really great friends! It will be awesome to have him in the same house!"

"Well, it's not official yet. It's something we're just talking about. Peggy is talking to Jake and Lauren today to see what they think. A lot will depend on them."

"Jake'll love it! I know it!" was Brody's boisterous response. Then, a bit more sober, "Maybe even Lauren'll think it's a good idea. She's such a brat! She's always leanin' on Jake and me, pretendin' she's so much more grown up and smart. She's only two years older."

"We're just going to have to wait and see what Peggy finds out, Brody. But please keep this to yourself. Don't discuss it with Jake or other friends until we hear from Peggy, okay?"

"Okay, but I hope it works out. I'd have someone to play video games with all the time! I wouldn't have to be tryin' to teach you how to play. You're not very good, you know."

"No, just another thing I'm not good at," said Julie with a chuckle. "Let me tell you something; I won't miss those video games at all! They drive me nuts!"

"Oh, mom, you're so old-fashioned," said Brody, laughing. "Everybody loves video games…everybody 'cept you, that is."

"As long as it doesn't interfere with your school work. Speaking of school work, how much do you have to do?"

"Not much at all, mom, honest! I have a short paper for English, a chapter to read for social studies and a little assignment for math…a couple of really simple problems to solve."

"Well, get to it. Then we'll have a nice dinner. Maybe we can even play one of those abominable games later."

Julie smiled and turned toward the kitchen as Brody replied. "Great! I'll get the work done. Then we can play Call of Duty," said Brody. "Really…Call of Duty?" Julie asked, turning. "That one again? Don't you have something else?"

"Oh, there are lots of games but none as fun as Call of Duty. Mom… please play that one? Please?"

Well, get at the homework. When it's done, we'll have dinner and talk about it. How about tacos?"

"Tacos? Great! From Taco Bell, right?"

"Yup, Taco Bell. Now get at the homework while I get some things done in the kitchen."

CHAPTER 10

While Brody busied himself with homework and Julie worked in the kitchen of their little apartment, Al worked at the precinct, clearing case files off his desk. The phone rang.

"It's Charlie," said the caller. "We've talked with the roommate. He hasn't seen Evenson since they were at Ed's last night. He thought Evenson had had enough to drink and went home. Goddamnit! It never occurred to him to look when he got home. We woke him. Asked him to look. Really…isn't that amazing? I ain't got any time for these goddamn irresponsible assholes, Al!" Al could hear him pounding on the wooden surface of his desk before continuing the angry tirade.

"The Pepin County boys are callin' Evenson's folks now. We'll know soon if they reached 'em. That'll let us know how soon we might get to talk to 'em."

"Keep me posted," urged Al. "Much as I am not looking forward to meeting the parents of what is probably another victim, I'm ready to do anything but this paperwork."

"I hear ya, man…goddamn paperwork…a pain in the ass! I'll let you know as soon as I know somethin'."

CHAPTER 11

After dinner, Julie cleared the table and stored the leftovers, checked Brody's homework, and goaded him into bed. She leaned over in expectation of getting a good night kiss from her son.

"Mom, I'm too old," protested Brody.

"Maybe you feel that way, but I don't," Julie retorted. "I sort of consider that one little kiss each night payment for space, food and clothes. I think that's a pretty good deal. Don't you?"

"Aw, mom, fine. But, I'm telling you, I'm too old! Just make sure when I have friends over, you don't expect any kisses! Promise?"

"Promise," said Julie, smiling as she tucked him in. She retired to the living room. The room, filled with hand-me-down furniture, was a mismatch of styles and colors, but she loved the randomness of it. As she sank into the sofa, she didn't even consider turning on the television set. She wanted to think.

Carefully, she replayed the news of the 15th drowning death over and over in her mind. *What would Peggy think*, she wondered, *if she knew how happy I am to see those jerks erased?*

As she pondered these answerless questions, the phone rang, interrupting her thoughts.

"Hello?"

"Julie, it's Peggy." Peggy sounded obviously excited. "I just talked to Jake and Lauren. They think the idea is great!"

"Really? Even Lauren?"

"Well, Lauren was her usual snotty, teenage self. After we talked about it for a while, she came around to the idea, particularly when I told her that the arrangement would likely allow a bigger and better place.,

Lauren's excited because I told her she might get the expensive things she always asks for."

"Fantastic!" said Julie. "Do you think she will get annoyed with us constantly being around? I mean, like anything else, I'm sure it won't always be sunshine and roses."

"Well, Jake will never get tired of having Brody around," said Peggy. "But yeah, Lauren will have her ups and downs. She's in that teenage, bitchy stage. I personally think havin' others around to share the pain of a hormonal teenager will be great."

Both women laughed and grew quiet, absorbed in their own private thoughts.

Julie broke the silence. "Are we sure we can put up with each other, given all the things we know? "Oh, for god's sake, will you cut that out," said Peggy. "You're not gonna talk me out of it, no matter what. I know what I want. I love what I know about you, Julie, and I want to know you even better. Sharin' expenses'll be good for both of us. I struggle to make ends meet. So do you. Maybe by puttin' it all together, we'll both be better off."

"I sure hope so," said Julie. I just don't want another disappointment. I'm not a very happy person, Peggy. I want happiness!"

"Trust me, girlfriend. You're gonna be happy. I'll make sure you're so happy you turn cartwheels in a skirt. Heck, we've always gotten along like family. Now, we're even closer. I want you in the room next to me. I want to be able to get a 'fix' whenever we feel like it. Don't you want that, too?"

"I do…I do," said Julie, "but I'd hate to see our friendship end because we get too close. You know what they say about having best friends as roommates. Don't you worry about that?"

"Not one damn bit," replied Peggy quickly. "I can't get you out of my mind. I've concluded I can't live without you bein' close. Heck, just talkin' about it gets me wet."

"I'm wet, too," said Julie, pausing before continuing. "Whoa. That came out of nowhere. I never thought I'd tell anyone *that*. But I do love what we have."

"Don't worry. We'll have some tense moments, I suppose, but if we take 'em one at a time and remember the love we feel, no challenge should be too big."

I wonder what Peggy would think if she knew that I feel actual joy when I hear about the drownings in La Crosse, Julie thought.

After a few more minutes of chitchat, the conversation concluded with a chorus of warm "I love you."

I really do love Peggy, thought Julie, as she sat alone with her thoughts. Things must change. If this new living arrangement worked out, either she had to put the past fully behind her and forget her hunger for revenge or she'd have to tell Peggy. Can she tell—even her best friend? Would she understand? These thoughts haunted her as she got ready for bed, turned off the lights, and slipped beneath the covers.

It was an odd feeling. On one hand, she had a great promise of love and companionship. On the other hand, she held conflicted feelings over 15 deaths.

CHAPTER 12

Back in La Crosse, Charlie and Al were at their desks. It was a gloomy Sunday with thick, dark clouds scuttling across the sky. Rick busied himself with getting ready for the autopsy. He hoped the family would allow the autopsy. Rick didn't know how he'd figure out these drowning deaths otherwise.

"The mother, father and a sister should be here in about an hour," said Charlie when Al answered the phone. "It's gonna be a late night. Want me to pick you up?"

"Sure," said Al, "I'll be here."

"Good. I'm gonna get going. I have to call Rick and let him know."

"Okay." "Let's hope that he and Pat will be able to get the autopsy going, said Al."

After he hung up, Al sat there for a moment, lost in his thoughts. Suddenly, he spun his chair around and opened a filing cabinet drawer with Drowning *Deaths* in big capital letters. The fourteen neatly organized files stood where he had left them earlier. The alphabetized tabs stared at him. Soon there would be another. He pulled out the Sorensen, Shawn file. He held it for a moment. *Buddy, you started all this. I wish you could talk…tell me what I'm overlooking*, Al thought.

He thumbed aimlessly through the rest of the files, his mind spanning the years since 1997. He thought about the deaths he had investigated. It was heartbreaking work to only offer the parents a simple statement: It was a tragic accident. Al wanted more answers, desperately. The terrible string of coincidences never seemed to end. The idea that he missed something major haunted him immensely. He put the Sorensen file away, closed the cabinet, stood, grabbed his parka and headed out to meet Charlie.

***

"We really *do* have to stop meeting like this," joked Al, somberly, as he climbed into the SUV.

They parked the truck outside the emergency entrance at the hospital and stepped into the night. The murkiness of the weather yet again matched their moods. Fog from the river had moved in overnight. Ghost-like figures moved in and out of the lighted entrance, hurrying to escape the cold, damp evening and enter a warm lobby.

The two friends walked down the hall, shoulder to shoulder, heads down, and then entered through a door. The doorplate read *No Entrance, Autopsy in Progress.*

Inside, Rick and Pat were waiting. They all exchanged somber greetings. "The parents should be here in a half hour or so. They will have a daughter with them. I guess Charlie and I will handle the introductions and the identification. We'll need your help when it comes to the autopsy, "said Al.

"We do our best to make it seem like the parents have a choice," he said, addressing Dr. Pat Grebin. "This time, given what you spotted, we have something more. Let's hope we don't have to use it."

"We've always expected more pushback than we've gotten," chimed in a somber Charlie. "Parents wanna make sure they do everything they can to put reason to a death like this. We'll handle the first part; it's a shitty job. Break in whenever you want."

"Coffee, anyone?" asked Rick, looking at his watch. "We just have time for a cup."

Nods all around, the four headed down the hall to the brightly lit, colorfully decorated cafeteria. They quickly got cups, filled them with coffee and grabbed a table in the corner.

Charlie slurped, grabbed for a napkin and blotted his lips. "Goddamnit! It ain't bad enough I have to live on this shit. Now, I burned my mouth."

Al turned to him with a stern look and Charlie quickly got the point.

"Oops, sorry Pat…er…I wasn't thinkin'."

"No big deal," said Pat. "My big worry is that small mark in the ear is not just another false alarm. Rick told me there have been other false hopes before."

Looking at him, she said, "I agree with you that creating false hope is the worst. Let's hope for more this time."

"Yah, false hope's a terrible thing," said Charlie. He squirmed a bit. "I keep tellin' myself to calm down. Goddamnit, it just doesn't work; we need a break!"

As the words hung in the air, the four colleagues, brought together by a senseless string of deaths, sipped their coffee in silence for a few minutes. The group rose without a word and headed back to work.

Four minutes later, a call from the admitting desk announced that the family had arrived. Al and Charlie walked to meet them. As they neared the entry, their steps slowed. This was the toughest part of the job. They steeled themselves.

Lars Evenson and his wife Goldene were an attractive couple in their late 40s and their daughter, Debbie, was beautiful and blonde. They were obviously distraught. Tear marks stained the women's cheeks. The man wore a tortured look.

"Folks," began Al softly, "we're sorry to have brought you here. We know the next few minutes are gonna be tough. Please know we will understand your reaction, whatever it is. Don't try to suppress feelings. We hate this, too."

Charlie took Mrs. Evenson by the arm. Al gestured to Mr. Evenson, pointing the way. The daughter fell in line. The five proceeded to the room to do the dreaded identification process.

The doctors sympathetically greeted the Evensons, introduced themselves, and explained why this was all necessary for a positive I.D. As the doctors started to move the white cover over the body, the Evensons moved closer. They stood rigidly as the shroud was lifted.

"Oh, my god!" screamed Mrs. Evenson. "That's Rolf…that's our baby!" As tears rolled down her pale face, her husband and daughter took her by the arms. Ken nodded, and all three turned away from the table. With the doctors leading the way, the small procession moved to a nearby conference room. The doctors and cops were quiet, waiting for the Evensons to compose themselves. The horror of the identification and confirmation of the terrible truth over, Goldene and Debbie sobbed quietly into Lars' coat.

After several minutes passed, Rick sat forward and rested his hands on the table. He began to speak in a soft and somber tone. "Much as we wish we could spare you this agony, there are several things we need to discuss. Do you need a little more time or should we proceed?"

"Go ahead," said Lars, his voice cracking. "It's probably best to get things over with."

"There will be papers to sign," continued Rick. "We have some questions, too. Is it okay if I go ahead?"

Lars Evenson nodded.

Among the papers to sign will be those confirming the victim's identity. Others will tell us who will collect Rolf's body. Before the release, we're hoping you will permit us to conduct an autopsy. That would help, we believe, answer a number of questions and bring some closure to how this happened," said Rick.

As the Evenson women quietly sobbed, Lars was silent for a minute. "Yes, we will want that. We need to know how this happened. But, Rick... Pat...will you be sure to send him home so we can have a normal service? His friends will want to see him one more time...and," trailed Lars. The doctors knew exactly what he meant.

"If you are worried about us doing anything that will affect the appearance of your son's face, let me assure you that will not happen. As we made our preliminary inspection, Pat noticed a mark within the left ear that we would like to take a closer look at, but there was nothing else above the neck that should cause any sort of intrusive procedure. If we find anything suspicious in the area, we will contact you before proceeding further."

"I guess that's fair," said Lars quietly. "Is that all you need?"

"With the exception of the paperwork, yes," replied Rick. "There will also be papers to sign indicating your consent to the autopsy. I'd like to put you in touch with our office manager to handle that. We also have chaplains on call, if you desire that service."

"I think we would like that," said Lars, his wife and daughter nodding in assent.

"That will be no problem," Rick assured them. "Let me get you to the office."

As the Evensons rose, Al also stood and spoke. "Deputy Berzinski and I will also have a few questions, if you don't mind. We will take as little time as possible."

The doctors shook hands with the visitors, ushered them to the office, and then quietly retreated to begin their grim work.

CHAPTER 13

Julie Sonoma drifted into a fitful sleep, tossing and turning, her dreams haunted by a collage of faces, ethereal images of drowning victims. Their faces often haunted her dreams.

Her night passed agonizingly. When she awoke, she couldn't shake the nagging thought that something was different about this death.

As she drove toward the clinic, her mind was in La Crosse. She thought about the latest death. A cacophony of car horns startled her back into reality. Realizing just in time that the horns were for her as she entered the intersection of North Arlington Heights Road and Euclid Avenue, she slammed on the brakes, stopping just in time to avoid colliding with traffic in the intersection.

"Oh, my god!" she thought. "I have to get it together."

As the light changed, she had composed herself sufficiently to travel through the intersection and turn into the employee parking lot of the Kahn Clinic.

The clinic was a multi-specialty practice employing 46 doctors and an equal number of P.A.'s. Each P.A. worked with a doctor. Julie was especially happy to be employed by ear, nose and throat specialist Dr. Jerome Esch, a handsome, middle-aged man with a great sense of humor and a phenomenal bedside manner. He was also especially good about sharing things with Julie and teaching her things that would make her more effective. She was now a master at needle selection, thanks to his lessons. She learned about the inner ear's sensitivity to injections because the blood vessels found there swiftly distributed fluid throughout the head. Dr. Esch had also instructed her in mixing anesthetics to achieve different types of sleep.

As she entered the employee break room, Peggy was already there, the constant cup of black coffee at her elbow as she talked animatedly to an attractive brunette.

"Julie, come here will you?" said Peggy, waving her over. "There's someone I want you to meet. This is Kelly Hammermeister. It's Kelly's first day on the job. And, guess what? She's a graduate of the P.A. program at La Crosse. I'm guessing you two will know lots of the same people."

Soon Peggy, Julie and Kelly were chatting like they'd been friends for ages. Kelly was a native of Eau Claire, Wisconsin, the daughter of dairy farmers. She had a sister and four brothers. Kelly was the youngest at age 31, the last to graduate from college and the first to find her way to the Greater Chicago Area for employment.

"It's really nice to meet some friendly people so soon," she said, her deep brown eyes flashing from Peggy to Julie. "I was worried about what people here would be like, but if they're all like you, this will be a great place for me."

Kelly was assigned to the other ENT specialist at the clinic and would be working in proximity to Julie, so the two women walked together to their area of the clinic. Julie introduced Kelly to the office manager, Sharon Walker and left, promising Kelly she would show her around the office and introduce her to others when she and Sharon were finished.

CHAPTER 14

Back at the Gundersen Clinic in Wisconsin, Rick had just hung up the phone.

"The paperwork is complete," he reported, turning his chair to face Pat. "Time to get to work. By the way I'm glad you're joining me on this one. If there's something to find, we'll find it. We all want answers."

"I'm hoping you'll let me take a look at that spot I found right away," said Pat, pulling her left glove and then her right glove into place, a gesture done countless times.

"Absolutely. We need to know if there's anything there, if a killer left behind a clue," replied Rick. "If we find something, it could impact everything else."

The body was positioned on its right side. Pat shifted into place. She moved the surgical light into place, focusing its intense light on the left ear, and illuminating a tiny spot just inside the entrance to the ear canal.

"See that," she said, pointing. "It definitely looks like a needle puncture."

Picking up a magnifying glass, Pat studied the spot for what seemed like minutes and turned to Rick. "Rick, take a look. It looks like there's bruising…and doesn't that look like a tiny speck of blood on the spot's far side, just above the puncture?"

She moved so Rick could take a look. He pushed the magnifying glass to a place where he could view the tiny spot up close. The doctor peered into the glass, moving it slowly back and forth several times. He pushed his chair back, sat up, and looked at Pat, astonished.

"I think you're right," he said. "There are definite signs of bruising, and there's a tiny fleck of what could possibly be blood. Let's extract a small piece of tissue that includes the spot, the surrounding bruised area, and the possible blood. The big concern I have is making the excision deep enough to give us some idea of the depth of the puncture. If we know the depth, we will know if it was made with a needle or not, and, if so, the needle size. Do you think you can remove an area of sufficient size to give us a good look without providing any sort of disfiguration?"

"Of course. I'm positive I can do that. I'm guessing that any wound will be easily masked by a bit of putty and a touch of makeup."

Pat gathered the necessary tools: a lamina spreader, scalpel, and forceps. Steadying her right hand, Pat carefully used the spreader to widen the auditory canal. She then carefully worked the scalpel into place beyond the tiny puncture mark. With a sure hand, she quickly made a small cut to the right of the mark, made a similar cut to its left and then completed the triangle, gently working the tiny skin particle loose before grasping it with the forceps and gently removing it.

The tissue sample was a three-dimensional pyramid. The puncture was in a very odd spot to be the result of an accident, unless the victim had been probing his ear with a sharp object.

"The specimen has a depth of about 1.2 centimeters and there is no break at its end," she reported as she examined the small tissue sample under the magnifier. "I have also found what appears to be a hair on the victim, and, unless I am mistaken, it doesn't belong to him. I found it just where his neck and shoulder blade meet. I suspect it hung there because it was under his shirt collar. That probably kept the river water from washing it away."

"Let's get the skin sample under the microscope. See if we can peel away enough layers to find the termination of the puncture. Perhaps there will be a clue there," suggested Rick, peering intently over her shoulder. "I think we should also do some scans on the hair. Do you agree?"

"I was going to do that," replied Pat. "Do you want to help? Or do you want to start the rest of the work?"

"I want to see what your exam produces. I'm gonna hang in here until you uncover the terminus of the puncture. Let's do that first. When that's done, we'll deal with the hair specimen."

Pat moved the sample carefully under a microscope. "It looks like it was made by an ultra-fine pen needle. Depending upon the pressure applied, this would place the depth short of eight millimeters," said Pat.

Working with extreme caution, she carefully positioned the microscope so she could peel away layers of the specimen and still observe the results. Her first dissection removed a portion of the tiny fatty layer within the canal. The puncture appeared to have been deflected by the elastic cartilage. Another tiny cut exposed what appeared to be the termination of the puncture. There was what appeared to be a minute disruption of the fatty layer beyond the end of the puncture.

"Rick, I think we have something here," she said without looking up. Pat moved her chair away. "Take a look and tell me what you see."

Sliding into position, Rick hovered over the microscope, tuning the focus as he moved in closer.

"Hmmm, yes, I see what you mean," answered Rick. His reply was nearly a whisper. "This is definitely a puncture mark. And there's a disturbance in the tissue at the end of the puncture. It appears a lot like the remains of an injection." The realization dawned on him. "Pat, this could be what we've been looking for. This could be a major find!"

As Pat sat down after Rick vacated the chair, she thought for a minute. "I'd like to call George Lee, an anesthesiologist. You know George, right?" As Rick nodded, she said, "We need someone who deals with injections on a regular basis. I'm betting George can either refute our suspicions or confirm that there is something here."

"Good call," said Rick. "Let's see if he's in."

He quickly picked up the phone and dialed.

"Is George in?" he asked after a few seconds. Smiling he turned toward Pat as he returned the receiver to its cradle.

"We're in luck. George just finished a surgery. They think he's probably still in the locker room. If they can find him, they'll send him over."

While waiting, the two doctors sorted out the rest of the work. Rick, it was decided, would work on the chest cavity while Pat completed the cranial exam. Her work, though, would wait for Dr. Lee's advice. In the meantime, she'd start analyzing the hair.

As Rick turned to the table, pulled the microphone into place, and began the Y incision, Pat slumped into the chair and put her head on her arms. "Tired," she mumbled.

Rick heard her and responded. "Yea, it's been a long day, and if you're on to something, it's gonna get a lot longer."

The double doors opened silently to admit a smiling Asian man. "You called?" asked Dr. Lee.

"Hi, Doctor Lee," greeted Pat as she rose from the chair. "We really need your expertise here. We've been examining another drowning victim. Rick has just begun the autopsy, but your expert advice is needed about something we found in the auditory canal of the left ear."

With Lee looking over her shoulder, Pat displayed the specimen under the scope, then moved so he could see: "It appears to me to be a puncture. I'm not nearly as good as you at identifying things like this, but I think it could have been made by an ultra-fine pen needle.

As he peered into the microscope, she told him, "I have some tissue specimens over here, too. I'd be grateful if you'd take look at those, too."

Dr. Lee bent over the microscope to take a preliminary look and nodded his head. He reached for the chair. Sitting down, he again put his eye to the microscope and began to talk, or hum, rather, to himself as he focused the instrument.

"I believe this is a wound caused by a needle," he reported without looking up. "Disturbance of the fatty tissue at termination of incision would indicate dispersal of some material, although disturbance is nearly invisible. I'm amazed you found it."

"The real questions now are," began Pat, "what made the disturbance? And if it was made by a substance, what substance?"

"Yes," responded Dr. Lee, "but I'm guessing the puncture permitted injection of some type of fluid into the layer immediately outside the auditory canal. Thorough examination of that portion of specimen could be helpful. I would also suggest thorough analysis of the stomach contents, although unlikely to produce anything. I think this injection was aimed at the auditory nerve and then to other nerves."

"Thanks," said Rick, who had just removed the stomach and placed it into an enamel pot. "As much as I can tell from feel, it likely contains only liquid, but we will send it on for a thorough look. And we'll look closely, too."

Dr. Lee left the other two to finish the autopsy which revealed no other abnormalities.

"It seems obvious to me from the contusions and lacerations that our victim made a short trip in an angry Mississippi," said Rick. "What we have to hope is the puncture you spotted will produce something."

"I'm on it," replied Pat, picking up the sample and walking from the room. Soon the slide containing the specimen was in the hands of Gundersen's top researcher Sarah Gile, who had a national reputation for her work with anesthetic agents. Pat delivered an exhaustive explanation. "This is going to take hours, maybe a day or two. Why don't you go home and get some rest? Check back when you come in tomorrow," suggested Sarah.

"Good idea." Pat then stopped back to tell Rick she was going to leave to get some rest. She found him washing up after concluding his work. Together they walked from the facility into a parking lot streaked by dawn's early light and the myriad of orange mercury vapor lights.

"See you tomorrow," said Pat.

"I think it's today," replied Rick, a tight smile creasing his lips. "Yea, I'll catch three or four hours and be back here by eight or nine. I want to be here when Sarah is done."

"Night," said Pat, opening the door of her car. She started the motor and began to drive toward the exit. She noticed Rick unlocking the door of his late-model Audi. She waved, then realized that he likely couldn't see the gesture even if he had been looking.

CHAPTER 15

Al and Charlie were also wrapping up their late-night office vigils. Al called his friend as he prepared to leave.

"Just heard from Rick," he reported. "He told me he might have something for us this time. Seems that Pat found a puncture wound in the victim's ear. She and Rick think it might have been made by an ultra-fine pen needle, whatever the heck that is. Apparently it's used in injections."

"Good," said Charlie. "Now maybe we can end this ridiculous coincidence theory?"

"Hopefully. Alright, I want to be rested when Pat and Rick call. I'm heading home to get some sleep. I'm gonna set the alarm for nine, which should put me back here about 10," finished Al.

"Great goddamn idea," replied Charlie. "I'll call when I'm back."

"Sleep tight, buddy! I'm just hoping I can sleep. Talk to you later." Al hung up the phone and went home.

CHAPTER 16

Just a few hours later, Julie started her work day, preparing for her patients. A shadow darkened her office, causing her to look up. The shadow was a smiling Kelly Hammermeister.

"The HR paperwork's done," said Kelly, smiling.

"Let me show you around," offered Julie, standing. Taking her visitor by the arm, she walked Kelly down the hall, stopping at each doorway to introduce her to co-workers.

After they had been through the department, Kelly looked at Julie quizzically. "You're not going to give me a test, are you? Right now, faces and names are a blur."

"Nope, no tests. You'll be a veteran before you know it." She handed Kelly off to the department receptionist, Harriet Willis. Julie returned to her office.

Suddenly, Julie looked at the office clock. *5:10.* The office had become eerily quiet as lights were turned off down the hall. She walked quickly to Kelly's office and asked her if she'd like to join her and Peggy for a glass of wine at an Italian place across the street. Kelly quickly agreed, reached for her coat and turned off her office light. The two set off to find Peggy, who worked in orthopedics under the surgeon Andrew Rother.

As the three women left the clinic, a stiff, northerly breeze made the air seem even colder than 34 degrees.

"B-r-r-r," said Peggy. "Winter's on the way. I could get along just fine without it."

"But," offered Kelly, "what would Christmas be without cold and snow? And what would fall be like without brisk temperatures and bright leaves? You wouldn't like to live in San Diego, would you? It's always warm and green there…boring!"

Julie agreed. "I wouldn't trade the Midwest for anywhere on earth. I love the change of seasons. I'd prefer a small town to the big city, but Arlington Heights is pretty darn nice…sort of the best of both worlds… small-town atmosphere with big-city amenities."

Soon the three women entered Luigi's, the favorite happy hour restaurant for Peggy and Julie. The womanly quickly discarded their coats, secured a table in front of the vast fireplace and ordered glasses of wine.

As the drinks arrived—pinot noir for Peggy and Julie, chardonnay for Kelly—talk turned to work and life. Kelly was divorced, a bitter separation, she said, and not anxious to be involved in romance any time soon.

"He was a jerk to begin with, then he drowned in the Mississippi two years ago," she said. "The loss was surprising but not devastating. I don't miss my husband, the SOB, that's for sure."

Julie almost spit out her wine, noting the similarity to her own story.

"Join the club," offered Peggy. "Each of us can tell the same story."

Silence settled over the table. Peggy broke the silence.

"Maybe we should get into the rent-a-dad business? Seems there are lots of people like us whose kids could use an adult male in their lives. But please, don't get any ideas. I've had all I want of married life. I miss the occasional caress and the extra paycheck, but that's more than offset by the bad times."

Soon the three were talking even more about their lives. Fueled by the coincidence of their circumstances and the wine, talk flowed freely. Julie didn't mention Shawn.

After each of the women had described her own experience with widowhood, they ordered second glasses of wine. After a sip of the refilled glass placed before her, Kelly asked the other two a question.

"Did you see the *Tribune* today? Seems there is another drowning victim in La Crosse…another kid. There have been so many, one or more each year. Coincidence seems a stretch. I always thought that when Tom died. He wasn't the kind to get wasted and wander away. He was drinking with college buddies, but they are pretty serious guys."

"I didn't see the paper," interrupted Julie, speaking quickly, "but I know there have been a long string of deaths." She glanced at her watch and exclaimed, "Ouch, 6:15! Brody, my son, is going to think I got lost. I need to dash. See you tomorrow." Julie headed for the door.

"Are you all right for a little while? My kids won't be home for 45 minutes. I have time to kill. I'd love to finish this glass of wine," said Peggy.

"Great by me," replied Kelly.

Peggy glanced at Julie's hurried exit out of the restaurant and sighed. "Kelly, you should know that the love of Julie's life drowned during their junior year at La Crosse. If Julie seemed tense when she left, that might be the reason."

"Oh, my god! I'm so sorry. That makes me feel terrible."

"You couldn't have known," replied Peggy, soothingly patting her new friend's arm. "I'm sure she'll tell you one day. Let her bring it up. It's a sensitive topic. Julie's a great person, but even though it happened years ago, you'd think it happened yesterday. When she brings it up, just act surprised."

CHAPTER 17

Driving home, Julie knew it was going to be one of those quiet nights. Brody would be home in about a half hour, hungry as usual. If this was a typical evening, he would wolf down dinner and head for his room and homework. He was a popular kid, so there probably would be time spent texting. She knew that would mean another night alone with her brooding, melancholy thoughts. Her pensive mood foreshadowed an unpleasant evening.

True to form, Brody rushed in a half-hour later and, while taking off his coat, asked the usual barrage of questions, "What's for dinner, mom? Will it be ready soon? I'm starved, and I have to get going over to Bill's. He and I are going to study. There's a math test tomorrow. I want to be prepared."

Bill was a neighbor from down the street with whom Brody had grown close over the few years they had lived in this apartment. Bill's father, Dan Hanson, was a handsome man about her age who had given off plenty of hints that he was interested in her. It was no use. She wasn't interested.

These were her thoughts as she cleared the dishes and cleaned the kitchen before settling down with a new David Baldacci book. He was one of her favorite authors, and, normally, time spent in bed with *him* would be a treat. Even Baldacci couldn't help Julie shatter her morose mood.

The thought of moving in with Peggy excited her for many reasons, not the least of which was the economic help for her and Brody.

With Peggy, she would have a family and the two of them could raise their kids together. She worried that her dark moods and thoughts of revenge would scare Peggy. *Could she turn them off,* she wondered? Would the feelings become overwhelming once she felt the first crisp, fall winds?

Could she control her emotions and the lust for revenge for the death of her lover?

These questions haunted her as she sat in near darkness while Brody studied at Bill's. Would she be able to sleep?

CHAPTER 18

Al, Charlie, Rick, and Pat eagerly greeted a new day. Would they finally learn today what caused these string of deaths?

Rick was the first person out the door. He hadn't slept well. When the first streaks of dawn crossed the sky, he was already out of bed and getting ready for what promised to be a long day at work. He hoped Sarah's overnight work would produce new information.

Al and Charlie also had restless nights. After getting ready for work, Al called to ask if Charlie wanted to join him for breakfast at the little place off Losey Boulevard.

"Coffee's gonna be enough for me," mumbled Charlie, yawning. "I didn't sleep worth a damn."

"I couldn't sleep either," replied Al, "but I think breakfast will do us good. Charlie, the notion of you passing up a meal is just not something I can fathom."

"Ya, guess you're right. See you at Ma's in a half hour?"

"Yup, I'll be waiting."

As Charlie walked in, exhibiting that freshly scrubbed morning look, Al was already buttering toast and getting ready to dig into a plate of fried eggs and ham.

"Couldn't you wait?" said Charlie, in more of a series of grunts than actual words.

"Well, I thought you'd be here sooner. Usually you can't wait to dig into Ma's pancakes...or is it going to be a waffle today?"

"I may have both, thank you very much! And bacon and sausage, too."

"What's that, Deputy Berzinski?" asked Ma Pritchard, wiping her hands on her apron. "Did I hear you say pancakes *and* a waffle and bacon *and* sausage, too?"

"Yup, Ma. It's gonna be a busy day. I have to help Al solve a case again…and—"

"And you're a growing boy. So I guess that 52-inch waist ain't yet fully grown?" asked Ma. "Pretty soon, you'll be buying your pants at Omar the tentmaker."

"Ah, Ma," said Charlie, cupping his hands to his mouth and whispering loud enough for everyone at the counter to hear, "We got another drowning. We think we're finally onto something."

"About the only thing you're onto Charlie is another notch in the belt. You're gettin' so big that soon you won't be able to move around," she lectured.

Breakfast finished and the good-natured banter of Ma's behind them, Al and Charlie got into their cars and headed to work. Lost in thought, Al maneuvered his Prius through moderate traffic while thinking about Rick and Pat. He wondered if there was news. He thought about calling them, but it was early and he'd be there soon enough.

Charlie was also preoccupied. He was thinking about the young Mr. Evenson and how bleak the holidays were going to be for the couple in Durand who raised him.

***

When Al arrived at his desk, there was a note from Rick, asking him to call his cell. He dialed the now far-too-familiar number. It rang four times before a drowsy-sounding Rick answered.

"Hey Al, thought it might be you. I've been trying to wake up since getting a call from our researcher about a half hour ago. Sarah Gile, the best researcher we have on staff, says one of the tests she ran—a stereochemistry examination that identifies agents according to the direction they deflect polarized light a test so obscure that she almost didn't' run it—picked up a trace of Etomidate. It's a short-acting intravenous agent used for general anesthesia and sedation. There's another substance involved, too, but Sarah hasn't been able to determine what. To be honest, I'm surprised she found the Etomidate. The drug usually breaks down so quickly, it's gone in a flash, but, for some reason, Sarah was able to find it…maybe because of where it was found in the ear canal."

Al considered all of this for a moment. "Rick, would the Etomidate have enough power to knock someone out long enough to get them to the river?"

"Not by itself, that's for sure. But one of the advantages of Etomidate is that it easily mixes with many other anesthetics to produce quick sedation in trauma victims. It's an initial sedative that's administered before the general anesthesia. It also allows the victim to communicate with their surgeons before unconsciousness occurs."

"Do you think Sarah will be able to identify other agents?" asked Al.

"She might, but even if she doesn't, I think we can at least suggest something other than accidental death. Etomidate is often taken recreationally because it creates a euphoric condition. If Sarah can identify drugs that were mixed with the Etomidate, it will tell us whether this was recreational drug use or murder."

"When will we know?"

"I'm hoping Sarah will be finishing up by the time I get over to her lab," reported Rick. "I'll be there in a half hour after cleaning up a few things. As soon as I know something, you'll be my first call."

"Thanks, buddy," said Al. He hung up.

Al called Charlie with the news.

"Goddamn, we better tie up loose ends on the other cases we're working, Al," suggested Charlie. "If Sarah identifies other drugs, we're gonna be busy the next few days."

"We sure are," agreed Al. "Assuming we have something definitive here, we need to think about exhuming bodies of other victims to see if there are traces of the same drug."

"Yeah, and if we find another with the same mark, that means we're talking about a serial killer here. The docs are gonna have to advise us on how far back we should reach. I sure as hell don't know how fast the drug disappears from a body. Then there's cremation. Those would be useless to us.

"I think we're gonna have to talk with Rick and Pat. They should be able to give us some advice about which bodies to test. I know examination of ashes can produce lots of DNA information, but we were told the traces of the poison disappear rapidly. About the only chance we have is finding more puncture marks that might have been missed in autopsies," said Al. He paused. "We better not get ahead of ourselves."

Both men turned silent. They busied themselves with paperwork while the clock ticked.

CHAPTER 19

Twenty minutes later, Rick strode toward Sarah Gile's lab. Stopping at Pat's office, he found the door locked. She had not yet arrived.

"Hi, Sarah," said Rick, entering a tastefully decorated and brightly lit lab space. "Anything new?"

"I'm…just…starting…to…find…out," came the halting reply from the researcher, who was bent over a microscope." Looking up, Sarah continued. "I suspect a combination of drugs. I think that would be needed to achieve enough drowsiness to get a victim into the river. I have some slide samples. They'll be finished soon. Hang around a few minutes. We can look at the results together."

Rick watched the younger woman work. Sarah was a master at skillfully manipulating the microscope.

"Okay, look at this," asked Sarah. "Tell me what you see."

Bending over the microscope, Rick studied the image. "It looks as if there's residue of more than one material. I know the Etomidate is likely responsible for the slight aqua coloring. I would have missed that if I didn't know what I was looking for. There also seems to be a faint tinge of a sandy-colored border…or am I just seeing things?"

"I don't think you are. It's slight, but I think that stain was made by some other agent mixed with the Etomidate. I'm betting the combination created incapacitation. The question is what else was used."

Just then the door opened and Pat walked in. She looked refreshed and dressed for a hard day. The jeans, sweatshirt, and tennis shoes suggested she was expecting a long day, too, and wanted to be dressed as comfortably as possible.

"Pat, check this out," said Rick, gesturing to the microscope. "Sarah and I think we've found something. We'd like another opinion."

Pat bent over the microscope, attaching her eye to the instrument as her long auburn hair cascaded forward. She tucked it back behind her ear and adjusted the eyepiece, focusing the scope. She inched closer, hand on the lens adjustment.

"I see a kind of aqua-colored spot," she said, her voice muffled by her position. "I suspect that's from the Etomidate. Then…there's just the faintest trace…of color that looks like the mark left at the outer edge of a paper burn…kind of brownish yellow, right?"

"We saw it too," responded Sarah as Pat looked up in time to see Rick nodding. "Now we need to figure out what it is."

"Is there anything we can do to help?" asked Rick.

"Not really," answered Sarah. "There's such a tiny bit of material I worry there isn't even enough to test. Figuring this out is going to take all the skill I have. Assuming I can pull something out of the sample, it won't take long. You can wait, if you want."

"I'm not leaving," said Pat, hands on her hips and her mouth drawn in tense lines.

"Nor I," echoed Rick. "Unless I can get you ladies something?"

"Coffee'd be nice," responded Sarah.

"If you can handle a milk, too, I'd like that," replied Pat.

"Two coffees and a milk…and maybe some mini-doughnuts coming up," said Rick, smiling as he headed for the door and walked toward the cafeteria.

"Go ahead, Sarah," urged Pat. "I'll make myself inconspicuous and watch you work."

Taking some glass slides and chemical-filled bottles from the overhead cabinet, Sarah carefully studied the specimen, moving the microscope's stage a bit lower to allow her to maneuver the material on the slide. Carefully, she utilized a scalpel to create a series of small specimen slides, then treated each with liquid from the various bottles near her right hand.

She gently moved the slides to the Vectra quantitative pathology imaging system. The device made quick work of sorting through the drugs that could have created the sandy tinge.

"Bingo!" she exclaimed, as the machine's light blinked from red to green. She studied the result. "We've got a hit; it's a dandy. The machine says the stain was caused by Midazolam. Now that's a nasty concoction. The jab of a quick sedation followed with a knockout punch. It's no wonder this guy drowned. It must have been a horrible death, too, because he would have been just conscious enough to know what was happening but helpless to do anything about it."

"I've heard of it," said Pat, "but I have never used it. What does it do?"

"It can be a nasty knockout drug," replied Sarah. "It's one of about 35 benzodiazepines, but this one in particular has a murderous use. It's been used as part of a three-drug cocktail, with vecuronium bromide and potassium chloride in Florida and Oklahoma prisons during capital killings. It has also been used along with hydromorphone in a two-drug protocol in Ohio and Arizona executions."

"What has?" asked Rick, returning to the lab and depositing two coffee cups, a milk and a tray of doughnuts on the nearby table. "I just caught the last bit of that. Tell me?"

Deep frowns crossed the faces of the other two docs as they thought of the young man's terror during his last moments.

"Sarah has identified another drug as Midazolam. And we know now that this victim was no accident. Looks like we've got a real, honest-to-god clue," murmured Pat.

Rick shook his head in agreement, then said, his voice barely audible. "At least now Al and Charlie have something to work with."

***

"Rouse here," Al answered in a gruff voice when he picked up the phone.

"It's Rick, Al. You and Charlie might want to get over here as quickly as you can; we have something for you."

"You're kidding! I've got a million questions. Are you sure?"

"Yup, we're 98-percent certain that young Mr. Evenson is no accidental victim. He had some help—lots of it!"

"Gimme a second to get Charlie and we'll be right over!"

Finally.

CHAPTER 20

In Arlington Heights, quiet settled over the Sonoma apartment. Brody had just gone to bed. Julie, tired after a long day of work, snuggled back into the corner of her sofa with the Baldacci book.

She couldn't focus on the book and became lost in her own thoughts. She reached for the newspaper to check the real estate section. There were several houses on North Hickory Avenue and a rental on North Illinois Avenue. Julie circled them and reached for her purse, tucking the newspaper inside. She'd show the ads to Peggy in the morning.

As she settled back onto the couch and pulled the throw over her lap, she thought about the houses. The one on North Hickory sounded interesting. She didn't know the area well. She knew it was upscale, relatively secluded, and featured big, old houses that once were home to the wealthy elite as the Chicago sprawl spread west from Lake Michigan. *If the house was anywhere near affordable*, she thought, *it might be a good one.*

She tried to concentrate on the book, but, try as she might, she just couldn't get into it. It wasn't because it was a dull read. Tonight, her thoughts swirled around La Crosse, Shawn, the other drownings, and her romantic interlude with Peggy. Finally, still lost in thought, she checked the doors and turned off the light heading for a warm shower and, hopefully, a good night's sleep.

It didn't happen. After tossing and turning for what seemed like hours, Julie got up, made a cup of tea and continued to think. She figured that a move with Peggy would be great for her and her son. If anything happened to her or to Peggy, there would be a solution for the kids. Even so, she wasn't sure that she wanted a committed relationship. It was nice to have the dalliance, but she was starting to wonder if Peggy wanted it to be something more. She hoped that Peggy felt the same way as her…that their time alone together was simply a way to lose themselves in pleasure for a few minutes. Maybe Peggy wanted no more than Julie did: a great friendship with a few benefits to relieve urges. Julie decided that before any move took place, she would have a visit with Peggy to clarify things. After all, it was a big move; both women should want the same thing.

CHAPTER 21

As dawn broke over a sleeping city of La Crosse, Al and Charlie were up and working. They had been at it for several hours. After talking with the doctors and Sarah, they were planning the best way to approach a number of things. The first issue was whether and how to announce a potential break in the case. Another was planning a visit to the Evensons to find more information regarding their son's friends and relationships. Finally, what were the next steps? How could they track down the killer in their midst? They needed to confirm that this was a serial killing and not just a single act.

"Al, I don't think we should allow the Pepin County boys to handle the next talks with the Evensons," suggested Charlie. "I think that's something that has to be done by either one or both of us. Maybe they'll be happy to hear it was something other than drunkenness."

"Absolutely," agreed Al. "I think we should do it today. I also think we'd better tell our bosses. They're gonna have to clear the decks for us. This one's gonna take some time and considerable energy."

Two hours later, the white unmarked car was headed north on Highway 35. They had gotten permission to focus all their efforts on this case from La Crosse County Sheriff Dwight Hooper and Police Chief Brent Whigg, who also promised whatever they needed to aid the investigation. Charlie and Al were told to spare no expense to get the job done.

First up was the Evenson visit. How would Goldene and Lars take the news that the Rolf's death was not accidental? Would they supply useful information?

Three hours later, they knew no more than when they left La Crosse. The Evensons expressed amazement at the news. According to his family, Rolf had no enemies. He was a popular member of the UWL junior class, just like his time at Durand High School. Everyone liked Rolf. He had numerous friends. All of this information matched what Charlie and Al heard in La Crosse.

As the unmarked car headed south, Charlie and Al traded notes. It was interesting and important, they agreed, that there had been no similar cases in other communities on either side of the river. Two towns of particular interest were Winona, Minnesota, and Dubuque, Iowa. Like La Crosse, they were college communities. Sure, Winona had tragic accidents involving students sometimes that became notable. The deaths of five St. Mary's University students when their car plunged off a road along the river several years earlier was the most recent case. But there had been no drowning reports of young males there. There was no pattern to the deaths in La Crosse, other than the victims were young men, most of whom had been drinking in bars near the Mississippi.

Comparing notes as they went, the trip passed quickly. Passing through Nelson, Wisconsin, they drove to Wabasha and caught the four-lane Highway 61 south toward La Crosse. Al held the car at a steady 70 miles an hour.

After passing Winona, Al raised the question of exhumation. "We're gonna have to take a look at other bodies."

"Yup, no question. I think we're gonna have to talk with Rick and Pat. They should be able to give us some advice about which bodies to test."

While Charlie stared at the river, Al reached for the car phone and punched speed dial. "Rick," he said, "Charlie and I are on our way home from Durand. No, nothing new. We do need to talk to you and Pat. Any chance we can stop by in about 20 minutes? Okay, see you."

"They'll be waiting," said Al. "They are as anxious as we are to move this thing along."

"Al, I'm just goddamned worried about screwing this up. We finally got the break we want but now our asses are on the line big time. One little fuck-up, and we're gonna be the laughin' stock of La Crosse, or, worse, we could lose a conviction."

"Don't even think about that," said Al. "It's not gonna happen. We're good, thorough investigators, Charlie. We'll get the job done. I believe that."

"Wish I did," grumbled Charlie. "Nothin' about my life is goin' very well these days. Charlene bitches at me every time she sees me. The kids are a pain in the ass. And these drownings are a bitch!"

"I know how you feel," commiserated Al, steering the unmarked car across the interstate bridge into La Crosse. "I know things are rough at home. Thank god I don't have trouble at home. JoAnne is wonderful and the kids are great, too. If we can solve this one, we're all gonna be on cloud nine."

"Geez, Al, we've been married 29 years, the kids are almost gone and each day it gets worse. Nothing I do is worth a shit. She complains about everything. Every time we fight I resolve to divorce her and then I'm too lazy to get it done. But I'm getting closer."

An hour and a half later, after talking to the docs, Charlie and Al squeezed into Al's cube, studying a sheet of paper.

"They said we could safely go back to 2008," said Charlie, his notes in hand, "and maybe to 2007. There was nothing in the stomach contents, which means that any trace DNA would be nonexistent. That means we need to check on Schneider, Darst, Shapiro and Hintzle. Which two do you want?"

"Makes no difference. What say we start with the undertakers?" suggested Al. "We can find out as much as we can from them. Then, if we find reason, we can contact the parents. How about I take Hintzle and Shapiro? That leaves Darst and Schneider for you?"

"Sounds good…where's a phone?"

Al pointed Charlie to a small conference room, then left to make his calls.

They reconnected 45 minutes later. The two men had been successful.

"Darst was cremated, so he's out. But Schneider is a good bet," reported Charlie. "The mortician said his parents asked that special care be taken in the embalming. They also bought the most expensive vault available, one that creates a vacuum. Shit, nobody'd give a crap about me. I'll be lucky if I get a pine box."

Al laughed, "I don't think it'll be that bad, Charlie. But that sounds like it could give us some great information. Both Shapiro and Hintzle were buried in basic coffins, but I'm going to suggest we skip over Shapiro, just because of the religious problems—he's Jewish, I confirmed—we might encounter with an exhumation. Hintzle's folks live in Kenosha. That will be my next call. Do you think we can do this over the phone?" asked Al.

"I think we have to go that route at first. Schneider is from Eau Claire," said Charlie. "I'll plan to get his folks on the phone. If they want to talk in person, maybe we can split up to get things going."

Half an hour later, the officers met up again, smiling. Both sets of parents readily agreed to cooperate.

"If we get our ass in gear, I think we could do Schneider tomorrow," said Charlie. "We should see what we can set up for Hintzle. I also think we should take Sarah, Rick or Pat."

"Great idea, I'll call the Kenosha mortician back. I'll see how fast we can get that one scheduled. Before I make the call, let's put together the paperwork. We'll see if the chief will work with his counterparts in Eau Claire and Kenosha to get what we need."

Two hours later, everything was ready. Both exhumations would be done the following day. Charlie and Rick would travel to Eau Claire; Al and Sarah would head to Kenosha. Judges in each of those counties had completed the paperwork with uncommon speed after hearing from the parents.

CHAPTER 22

Julie arrived at work early on Tuesday. She showed Peggy the ad for the house on North Hickory. Peggy thought it looked great.

"How about we view it after work?" Julie asked.

"I think I could make that work. Lauren has dance practice and Jake is supposed to get right home and mow the lawn. I'll check my calendar, but I think I'm free."

"Excellent, I'll call the realtor and see if we can view the house then."

Julie walked to the ENT department, put away her lunch and purse, and began to prepare for the day. Toady was not be a surgery day, so it'd be fairly easy, but Dr. Esch had a full appointment schedule.

She sorted files to make sure everything was in order. Dr. Esch was a kindly man but also demanding—something she discovered on her first day—but they were a good team. In addition to being her boss, Dr. Esch was also a father figure. When he found out that Julie was a single mom, he made sure to always be available for advice. He also went out of his way to provide little perks, rewarding her for good work and appreciating that her life was sometimes hard. If Brody was ill, he let her stay home, and if she arrived late, which rarely happened, he never held it against her.

As Julie sorted files, the phone rang.

"I'm free," reported Peggy. "Lauren will see to sandwiches for the kids. Jake was thrilled at the prospect of having help with the lawn."

"You can bet," said Julie with a chuckle, "that both are plotting the quickest way possible to get to those video games."

"Well," suggested Peggy, "give the realtor a call. See if we can do it today.

The morning sped past. When Peggy met Julie in the lunchroom, Julie hadn't yet had a chance to call. "I'll do it before we leave here," she promised. "I brought the number with me."

Sandwiches consumed and a second cup of coffee poured, Julie dialed her cell phone.

"Is this the realtor for the house on North Hickory?" she asked as Peggy listened. "My girlfriend and I are thinking about moving in together, so we're house hunting."

Peggy could hear the voice on the other end of the line say they would love the house. It was in a great neighborhood, near schools and shopping areas. Lots of kids in the area.

School? Peggy pondered the thought. *I wonder what school the kids would attend? A shift at this age,* she thought, *would be tough. We'll cross that bridge later.*

"Okay," she heard Julie say, "we'll meet you there at 5:30. Thanks so much."

"We have an appointment," she reported, realizing Peggy already knew. "You overheard, didn't you? I thought so."

"While you were talking," Peggy said, "I was thinking about school. Do you suppose the kids have to change schools?"

Oh, never thought of that," confessed Julie. "Brody wouldn't like changing."

"Neither would Jake or Lauren, murmured Peggy.

"Do you think I should check?" asked Julie. "I'll do it on break. I'll call the school."

"Good idea. See you after work."

When afternoon break rolled around, Julie called Roosevelt Junior High School and talked to the receptionist. She was transferred to the principal, Joel Jensen, whom she knew.

When she and Peggy met in the parking lot at 5 o'clock, Peggy was eager for the news.

"It's not good," lamented Julie. "I spoke to Joel Jensen and he told me that the kids would be in different schools than they are today—Madison for Brody and Jake, Washington for Lauren. That's a deal breaker, don't you think?"

"God, can you imagine Lauren's reaction? She's really tight with her friends. Most of them are on the dance line. I don't think I'm ready to take that one on."

"Agreed," Julie said, "but I do think we have to look at the house. The realtor sounded very nice. She's probably there already."

After the 20-minute drive, they pulled up to the curb. Peggy laughed. "Guess we shouldn't have worried. This looks like something Frankenstein would have built," said Peggy.

Julie and Peggy were both laughing as they got out of the car. As they walked, a middle-aged blonde, pretty in a contemporary way, rushed to meet them. Bright shades of red and blue streaked her hair. She was dressed in a short, red skirt, blue leggings, a white blouse and blue blazer. The outfit was striking on her shapely body.

"Hi, you must be Julie and Peggy," she greeted. "I'll bet you're Julie." She pointed to Julie, who smiled and agreed.

"That means you're Peggy. Great! Barb Romney. Nice to meet you! I'm guessing, though, that seeing you, this may not be what you want. It could be a nice house, but it's sadly outdated. It's gonna need a lot of work. Are you up for that?"

"You know, Barb," began Julie, a frown crossing her face, "this afternoon I made a call I should have made first. There's really no sense looking inside. We found out our kids would have to change schools. That's a deal breaker."

"No problem," said Barb. "So, let's talk a bit about how I might help you. How about a drink? There's a little wine bar down the street. We can chat and figure out what houses might work for you."

"A glass of wine would be great," said Peggy quickly, looking at Julie. She nodded in agreement.

"Ok, follow me. We'll be there in a flash."

Julie followed the bright, yellow Mustang to the quiet little wine bar down the street. A bottle of pinot region on the table, the three were talking animatedly.

"We want something nice in a quiet neighborhood," began Peggy.

"And there should be kids around," chimed Julie. "We definitely need five bedrooms…or," she looked at Peggy, "maybe Brody and Jake could share?"

"They'd play video games all night. Let's shoot for five. Oh yeah, if three bedrooms were apart from the other two, that'd be terrific," suggested Peggy.

"What about a guest room?" asked Julie.

"If six bedrooms puts a house out of reach financially, we'll get along with five," said Peggy. "We can afford something nice, but not extravagant."

After sharing the bottle of wine, the three grew more and more friendly. Barb promised she would give their situation her immediate attention. "It's a good time to be buying," she said. "But that means it's not a good time to be selling. It's like farming. I grew up on a farm and it was either too dry or too wet, too warm or too cold. In real estate, if it's great for buyers, it's not so good for sellers. But let me see what I can do."

Feeling just a tiny bit tipsy, the three parted. Julie and Peggy got into the car. "I really want this to work out, Peggy. But now I'm discouraged," said Julie.

"C'mon, get your chin up," urged Peggy, patting her on the shoulder. "Let's not give up before we have even really tried. I think Barb will come up with something. How about we let her worry about that and we try to get safely home? The kids already ate but I'm starving."

"Okay," said Julie. Her voice still carried the twang of discouragement. "How about KFC? Can we go to your house? It's on the way and Brody's at your place."

"KFC it is. I'll buy," replied Peggy.

When they pulled into Peggy's driveway, Brody and Jake rushed up. "How was it?" asked Jake. "Yeah, how was it?" said Brody.

"Where's Lauren?" asked Peggy. "It'd be best if we could share the news with all three of you at once."

"Aw, mom, that's crappy. Lauren's still at dance. She may not be home for an hour yet. She rushed home, made us sandwiches, bossed us around, and left for practice. It's shitty to wait," said Jake.

"Jake Russell, don't you talk like that!" admonished Peggy. "Your sister should be here too, and you know it. Is the yard mowed? It better be!"

"I'm sorry, mom," said a contrite Jake, softly. "Sometimes I don't think." He brightened. "But Brody and I got the grass cut and the trimming done. We even took the clippings to the dump place down the street. We swept the sidewalk and everything."

"Wonderful," said Peggy.

Jake and Brody went directly to Jake's room to play X-box. Julie and Peggy busied themselves in the kitchen. Peggy opened the fridge and took out a bottle of chardonnay.

"Ah, I'm not sure that's a good idea. I already feel the results of earlier. I drink some more, and I may not be able to drive," said Julie.

"Then you'll stay here," said Peggy. "I can lend you a nightgown. You and Brody can be up early enough to go home and get ready for work and school."

"That might not work," said Julie. "Dr. Esch has a big day tomorrow. I'd better not be hung over."

"C'mon, just a little," offered Peggy. "It'll do you good."

"Okay, maybe one little glass."

One led to two and two led to three. Both Peggy and Julie were giggling like schoolgirls when Lauren walked in.

"Looks like you've been at it a while," said Lauren. "Mom, maybe you should cool it a little."

"Aww, honey, we just had a couple of glasses. Drop your stuff. Jake and Brody are anxious to hear what we have to tell you."

"Be right back!" said Lauren, walking from the room to take her things to her room.

Julie and Peggy had a fourth glass of wine with dinner. By the time clean up began, they were more than a little drunk.

"You better stay," said Peggy, thickly, as she wiped and put away dishes Julie washed.

"Guess you're right, but I'd better get to sleep early. Tomorrow is a really big day."

"Soon as the dishes are done we can shower and get to bed. I hope the kids will follow suit and not stay up all night."

As Lauren studied in her room and the boys played a video game, Peggy and Julie showered together.

"God, you have a great body," said Peggy, looking Julie up and down.

"Me? Are you kidding? You're the one with the body. Look at you. Your breasts are huge…and I'll bet they're as firm as they were in high school. Every time I see you nude, I get turned on," confessed Julie, a bit embarrassed by the admission.

"How about I wash your back?" whispered Peggy. "Maybe I can rub some of that stress away."

"Mmm, that's wonderful. You have great hands," mumbled Julie as Peggy began rubbing her shoulders, working her way down across Julie's back before moving to her tummy and up to her breasts.

"Oh my!" said Peggy. "Your nipples are so hard!"

"And so sensitive, too," said Julie, turning to face Peggy. Peggy immediately drew her close and began to kiss her deeply. "If you keep that up, I may never want to go home!"

"That'd be okay with me," said Peggy, softly. "I'd like to have your body next to me every night."

Her fingers wandered down to the patch of fur beneath Julie's navel. Peggy worked her index finger into the slippery slit and began to probe farther.

"Uh," gasped Julie, "that's so good…so, so good. But, Peggy, tonight I'd like to make love in bed. Is that okay?"

"Absolutely. Whatever you want."

"Let's talk in bed," suggested Julie.

Each woman busied herself with scrubbing the other and no spot was omitted. Nipples grew hard and nether regions grew slippery until neither could wait to get to bed. They toweled each other briskly, quickly donned nightgowns and crawled beneath the covers. Peggy turned out the light as Julie snuggled into her.

"Tell me, Peggy," began Julie, "where this began for you. Did you always want women? Am I the first?"

"No, not the first," replied Peggy, "but the best…the best by a long, long way. I had a girlfriend in high school. We messed around a bit, but it was just, kind of like, watching each other and telling each other what we felt. We touched each other a few times, but nothing heavy. There was a roommate in college that I made love to a few times. It was just kind of appeasing raging hormones. We were definitely not in love. Matt came along, and he took care of every need I had. He was so damn horny… and I loved it. We made love everywhere…day and night, inside and out. How about you?"

"It began with you," admitted Julie. "Sex was hardly ever on my mind until I met Shawn. He was so wonderful, Peggy, I just miss him so. We had a great relationship. He was genuine, honest, beautiful, and kind—my superhero."

"I guess you felt the same way I did when Matt was killed. He was my world, Julie. We never got over the 'first love' stage. We were like two high school kids in the backseat of a car right up until he died. I got so lonely. It was unbearable."

"I've gotten along fine," said Julie, thinking. "I might have looked at girls with mild interest, but I would no more have thought of making love to them than I would climb Everest. Brody became my life. Shawn and I made love only six or seven times, but that was wonderful. Before that, no one touched me. I didn't masturbate until long after Shawn drowned."

"I think I've been playing with myself since I was born," said Peggy with a laugh. "I'm just one of those always ready women."

"You made me understand that love with a woman can be good," said Julie. "I love it, but every time we do it, I feel guilty...feel like this has to stop. I feel that way now."

"Why is that?" asked Peggy.

"My family is very religious," admitted Julie. "We preached about the sins of same-sex involvement. And now I love it...but I think it's wrong."

"I don't. I could live with and love you forever," responded Peggy in a soft voice. "But I know where you are. I'll do whatever you want, you know that. When you say it can't happen again, I'll agree. But I'll feel terrible."

"I don't think that will happen soon," replied Julie. "But, Peggy, I'm not a lesbian. I'm just... sometimes needy. You're the only option I turn to for release. If you can live with knowing that, I'm fine."

Peggy's answer was to kiss her deeply, pull Julie even closer, and hug her tightly.

"You are wonderful," mumbled Julie, her hands moving across Peggy's breasts and hugging her back. That's the way they fell asleep.

CHAPTER 23

Julie and Peggy were still asleep at dawn on Wednesday. Rick and Charlie were already out of bed long before dawn.

In Eau Claire, Charlie and Rick waited at the cemetery for men and equipment. An hour later, the vault containing Schneider's body had been opened. The casket was ready to be hoisted out of the ground. At the same moment in Kenosha, work began at the cemetery.

Schneider's body was swiftly moved to Oak Leaf Surgical Hospital. Rick and Charlie, already in gowns, began their work. They moved the body to the operating table, turned the lights on, and Rick moved the body to get a close-up look at the left ear.

Almost as soon as he moved the body, Rick exclaimed, "Unless I'm mistaken, there it is…although smudged…the same kind of mark we saw on Evenson. I'll remove a bit of tissue. We'll test more thoroughly later, but I think Schneider may have died the same way as Evenson."

Less than an hour later, just as Hintzle's casket was unearthed several hundred miles away, Rick confirmed his view. There was a mark in roughly the same place. Although trace evidence was long ago destroyed, the evidence was conclusive. Both men were murdered.

Shortly before noon, Sarah stepped back from Hintzle's body and turned to Al. "You saw it, right? The very same kind of mark. Approximately in the same place as the mark on Evenson," she said. "I saw it all right," agreed Al. "Given the news from Eau Claire, we're looking for a serial killer. The only missing piece is how many of these 'accidents' were murders. I'd bet all 15 of them. We'll never know unless we find this killer and get him or her to confess."

"How likely is that?" asked Sarah.

"Unfortunately, I think our chances are about 10 percent—20, tops," guessed Al. "I suspect the killer is very smart. The lack of evidence suggests thorough planning."

"I suppose you're right," agreed Sarah, "but we may have enough evidence to pin down a few more things. That should be helpful. Etomidate and Midazolam are not common, and there are only a few places where they can be found in La Crosse. Someone skilled enough to compound those two has to be a doctor or at least have had medical training. I'll see what I can do."

"I know you will. It's a long road ahead, one that may not have an end," said Al.

"I found something else," said Sarah, smiling and holding up a plastic bag. "These hairs clearly are not Hintzle's. He has dark hair. These ones are a distinctly different color and length. I need to set up up more testing. Maybe these hairs will lead us to something."

CHAPTER 24

Julie and Peggy were up at 6 on Wednesday, talked over coffee, and woke the kids at 7. They showered, dressed, dropped the kids off at their schools, and arrived at work before 8. As they walked in, Julie lamented the housing situation.

"I sure hope Barb can come up with something," she said.

"She seems pretty resourceful. I'll bet we'll hear from her soon—maybe even today," replied Peggy.

The pair parted at the reception desk. *It would be a surgery day* Julie thought. She'd be busy. On these days, she assisted the doctor during the procedures. The schedule began with a complicated surgery. Dr. Esch removed a cancerous tumor from the nostril of a young man. In fact, the patient wasn't much older than Brody. It made her shiver.

As the morning wore on, three surgeries were completed. The first one had gone well. The doctor removed the tumor, the excised tissue around it indicating the cancer had not metastasized. The second surgery was a routine endoscopic sinus procedure. The third one was a bit more complicated. Dr. Esch was one of the best salivary gland surgeons in the nation. His method of accessing the gland was unique. His development accessed the gland with the endoscope, which made the surgery far less complicated and the recovery quicker and easier.

The surgery ended a few minutes before 11:30.

Julie cleaned up the surgery room and put the tools in the sterilizer. By the time she finished, it was noon, lunchtime. She met Peggy in the breakroom. Over sandwiches from the vending machine and cups of coffee, they talked more about housing.

"Nothing yet?" asked Peggy.

"Nope, no messages. I checked before walking over. I'm anxious to hear something…anything."

"Maybe this afternoon," suggested Peggy.

"Maybe."

Dr. Esch always saved the more routine surgeries for the afternoon. This meant a crowded schedule. This afternoon was no exception. Time passed quickly as they worked through five procedures.

Cleanup complete, Julie arrived at her cubicle. The desk was full of papers. She hoped a message from Barb would be among them, but no such luck.

***

The evening passed in typical fashion. She and Brody had mac and cheese, a salad and fresh-baked rolls. After she cleaned the dishes and kitchen, Julie focused on Baldacci while Brody studied in his room. Julie read for a while, reminded Brody not to stay up too late, then turned off her light. Sleep came quickly. The night was restful with no haunting dreams.

CHAPTER 25

A few hours earlier, Charlie and Rick pulled into the hospital parking lot in La Crosse. The sun had already slipped behind the bluffs of Minnesota and night was closing in. In spite of the darkness, the men felt upbeat. They believed they had taken another major step in determining the cause of these mysterious deaths.

As Rick prepared to move the samples from Jon Schneider's body out of the car and into the lab, Charlie dialed Al on his cell.

"How's it going over there, buddy?" Charlie said. "And where are you?"

"About an hour from La Crosse," said Al, "and when we get there, we'll have plenty of work to do."

Charlie heard Sarah clearing her throat loudly.

"Uh, I mean Sarah and Rick will have lots to do," Al replied.

"In addition to the puncture mark, Sarah also found some long, light hairs on Hintzle's body. They are clearly not his, so we brought them with us, hoping they might be another clue. I'm anxious to find out if Hintzle's body also contains Etomidate and Midazolam. If so, I think we can safely conclude that we are dealing with a killer or killers.

"We have a news conference, tomorrow," Charlie said. "In the meantime, we should put out an all-points closed communication, a private communication to law enforcement agencies, to determine if there have been any other mysterious drownings in places like Wisconsin, Minnesota, Iowa or Illinois. Lots to do, partner. Guess it will be another late night." He changed the subject. "Are you coming straight to the hospital when you get back? If you are, maybe we could ask the sheriff and chief to meet us here for a debrief?"

Al thought for a moment. "That sounds like it would work best. Since you're back, can you alert them?"

"Happy to do it. I'll get them on the landline. No unwanted ears that way." Al hung up. Charlie hurried through the clinic doors to join Rick in the lab. Arriving in the brightly lit room, he hung his coat on a hook, moved to the work station that Rick was using, and looked over Rick's shoulder.

Without turning, Rick continued his work. "Charlie, do you see this faint stain?"

"You mean the milky trace?" asked Charlie.

"That's the one. That milky film is not indicative of either Etomidate or Midazolam," he said, intently studying the magnified image. "It indicates an anesthetic, though. This milky stain is Propofol. It was pulled from the market because its effects were found to fade too quickly. That created some embarrassing moments. Propofol is powerful, though. It's known as the 'milk of amnesia' because of its impact and color."

He continued. "If someone wanted to create short-lived unconsciousness, accompanied by severe pain during injection, Propofol would be the drug to use. If Propofol were used in this case, as I suspect, the drug combination will differ from those used in Evenson. We'll also have the samples from Sarah and Al. They might tell us something, too."

By the time Al and Sarah joined Rick and Charlie, the group expanded to include Pat and Dr. Lee.

"Guess we're the gang of six," quipped Rick, as Sarah hurried to the lab table with the case containing things she had taken from the body of Phil Hintzle. She opened the case, extracted some slides, and gingerly clamped one into place on the microscope stage.

"See this mark?" she asked, flashing the image on the wall's television monitor and using a pen to point. "This seems consistent with the puncture wound found on the body of Mr. Evenson."

"And Mr. Schneider," interrupted Rick, quickly bringing Sarah and Al up to speed on the results of the tests he had run on the Eau Claire samples. "Let's see if we can find any substance traces on your samples."

As Sarah clamped the third slide into place, Rick moved to her side. He was astonished. "There…there it is! See that milky white stain. You have to look hard. It's barely visible. I think that was made by Propofol, and, if it is, our mystery just deepened."

Seeing the frown on Al's face as he turned back to the group, Rick explained, "As I was looking at the samples from Schneider, I found a similar stain. Tests confirmed it as Propofol. It's a powerful but short-acting anesthetic that is administered with great pain to the patient. Its use was discontinued for that reason, in addition to its short-acting timeframe. If the Kenosha sample shows Propofol, we will have a complication on our hands. In Evenson we found Etomidate and Midazolam, but no Propofol. So either our killer changed drugs, which is rare in serial cases like this or…"

The interrupted answer to that thought silenced the room. No one wanted to think of the alternative. Suddenly, the phone rang, interrupting the silence. Rick answered and spoke briefly. "The sheriff and chief are here. They'll be right down."

"Yeah, we have to plan a news conference," said Charlie. "Al and I thought it would be just as well for them to hear the news from you folks rather than getting it secondhand."

"We may have news they don't want to hear," responded Rick. "Propofol and the hair indicate this isn't going to be an open and shut case. I'll explain when they get here."

"We'll have to do it as quickly as possible," replied Al. "We have to get the news conference set. Before that, we'd better have all the facts."

A knock sounded on the door and two large men entered. Sheriff Dwight Hooper was a tall, slender, raw-boned man. His features could have been chiseled from granite. His personality suited his physicality—he was a man who wanted answers to his questions and wanted them with no superfluous detail. La Crosse Police Chief Brent Whigg was just the opposite. Although he stood slightly more than six feet tall, he was a wide and solidly built man. His round face was ruddy, a feature accented by his Magnum cycling sunglasses that adjusted to the bright lab lighting. Both men exuded confidence. Neither of these men tolerated nonsense.

The lawmen went around the room, greeting those they knew and introducing themselves to those they didn't. After formalities, they got down to business. "So, what've you got?" said Whigg.

"More mystery," replied Rick, gesturing the newcomers to sit down. He moved to the front of the group.

"As you know," Rick began, "I was with Al and Charlie when they recovered the body of Rolf Evenson from the river on Saturday. When we got back here, I asked Pat to help with the examination. She found what we've been looking for. A faint but visible puncture wound was inside the left ear. Dr. Lee later confirmed the mark as a puncture wound, probably created by a hypodermic needle. By working together with Pat and Sarah, we found traces of what we have now confirmed as Etomidate and Midazolam. These are two strong sedatives that used together would quickly render the recipient groggy and unresponsive. In surgery, these two drugs would be used to make a patient unconscious before a doctor administers a stronger, longer-acting sedative. Al and Charlie arranged to have the bodies of two additional drowning victims exhumed so we could check for more evidence. We advised that going back farther than four years would probably be useless, given the likely condition of the bodies.

"This morning, Charlie and I were in Eau Claire as the body of Jon Schneider was exhumed. Sarah and Al were in Kenosha for the exhumation of Phil Hintzle. In each case, we found the same type of mark inside the left ear, also made with a hypodermic needle. When we got today's samples, the case gained another mystery. We did not find traces of Etomidate and Midazolam. We found traces of Propofol, a powerful sedative withdrawn from the market in 2004 because it created short-term unconsciousness and caused great pain when administered."

"That's significant," continued Rick, "because serial killers generally adopt a consistent killing pattern."

"Are you saying we are dealing with two different killers?" broke in Sheriff Hooper.

"I—we—are not saying that," said Rick. "What we *are* saying is that serial killers generally stay with the same modus operandi. That means the person or persons would likely use the same drugs consistently."

Al chimed in. "We know that in three cases, the death by drowning was likely aided by drugs. We also know that if drugs were used in the same manner as Evenson, Hintzle, and Schneider that the injections were in the very same spot inside the left ear. We are leaning toward one killer."

"Given the method and the site of the punctures," said Rick, "I'd bet on one killer—a right-handed killer. The use of three different drugs does add a bit of a challenge."

"Why right-handed?" asked Hooper.

"My guess is," reported Rick, "that the injections came from behind the victims."

"Makes sense, I guess," agreed Hooper. "But why would someone switch drugs?"

"There could be many reasons, I suppose," replied Rick, looking toward the doctors and Sarah for confirmation. "Perhaps the removal of Propofol from the market eliminated access. It could also be that the pain during injection caused victims to make too much noise or struggle too severely. Maybe Propofol did not last long enough. It could be a hundred other reasons; pick one."

"Reasonable points," agreed Hooper. "You know that we're calling a news conference in the morning. We want to provide as much information as you're comfortable with." As he said that, he looked around the group. "So we need to figure that out. We also need to decide who's doing what."

"I'm sure that Al and Charlie can take care of those things," said Rick. "You should also know, though, that Sarah found something else. As she examined Hintzle's body, she found some long, light-colored hairs in his hair. We're not certain he drowned. It could mean hundreds of contacts and hours and hours of lab time."

"But it'll be worth it if we find the person or people we're looking for," said Hooper, almost as if he was talking to himself.

An hour and a half later, the group reached an agreement on what information would be shared. No one would mention the hair, but Sarah would perform a full DNA workup on the specimen.

Before the news conference at 9 a.m., there was plenty to do. Hooper and Whigg would inform the media and contact the general managers of the radio and television stations and the editor of the *La Crosse Tribune*. Al and Charlie would contact next-of-kin of each of the victims to give them a heads-up about the new findings and how they'd use this information. The doctors and researcher would prepare a document using simple language, describing what they found and the significance of each item. Al would also talk to Hintzle's parents and the morticians at Sanford and Brown Funeral Home in Kenosha. They might need hair samples from everyone there and all family members, as well as the people who were with Hintzle the night he died.

After the group finished, Al and Charlie headed back to police headquarters at 400 La Crosse Street to begin their calls. Al, suddenly concerned, spoke. "Charlie, we forgot to suggest the closed communication to the other departments."

"Get a hold of Whigg," urged Charlie. "He'll take care of it."

That detail satisfied, the work began for what would be a very busy Thursday.

CHAPTER 26

Just before noon on Thursday, Julie's phone rang. "Hi, Julie," said Barb. "I've found three houses that you might like. None of them would require a new school district. When are you and Peggy free?"

"Gosh, I'm not sure about Peggy, but I could go after work," she said, looking at her watch. It was almost quitting time. "Wow, it's already almost 5. Is tonight an option?"

"I could make it work. Check with Peggy and call me back. The sooner you let me know, the better. I'll need to make a few arrangements at home," said Barb.

Peggy was free. They set up a meeting for 6:30 at Barb's office.

Three hours later as the clock edged its way toward 10, Julie and Peggy were discouraged. After seeing all three houses, they had not liked a single one. Thankfully, both Peggy and Julie, unknowingly, had the same taste in homes. When one didn't like an aspect of a home, the other felt the same way.

"Don't worry," replied Barb when Julie expressed her discouragement. "We'll find it. We'll just look a little longer. Maybe we'll find something new to look at during the weekend. I have lots of open houses. But none of those will work. We sometimes get calls for new openings on the weekend. The Multiple Listing Service also meets on Tuesday. I'll bet we will find something then."

"Oh, Tuesday," moaned Julie. "That seems like forever."

"Finding the perfect house isn't an easy job. But it will happen. It always does," assured Barb.

"Well, I guess I'll just have to be patient," said Julie with a sigh.

Later on, she talked with Peggy on the phone. They were anxious but they didn't want to compromise for anything less than a perfect home. After the long day at work, they decided to do something fun for the weekend. Peggy suggested they spend the weekend together.

"I love our time together, Peggy," said Julie. "But remember what I said. My biggest worry is the kids catching us messing around. I think it would really confuse Brody."

"Lauren and Jake's world would be rocked, too," said Peggy. "Don't worry, that won't happen. Think of how fun a campout will be! We could even do some organizing and packing. When we find our dream house, we'll be ready to move."

"Now that's an idea I can buy," said Julie, a smile breaking across her face. "A campout and packing party. Sounds like fun!"

CHAPTER 27

Thursday, November 17, 2011. Today was a busy day in La Crosse. The day dawned sunny without a cloud in the sky. Both Al and Charlie were up earlier than usual. Breakfast never crossed Charlie's mind as he raced to shower, shave, put on his best suit, and tie his tie. Al was a bit more cool and collected, as always, but he couldn't control his nervous excitement, either, for this big day. As he showered, he said a silent prayer that this conference signaled the end of these drownings, the deaths that plagued La Crosse for 15 years. He also dressed carefully. As he prepared to leave home, he called Charlie. He wanted to meet Charlie for breakfast at Ma's.

"I'll meet you there at 7:30, but I don't think I'm up to a big breakfast. I doubt I could keep a big Ma's breakfast down," said Charlie.

Al agreed. Still, both men acknowledged that getting something to eat before all of the action was a good idea.

"I doubt there will be much time to eat after the news conference," pondered Al.

"No kiddin'. We'll be busier than a goddamn one-armed paper hanger," replied Charlie. "See ya at Ma's."

By the time the two met for breakfast, Charlie, unsurprisingly, recovered his appetite. As usual, he ordered enough food for a railroad crew. Al ordered just one pancake and two strips of crispy bacon.

"Seriously, Charlie, how in the hell can you eat so much?" Al looked at Charlie's less than svelte figure.

"I have to keep up my strength, you know," replied Charlie.

"And my livelihood," came Ma's voice from the pantry. "Without you Charlie, I would have closed long ago."

"Enough," said Charlie gruffly. He stared at his plate. "Ma, where are my waffles?"

The tiny and round elderly woman, who resembled Mrs. Santa Claus more than a cook, emerged from the kitchen, balancing two huge platters of food. A tiny plate sat precariously atop these huge platters, containing a single pancake and two crispy strips of bacon.

"There," said Ma, dropping the plates to the counter with a clank. "I hope that will be enough food to satisfy you until noon. Charlie, just how in the heck do you get anything done? If I ate like that, I'd be asleep until supper time, to say nothing of the disgusting sounds I'd make."

"Aww, Ma," Charlie protested, "a growin' boy has to have his food. And we know how to free the gas noiselessly."

"Charlie, you're shameless!" "What are you, 400 pounds? What you eat multiplies my bottom line by three and costs me four times as much in furniture repair. Look how those counter stools are slumping," said Ma.

"I'm 382, thank you very much," said Charlie after swallowing. "Those stools have been slumping since before I was born."

"Charlie, does your wife ever win an argument with you?" asked Ma. "You just have to have the last word, don't you? Well, you know what, I'm gonna let you have it so I can get some work done."

After Ma walked off, Al turned to Charlie. "Are we ready?"

"I can't think of anything we overlooked. I was awake most of the night thinkin' about it, to be honest," confessed Charlie. "I think we have all the t's crossed and i's dotted. Why, did you think of somethin'?"

"No, I think we're set. But unless you pick it up, we're going to miss the show."

"Another wise guy!" But Charlie began to stuff the food in his mouth at such a quick pace that Al wondered if he was even chewing.

After wiping his mouth and punctuating the action with a burp loud enough to rattle the windows, Charlie drew a snort from Ma. The two men got up and headed outside, going over a few details.

"I'm gonna head to the office for a few minutes," said Charlie. "I'll see you at 8:30."

"Don't take too long," said Al, looking at his watch. "It's already 10 to 8."

"I'll be there. Don't worry about that."

***

The 9 a.m. news conference was held in the small auditorium at City Hall, a perfect space for today. The auditorium had ample room for cameras and great acoustics, but it was wired as well for as many microphones as needed. No one would miss the big news. When Al got to his office, he dropped his coat and went to check on the auditorium. Everything was in place, so he went back to study his notes.

At 9 on the dot, the small group of officers and medical personnel, shoulder to shoulder, entered the hall with Sheriff Hooper and Chief Whigg leading the way. They arrived at the chairs on the stage at the front of the room. After finding their seats, Whigg stepped to the podium and addressed the crowd after a somber welcome.

"As you know, Deputy Charlie Berzinski and Detective Al Rouse answered a call Saturday morning that led, sadly, to the recovery of a drowning victim, a male in his 20s. This was the 15th recovery of this sort, dating back to 1997."

"The 15th body was identified as a 21-year-old junior at the University of Wisconsin-Lacrosse. His name was Rolf Evenson. He was a native of Durand, Wisconsin, and the son of Durand residents Goldene and Lars Evenson."

"We now have evidence that at least three of these deaths—and likely all 15—were homicides and not accidental drownings, as we had previously concluded."

The statement caused a roar to break out in the room. Broadcast reporters and print journalists scribbled feverishly.

Raising his hand for quiet, Whigg continued. "We believe we are looking at a solitary killer here because these methods were consistent in the three bodies that we were able to test."

As the news conference continued, it was obvious by their fidgeting that the reporters had lots of questions. However, they sat respectfully and listened as each of the presenters told the portion of the story assigned to them.

An hour later, Chief Whigg was back at the podium. "Before I open it up for questions, Sheriff Hooper and I have one more announcement. I am pleased to report that the Wisconsin Sheriff's Association, the Wisconsin League of Police Officers, the Wisconsin Trial Lawyers Congress, and the La Crosse Crime Stoppers Organization have pooled their resources and are offering a $100,000 reward for information leading to the arrest and conviction of the person or persons responsible for these heinous acts. Now, let me thank you for allowing us to roll out the facts as we know them. We are ready for questions. I promise you we will be here as long as it takes to answer them."

Whigg waved for Hooper to join him at the podium. "The sheriff and I will take turns fielding questions. We will direct them to our colleagues and the medical personnel. We want you to have accurate information. Undoubtedly, questions will be asked that we will be unable to answer. We ask respectfully for your understanding. Sheriff…"

"Martha," said Sheriff Hooper, pointing at Martha Johnson of WKBT-TV.

"Sheriff, am I wrong in assuming that the mark Dr. Pat Grebin found could have been observed in other victims if the previous investigations had been more thorough?"

Before turning to Pat for more information, Hooper responded. "Martha, I believe we should be saluting Dr. Grebin rather than suggesting her colleagues were ineffective. You need to understand that the mark Dr. Grebin found was so tiny that it was almost invisible to the naked eye."

It went on like this for the next hour, and they answered every question. It was 11:05 when no more hands were raised.

"So that's it," said Whigg, surveying the audience. "In closing, let me tell you that we are committed to sharing every vetted and viable piece of information. It should be obvious that we need your help. Thank you for coming and thanks for your undivided attention."

For the first time in the group's memory, reporters sprinted for the doors. This was the biggest story they had ever covered. It became obvious that fielding and responding to questions was going to be a gargantuan task.

"Dwight," said Chief Whigg, "I think we'd better get together and decide how to deal with this in the future."

"Good idea," agreed Hooper. "We've only dealt with city media. You can bet La Crosse is going to be swimming with national media very soon."

"And," said Whigg, we have the Division of Criminal Investigation arriving this afternoon."

Whigg was referring to the much-maligned state of Wisconsin bureau that assisted with major investigations. Many lawmen in Wisconsin questioned if this bureau actually helped solve cases.

The two men left together, still sorting out the details.

CHAPTER 28

During their Friday morning break, Julie asked Peggy if she had heard from Barb. She hadn't. "Not sure why I'm asking," said Julie. "Guess I'm just anxious."

"I know what you mean. I'm also impatient," answered Peggy. "I'm ready to get settled into our new life."

When the clock struck noon, Julie tidied up some papers, headed to the break room, and took out the sandwich she had brought from home. She found Peggy and Kelly involved in an intense discussion. Arms flying, Kelly seemed to be relaying information to Peggy.

"Oh, great, you're here!" exclaimed Kelly, looking up. "We were just talking about you when I told Peggy about what I heard this morning."

"What's that?" inquired Julie.

"Did you hear about the news from La Crosse?" She was visibly excited. Without waiting for Julie's response, Kelly continued her news. "Police said yesterday that the string of drownings that began when we were on campus are the work of a killer or killers, *serial killers*. Can you believe it?"

Julie's world stopped. She was sure the look on her face would confuse Kelly and Peggy.

"Not accidents," she stammered. "What do you mean? What did they say?"

"The police said that in the bodies they checked, they found evidence that pointed to murder. Apparently, some dynamite La Crosse doc found something in the ear of the latest victim. The tests showed the use of drugs. The theory is the killer used drugs to help get the victims to the river."

"Really?" said Julie in disbelief. "How could they possibly know that?"

"Well, I guess this doc is really good because she found the stick mark. They dug up the bodies of two other men who drowned. I guess they found marks in the same place. You know what's spooky about that? I thought only a few people knew that information. I thought I might be among the very few who know that the ear canals are great places to administer sedatives. I have been doing injections there for as long as I can remember, probably for the same 15 years that these deaths occurred."

Julie sat in stunned disbelief. The fact that officials in La Crosse determined the drownings as homicides greatly disturbed her. So were Kelly's comments about delivering intravenous injections in the ear. Was it possible that Kelly knew more than she was letting on? No, it couldn't be. She dismissed the idea.

But Kelly's next words were even more disturbing.

"What I'm really wondering is if someone I told about my method committed these murders," said Kelly, a worried look on her face. "I sure haven't kept it a secret."

That sent Julie's thoughts racing. *Did I hear about the ear canal from someone? I don't think so, but maybe I did. And if someone told me, what will they think when they hear the news? Will they remember they told me? And if they remember, will they tell the police?*

Her mind continued to race, sweeping away pleasant thoughts about moving and how happy Brody would be if she and Peggy found a new home. Suddenly, her world had been turned upside down. The news from La Crosse was enormously disturbing—threatening, even.

Julie was so focused on her thoughts that it took Kelly three times to get her attention.

"Wha…what?" asked Julie as her thoughts returned to the conversation.

"I asked you three times if you think someone I told about my method could have done the crime," said Kelly, smiling. Her tone became a bit more chiding. "But you were in dreamland. Where were you, Julie?"

"I was thinking about something Peggy and I are working on," she stammered. "It's pretty important to my son. All morning I have been losing concentration whenever it enters my mind."

Kelly's eyes met Julie's for a long moment before she broke the silence. "Good. For a moment, there I thought you were back in La Crosse. You were in a mysterious place, Julie."

"N-n-n-no," said Julie hesitantly. "I was thinking about Brody."

"Well, for a minute I thought you were the Queen of Drownings," joked Kelly. Julie didn't find it funny.

"Don't ever say anything like that, Kelly!" she exclaimed. "That was a terrible thing to say!"

"Don't be so serious," chided Kelly. "I was just kidding."

"Well, maybe you should find out some of the facts before deciding to be a jokester," retorted Julie, gathering her things and fleeing the room.

Kelly turned to Peggy, a bewildered look on her face. "What did I do? I didn't mean to upset Julie."

"Y know, Kelly, that Julie's lover, Brody's father, was one of the La Crosse drowning victims. Your comments probably hit a nerve. She's very sensitive whenever news like this comes up."

"Oh, God. You're right. I'll apologize when I see her next."

Back at her work station, Julie tried to shake off the terrible feeling that someone, somehow, *knew* that she delivered anesthetic injections in the ear canal. It seemed like Kelly was too familiar with her. It unnerved her. All afternoon, she did her job in a distracted, robotic fashion. As she sat at her desk, her mind was 300 miles away in La Crosse near the Midway Motor Lodge. Images of a dark and swiftly flowing river's shores burned in her mind.

A shadow fell across the desk. Looking up, she saw Kelly.

Before she could say anything, Kelly's face took on a look of concern. "Julie, I'm very sorry. I never meant to upset you. Peggy reminded me about your loss. I feel like such a moron. I am so sorry…"

Her voice trailed off as Julie held up her hand.

"It's okay, Kelly, really. I know I'm very sensitive when it comes to Shawn, my son's father. I don't think I'll ever get over it. Whenever I look at Brody, I see his father. As wonderful as it is to have a bright, young son, it hurts to see his father in his face and think about what might have been. That damned river!"

"Oh, Kelly, there I go again," lamented Julie, tears rolling down her cheeks. "Forgive me. This has nothing to do with you or what you said. It was just the time and place your words took me to. I'm happy to have you as a new friend. Someday, when we know each other better, I'll tell you about my time in La Crosse, especially that one terrible week in November. But, for now, I'll try to pull myself out of this funk and think of better things."

The two women went their separate ways. Julie was involved in three procedures and also took care of six office visits. The next time she looked at the clock, it was 5:10 and the office had begun to empty.

She dialed Peggy's extension. "What time do you want me over?" As Peggy talked, Julie nodded and smiled. "Great. What can I bring? No… not nothing. Please let me bring something. Buns? Okay. I'll stop at the bakery on my way home. How about I pick up doughnuts for tomorrow. Okay, I'll do it. See you in a bit."

When Julie steered her black GMC Terrain into Peggy's driveway, her friend was waiting. She waved to Julie from her porch. Julie grabbed several packages filled with pastries and a bag filled with fresh clothes for her and Brody. Peggy held the door. Julie deposited the packages in the kitchen, turned and embraced her friend.

As they walked inside, the topic of money came up. "I'm nervous that we'll find exactly what we want and we won't be able to afford it. I know you have many more resources, but I can't have you pay all the bills," said Julie.

Peggy winked at her friend. "How about we cross that bridge when we come to it? If we find exactly what we want, we'll figure it out."

"But, Peggy, you have plenty of money," said Julie, staring into space. "I have to figure out how I can afford a house and take care of other things, like Brody's college education."

"We will work it out," promised Peggy. "And once we settle into a place, it will be the beginning of a new and wonderful life for us. Imagine what it would be like to have the opportunity to share a bed every night and do all the things lovers do: a touch, quiet kisses, and passionate love anywhere in the house."

Julie broke out in laughter. "I think you're forgetting three things named Brody, Lauren, and Jake."

"I suppose I am, but the kids are gone all the time. We'll be home alone a fair amount."

"That worries me most," admitted Julie. "I love the thought of closeness and intimacy, but I worry that we'll get caught. I think of that all the time. And I wonder…"

"If talking to the kids about our love makes sense?" said Peggy, finishing the sentence.

"No, never!" shot back Julie. "I told you that. I never want Brody to know. That means Lauren and Jake can't know either."

CHAPTER 29

As the Friday morning workday began in La Crosse, Al and Charlie were at their desks early, looking over files and notes to see if they could piece together any possible theories.

A mile south, in the basement of Lutheran Hospital, part of the Gundersen complex, Rick and Pat were having coffee with Sarah and discussing the drownings.

"After we log our notes, and I run tests on the hair—I have one follicle that appears complete—let's get together, look at the results, and then decide what our next steps will be," said Sarah.

"Great idea," agreed Rick. "Okay, I have some things I still need to itemize and catalog. I'll post those within the hour. How about we get together for lunch to see if we've found anything?"

"Great," agreed Sarah. Pat nodded, and they all went their separate ways.

***

Al and Charlie talked several times during the morning. Each time, they just wound up more frustrated with the lack of solid evidence.

"Goddamnit, if there is anything there, the docs are going to have to find it!" thundered Charlie. "To be honest, I haven't found a fuckin' thing that we didn't know already. We know someone facilitated the deaths, but we have no idea about who and no goddamn idea about where to go next."

Al agreed. "How about I check with Rick to see what they're up to? If they're in the same boat, we have a big problem."

"It's maddening. We know just enough to be totally fucking confused. This confusion, it seems to me, is leading to wild-ass activity that most likely will get us nothing but more confusion. But checking with Rick is great. Get back to me when you've talked to him. I hope to God he has *something*!"

"Sure thing. Talk to you soon."

Ten minutes later, Al had received an update from Rick, returned a call to Charlie and arrived back at work, clearing a mountain of paperwork and pay vouchers from the recent trips. Rick's examinations turned up nothing.

***

A few hours later, everything changed. Sarah discovered a note entry regarding a hair from the collar of Rolf Evenson's shirt. Rick's tests identified this hair as female. Sarah searched further, discovering that the unknown hairs found in Hintzle's hair also tested female.

When she and the doctors got together, Sarah listened to Rick and Pat's reports, basically saying they had nothing new. She sat quietly for a minute before speaking. "How about the hairs found on Evenson's shirt and in Hintzle's hair? We've logged them as female. Doesn't that seem odd, given the rest of what we know? Both victims were in bars with male friends, weren't they?"

"They were," Rick agreed. "I think Charlie, Rick and I assumed the hair was either from their girlfriends or other friends. I know that Rolf and his girlfriend were close. His parents told us about her. They said when they told her, she completely fell apart. I don't know much about Hintzle. Maybe we should have checked that hair more closely."

"I'll give Al a call and see what he can tell us," said Rick. He took his cell phone and hit speed dial.

The women heard Al's loud hello, then listened as Rick described the issue. Rick hung up. "Al says the girlfriend isn't a suspect. He said when he and Charlie talked to her, she was so distraught they had to interview her several times before finally concluding that she had nothing useful to tell them. But just to be sure, Al is going to see if they can reach her for a DNA sample."

Evenson's girlfriend worked at Wine Guyz in downtown La Crosse. Her roommate told Al she was working the day shift and they could find her there.

They did. Janet Logan saw them the moment they entered and hurried over.

"Is there something new?" she asked excitedly. "I keep hoping you will find something beyond a mindless stupor that led to Rolf's death. Much as I hate to even think about it, the news conference seemed like an answer to my prayers. You do think someone killed him, don't you?"

Looking at her intently, Charlie's voice softened. "Janet, that's what we're here about. You know we found evidence suggesting foul play. We also found another possible clue. That's what's on our minds. We found a female hair on the collar of Rolf's shirt. We're wondering if you would be kind enough to provide us with a DNA swab?"

"You…you think I had something to do with it?" Janet asked, backing away. "That's just…"

"No, no, Janet, nothing like that," broke in Rick, reassuring her. "We just want to make sure that the hair we found does not belong to you. The more people we can rule out, the more we can focus our investigation and hopefully find the person who did this."

At this, Janet seemed to relax. "That's all?" she asked, the frowns of concern beginning to disappear.

"That's it," said Charlie, a hint of a smile cracking his lips.

"So what do you need?"

"I'll just take this swab," explained Al, withdrawing a small, plastic container from his pocket. A small wooden rod projected from the container. "Run it around your mouth. Then we'll compare it to the hair. That will help us to determine if the hair's yours or someone else's."

Janet opened her mouth. Al quickly opened the canister, ran the swab around her mouth and returned it to the container.

"Thanks a million," said Al. "We'll keep you posted."

As the two lawmen left Wine Guyz, Charlie suggested going to Gundersen to drop off the sample.

"Good idea," said Rick.

Ten minutes later, they were in Rick's lab. Pat and Sarah were also there. "Let's take a look," said Rick, handing the container to Sarah. "Back in a while," she said, hurrying from the room.

Two hours later, she was back. "The hair does not belong to Janet. We're gonna have to keep looking."

Charlie and Al left to return to work. Two hours later they were back at Gundersen, summoned by Rick to get back ASAP.

"What's up?" asked Al.

"We have something," reported Rick. "Sarah found a pattern. She viewed DNA evidence collected from the five most recent drowning victims. She discovered a hair found on the clothing of Garth Thomas, who died in 2006, that matched the one taken from Evenson's shirt. We're still awaiting the test on Hintzle."

Rick and Charlie looked dazed. They slumped into office chairs.

"That was our reaction, too," said Pat. "We didn't believe it, but Rick and I ran our own tests. Both of ours confirmed Sarah's findings."

"So that means," began Rick, "that we're looking at…a female killer?"

"Or at least a female accomplice," interjected Pat. "We're betting this woman either gave the injections or helped distract the victims. We wish we could tell you more. But the two hairs are all that we have. Perhaps your databases will help?"

"We'll be checking those today," assured Al. "We can divide up the work to make sure that we touch everything that's out there. We'll start with North America. If necessary, we'll search the globe."

"In the meantime, we'll look at everything we have on file," said Rick. "Maybe there's something else out there. If there is, we'll find it."

Just then the door opened. Sarah hustled in. "It's a match…it's from the same person as the hairs found on Evenson and Thomas."

Al and Charlie gone, Rick, Pat, and Sarah planned their work for the day, hoping the schedule would remain quiet enough for additional searches. They wanted to identify the hairs' owner as soon as they could.

CHAPTER 30

As the weekend arrived, no call came from Barb. While they waited impatiently, Peggy and Julie decided to spend the weekend together again.

Friday night was fun. The kids went to the opening basketball game at Washington and arranged to get a ride home with friends. Meanwhile, Peggy and Julie behaved like school kids. Peggy built a fire in her fireplace. The two roasted hot dogs and finished off their picnic with s'mores.

"Just like high school, don't you think?" said Peggy. "God, we used to have fun at bonfires. We'd make out like crazy. There were blankets all over the campground."

"I never went to a bonfire," said Julie. "Never wanted to. They called me the iron maiden." She paused and thought for a bit. "But if I could have gone with Shawn, I would have loved it."

Silence enveloped the room. Minutes went past. Each woman was lost in thought. Finally, Peggy broke the silence. "Listen to us! Just a couple of schoolgirls. C'mon over here."

As Peggy stretched out her arm, Julie slid over. Soon, she snuggled into Peggy's shoulder and was kissing her neck.

"You always smell so good. You smell good all over."

"Now who's pushing?" asked Peggy. "Was that some sort of invitation?"

Julie thought for a while. "I guess it was," she admitted. "I think I'm a little…how do they say it? Randy? Is that the word?"

"It's a word. It means horny, honey. If that's what you are, I will be happy to take care of it."

Julie snuggled closer and the two kissed some more. Peggy's tongue probed deeply. When Julie moaned, Peggy's left hand cupped her friend's breast. She could feel the nipple grow hard as she continued to kiss her friend. Julie moved forward, turned toward Peggy and put her right leg over Peggy's leg. As the kisses continued, Julie pressed against her friend's leg, eased up and pressed again.

"Is that a signal?" mumbled Peggy.

"It is. I feel hot all over."

Peggy's hand worked its way into the top of Julie's jeans. When Julie sucked in her stomach, Peggy took advantage of the opening to move her hand farther down. She felt Julie's luxurious pubic hair and began to play with it, winding it around her index finger.

"Um, your hair is so soft. It's long enough to braid. Maybe I could do that one of these days."

"I don't think it's that long," replied Julie, breathlessly. "What you're doing tickles. Lower, please. Oh, that's it—right there…right there…oh."

Julie was now straining against the back of the couch, trying to give Peggy easy access.

"You're so wet. You're just dripping!"

"Keep your finger right there. Yes, right there. Oh, a little harder… that's it. Move your finger up and down, Peggy—oh, yes."

Julie reached down, unbuckled her belt, popped the snap on her jeans and slipped the zipper down.

"Much better," she moaned as Peggy's fingers moved with greater freedom. That's all it took. Julie came with a burst of moans. Peggy held Julie tight and pressed her finger into her slit, remaining motionless until the spasms stopped.

"Do you want me to repay the favor now?"

Peggy smiled and stroked her friend gently. "I'll take mine later, if that's all right with you. I like it when we're in bed. Then there is total freedom. I like that best."

"Fair enough," responded Julie, lazily. "I should be recovered enough by then. You know, I like getting, but it's just as much fun to give. I love the taste of you."

"I can't handle much more of this talk without taking you to bed right now," snickered Peggy. "Let's talk about the move. We're pretty certain we'll find something soon, right? How about we get up early, eat breakfast and spend time packing? We can start here or at your place, doesn't matter to me."

"I like it. Might as well start here. We can go to my place in the afternoon or on Sunday, whenever we finish here."

As the two friends sat and talked, the clock crept toward 10 p.m.

Julie looked at her watch. "Gosh, it's almost 10. What time will the kids be home?"

"Any minute now, I think," said Peggy, assuredly. "I'm pretty sure Lauren will exercise all of her bossy tendencies to make sure the boys are towing the line."

Not five minutes later, the door opened. Jake and Brody burst into the room. Both were excited. Seeing Peggy, Jake exclaimed, "Mom! Are we good? That Brady kid is unbelievable. He had 30 points tonight!"

Brody quickly affirmed the team's talent. "They are really good, Mom! Doug Brady is *really* good, but he's not the only one. There are six or seven great players."

The oh-so-sophisticated Lauren walked in, sat down, and crossed her legs. "The team has some talent. But boys are so immature. Brady had four fouls, two others fouled out, and they had two technical fouls. They can't control themselves."

"Okay, enough about the game," said Peggy. "It's late. There's some microwave popcorn in the cupboard and cake left over from last night. Help yourselves. Then you'd better hit the sack. And I don't want to hear any complaining. It's been a busy week and next week might be even busier. Julie and I are going to start packing tomorrow. We could use some help. I might even be willing to pay."

"Alright!" shouted Jake, slapping his hand on the table. "We'll be happy to help, won't we, Brody?"

"Sure we will, especially if we can make some money. That's cool."

The kids went to the kitchen. The familiar noises of the microwave began. Twenty minutes later, when Peggy and Julie went to check, the cake pan was empty, there were three large bowls with unpopped kernels, and three empty microwave popcorn bags on the counter.

"Lauren and Jake, get your butts down here!" shouted Peggy. "You know better than to leave a mess like this. I want it cleaned up…now!"

"Brody, you get down here and help!" echoed Julie.

Soon the kitchen was spotless, the three kids were off to bed, and Julie and Peggy had undressed, washed up and slipped into nightgowns. Thirty minutes later, Julie had paid off her IOU. Peggy nearly purred like a cat. Julie was exhausted, but she loved the taste on her lips. Soon, she was fast asleep in Peggy's arms.

CHAPTER 31

The work week didn't end on Friday for Al and Charlie. When midafternoon rolled around on Saturday, they had been at work all day, probing all of the police and fire databases in the region. Charlie scanned the database focused on people implicated in criminal activity and then shared with Al the names of everyone they knew that could be involved.

This search was the first one they had done, and while it took only a couple of hours, it turned up nothing. The men expected this outcome.

"I think we have to focus our efforts around CODIS," suggested Al. "I think it's our best bet, don't you?"

CODIS was a system developed by the federal government in the late 1980s to store DNA in national, state and local databases. It maintained DNA profiles obtained by the various systems, storing them in a series of databases available to law enforcement agencies across the country. CODIS can also link evidence obtained from various crime scenes which helps in identifying serial criminals.

"CODIS is our best bet," agreed Charlie, "but the goddamn forms are going to be no small job."

"Yeah," said Al, "but there's really nowhere else to look. We don't have a name. We don't have a suspect. All we have are a few hairs."

"And we have eliminated family, friends, and morticians, either by the color of their hair or samples they gave us," said Charlie. "The only person we haven't found is the girlfriend of the initial victim, Shawn Sorensen. But we haven't looked very hard either."

When Al downloaded the CODIS results, the look on his face told Charlie everything he didn't want to know.

"No fuckin' hits, I guess," he said as Al studied the printout.

"Not a thing," said Al. "I guess we aren't dealing with a known perp."

"What haven't we looked at?" asked Charlie, closing his eyes and thinking.

"Well, we haven't missed any of the national crime databases," responded Al. "I'm sure there are others out there, but that would be like searching for a needle in a haystack, wouldn't it?"

"I guess it would," agreed Charlie. "But—hey, wait a minute. We are likely dealing with someone who knows a good deal about medicine and medicines. Shouldn't we search the healthcare databases?"

"Great idea, Charlie," said Al with a smile. "Every year or two you come up with one of those."

Both officers turned to their computer screens, found a list of health care databases online, and then focused on the ones that included DNA.

An hour later, 17 more queries were underway. Charlie was ready to eat.

"Christ, I'm hungry. My belly button's tapping a tune on my backbone. Why don't we let the computer chew on this while we go out for a bite?"

"You're always starved, Charlie," said Al with a laugh. "And what would rescue you from starvation?"

"Well, I'm kinda in the mood for one of those French dip sandwiches at the La Crosse Club," answered Charlie. "You do still have your membership, don't you?"

"You're a classic," said Al, shaking his head. "You know damn well I have a membership. You also know that if we go there, I'm obligated to pay. When are you ever going to buy?"

"Aww, c'mon, didn't I just buy at Ma's?" asked Charlie.

"Yea, I think you did, Charlie. As I recall, it was about two years ago."

"Get outta here! It hasn't been two years. If you're that fuckin' stingy and determined to deprive a friend of a French dip, hell, pick the place and I'll buy."

Satisfied now, Al changed his tune, "Grab your coat, let's go."

As Al steered the unmarked police car toward the river, Charlie wanted to know where they were going.

"It's gonna be the La Crosse Club," replied Al. "Not because I'm giving in, but because you have my mouth watering for a French dip, too."

An hour and a half later, the two were back in the car. As Al prepared to turn the car around, Charlie emitted a world-class burp. He rubbed his stomach. "Not a burp, just a goddamn good French dip."

"Charlie, have you no couth?"

"Couth? Of course, I don't have couth. I take a shower every day and scrub my hair and body real good."

"Couth means manners, Charlie. Not cooties."

"Well, whatever, but you gotta admit my idea to go to the club was a goddamn good one."

"It sure was," said Al, "and it hit me damn hard in the wallet. The next time it'll be my choice…and I'm pickin' an expensive place!"

They were still chuckling when they got back to the office. The printer was spewing paper. All of the searches they had ordered before leaving for lunch were back, and not a one of them had produced a hit.

"Charlie, it looks like a dead end," said Al. "Let's call it a day. Perhaps if we think about it on our own, we'll come across something helpful."

Charlie agreed, turned, and walked to the Sheriff's Department, just a few blocks to the southeast. As he walked, the sun brightening an otherwise bleak walk, he thought yet again about what might have been overlooked. Just as he opened the door, he wondered if a search of the DNA databases of foreign countries might be helpful. He supposed it was possible that the perp participated in some sort of health exchange or was wounded in the service.

Working alone, Charlie queried the United Kingdom's National DNA Database, the largest in the world. He also accessed Interpol's National DNA Database.

***

By the time he was done, it was 5:20 p.m. A good time to quit for the day, he decided, since he had literally been working round the clock since the discovery of Rolf Evenson's body. He checked out at the central desk and headed home for, hopefully, a great meal and a goodnight's sleep.

As he drove, he called Al on his cell and told him about the orders.

"God, Charlie, you are amazing!" praised Al. "That's a great idea… two in one day. You are now paid up for the next decade."

"Aw, Al, stop," replied Charlie. "I'm trying to help here and you make me sound like a country bumpkin."

"Well, if the shoe fits," replied Al, laughing.

"I've had enough abuse for one day," snapped Charlie. "Now I'm headin' home for a few more shovels of it from my wife. I'm done for the day, Al. So just stick your rude comments up your ass."

"Charming." Al hung up.

As the phone clicked, Al laughed to himself, thinking just how fortunate he was to be working with Charlie. He really was a great guy, despite his ribbing. He was self-deprecating and always willing to laugh at himself. *Yes*, Al thought, *I'm a lucky guy: Charlie at work and a great family at home. Now, if we could only catch this killer.*

CHAPTER 32

Julie awoke with a start. She was in bed with Peggy, wrapped in a sleepy embrace. Peggy's long, blonde hair cascaded down Julie's side. Rays from the rising sun gave her skin a glistening sheen. Julie thought back over the previous night. *Ecstasy*, she thought, remembering the orgasms they created. *Yes, she needed the release as much as her friend*, she realized, suddenly aware of the sweet ache that filled her. *Could female love really create the same sort of next-morning feelings as sex with a man?* She experienced these feelings, a long, long time ago. Now, Peggy reawakened her desires and brought back sweet aches in, the morning after a night of passionate lovemaking.

"Mm," mumbled Peggy, snuggling closer to Julie. Her lips reached out to embrace her friend. "Quite a night, wasn't it?"

As they disentangled, Peggy rolled toward her. "Julie, can I ask you something?"

"Sure…anything."

"Do you ever miss, you know, the feeling of a man's penis inside you? Please be honest."

"Remember, I only had that happen on a half dozen occasions, and it was so long ago, it's hard to remember. I remember Shawn, but that part of him is vague. I don't know if I miss it or not, I'm just happy that you make me feel alive again," whispered Julie.

"I don't miss it either," confessed Peggy, "but I thought if you did, then we could see what we can do about it."

"You mean like finding a man?" replied Julie, giggling.

"Well, only if you insisted. You know, there are other ways," said Peggy. "Some sex toys are built for woman-to-woman contact."

"Oh, but I think that would feel so fake," said Julie. "I love it the way that it is. I'm totally satisfied. The only thing I worry about are the kids. What they would think, you know?"

"Right now, I think we should get up and get started on packing. We have lots to do. You don't seem to think we are going to get the kids to help."

"Yeah, I guess you're right, but I could stay here all day," said Peggy.

"So could I," mumbled Julie, nuzzling Peggy's neck. "But that isn't going to get our work done."

Her less-than-soft bite had Peggy sitting up in seconds.

"What was that about?"

"Just a love nip to get you moving," said Julie, giggling. "If the kids are going to sleep until midafternoon, think of all the fun we can have getting our work done."

The pair had fun, that's for sure. They worked and played, inventing little games to speed up the tasks. Before 2 o'clock, all of the items in Peggy's house were marked with colored tags, green for the things they would keep and use, red for the things they would discard, and yellow for the things they would keep but store.

Peggy made a delicious shrimp salad as Julie finished up the assignments. They woke the kids, fed them, and told them that Peggy and Julie would be working at Julie's house for the rest of afternoon and evening. The two women left together after giving Lauren some money, telling her to buy fast food for herself and the boys.

"I'm thinking they know…or at least suspect," said Peggy as they drove. "It's hard for me to imagine Lauren refusing our request to help. The fact that she would opt to stay with the two boys tells me she thought we should be alone."

"Interesting observation," said Julie, nodding. "When you think about it, we haven't been very secretive. Kids are actually much more observant than we often think."

"Really doesn't matter," said Peggy. "We must sit them down and talk to them about us, and the sooner, the better. If they already suspect it, the talk might make it easier."

Peggy started laughing heartily.

"What's so funny?" asked Julie.

"Well, I don't know how it was with you, but when my mom got around to talking to me about the birds and the bees, I had been sexually active for three years and masturbating for five before that. I think she thought I knew, and that made it easier for her. How about you?"

"No one told me anything," admitted Julie. "They didn't have to. I was a good girl. My folks knew it, and so did everyone else in Alma. What little I knew before you, I learned from Shawn. I don't know how he compares to others, but he was very gentle. He seemed to know I was clueless. He made it easy. He was soft, gentle, took lots of time, and made sure I was satisfied. The only thing I didn't like was the quick exit when it was over. I wished he'd stayed inside me and talked to me. But no, it was roll over, wipe himself off, throw me a towel and put on his clothes. I always wanted more."

"Most people's first love is like that, I think," mused Peggy. "My first time was in the backseat of a car when I was a sophomore. He came *before* he got it in. What a disappointment. The second, third, and fourth times weren't much better. I stuck with it and he finally came around. When that happened, I *came* around, too. After that, he talked his little head off, and I never had to worry about boys after that. They kind of stood in line."

"God, Peggy, didn't you worry about getting pregnant?"

"Not at first. When I missed a period, I was paranoid. I ran up and down stairs. I took hot baths, followed by cold showers. No one was happier than me when a month later, the dam broke. I was so relieved; I promised I'd never do it again. That lasted about eight days. I just really couldn't get along without it. I made a lot of guys happy."

"You make me laugh," said Julie. "And then I get a little jealous, too."

The talk went on as the women began to mark items at Julie's. Peggy studied the little marks on all the items. "You know, we're not gonna have a ton of space. We're going to have to start prioritizing. Maybe, we should start using color-coded post-its and then if we have not enough room, we'll know what goes first."

"Great idea," said Julie. She grabbed the color coded sticky notes.

They busied themselves, working briskly until 7:30. They were about half done, but they were also hungry and thirsty.

"Do you have any wine?" asked Peggy.

"Sure, red or white?"

"I'd like a nice pinot noir," said Peggy. "And what would you say to a pizza?"

"I'd love it. Sausage and mushrooms?"

"Sure, but let's add peppers and onions, too."

"Let's eat here," suggested Peggy. "When we're done, we'll head back to my house to sleep. Sound okay to you?"

"I guess, but I could stay here, too. Maybe I should…"

"No, you should not. You should sleep at my house. If you want to sleep in a separate bed, fine. The kids are at my house. We should be there too."

"Why don't we sleep here? Can't Lauren keep the boys in line? If we slept here, we'd have privacy. When we get up tomorrow, we can eat breakfast and get right to work," suggested Julie.

"I'm not sure. Do you really think it's a good idea to leave the kids alone? I do think Lauren's responsible, but I've never left them alone overnight before. I'd love to be alone with you. Yet, I'd be terribly worried about the kids," admitted Peggy.

"Maybe you're right," agreed Julie. "Okay, let's get some food—takeout or cook—and get to your house. It's already getting late."

"I think takeout. If we make supper now, we wouldn't get to bed until midnight, "said Peggy.

"Agreed. Want to call the pizza place? One for us and two for them?"

Peggy smiled. "They'll love it, and they'll love you for suggesting it."

CHAPTER 33

Al had intended to take Sunday off. He knew he owed his family a day with them. His wife JoAnne was beginning to complain about his absences. While she understood the complexities of his job, especially now that there had been a break and he was hunting a killer, she worried for him. She felt he'd become too wedded to his job and didn't have any time for his family. She also worried about his safety.

Even before the La Crosse detective opened his eyes, he began thinking about the database queries Charlie started before leaving the office yesterday. *Maybe*, he thought, *I could just sneak out and take a peek. It's pretty unlikely we would have any hits, anyhow.*

He gently moved toward the side of the bed. He had one leg on the floor and had begun to sit up when his wife spoke. "Al, for God's sake, it's 5:30. Just where are you going at 5:30?"

"Well," he began, "I thought maybe I could sneak down to the office to check on the database queries Charlie asked for. I doubt there will be anything there, but I'd like to know for sure."

"Go then," she said. "You might as well get it over with. If you don't do it now, you'll be absent all day, anyhow, even if you're here!"

"I suppose that's right." "Tell you what, you lie back for a little nap. When I get back, I'll wake you for a little sugar time. Sound good?"

"Al, all you ever have on your mind, is work and sex. But, yes, a little Sunday morning sugar would be great. If you haven't forgotten how?"

"JoAnne, how could I forget? I have the best piece in town. Don't think I'd forget that."

"Just how would you know I'm the best in town? I mean, it's what *all* the guys tell me, but how do you know?"

"What?" stammered Al. "What guys?"

"Oh, for God's sake, Al," said JoAnne, laughing. "Do you really think I'd mess around on you? Give me a break. You're pretty damn good, too, but it's been ages. So, please don't let me down again!"

Al rushed through a shower, shaved, dressed and was out the door in 20 minutes. Ten minutes later, he was in his office. After checking his desk and, thankfully, finding it as he had left it, he walked a few steps to the printer connected to database queries. He was surprised to see a mound of printout paper lying on the floor under the printer. Assuming the paper contained responses to Charlie's queries, Al picked up the stack and casually paged through it.

There it was!

"Well, I'll be damned," muttered Al out loud when he saw the words *Match Found*. Looking closer, he saw this was a response to the query to the United Kingdom National Police Database. KNPD was one of the most expansive databases in the world. Most people knew it as Gene Watch.

Almost afraid to believe what he had seen, Al rushed back to his desk with the printout and began to read. The more he read, the more disheartened he became.

Indeed, there had been a DNA match to the hairs found on two of the three bodies. But—and there always seemed to be a 'but'—the identity of the person was impossible to ascertain, according to the report. The hairs belonged to a U.S. citizen who was on a mercy mission to West Africa during the Ebola outbreak. The databases in Liberia, Guinea, Sierra Leone, Nigeria, and Mali were unreliable to begin with, stated the report, and, in this case, the sample was taken during the peak of the chaos. Therefore, no name was attached.

"Dammit!" shouted Al, slamming his hand on his desk. "How the hell can something be that mixed up?" He sat and thought for nearly an hour and then reluctantly dialed Charlie, who he knew was also hoping to enjoy a Sunday with his family. The two men talked for 20 minutes. "Tell you what, give this some thought in your spare time. I'll do the same. By tomorrow, maybe we will have come up with something," said Al.

"Give it some thought in my spare time!" said Charlie, indignant. "You know damn well that I won't be thinking of anything else today. Goddamn, Charlene is going to have my ass. The kids aren't going to be happy, either. But hell yes, Mr. Rouse, I *will* give it some thought!"

Al puttered around his office for another hour, tidying up things here and there. Totally dejected, he departed for home, expecting a very trying

Sunday. Even the thought of Sunday morning sugar didn't brighten his mood.

He was wrong about that last thought, though. JoAnne was at the top of her game. She had sent the kids to church and Sunday school. "C'mon, big guy! Let's exercise that little guy!"

Al reacted immediately. "Hey, little guy? What the hell is that? I haven't heard any complaints before."

"Oh, didn't you hear, Al? Size matters. It's been all over the papers these last three days. Guess you haven't had time to pay attention."

Al quickly dropped his pants, stepping on the legs to get out of them. His shorts quickly followed. Before she knew it, he was in bed and on top of her. He entered her in a rush. When she exclaimed, he let her know in no uncertain terms what he intended.

"I'm gonna show you just how this 'little fella' can be!" He did show her—over, under, and over again, until they were both exhausted.

Laughing, she finally pushed him away. They were both panting heavily.

"Al, where…have…you…been saving that? You had me right from the start!"

"Just like I always did…ever since you were a sophomore," said Al, preening.

"Sophomore? I'll give you sophomore. You have one bad memory, Detective Rouse. You didn't get it until four days after graduation."

An amazed look broke out on Al's face.

"Four days after graduation? Jo…I swear to God you're in the advanced stages of Alzheimer's. It was in January of our sophomore year after a basketball game. I scored 27 points in that one."

"Well, you sure as hell didn't score after the game," lectured JoAnne. She thought for a moment. "Well, it might have been at the end of our junior year."

"You're crazy!" he said, laughing. He then picked her up and sat her down on his erect penis. Again, she gasped. "What do you think I am, a pinball machine?"

"Oh, complaining are you?"

This time there was no comeback. His wife, it seemed, was occupied with other things. It didn't take long before her moans threatened to wake the neighborhood.

"Jo, quiet!" he urged. "You're gonna wake the dead."

"The dead? He's been awake for nearly an hour," she said, pointing below his waist. "That's a new record, I swear. I'd love to break it again tonight if you're up to it."

"Crap, you're never satisfied," lamented Al. "But…sure…I'll do my best to make you happy again tonight. Then will you cut me some slack? It's gonna be a helluva busy week."

JoAnne thought for a moment. "I'll think about it. I'm not so sure I want to cut you any slack. I've had a very good time this morning. Now quit patting yourself on the back and go make all of us some of your famous waffles. The kids'll be home soon."

"God, woman, you are never satisfied. Isn't it enough that I work my ass off day in and day out?"

She craned her neck just a bit. "Al, I feel it only fair to report to you that you still have an ass. Perhaps you worked some other part off?"

"I'm outta here! Waffles, fresh orange juice, bacon…and coffee for you and me!"

Quiet settled over the bedroom as JoAnne roused herself, put on a sweatshirt, some jeans and headed for downstairs.

At Charlie's house, things weren't going quite so well. He and Charlene had been up since 7:30. The argument that had begun the night before continued immediately.

"You left your clothes on the floor again," snapped Charlene, looking at the heap next to the couch where Charlie had slept—again.

"And just what the hell would you have me do with them? I wind up sleeping on the goddamn couch every night and the last time I looked, there's no closet next to the couch."

Hands on her hips with lightning sparks in her eyes, Charlene took a deep breath. "Charles, this life is sure not what I opted for when we got married. You're married to your job and Al. Neither I nor the kids get anything from you. You're up early and gone before the rest of us are awake. You come home after dark, bitch about no supper and stomp out to find something somewhere else. God knows what else you might be finding. And you know what, Charlie? I don't give a shit! I really don't. I just wish you were gone so we could have some peace. Maybe I could find someone who would think that I'm as important as his job!"

"Aww, Charlene, you always make it worse than it is. You complain about everything. How do you think that makes me feel? If you want me out, I'll be happy to leave. Hell, this is no marriage any way. When's the last time we slept together? A year ago…or maybe two?"

"That's just like you, Charlie. Everything becomes a matter of sex. Well, there's not going to be any sex around here. Not now! Not ever!"

Charlie stared at her for a long time and then spoke softly. "I said slept together. I didn't say screwed. I'm sick of sleeping on the goddamned couch. And I'm sick of your bitchin' about everything I do or don't do. You know what, Charlene? You can stick it where the sun don't shine. I'm outta here! And maybe I won't be back!"

As Charlie turned to leave, Charlene's voice followed him out the door. "And just who the hell do you think cares? None of us even know you any more, you asshole!"

Charlie got into his SUV. He started driving and thinking. It had been like this from the beginning for Charlene and him. He'd gotten her pregnant their senior year in high school, and she had the baby before graduation. She came from a family considerably more well off than Charlie's, and the nagging about money and things they didn't have began almost immediately. She refused to work or cook. And sex? There was none. *Why the hell*, he thought, *had he put with it. He liked his job and hated his home life. Time to do something about it.*

As he thought, he paid little attention to where he was until he rolled into the town of Westby 45 minutes later. He spotted the Westby House B&B, realized he was hungry and decided to eat. It was already approaching 11 when he walked into the dining room. The B&B was serving what appeared to be a substantial brunch. As with all things, Charlie knew eating would make him feel better.

He darn near cleared the buffet of food. Mary, the proprietor, looked on in awe as this substantial man made trip after trip to the food bar. It was nearly 1 o'clock when he leaned back in his chair, took a big breath and rubbed his stomach.

"Mam, that was mighty good," said Charlie. He thought for a second. He couldn't think about going back home. "What's your room rate, by the way?"

"I've got one room left," reported Mary. "If you want to take a nap, I'll give it to you for half price. You can stay the night, if you want. Better let me know now, though, so I can make sure I have enough food to feed you dinner."

Charlie was relieved that as she talked, Mary beamed. Her smile made him happy, and he smiled, too. "You know what, ma'am, I'll take that room…for the night. Any place nearby where I can buy deodorant, a razor and shaving cream?"

"Right across the street," said Mary, pointing. "Torgerson Drug has everything you'll need. You from around here?"

"Yes, Mam. I'm from La Crosse. Sheriff's Deputy Charlie Berzinski at your service!"

Charlie stuck out his hand. Mary took it and shook it briskly. Soon the two were talking like old friends, and Mary found herself feeling sorry for the big but seemingly gentle man who was, obviously, distraught over his personal life He told her about the drownings. *His work life ain't so good, either*, she thought.

"Charlie, go get what you need across the street. Then come back and take a nap. I'll cook up something for supper that'll put a smile on your face!"

"Ma'am," offered Charlie, smiling. "Food always puts a smile on my face. Not sure about today, but you go ahead and give it a try."

"I will, young man," promised Mary as Charlie left and walked across the street to Torgerson. He returned and got directions to the room, which, as it turned out, was at the back of the large Victorian house. The room was as quiet as a graveyard. Charlie shrugged out of his clothes, laid down without uncovering the bed, and almost immediately fell asleep. Quiet snoring filled the room. .

CHAPTER 34

Back at Peggy's house, the women were hard at work. They had been up early and immediately started packing.

"If we get the job done, we can play," quipped Peggy, drawing a nod from Julie.

As Sunday afternoon rolled around, they had finished with most of the packing and organizing on the first floor. They would keep some things, but they also earmarked many things for sale.

After a late lunch at Peggy's house—BLTs that Lauren, Brody and Jake managed to get out of bed to eat—the three kids stumbled to the living room to watch TV. Julie and Peggy finished the dishes, and then set out to work at Julie's house.

They finished what little there was to do in the kitchen quickly. Most of Julie's things were hand-me-downs. All of those items were earmarked for sale or disposal. The spare bedroom was much the same, except for the antique rocker that had belonged to Julie's grandmother. It was a family heirloom. Peggy moved on to Brody's room. Julie busied herself in her room, taking advantage of the opportunity to toss lots of things that accumulated in drawers or she no longer wore. By the time they finished these tasks, the clock was approaching 4 p.m.

"Tell you what," suggested Peggy, "how about I take the bathroom and you take the back storeroom? Those rooms shouldn't take long. After that, we can look at the garage."

"There's nothing in the garage. A few old tools, maybe, several empty boxes, a snow shovel or two, and a rake. Most of those items I'd throw out," said Julie. "The garage should take no time at all."

While Julie was busily marking things to save or pitch, Peggy busied herself in the bathroom.

Suddenly, Peggy appeared at the storeroom door, a fairly large cardboard box in her hands. "Girlfriend, what the heck is this?" asked Peggy. "It's full of hypodermic needles and other medical supplies. Lots of drugs, too. What's that all about?"

Embarrassed, Julie's faced turned red. "It's all from when I worked with my dad. He compounded lots of drugs. I picked up the habit. During college, I experimented with compounds. I suppose that I hoped I might find something useful, a better sedative, maybe."

"I see," responded Peggy. Her tone was hesitant.

"Really, it's just a hobby I picked up years ago. I suppose the stuff stayed in the bathroom."

"If you say so," replied Peggy in a brisk tone. "Some of this stuff looks pretty new, though."

"I might have added a few things several years ago," replied Julie. "I haven't used that stuff since."

Julie looked at her friend, pushed a lock of hair out of her eyes, and rested her hands on her hips. "I decided, Peggy, that I would keep absolutely no secrets from you. I want to be an open book for you. I don't want there to be anything you don't know. To be honest, there are several things that I want to talk to you about, but not today. Soon, though."

"Okay," said Peggy, a smile spreading across her beautiful face. "Having you close to me is all I really need. I just hope you don't meet someone else in the meantime and leave in a flash."

"Don't be silly," said Julie reassuringly. "The only way we'll ever be separated is if something beyond our control comes along and takes one of us away."

Julie's response seemed odd, but Peggy let it go. As the two women sat on the couch chatting, they were interrupted by the phone.

"Must be the kids," guessed Julie. "I'll bet they're wondering about dinner."

She picked up the receiver. "Hello? Oh, Barb," said Julie, excitingly looking at Peggy and shrugging her shoulders. "I hope this call means you have something for us. You do? Okay, tell me. Peggy is here, too. She's as interested as I am. I'll put it on speaker."

"You have to be kidding!" she exclaimed as Barb paused, apparently to take a breath.

"I don't believe it," said Julie to Peggy. "Barb was at an open house today and met an older lady who has a great house. She's too old to take care of it properly. It's too big. She told Barb she knows the house would command a great price. She also knows the market probably has few buyers who can afford it."

"Yes," replied Julie. "She told Barb the most important thing to her is having the right people—people who will like it and care for it like she and her late husband did. She said she is willing to sacrifice price to get the right people. Even better, the sooner she can move, the better. She rented an apartment at an assisted living facility."

"Barb wants to know if we can look at it tonight?" said Julie, excitedly.

"We'd better calm down," suggested Peggy. "We don't even know where this house is. We don't know if the kids have to change schools. We don't know how much it is. Let's not get way ahead of ourselves here."

Barb told them the house was at 6807 North Kennicott. Although they didn't know where Kennicott was, Barb explained it was near Haley Park. They knew where that was. Barb disclosed some really good news. The kids would not have to change schools because she already checked. Unfortunately, there also came some bad news. The house was listed for $750,000!

When they heard that, both women went ballistic.

"Barb, that's ridiculous!" exclaimed Julie. "There is no way we can afford three quarters of a million. It's out of the question!"

Barb was almost screaming as she urged them to calm down. "Jeepers, calm down! Let me explain!"

"Now, let's go over this slowly," said Barb. "The owner is asking $750,000. The house is clearly worth that or more. However, the owner is also *more concerned* about finding the *right* buyer than the price."

Peggy and Julie nodded at each other. Peggy spoke. "Barb, give us 15 minutes to try and get our arms around this. Yes, I'm sure we're going to want to see it, but tonight? Is tonight really a good time?"

After Barb reassured them that she and the owner were available and anxious for them to see it, the conversation concluded.

Julie looked at her friend. "A house worth $750,000. God, what are we thinking? It's way beyond our reach. Seeing it probably isn't a good idea."

"But Barb said the owner is willing to make the price affordable to the right buyer," said Peggy. "I say we look at it. Heck, let's do it. What do we have to lose? If it's beyond our reach, we say no. Besides, I'd enjoy some time away from this packing."

While Julie agreed, she wasn't so sure. "We're not really dressed for real estate viewing. Look at me! Look at you!"

Laughing now as she looked in a mirror, Julie saw the smudges on her face and dirt on her shirt. She turned back to Peggy and laughed louder. "Girlfriend, you're a mess!"

Peggy looked in the mirror and burst out laughing. "Man, am I a mess. I'm filthy. You're right, no house hunting tonight. Maybe, we could at least drive by it on the way home and then look at it on Monday if we like it?"

Julie started laughing again. "6807 North Kennicott is definitely not on the way to your house. But, you're right, let's drive past it. It would be good to get an idea of whether we like it or not, at least from the outside."

Peggy went back to work while Julie called Barb. An appointment arranged for Monday evening, Julie got back to the work remaining in the backroom. Peggy was busy in the bathroom. Soon, the work was finished. The women were ready to end their work day with a drive to North Kennicott. Peggy called the kids and told them they would pick up dinner. She succumbed to pleas for Papa Murphy's pizza.

"Pizza! All they ever want is pizza," lamented Peggy. "How about we stop at Sammy's and pick up something other than pizza for us?"

"That would be great. How about spaghetti?"

"Love it; let's get out of here."

Soon, Peggy's SUV headed toward Haley Park and North Kennicott. They passed the park, now quiet, everyone likely inside for Sunday dinner. Peggy made a right onto North Kennicott and pointed out that the house would be on Julie's side. The street was filled with stately brick homes, all of them set back from the street and above it. All the lawns were beautifully landscaped and featured large trees, most of them maples. A few still bore colorful leaves not yet blown away.

"Oh gosh," said Julie. "Peggy, this is beautiful. I hate to even look. We're way out of our league here."

As they rounded a bend in the street, ahead of them stood a stately, three-story brick house, its white trim sparkling in the light of the setting sun. Its lawn was manicured. Set back from the house was a large building that looked to be more than a garage, although it obviously contained space for vehicles. The wide concrete driveway wound up the hill. Everything about the house was well kept; it was a charming reminder of how wealthy Americans once lived.

"Have you ever been to Newport, Rhode Island?" asked Peggy.

"No, never east of Ohio," replied Julie. "Why?"

"This reminds me of Ocean Drive in Newport," explained Peggy. "Newport has the greatest collection of mansions you've ever seen, built by folks named Vanderbilt and Astor. This house would be right at home on Ocean Drive."

"That means that there is no way I can even consider this. It's way out of my reach."

Peggy turned into the driveway and headed the Toyota SUV up the hill.

"Peggy, what the heck are you doing!" shouted Julie. "This is trespassing. We'll end up in jail!"

"Relax," said Peggy, laughing, "we'll just go up, take a look at the backyard, turn around and come down. If anyone calls the police, we have a perfect alibi. We're prospective buyers."

"In your dreams," lamented Julie. "We're gonna fall in love with this place and then we're going to be heartbroken when we find out we can't afford it."

When they saw the backyard, they were blown away. There was a pond and artificial waterfall in one corner. Gardens seemed everywhere. Mums, asters, and kale provided a blaze of color. What, undoubtedly, was a vegetable garden had been covered with leaves from the collection of large oaks and maples. It seemed logical because there wasn't a leaf on the grass, which still maintained its fall green.

I can't ever imagine living in a house like this," said Julie slowly. "I'd have to marry a billionaire to have a house like this and that's not gonna happen."

"I sure hope not," said Peggy, looking over her shoulder to back the car toward the garage, carriage house or whatever the heck it was called. "I'm not ready to lose you to a house unless I come with it."

They turned to look as they went down the drive, made the turn onto North Kennicott and headed for Sammy's. Spaghetti and garlic bread in a carryout bag, they stopped again at Papa Murphy's, picked up two large pizzas, and drove toward home.

The kids, of course, were ravenous. The pizzas disappeared in a flash, and so did the sodas. When those items were demolished, Jake and Brody hovered over the spaghetti, waiting to see what might be salvaged. There was plenty left. It disappeared as quickly as the pizza.

When dinner was finished, Peggy and Julie told the kids to clean up the dishes. The two women sat and talked for a while about the day, the house, and the fact that they could never afford it. The dishes done, Julie and Brody headed home. Since Brody had no homework, they went straight to bed.

CHAPTER 35

When Al arrived at his desk Monday morning, he booted up his computer and went to get a cup of coffee from the nearby Keurig while the computer stubbornly groaned its way to life. *Damn*, he thought, *why can't machines have some sense of urgency?* He suddenly remembered the circumstances and chuckled to himself. *No need for urgency*, he mused, *unless they came up with something more on the DNA search.*

When the computer was ready, he checked his emails. He had received 21 emails on Sunday. Fifteen of them were from Charlie. In the last one, he apologized for the flurry of messages. However, Charlie wrote that many emails were better than losing a thought, thanks to an aging memory.

Al shared his friend's sentiment. Both men determined that Sheriff Hooper and Chief Whigg should contact the FBI Federal DNA Database Unit. The feds should explore the situation with officials of the UK's National Database.

The two lawmen met with their bosses 30 minutes later, catching them at the close of their morning news meeting. The four men went to a conference room to talk.

Al outlined the situation with as much detail as he could, emphasizing continually that the key to the identity of the killer was likely somewhere in these computers in London. Hooper and Whigg understood and it was obvious they wanted to help. However, this was new territory for them, too.

The nearest FBI field offices were in Rochester, Minnesota, and Madison, Wisconsin. The group decided to ask for help in Madison since it was larger. It was the capital of Wisconsin and, probably, better staffed. Hooper and Whigg, armed with a briefcase full of papers, set off to call the Madison FBI. Al and Charlie, left with nothing to do at the moment, headed toward their desks. In this short span of time, their desks had now disappeared entirely beneath case files, both new and old. The motivation to work on other cases just wasn't there. Al wandered to the chief's office to see if there was anything new.

"C'mon in, Al," said Whigg. "I'm hoping to have someone from the FBI and from the U.K.'s home office on the line with me and Sheriff Hooper any minute. How about you listen in?"

"You couldn't keep me away," muttered Al, "but what about Charlie? Will the sheriff include him, too? He should because Charlie has worked darn hard on this case. He also seems really down this morning. I'm not sure if it's the case or his family life. I don't think either is going very well at the moment."

Finally, the phone rang, and the chief quickly answered it. Soon, the La Crosse contingent—including Charlie, Rick and Pat—was deep in discussion with officials in D.C. and London.

The three U.K. participants were Lord Bates, Parliamentary Undersecretary of State for Criminal Information; Lynn Featherstone, Minister of State for Crime Prevention, and Mike Penning, Minister of State for Policing, Criminal Justice, and Victims. The officials understood the situation immediately.

"We've had situations like this come up before, unfortunately," replied Lord Bates. "Records in the African countries are scattered and poorly kept. Lynn and Mike have had some luck on occasion using their backdoor channels. Of course, we do best when we have some history of involvement."

"What I can assure you of is this: If the Mercy Mission delegation spent time in or had contact with Sierra Leone, I am confident that we can provide additional information," said Bates.

He continued. "I am also wondering if your early connections to Liberia might serve you well with officials there."

They conversed for another 10 minutes. When the call ended, the group decided that Featherstone and Penning would check Sierra Leone for information on health care exchanges involving anyone with La Crosse connections. In addition, the FBI's Acting Information and Technology Branch Executive Assistant Director, Dean E. Hall, would work with members of his unit to see what they could find in Liberia.

The La Crosse contingent all agreed that it had been a good call. If there was any information to find in the two countries, it would likely be found by this team.

Al and Charlie returned to their desks, back to the agony of waiting. The workday's hours marched along. When the work day ended, they met for a beer at the Logan Tavern on Caledonia Street, near the river in downtown La Crosse. Tired and out of patience, it was a mostly silent meeting. Al finally broke the silence.

"Charlie, I'm on pins and needles. One minute, I think we are close to solving this sucker, and the next minute I'm pretty sure this killer or killers will go free. If that ends up happening, I'm not sure if I can stay with law enforcement. This one has really gotten to me."

"So, just what the hell are you going to do?" asked Charlie, glumly. "If anyone's leavin', it'll be me. I've just about had it, Al. Things at home are terrible. This case is tearing me up. I'd be better off workin' at Fleet Farm, tending bar, or maybe there will be somethin' for me in private security services."

"C'mon, Charlie," responded Al, "even if you could be a good clerk or bartender, you'd hate both of them—not enough action. Like me, you were born to be a cop. My guess is, that you'll be a cop you will be until the day you die, hopefully many, many happy years from now."

"S'pose you're right," agreed Charlie. "But cases like this just drive me nuts. I walked out on Charlene yesterday. I spent the night in Westby. I went home this morning to shower, shave, and get into uniform. It was like a cave in Alaska, dark and icy. I just can't take it anymore."

"I know what you mean about the case, but this is the first one of these we've had, thank God," reminded Al. "As for your home life, I can't say much. What are you going to do?"

Charlie stared into his beer so long, Al thought he was crying. Finally, Charlie spoke, still staring at the glass. "I'm not goin' home, Al. It's just too fuckin' terrible. I guess I'll go back to Westby. The gal that runs the B&B is one goddamn amazing cook. We get along good. Maybe I'll marry her and get fat and lazy doing chores around the house while she cooks for me and the guests."

"You cut me up. When it involves your stomach, you're a happy guy. If Westby makes you happy, stay there for a few days. Maybe the cooling off period will do you and Charlene good. But it's Thanksgiving in a couple of days."

"Shit, Al, she doesn't need to cool off. It's like she makes ice cubes in her panties. We're just an ice machine and a garbage can passin' in the night. It ain't fun. Well, I ain't gonna solve anything here, and my stomach's growlin'. Mary told me she's making pot roast for dinner. Now there's a winner! How're things with you and JoAnne?"

"She's pretty happy with me, to be honest. I promised her a little sugar yesterday after I sneaked into the office to check the queries. I gave it to her good. She was glowing. We had a great dinner last night and then did it all over again."

"You know, you have the best goddamn wife of all time," said Charlie. "If JoAnne was mine, I'd never have a job. We'd just stay home all day and screw our goddamn brains out."

"Hey, easy now. Sex is a good thing, but not if it's a constant thing," replied Al, smiling.

As Al opened the door. Charlie finished his beer, picked up his coat, and followed his friend into the late November rain. "God," he said, "couldn't you give us a little sunshine? It's hard to be upbeat when the weather is lousy. Look it, Al; even God is mad at me. Sex might be a good thing but not when it's nonexistent. Maybe I'll just look at Mary's ass and dream. She's got a great caboose."

"Just be careful, buddy. I'd suggest not screwin' around too openly until you have this home thing sorted out."

"Yea, you're right. Not to worry. All I got is dreams. Hell, I'm not even sure I can get it up!"

"Well don't try to answer that question tonight, okay? See you tomorrow."

"Sure, I'm sure I'll be the same bundle of joy I was today!"

The two got into their cars. Both were laughing. Charlie drove toward Highway 14 dreaming of pot roast. Al was dreaming of something just a little hotter.

CHAPTER 36

Later that evening, Julie and Peggy were concluding another busy day. They met with Barb Romney and decided at least to view the house. If they didn't like it, fine. If they did, they figured that Barb could do some negotiating on their behalf.

"If we're going to look at the house after work, I need to let Brody know," said Julie.

"Why not text him about what we're up to? He can go over to my house after school if he wants," suggested Peggy.

Julie quickly sent a text to Brody, telling him the plan. She got an immediate response.

Mom, gr8 news. When can I c?

Take you over if a realistic option. Know more when I see you. Love you!. Luv u 2.

Peggy was in Julie's office promptly at 5 p.m. Both women were excited as they walked together to the parking lot. Perhaps it was the promise of the future, but the large, three-story brick home looked even better today. As they drove up the drive, the two friends talked animatedly.

"Could it really be this great on the inside?" Peggy wondered out loud.

"I am kind of hoping it isn't," replied Julie. "Peggy, I just can't afford something like this."

"Why don't we take a look and see what it's like?" "If we really like it, we can see what the owner has in mind. If it's too expensive and beyond our reach, we'll shed a few tears and move on. Okay?"

"I guess so," said Julie.

Stopping behind the house and in front of a large, four-car garage, they saw the living quarters above the garage. They were, clearly, very spacious, and the lawn was even more expansive than what they'd seen the day before.

"Can you imagine getting the boys to cut the grass?" asked Julie, laughing nervously.

"Not really," admitted Peggy, "but isn't it beautiful? I can't imagine anything more terrific. I'm saying a little prayer that the inside is just as great and that we can afford it. I hate to admit it, but I think I have kind of already bought it. And I haven't even seen the inside yet. You're right that neither of us can afford $750,000."

Just then, Barb drove up. She led them to the back porch. "This is a great house and a *great* deal!" preached Barb. "At $750,000, it's a steal, particularly since there is a beautiful apartment atop the garage."

Yes, it *was* typical real estate agent hype, but after the tour ended, Julie and Peggy had to agree with Barb's assessment. It was gorgeous—six bedrooms, five baths, a beautiful, modern kitchen, and spacious living spaces throughout the house. After looking at the apartment above the garage, which was bigger than either of the properties in which they currently lived, they were sold. Everything was perfect—except for the price.

"How much," began Julie, haltingly, "might…the owner…be willing to negotiate?"

"Gosh, I'm not sure," said Barb. "It's been on the market a while and houses aren't moving very well, as I told you. The clientele for a house like this is limited. Even so, this house has already been discounted to the point that I think it *has to* sell. The owner is a very nice lady, and she seems determined to sell this house to the right people."

"We'll talk about it," said Peggy, "but I'm afraid it's gonna be too much of a stretch for me."

"And it's way, way beyond me," admitted Julie, a little relieved that Peggy admitted her financial status first.

"Tell you what," said Barb. "Why don't I visit with the owner? I'll tell her about you. If she asks, any idea what you can afford? Have you talked to your bankers?" After Peggy and Julie shook their heads, Barb continued. "I'll find out what the owner might consider. How about you talk to your banks? See what might work for you. Until you do that, we're flying blind. Meanwhile, I will let you know if any other buyers come along. After you know your bottom line, we can talk with the owner."

The three said their goodbyes. Julie and Peggy got into their car and prepared to depart. Peggy spoke before starting the car. "It is just perfect, isn't it? I am going to be heartbroken if we can't work something out."

"It is perfect," responded Julie, wistfully looking out the window. "I love it, too; I want it!"

They stopped at Subway for sandwiches, and then drove to Peggy's house. They ate with the kids, tidied up the kitchen, and then Julie and Brody got ready to leave. Just as Julie put on her coat, the phone rang.

Peggy answered, put her hand over the phone, and spoke. "It's Barb. She's talked to Genevieve, the owner."

Julie took off her coat, sat down, and tried to follow the conversation from her side. It was pretty hard to piece together only bits and pieces. All she heard were "good," "great," "wonderful," "oh?", "really," and, finally, "exciting!"

Peggy hung up, seeing Julie's expectant face.

"Barb told the owner what she knew about us and our families. She also told her that we likely couldn't afford $750,000. This is where it gets really exciting. Luckily, Barb told her that she thought we were that kind of people. Genevieve—her last name is Wangen—wants children in that house again, which is fantastic. She wants to meet us ASAP! Can we meet her tomorrow after work?"

"Gosh, I don't see why not," replied Julie. "Either she likes us well enough to make us one damn good deal or we move on. Better we know sooner than later, right?"

"It is," agreed Peggy. "I'll call Barb back and tell her we can make it tomorrow night."

"Brody and I are going home to bed replied Julie in a tired voice. "See you tomorrow!"

***

As Julie and Brody drove home, she told him about the house, making sure to stress the likelihood they could never own it. She told him that as much as it would be wonderful and at a great price, it was just not affordable.

"It's hard to know that the house would be perfect for all of us," said Julie. "I try hard to make life good for you, Brody, but the truth is that I know you don't have all the things you want. This is probably going to be another one. I'm sorry."

"Mom, please don't feel bad. We do great. If I was old enough, I would help more," replied Brody. He really was wise beyond his years. "Someday mom, I'll buy you a mansion with servants, even. You work too hard."

"Honey, I love you and I love my job. I just feel bad when I can't do everything for you that I'd like to."

"Mom, you give me everything I need," replied Brody, patting her on the shoulder. "Please, don't be sad. I like our apartment. If we can get a house with Jake and his mom—even his snotty sister—that would be great. If it doesn't work out, no big deal."

"You are wonderful," said Julie, reaching over, pinching his knee, and thinking how much he was like his father, a wonderful young man.

***

Julie and Peggy were at work early. A nervous excitement permeated their day but didn't make the clock move any faster. The hours dragged past. They spent lunch discussing the house, what-if's, maybes, and maybe nots. When, at last, 5 p.m. rolled around, the women were in their coats and out the door in a flash. Peggy drove them along the now familiar route to North Kennicott.

They pulled into the driveway at 6807 North Kennicott, excited but apprehensive.

Barb's car was in front of the garage. They saw her standing outside with an elderly woman who had a wide smile. The woman greeted them from the back porch.

Genevieve Wangen was a bright, spritely, 79-year-old woman. She was in remarkable condition. Muscles bulged under the sleeves of her dress, and her legs were also strong and muscular. She was a delight. As bubbly as Barb and just as entertaining, she put Julie and Peggy instantly at ease. She told them about the house and how she came to occupy it.

"I didn't raise six children here," admitted Genevieve. "But, six children were raised here. My Henry was married before I met him. He and his late wife, Charlabelle, raised their family here. Harry was an engineer—a damn good one, too. He could design and make anything. You should see some of the things he made for me."

"We met three years after Charlabelle died. Their children were already grown and gone. I came to love them as my own, and, thankfully, they think of me in the same way. It could have been ugly. After all, this was their mom's house that I was squatting in. I'd have been upset if I was them, but they were wonderful. They came back often after Henry and I married, but I don't see them as much since Henry passed. To be honest, my Henry and I rattled around in this big, old house for 12 lovely years.

Henry died of pancreatic cancer. It took him fast. He was diagnosed one day and dead only three weeks later. I was devastated. I turned to other things. I tried to get in better touch with my past; I had a tough childhood that I tried to forget. Alone for the first time in a long time, I decided it was important to explore my past."

"I reconnected with family I had not seen in years. I researched my roots and found out some fascinating things about where my family came from and what they did. I decided after life became better, that I needed to be healthier. "These," she said, flexing her arms, "are the result of strenuous workouts, four days a week. I also got back into my old hobby—creating drugs. You should see the lab my Henry built me. Well, listen to me; of course, you will see it."

She told them that her experience with compounding, a lost art, had created a new occupation. She thought of it as a hobby. She created anesthetics for several veterinarians, and that led to more work with, even, a few docs that the vets knew. Julie told her that she, too, had a background in compounding. Genevieve was interested and soon they were visiting like long lost relatives.

Julie and Peggy immediately bonded with the older woman. They discovered they had much in common. Genevieve had a nursing background, kept up with developments in the health care field, and loved children. In fact, she demanded, nicely, of course, when Peggy and Julie had finished another walk-through and visited with her for a few minutes more that they bring Lauren, Jake, and Brody to view the house.

"My dears, there's no sense talking about what might be until your children have had a chance to see the house. They need to decide if they would like to live here. I have just met you, but I would love for you to have this house. Julie, I know you are concerned about the cost, thank you for sharing that information. Don't worry; we will try to work out some sort of agreement."

Genevieve's upbeat mood was infectious. Peggy ran home to collect the kids. Julie and Genevieve continued to visit. Barb smiled as she listened. It was obvious that the two women had much in common.

"Tell me about you, dear," said Genevieve. "I am very interested in who you are and what you do."

For the next half hour, Julie and Genevieve talked as if they had known each other for years. Julie told her about growing up in Alma, Wisconsin, and was fascinated to hear from Genevieve that she had friends there.

"They are long retired now," said Genevieve. "Mabel and Ray Hanck. Mabel cooked at the school. Ray drove a school bus and did odd jobs."

"Oh, yes, I know them well. Ray did odd jobs for my father at the drugstore. Mabel baked the best bread. They lived almost next door, just a vacant lot between our houses. I'd get off the school bus, smell the odor of baking bread, and wander to their door to see how Mabel was. She knew the game because she always had a slice of bread ready for me, smeared with fresh jam. Raspberry was my favorite. How do you know them?"

"Mabel, Ray, and I grew up together in Westby. Mabel and I were best friends all through school. Then I went to college and married my first love. We had just celebrated our 22nd anniversary when he died of a heart attack. I met Henry at a dance in La Crosse. We saw each other a few times here and there. After attending our second dance together in Richland Center, as I remember, we began talking on the phone every day. Two years later, we married and I moved here. He had a job at the Chrysler plant up the road. Mabel and Ray dated all through high school. They couldn't wait to get married. One month after graduation they tied the knot."

Genevieve chuckled while remembering her past. "Oh, my, it's so good to share memories. I miss my Henry, but I know he'll be waiting for me one of these days. Then we'll be together again."

"Are you lonely?" asked Julie. "You know, regardless of whether this works out here, I hope you and I will visit often."

"I'd love that. I'm still able to get around well; I even have my own car," said Genevieve, smiling. "It's a 1987 Chevy and it only has 8,500 miles on it. Runs like a dream. I suppose the day will come when I have to give it up, but, for right now, it's nice to have the freedom to come and go as I like."

The conversation turned to Julie's job. "Did you say you worked for an ENT specialist?" asked Genevieve.

"Yes, I do. Dr. Jerome Esch is a really nice person, a skilled specialist. I think he keeps the ENT practice alive at Kahn. But, that's just my opinion."

"I worked for a dermatologist. I did it all," admitted Genevieve. "I even administered the anesthetic for same-day surgeries in the office. We did a lot of those…tons."

"Interesting," said Julie. "My dad was a pharmacist. I spent a lot of time looking over his shoulder. I got pretty good at compounding. Dad did a lot of his own mixing. What kind of drugs did you use?"

"Propofol was my drug of choice," responded Genevieve. "It was really an art to do it right because it hurt so much during injection. I finally began to use a bit of lidocaine as a prep, and then actually mixed a little of the lidocaine with the Propofol during the injection to reduce the pain. I got so good at it, the patients hardly even noticed."

"Was that injected into the arm or did you run it through an IV drip into a vein?"

"I used the IV drip most," replied Genevieve. "But, you know what I found out? I found out that for minor work around the face and head, an injection into the ear canal was really effective. The area wasn't very sensitive, so the prep for eliminating pain was vastly reduced."

"I administer anesthetics for Dr. Esch, too, but I only use the arm."

"Give the ear canal a try. I think you'll find it works great and fast. You'll have to experiment with the dosage, though, because while it works really fast, patients come around quickly, too," advised Genevieve.

"I don't use Propofol," replied Julie. "I don't even think you can buy it anymore. I use a combination of Etomidate and Midazolam, but those drugs seem to have the same qualities as the drug you use. They act fast when going under and coming out."

"No Propofol, huh?" Genevieve asked in a way that indicated she couldn't believe it. "It's a darn good thing I stocked up before I retired. I use it whenever I have major problems sleeping. That doesn't happen often; maybe a couple of times a year, so I have enough that I'll never run out. When I inject it, I stick the needle, one of those new ultrafine needles, into my ear and off I go into dreamland."

As Julie opened her mouth to respond, the door opened. Brody, Jake, and Lauren almost ran into the room. They were obviously excited with everyone talking at once. They loved the outside of the house, and they couldn't wait to see the inside. All three kids wanted a dog.

"We've all wanted a dog for a long time," Lauren told her mother and Julie. "We'll share it and we'll also care for it, too. A dog would be a great idea. Mom, please?"

"One thing at a time," replied Peggy. "The first thing you need to do is introduce yourselves to Mrs. Wangen. She owns the house that we might want to buy."

The three children, now on their best behavior, introduced themselves to Mrs. Wangen. They spent time answering her questions about where they went to school, their likes and dislikes, their favorite pastimes, and what kind of students they were. Brody and Genevieve hit it off especially well. They seemed as if they had been friends for years.

"It's really important in today's world," advised Genevieve, "to do well in school. When I was your age, jobs were plentiful. You didn't need to have a good education, necessarily. It's not like that now. Now, employers want people who excel in the classroom and with other interests. Sounds like you folks are preparing well. Stick to it; it's important."

With that, Barb tapped her watch, causing Genevieve, Julie, and Peggy to glance at their watches.

"My goodness," exclaimed Peggy, "where has the time gone? It's almost 8:30 and you haven't seen the house yet."

The three kids looked glum, but they brightened considerably after Barb spoke. "How about I show you around while your moms visit with Mrs. Wangen?"

"Sounds great," chorused all three children. They followed Barb from the kitchen into the dining room and then on into the living room.

"They're going to love it," predicted Peggy, an opinion that Julie shared.

"I know they will. Now, we have to figure out whether we can swing it," reminded Julie.

"Now, now," said Genevieve, gently. "If the kids like this house, we will make it work for you. My Henry had a really good job. I have more money than I will ever spend. Having someone I like in the house is important to me. The only thing I have to worry about is not appearing to sell the house too low. If I did that, it would not be fair to my neighbors, since their property values would go down. They're good people. You'll love them, so we just have to be creative to make things work for everyone."

Twenty minutes later, the quartet led by Barb was back. Brody, Jake, and Lauren were even more excited.

"We agree. It's perfect," reported Lauren. "We even found our rooms and we all liked a different one! So there won't be fights. We need to buy this house! We must, mom! We must!"

"I agree!" exclaimed Brody. "This is fantastic, mom! We have to work it out. Mom, maybe I can get a job. I can help out that way." He looked at Genevieve. "Mrs. Wangen, you'll have to visit. None of us has a grandma. We've decided that we'd like to adopt you."

The smile that spread over the homeowner's face told the whole story. Brody's comment had sealed the deal.

"Okay," said Genevieve, "that's a deal. I'll be a surrogate grandma. I have lots of experience. I have 24 grandkids that I call my own. You must promise to visit me at Highland Estates as well."

The beaming smiles on the three young faces told her the answer.

"And now," began Genevieve, broaching the subject at hand, "it's time for you folks to get on your way. Barb and I will talk this evening. She will have information for you in the morning."

On the ride home, Brody chattered like a parrot. He told his mother how much he wanted the house, how much he didn't want her to worry about another thing, and how he'd get a job—two if necessary—to help out. The conversation was the same in Peggy's car. The two friends talked later, agreeing that they would try their best to work out a deal. Both of them went to bed, afraid to dream of owning the home. Still, they were happy that it could even be an option.

CHAPTER 37

November 22nd dawned as an ugly day in La Crosse. The wind had blown ferociously all night from the north, and as light fought its way through the heavy clouds, the clock reached for 7. Raindrops mixed with snowflakes. The forecast called for rapidly dropping temperatures throughout the day. A major snowstorm was expected to push its way into the region as the day progressed.

At Ma's by 6:30, Al and Charlie talked as they ate. Charlie, for once, had a more normal breakfast, although most people, still, would have called it gigantic.

"The chief called the house at 5," said Al. "He suggested that we join him and the sheriff in the chief's conference room after breakfast. He thinks using the day to consider all of the angles we have to investigate is a good idea."

"I actually think that's a pretty solid idea," said Charlie, thinking about all the things that they didn't know. "Tomorrow is the day before Thanksgiving, the whole country is on the move, and it would be nice to go into the holiday with some goddamn idea of where we're headed."

"Okay," agreed Al. "I have to admit that sounds like a better idea than what I had planned. We've got the whole damn family coming over for Thanksgiving. Planning today will help get me out of the chores that JoAnne will want me to do."

"So, let's drive down to your headquarters like the good little cops we are, make nice with the bosses, and help put together a comprehensive plan for after the holiday," suggested Charlie.

Getting up to leave, Al threw a balled-up napkin at Charlie. It bounced off Charlie's forehead, settling into the nearly full coffee cup just as he raised it to his mouth.

"That's a three!" shouted Al. Charlie, looking at the coffee stain growing on his white shirt, wasn't quite so ecstatic.

"Nice shot, asshole!" barked Charlie. "Look at what you've done to my shirt, and this is the first time I've worn it! Remember, I'm a man without a home. Shit, I was counting on getting a few days out of this shirt."

"In case you haven't figured it out," said Al, adopting a studious pose, "there is something called dry cleaning that will make the shirt look good as new. There are several shops around La Crosse."

"Listen, smartass," rebuked Charlie. "I know all about dry cleaning and things like that. But it sure as hell would've been nice to get two or three wears out of the shirt."

"Charlie," said Al. "You've never owned a shirt that didn't go at least five wears between cleanings. Most of them serve as a catalog of the things you've had to eat for the past month."

As Charlie, fuming now, reached for his coat, Al wisely beat him out the door. "See you at the station," said Al as he hurried to his car.

When Al walked into the conference room, he was astounded to see the mountain of material on the table. The chief looked at him and smiled. "This is all we have. I propose that we get started."

Charlie walked in. "Ah, I see you wore your best, clean shirt today," said Hooper, chiding his deputy.

"Don't start, just don't start!" fumed Charlie. He looked at Al. "Keep your goddamn mouth shut!"

***

Six and a half hours later, Al raised his head from the table and looked around him, amazed to see a transformed room. It had morphed from a collection of loosely stacked files to a collection of orderly, organized files and notes. The whiteboard was covered with slips of paper and post-its. The biggest change was a 10-step plan on the whiteboard.

"Tell you what," said Whigg, "why don't we take a stretch? We've been at this pretty hard. I've ordered some lunch. It should be here soon. We can eat, relax a bit, and then wrap things up. Sound good?"

"Sounds like a plan," said Hooper, smiling. "My neck feels like someone crunched it together. I'd welcome a break."

"I'm just gonna organize this last stack," offered Charlie. "A whiz and a sandwich will be good."

By the time Al and Charlie returned from the restroom, lunch had been delivered. The chief and sheriff were already digging in.

A half hour later, what once had looked like a beautiful feast of barbecued ribs resembled the whitening bones of a long-dead cow in Nevada. There was little food left. The four people around the table appeared satisfied, stroking their stomachs.

"I suggest a 15-minute break," said Al. Everyone agreed that another break would be good.

Fifteen minutes later, the group was back together. The plan was in its final form.

Everyone agreed to take the holiday. This break gave them the chance to see what the folks in the U.K. and at the FBI might find. If they found something, Charlie and Al could work on it. This meant their schedules had to be cleared. Both the chief and sheriff named the people who would take over their caseloads. It was hoped that if the new database inspections unearthed anything, appointments could be set for next week.

With their plans set, the four lawmen left work, again in the darkness, wishing they had a break in the case. They felt the satisfaction of a hard day's work.

CHAPTER 38

Julie and Peggy had their customary cup of coffee before work on Tuesday. No one else was in the Kahn breakroom, so they had a chance to talk. They agreed that each one would check with her bank to put together a financial plan. They wanted to see if there was any way they could afford the house on North Kennicott. They had begun to think of this house as their own.

Each one made the initial calls during the mid-morning break. Peggy was pleasantly surprised after talking to her banker, George Sanford.

George told Peggy that her borrowing capacity was $680,000, a figure far beyond what she expected. Julie, meanwhile, discovered that the maximum amount the bank was willing to lend to her was $230,000. She would have to secure part of that loan with the money she put away for Brody's college education.

"If you're thinking about spending in the neighborhood of $250,000 for a house, Julie, I think we can make it happen," said her banker. "But, in order to come up with the down payment on that kind of purchase, you will need to dip pretty deeply into your savings, including your 401K and Brody's college fund. Even with the down payment in place, the monthly payments are going to be killer."

"So, you're thinking I'm foolish to consider it?"

"No, not foolish, but you will be making a major commitment to a house, which means you will have to give up other things. I can't make the choice for you, but I can make sure you understand all of the details. The rest is up to you."

The hour and a half until lunch dragged for both women, each anxious to share what they learned. Even though Peggy had the happiest message, Julie was thinking that they just might be able to swing the deal. After the two women relayed their bankers' information, Peggy sat thoughtfully for a moment before speaking. "Julie, I knew our circumstances were different, but this is the best idea I think we have had. I don't want you to think that you have to give up on the plan because you are concerned about Brody's college fund. Tell you what, let's call Barb and tell her that we'd like to meet with her and Genevieve. Maybe we'll be pleasantly surprised at what they've worked out."

"Okay," said Julie. "I want to pay my share and Brody is dead set on us buying the house. To make that happen, I'm gonna have to rely on you more than I want to."

After putting lunch bags away and tidying up the break room, Peggy offered to call Barb to set up a second visit. Not even a half hour later, she hurried into Julie's work area, excited to tell her the good news. "Even before I told Barb that we wanted to meet with Genevieve, she said the woman wants to meet with us. Barb said again that it's very important to her that people she likes get the house. It sounded like she might be thinking of something that would be good news, although I'm really afraid to say that."

Julie thought for a moment and looked at her friend. "You know, the kids have already fallen in love with it. How about we take them with us? That way, if it doesn't work out, they will understand why and how hard we tried."

CHAPTER 39

"Hey, honey," greeted Al as he walked in the backdoor of his house. "How about we have dinner out tonight, maybe see a movie? You're gonna be really busy tomorrow, getting ready for Thanksgiving and the descending crew of ravenous folks. Besides, I want to ask you a couple of things, and there's also the raincheck."

"Al, you are one broken promise after another, you know that?" His wife of 28 years chided him in a teasing tone.

"Since I have nothing planned for dinner and you're home early, let's go out to eat and see *Unbroken*. Now, why don't you sit and watch TV while I go upstairs, freshen up, and slip into something I can wear out to dinner."

"I'll be right here when you come back," promised Al, settling into the couch and kicking his shoes off so he could lie down.

When JoAnne returned half an hour later, Al was snoring softly, a contented look on his face. She knew how hard he had been working on the drowning cases. She didn't have the heart to wake him. JoAnne went back upstairs, put on comfortable clothes, and went downstairs to make dinner.

Al slept contentedly until around 7 p.m. He woke up to darkness outside and wonderful smells emanating from the kitchen. *Liver and onions? Could it be? JoAnne hated to make liver and onions. But it sure smelled like liver and onions.*

As Al struggled into a sitting position, JoAnne's voice greeted him from the dark. "Welcome back, honey. I just didn't have the heart to wake you. I'd been planning to make you liver and onions one of these nights. I had the stuff for it, so I thought we'd pass on dinner out and a movie in favor of eating in and dessert in bed. Besides, if I'm going to stink up the house with liver, it might as well be before a day when the smells of turkey and dressing will overcome the liver."

"Now that's an offer I can't refuse. Let me get out of the suit and tie and I'll be down for dinner. I'll be good to go later. You can count on it."

"You'd better be!"

While Al was upstairs changing, the phone rang. JoAnne answered it. It was Charlie. "JoAnne, Al is the last person I wanted to disturb, but I knew that if I didn't get to him on this, he'd have a fit."

"You know, Charlie, you're almost as good as an alarm clock. Now what the heck am I going to do with Al's favorite meal of liver and onions? Even the dog won't eat it. Al's upstairs. I'll get him."

Putting down the phone, she shouted up the stairs. "Al, it's Charlie. Sounds important. So important that I suspect the liver and onions will be in the garbage tonight."

"Not on your life," said a breathless Al, thundering down the stairs and grabbing the phone. "What's up, partner?" The two talked for several minutes. "Let me take a few minutes for some dinner and I'll see you downtown. Oh, you're in Westby already? Okay." Raising his voice for JoAnne's benefit, he almost shouted. "But Charlie, I have to be home early. JoAnne has something special in store for me and I promised I'd be around. Good…great. See you in an hour." Al hung up the phone.

"What's Charlie doing in Westby?" asked JoAnne. "Is he on assignment there?"

"Nah, that's what I wanted to ask you about. Charlie and Charlene are having problems.

Charlie stayed in Westby on Sunday night and last night, and he's staying there again. He says things at home are terrible. He figures it's over between him and Charlene. I was hoping, maybe, we could invite him over for Thanksgiving. I'd sure hate to have him spend the holiday alone in a hotel room."

"Well that's not gonna happen," said JoAnne, firmly. "Charlie is welcome here. You know, Char has become an enormous pain. It's like nothing is good enough. She's always complaining. When we played cards at Debbie's last week, she made everyone think Charlie is the biggest jerk in the world. I hated it."

"Charlie says she's been on a tear," replied Al. "I'm just not sure what to do about it."

"Well, I know what to do about it. I'm gonna call Char tonight and try to make her understand how good she's got it. God, the guy is a great guy. At least, I think so. I think she must be going through her change or something. She's just not the same person," said JoAnne, sharply.

"Can that happen when you're only 40?" asked Al. "I don't know much about those things, but you're not there yet, are you? You're 10 years older."

"Al, the things you don't know about women would fill a book. There's no magic age. Yes, I *am* going through it. Guess you haven't noticed how sometimes I sweat like crazy. The next minute, I'm piling on covers."

"Well sure, I did notice. But heck, JoAnne, what's new about that? You've always been cold one minute and hot the next."

"Well, anyways, let's get you fed. As for Charlie, if he's not eating at home Thursday, he'll be here. Now, what did Charlie have to say about the case?"

"The Brits came through," said Al.

"I sure hope they have what you want," said Joanne, her words trailing behind her as she turned into the kitchen and began to get dinner on the table.

Al wolfed down his dinner and then kissed her deeply, promising that it was a small down payment. He'd be back later for the rest. As he grabbed his coat and headed for the door, he grabbed her behind, giving it a substantial pinch before he left the house.

***

Ten minutes later, he was at police headquarters. Charlie's SUV was already in the lot. Al rushed into the building, got to his office, and stopped when he saw Charlie. "What's up? What's goin' on? Whadda we know?" shouted Al.

"Al…Al…Al, stop!" exclaimed Charlie. "Calm down. The sheriff and chief are in the chief's office waiting for us. How about we go there?"

"You're right," said Al. "I am really excited. This time I just have a good feeling."

Al and Charlie covered the distance to the chief's office in record time. When they walked into the outer office, they heard Whigg yell at them to come in. They rushed into his office and stopped breathlessly, mouths gaping open at the sight of the stack of computer printouts on his desk.

"We haven't touched a thing," said Whigg. I picked these up from the printer, brought 'em in here, and put 'em down right where you see them. Right, Dwight?"

"That's the truth, Brent," said Hooper, looking at Charlie and Al. "We thought you'd probably come in here shootin' if we messed with your case."

Shrugging out of their coats and tossing them onto empty chairs, the two men settled into their own chairs. Al picked up the stack of papers, and, seeing that there was a copy for each of them, carefully handed them around.

The room grew quiet as the four began to read. A few grunts and the sound of "I'll be damned" were all that broke the silence as the four devoured the stack.

"Well look here," said Al, studying the cover letter from Lord Bates. "We don't have just one name, we have two, and an outside third, as well, I see now."

They studied the printouts. They showed a match for a Julie Sonoma and a Kelly Hammermeister, both graduates of the University of Wisconsin-La Crosse physician assistant program. They had both joined Doctors Without Borders and traveled to Sierra Leone, Kelly in 2007 and Julie in 2009. In addition, there was a third name, Genevieve Wangen. She had served as a nurse in Africa during the time that the drownings occurred. Genevieve Wangen, nee Smith, grew up in Westby, Wisconsin, only 26 miles from La Crosse. Mrs. Wangen graduated from the University of Wisconsin-Stevens Point.

"The plot thickens," said Al, his hands behind his head. "So, where does the tangled web lead from here?"

"I'd suggest it leads straight to you guys," said Charlie, looking at the sheriff and chief. "Because unless it does, we'll be in deep shit."

"Okay, so we have three women. Each or all of them could be the source of the hairs found on three of the bodies. What're the odds of all three living in Arlington Heights, Illinois? Something like 25 billion to one, right?" asked Hooper.

"It's amazing," said Whigg, winking at Hooper. "We don't even have to waste your talent on the search. It seems like Al can head down to Illinois on Monday to talk to the three women. Sound like a plan, Dwight?"

"Absolutely," said Hooper. "I appreciate your nominating Al, because I'm out of 2014 budget. I can't even afford the gas for the trip."

The two veteran lawmen turned back to the printouts. Al and Charlie looked at each other in amazement.

"Are you kidding?" began Al. "We need all the hands we can muster for this one. Why would you pull Charlie off?"

Charlie, looking like a disciplined basset hound, sat silently with his head in his hands.

"Al," said Hooper, "as much as I'd like to have Charlie go with you, I just can't afford to have him gone. I can't afford the trip, and I can't afford to let the case files pile up on his desk. We're shorthanded. I just can't spare him."

"I've argued with Dwight ever since the reports came in," said Whigg. "I even volunteered to pay Charlie's way, not that we're flush around here either. He's made me understand that the people he has available are just too few to handle the current caseload. Much as I hate to say it, I both understand and agree with him."

The conversation about next steps continued. Al had the assignment to visit Arlington Heights. Charlie said little, growing more and more morose. "So, Charlie," said Hooper, "this should mean that you can put some time in on that rustling case at Bangor and the armed robbery up at O'Dell's General Store in Stevenstown. Sound good?"

"I guess so." Charlie's response was so faint it could barely be heard. The scowl on his face could have broken 10 dozen eggs.

The conversation wrapped up shortly. The chief, sheriff, and Charlie rose to leave. Al was intently gathering up the papers on the desk, his face as red as Rudolph's nose.

Outside Al's office, the sheriff and chief bid each other goodbye, tipped their hat at Charlie, and started for the door. They had taken only three steps when Sheriff Hooper's booming laughter broke the silence. Suddenly, the chief was laughing, too. Al poked his head into the hallway to see what was happening.

"It's been pretty tense around here, Charlie," said the chief. "You seemed a ripe target to break up the tension."

You…son…of…a…" started Charlie, getting to his feet. He stopped, realized what a great pawn he'd been, and began laughing, too. Soon, everyone in the office was laughing. Charlie was making vile threats about the things he would do to get even.

It showed, Al thought, *that even in the most trying of times, a laugh could be had in a good cop shop.*

"Sorry, Charlie, my friend," said the sheriff. "It was just too good to pass up."

"And you fell for it hook, line, and sinker," broke in Whigg. Everyone was laughing again.

***

An hour later when Al and Charlie walked out of the office, they were two happy men, buoyed by fresh leads in what had thus far been a completely mystifying case. *We might be close to solving this one,* pondered Al. Even though there was now a ton more work to do, Al and Charlie approached it at ease. The uptight feelings they had shared were gone. The investigation was moving again.

"Where are you going to stay tonight?" asked Al.

"Westby," replied Charlie. "I sure as hell can't go home."

"Want to stay at our house? We've got plenty of room," offered Al.

"Thanks for the offer, buddy, but I'm goin' to Westby. I have my clothes there, a good bed, and the things I need to get ready for work. And, no offense to JoAnne, but Mary makes the best damn waffles in the world. I'll have some of those in the morning."

"Well, get some rest. Now the fun begins," finished Al as the two friends got into their vehicles, started the engines, and headed away—one to home and one to Westby.

CHAPTER 40

When Julie and Peggy met for lunch on Wednesday, each of them was excited to report on their progress. As they talked animatedly about packing and making arrangements to sell certain items, Peggy's cell phone rang.

Glancing at it, her brow furled. "Barb," said Peggy. "Let's hope nothing has gone wrong."

"Hi, Barb," said Peggy, putting a smile on her face in the hope that it would show in her voice. "Is everything all right?"

Julie watched as Peggy's face told the story: everything was not all right.

"I see. So, what do we do about that? We are so in love with the house, we would hate to give it up now. I think we have even moved in already in our minds."

While Barb talked, Julie was somewhat reassured as Peggy first nodded, then smiled, and finally spoke. "I can't imagine why that won't work. Let me ask Julie what she thinks. We were just having lunch and discussing preparations for the move."

Covering the phone with her left hand, Peggy turned to Julie. "Barb says that they have bumped into a bit of a problem with the sale price." Seeing Julie's disappointed look, Peggy hurried on with her explanation. "No, no, Barb says it can be worked out. Apparently, when she and Genevieve approached Genevieve's banker, they were told that reducing the price so dramatically could, and likely would, cause a big drop in value of the nearby properties. Remember how Genevieve told us that she was worried about that?"

"So what do we do about that? You know that I can afford a bit more, but not a whole lot more."

"Barb wants us to meet her and Genevieve for dinner at The Fireside to discuss a possible solution. She is sure we will like it. Can you be free for dinner?"

"Of course. How could I miss it?"

"We'll be there," said Peggy, ending the conversation. "We'll see you at 5:30."

"How do we work this out?" asked Julie, looking forlorn. "This sounds like it could be a huge problem."

"Let's not panic yet," suggested Peggy. "Let's see what Genevieve and Barb have to say. If the news isn't good, then we can start to worry."

"Good advice," replied Julie. "See you at 5. What about the kids?"

"I made marinara sauce last night," said Peggy. "Lauren can cook the pasta and make a salad. Brody can eat with Lauren and Jake."

"Sounds great," said Julie. "I'll text Brody now."

"Good idea," said Peggy. "See you later."

After a slow afternoon for Julie and a hectic one for Peggy, the two friends met in the parking lot to head over to The Fireside.

They arrived a few minutes later. Genevieve and Barb were waiting at a table in the rear of the dimly lit dining room. The restaurant was decorated in subdued colors, accented by gold woodwork. Light came from expensive-looking chandeliers. Each of the four dining room walls featured a large fireplace. The wood from the fires crackled as the hostess led Julie and Peggy to the table.

After the group exchanged pleasantries, Barb began. "I imagine my call today has you both worried to death. I should have explained, but I wanted Genevieve to have that honor."

"Why don't you do the preliminaries," suggested Genevieve. "I can try to explain what we propose after they know more."

"Okay, then, the preliminaries," began Barb. "When Genevieve went to the bank to explain that she was selling her house and how she was going to do it, the bank manager thought of something we were worried about. By reducing the price too much, all of the houses in the neighborhood would suffer a decline in value. We did some quick thinking. I consulted some of my partners. We came up with something we think you'll both like."

Barb nodded to Genevieve who continued the conversation. "We think that we can take care of the value problem by selling on a contract for deed. You will pay me $250,000 when we close. The difference of $475,000 will be financed in a contract for a deed. Isn't that how it works, Barb?"

"You've got it," said the realtor, nodding at Genevieve to continue.

"What we will do is set the payments at $11,250 a year for 10 years. Assuming I am still alive 10 years from now, there will be a balloon of $362,500. At that time, we'll redo the payments. I have a thought about that, too. When I die, the contract will end. You will own the house free and clear. How does that sound?"

"I hate to talk about Genevieve dying," lamented Julie. "It seems so morbid."

"My dear, I've lived a good life. I think this old body has a number of years left in it," replied Genevieve, smiling. "The plain truth is I want you two to have the house. Julie, I know you're worried about lots of things and I want to help out. Thanks to Barb, we have a plan to get it done."

"It's…fabulous," began Julie, haltingly, "but how does it work after…

"After Genevieve dies?" finished Barb.

"Yes," replied Julie. "After Genevieve dies."

"Pretty simple," explained Barb. "When Genevieve dies, the contract is paid. No more payments are required. The house will belong to the two of you, free and clear."

"Wow!" exclaimed Julie. "That's unbelievable. How can we thank you?"

"You already have, dear," said Genevieve. "It was considerate of you two to let me meet your children. They are so nice. And polite, too. I have 24 step-grandchildren, and none of them treat me as nice as your children. Each of my step-children is more than comfortably well off. None of them need any money. That means I can do anything I want to do."

Noticing frowns on Julie and Peggy's faces, the older woman reassured them. "Now, don't worry. The children have been told. Not one of them had a problem. All six were delighted."

"I don't know what to say," said Julie. "How can we ever repay you?"

"Just stay in touch. Invite me by once in a while," said Genevieve.

"Count on it," said Peggy. "The kids love you, too."

"Well, if that seems okay, just one more detail and we can order." Barb held her wine glass up and proposed a toast. "To lasting friendships and a happy, healthy and rewarding future for all," toasted Barb.

"Hear, hear!" chorused the three friends.

After dinner was eaten, the four friends stood to say goodbye. Barb promised to be in touch the day after Thanksgiving to schedule the closing.

"This feels like a dream," said Julie, turning toward Peggy. "Maybe we can be moved in time to celebrate Christmas there."

"Oh my gosh!" exclaimed Peggy. "Tomorrow is Thanksgiving. I haven't given one thought to it."

She looked at Julie. "What are we going to do?" Peggy turned to Barb and Genevieve. "What are you doing?"

"Well, they say they are having a great Thanksgiving dinner at Westminster, the assisted living facility," said Genevieve, sadly. "But it just isn't going to be the same. I've met some friends there, but Thanksgiving is for family, and my family is far away."

"I'm in the same boat," admitted Barb. "Gen, how about you and I go somewhere for dinner?"

Genevieve thought for a moment and smiled. "I'd like that. That would be nice."

Listening to all of this, Julie had to make a better suggestion. "Absolutely not! You are not going out to eat. Peggy and I haven't made any plans yet, so how about all of you and the kids come over to my place."

Peggy started laughing. "Great idea," said Peggy. "And just what are you going to serve? And what are you going to cook it in? We packed all the cooking utensils and most of the dishes."

Genevieve spoke up. "I have a better idea, I think. What would you say to Thanksgiving at the house? It's just the way it was when I lived there. There are pots, pans, dishes and silverware. All we'd have to do is pull a few sheets off the furniture, I think it would be great fun!"

"Thanksgiving at the house. What a nice ring to it. I think it'd be great!" said Julie. Peggy agreed, and the four women set off to plan for the following day.

***

On the way home, Peggy brought up a different subject. "You know Julie; it would sure be nice if you stayed over tonight. I must admit, it seems a very long time to me since we…"

"I'd like that. Popcorn, pop, a movie, and a late-night snuggle. I'm up for that," said Julie.

It was a great evening. The children were delighted at the notion of spending Thanksgiving in their new house. Lauren, unusually helpful, said she would get up early with her mom and Julie to start cleaning the house while the rest of them cooked.

Jake and Brody got into the spirit of things too, saying that they would run errands for their moms and Lauren.

Peggy and Julie looked at each other and smiled. *Was it possible*, each wondered, *that the house would bring the children even closer together?*

CHAPTER 41

Al and Charlie worked together all day on Wednesday. They met for breakfast at Ma's, as usual, and arrived at Al's office before 8 a.m. to prepare for their visit with the women of Arlington Heights the following week. They needed to have everything organized and planned out perfectly so their bosses couldn't say no.

They studied all of the printouts from the database, including the rest of the evidence they'd collected about the women. They located their houses on the Arlington Heights map, and they found out as much about them as they could from internet sources. The Arlington Heights police had been unable to provide anything to them except names and addresses. None of the women had a police record of any kind, not even a single misdemeanor.

With the help of the Illinois police, they were shocked again to discover that two women worked at the very same place, the Kahn Clinic. Even more intriguing was that they both worked in the ear, nose, and throat specialty area.

Al studied one of the printouts. "Two of these women work in an area of medicine where they'd need to know how to give injections, and where they'd be working with and around the ears. Are we dealing with more than one killer here?"

"Maybe," said Charlie. "I'll tell you one thing: I am damn sure that we're comin' home with a confessed killer next week. And yeah, maybe two. One of these two—maybe both—will probably sing like a bird when we tell her what we have."

Studying the information again, Al pointed out that Kelly Hammermeister rented an apartment above a flower shop near the clinic. Julie Sonoma was a couple miles from the clinic in the downstairs apartment of a duplex. Kelly, they found out, had not been with Kahn for very long, having moved there just a couple of weeks earlier. Julie was the mother of a child, Brody, going on 15. There was no record of either woman being or having been married.

"It's certainly a lead," admitted Al. "It looks good, for sure. But we haven't met either one. We don't know if they will have alibis. I'm just not willing to be too hopeful until we've met them."

With noon approaching and the plan, at least, laid out in skeleton form, Charlie put down the papers and announced that he was ravenous.

"You're hungry?" exclaimed Al. "Charlie, you just ate a huge breakfast three hours ago."

"It was more like four hours," said Charlie, woefully. "Stop riding me about it."

"Okay, okay, we'll go out in a minute."

The phone rang outside the room. "Call for Charlie," said the receptionist.

"It's for you," said Al, handing the receiver to Charlie.

There were a series of maybes, followed by a few yeses. "Maybe, I'll let you know later," said Charlie. He hung up the phone, a scowl on his face.

"Trouble?" asked Al.

"Nah, just Charlene. She was just as goddamned bitchy as she always is, but she's *guilty* about me being alone on Thanksgiving. Wants me to come to the house. That's a bunch of bullshit. I'll bet you a million bucks she's getting shit from the kids and tryin' to get her ass outa the fire."

Al studied his friend for a moment before offering again. "Charlie, you shouldn't be alone tomorrow. I think you belong with your family. But if you don't think you can do that, c'mon over to our house."

"I was lookin' forward to Mary's cookin', no offense to JoAnne. Charlene ain't much of a cook. Come to think of it, maybe that's it. I always do the cookin'. I'll bet that woman knows she can't make dinner. She doesn't wanna disappoint anyone. Goddamn it, that'd be just like her."

"Charlie, don't be so judgmental. Maybe, she does want you to cook. So what? Why don't you think about your kids? Don't you want to see them?"

"Well, sure, but they'll probably just grill me about when I'm moving back in. They're probably feelin' sorry for their ma. I get that—she's their ma, but I'm just not up for that."

"Well, you have to make up your mind. I heard you say you'd call back. Remember, you're welcome at our place, too. I'd like to know before the end of the day, though. I might have to run and buy another bird."

"Goddamnit, Al!" yelled Charlie. "All you fuckin' do is bitch at me or tease me about my eatin' habits. I like to eat! So what's it to you? Here's my answer. I won't be at your fuckin' house. So you won't have to buy another bird!"

With that statement, Charlie got up, grabbed his jacket and hat, and stormed out the door. "See you after lunch," said Al. His words trailed behind Charlie.

Wow, thought Al, *he's really in a mood. Not like him at all to walk out of anything in a huff. I wonder if it's just his battle with Charlene or something else. Guess I'll have to wait until after lunch to find out. Is he mad at me? That wouldn't be like him, either.*

Al decided to go out for a while, too, but the receptionist walked in and told him a number of the guys were ordering pizza. She wanted to know if he'd like something. He ordered spaghetti and meatballs, heading back to his office to work.

Al was about halfway through his spaghetti when Charlie walked back in, hung up his jacket, and slumped into his chair. "Sorry, Al. Didn't mean to take my troubles out on you. I'm just really pissed about my home life. All through lunch, I thought about what you said. I decided I'm gonna give it another try. But I'm gonna make sure that Charlene understands that some things are going to have to change," said Charlie.

He crossed his arms across his chest and leaned back, almost waiting for Al to argue with him.

"Get the chip off your shoulder," said Al, laughing. "I knew you were on edge. I took no offense to what you said. This is a stressful time for all of us, but especially for you. I'm pleased you're going to give your home life another shot. It is the right thing to do, Charlie. But I want you to know that I will support you 100 percent in whatever you decide. No questions asked. Fair enough?"

"Thanks, Al. The way I behaved bothered me all through lunch. Believe it or not, it bothered me so much that I didn't eat. I sat on a bench down by the river. Watched the water go by and thought about things. Life's a bitch right now. But I ain't helpin' the situation, either. So when we have a moment, I'm gonna call Charlene and tell her I'll be there."

"Do it now," said Al, gesturing across the hall to the empty and dark conference room. "Just turn on the light and shut the door. Dial nine to get an outside line."

"Whaddaya think I am, a kindergartener?" asked Charlie, smiling. "I've made calls outta that room for 15 years. I know the goddamn drill, Al!"

"Okay, okay, just get it done so we can finish up here. Maybe, we can even have a beer on the way home."

"Now there's an idea! Back in a flash!"

Charlie returned 15 minutes later, crestfallen but determined to see it through. "She was a bitch," reported Charlie. "I'm damn certain the only reason she called is to make sure she has a dinner to serve to her folks, brother, sister, and their kids. Ya, know, Al, I get tired of feedin' Charlene's family. They never even say thank you. And Char'll wanna do it all over again at Christmas. Oh well, like you said, we each have to give a bit, and I don't imagine I am a prince to live with."

"That's better, Charlie. If you can use that frame of mind, you should be able to tell her about the things that irritate you," said Al. "On personal things, I mean."

"She never gave me a chance. When I finally got a goddamn word in, I told her I wanted to stop by tonight to have a heart-to-heart. She told me I wouldn't have time because I would have to go and buy the groceries. Now, don't you think that's one goddamn thing she might be able to do? Shit, she is lazy, obstinate, and cruel."

Al looked his friend in the eyes and thought for a while before giving some advice. "Charlie, you don't sound like you are cutting her much slack. Yes, she could have—should have—bought the groceries. She could be bending over backwards to make you feel welcome. But, you could be doing things better, too, I think. My advice is to stay cool. If you're gonna blow up, count to 10, go outside, or kick the dog, but whatever you do, don't explode to Charlene, or, at the very least, in front of your company. I sure hope this works out. You've been miserable; I know that. I'd like to see you happy-go-lucky again. But like I said, you know that Jo and I will stand behind whatever decision you make."

"Al, you and Jo are great. I'm just lucky to have you two as friends. Life can be fuckin' miserable sometimes, but I always enjoy workin' with you."

"Well, let's crack it. Put the plan together and get out of here in time to have a beer."

"And then I can go and face the music. I'm stayin' in Westby, though. No goddamn way I'm stayin' at the house right now."

They worked on the plan diligently. When they finally looked up, it was 3 p.m. and as dark as if someone had turned off the lights. Dark, scudding clouds bustled across the sky, every now and then dropping a flurry of snowflakes.

"Will you look at that?" commented Al. "Snow for Thanksgiving. Remember when you were a kid, Charlie? We always had snow for Christmas, right?"

"Yup, we'd play outdoors until it was time to come in for dinner. One Thanksgiving, I got my goddamn lip cut when I was hit by a sled. Damn thing swelled up so much I couldn't eat. That was painful."

Al burst out laughing. "I'll bet not eating was the painful part!"

"Goddamnit, I was talking about the pain in my lip, you asshole! Now cut it out. Ease up, it's the holiday season. Be nice. If you know how!" snapped Charlie.

Al stood, stretched, and reached for his jacket. Let's get outta here and get a beer. We got some real work done today, partner."

"Sure as hell did," agreed Charlie. "We can take Saturday off and head for Illinois on Monday."

Holding the door open for Charlie, Al replied as the two walked out. "Should be quite an interesting trip.

It had been a good day, Al thought. *He felt ready for the trip, certain that the surprise visit and their questioning of the women would be sure to shake the truth loose.*

CHAPTER 42

Up early on Thanksgiving morning, Julie and Peggy showered and then loaded the car with the groceries they had bought the night before. They set out for Genevieve's house, anxious to get to work on dinner. There was dressing to make, turkey to stuff and place in the oven, vegetables to prepare, and pies to bake.

Those early tasks finished, Julie left Peggy to the pie. She started uncovering furniture and tidying up the place in anticipation of their guests for the holiday feast. Peggy was pleased when Julie joined her in the kitchen 25 minutes later, helping herself to coffee and sitting down on a nearby stool to watch.

"I thought earlier that maybe you were going to sleep in," said Peggy. "I was so careful to sneak out without waking you."

"If we had any thoughts of sleeping in on Thanksgiving, we must have been dreaming," said Julie.

"Agreed," replied Peggy. "But I definitely slept well after we finally got to bed. I was hoping to snuggle more, but I was asleep before I knew it."

"You were exceptionally quiet," agreed Julie, "but I had kind of a restless night. No reason for it…just kind of a sense of foreboding…a sense of the sky falling in. It might just be my nervous nature, being paranoid about the house deal."

Peggy smiled before replying. "I think the house deal is solid. So put that out of your mind. The financial arrangements are more than fair and allow you to participate without giving up anything. I just don't see how it could be about the house."

"Maybe, it's just that I so badly want Genevieve to feel as if we are doing as much for her as she is doing for us. I worry about that."

"Genevieve promoted the idea of us buying the house," said Peggy. "If we're worried, why not offer her the carriage house free of charge? We can afford to do that. The house arrangements are outstanding and we won't need the money. Maybe, we could even get a lift. It's like a little chair for her to sit on and ride up to the apartment. What do you think?"

"I love it!" exclaimed Julie. "Maybe we can bring it up at dinner. Great idea!"

As fast as the joy overtook her, the black mood settled back in. Peggy noticed it and confronted her, wondering why her friend couldn't keep a smile on her face.

"I know, I know, it's silly," agreed Julie, "but it's just like there is a black cloud hanging over my head."

"I think you are mistaken. I think that cloud is a rainbow and you are simply color blind," replied Peggy, smiling. "Now, how about helping me here so we can enjoy a great Thanksgiving dinner?"

A half hour later, the turkey was in the oven and the other food laid out, the two friends sat at the kitchen table, sipping coffee and talking.

"What would you think of Kelly living here, too?" asked Julie.

"Interesting question, but I don't think it's a topic for today. If things go well, and if Genevieve and Kelly take to each other, we can think about it That's Genevieve's call. If she brings it up, great. If she doesn't, let's let it go until she does."

"You always make things sound so simple," said Julie, hands propping up her head as they talked. "I guess I worry too much."

"You do! How about you stop it, and we'll just let it unfold. Work for you?"

Julie smiled, nodded, and felt the tension release from her shoulders.

Three hours later, hair combed and dressed for dinner, Julie felt like a new woman. She chuckled to herself while dressing, thinking that it was almost as if they had already moved in. She and Peggy had brought clothes and used the bathroom to clean up. As she left the bedroom, the smells coming from the kitchen were overwhelming. Her stomach rumbled in anticipation of the feast ahead.

As she straightened up napkins and silverware on the table, the doorbell rang. "I'll get it!" Julie yelled to Peggy, heading for the door. She greeted the smiling and bundled-up duo of Barb and Genevieve.

"Well, look at you," said Julie, taking flowers from Genevieve and a bottle of wine from Barb. "You've brought gifts! You weren't supposed to."

"It's the least we can do, dear," offered Genevieve, who sniffed the air. "Hmm, something good is cooking."

"Well, if there is, it's due to no skill of mine," said Julie. "Peggy's the cook. She's in charge of whatever it is we're having. Beyond the turkey, I'm lost."

Genevieve's and Barb's coats hung in the closet, Julie escorted them to the sitting room. The doorbell rang again.

"Oh, that must be Kelly Hammermeister, a woman who works with us," explained Julie. "We invited her because she is alone for the holiday, too. Let me get the door. I'll be right back."

Kelly was waiting on the doorstep, looking radiant.

"Hi there," greeted Julie. She groaned in a light-hearted manner. "Oh no, not again. Everyone arrives bearing gifts. You weren't supposed to bring anything, but thank you. It's so nice to have you here. C'mon in; let me get your coat." She took the wine bottle from Kelly and escorted her to the sitting room to meet Genevieve and Barb. As they entered the living room, Kelly glanced around, awestruck.

"Oh, my Lord!" gushed Kelly. "Is this really the house you're buying?" When Julie nodded, Kelly looked around again.

"This isn't a house. It's a mansion! Either you make a lot more money than I do or you and Peggy have sugar daddies I don't know about."

"No sugar daddies," said Peggy, who had joined them. She spoke firmly but with a smile on her face. "There are no men involved, and that's the way we like it."

"Well, come on in and meet Genevieve and Barb. We'll tell you the house story before dinner," said Julie.

Wine was poured, a light Chardonnay from Napa, and, soon, Barb, Kelly, and Genevieve were visiting like old friends. Soon, Peggy returned with the children. They had showered and dressed up. They joined the group in the living room. As they waited for the turkey to finish roasting, Julie and Peggy told the story of Genevieve's beneficence.

Genevieve talked expansively about her days as a med tech. She astounded Kelly by telling her that she had worked, many years before, in the same compounding pharmacy where Julie had worked. Kelly knew it well. She was enthralled when Genevieve talked about her interest in sedative styles and results. Eventually, she got around to talking about her life with Henry and how he had built her a laboratory right here on the estate.

Everyone wanted to see it, but, just then, Peggy announced that dinner was being served. Julie escorted them into the dining room. Genevieve promised a tour after the meal.

Everything was delicious. Peggy was an accomplished cook, and each of the dishes reflected her culinary artistry. Few words were spoken after the dinner prayer, offered by Genevieve, as eight hungry people gorged themselves on turkey, wild rice stuffing, mashed potatoes and gravy, green bean casserole, sweet potatoes, and corn. There was also an assortment of relishes, three kinds of olives, dill and sweet pickles, candied applies, and other items. It was a splendid feast for a splendid home.

All in all, it was the most rewarding Thanksgiving meal Julie had ever eaten. Brody demonstrated how much he loved the cooking by demolishing three helpings of everything while everyone else was eating their firsts. When everyone had eaten their fill, Peggy announced she was serving three kinds of pie: pumpkin for the traditionalists, butterscotch for the adventurous, it was the preferred pie in her house, she said, and lemon meringue, Julie's favorite.

The group decided to take a little break before dessert, and Lauren, Brody, and Jake talked Genevieve into leading a tour of the garage.

After showing them the comfortable but unfurnished two-bedroom upstairs apartment over the garage, she led them downstairs to the work bench. A full array of tools hung on the back panel, each correctly labeled. Genevieve wasn't thinking about the tools.

She bent to study the panel beneath the bench and then turned to Julie. "See right there…that little button? Push it, dear," said Genevieve.

Julie did as told. When she depressed the button, the tool bench slid aside, revealing what appeared to be a fully equipped compounding laboratory.

"Oh my!" exclaimed Julie, trying to take it all in. "May I go in?"

"Of course, dear. By this time next week, it will be yours. You might as well get used to all the little somethings this house has, secrets to be revealed as I like to think."

For the next hour, Julie, Peggy, Kelly, and Genevieve explored and talked, the younger women captivated by the magic the little lab revealed.

"This was my special place," admitted Genevieve, pointing at the compounding area of the work surface. "I concocted a number of great sedatives here. Some were used to put down the occasional rat or mouse that came around. I made some for a large-animal vet, who said they were the best he ever used. I even compounded a few sedatives for Dr. Bjorn

Svendsen over in West Allis, Wisconsin. He apparently was bothered by a couple of bad boys from Beloit. All I know is, he told me the meds had worked like a charm."

Julie and Kelly were especially awed by what they saw. When the group was back in the main house, Julie asked Peggy if she could bring up offering the apartment to Genevieve, if the opportunity came up.

"Sure! Just make sure she knows that we love her and want her to benefit from her great gift to us."

Julie added another idea. "Genevieve and Kelly seem to hit it off. What do you think? Ask her, too?"

"I thought we had this discussion," said Peggy, some irritation growing in her voice. "If there is a right time, it's not now. We don't know her well enough and neither does Genevieve. Get off this kick. Do you have something going with Kelly or what?"

"Of course not!" said Julie, hurt by Peggy's comment. "I just thought it… Just forget it!"

"Let's not fight," replied Peggy. "It has been such a good day. Let's not ruin it. I'm sorry, Julie. I just don't think we're ready yet."

"I guess. But it's still a good idea," insisted Julie. "It's just that we have been so lucky…I'd kinda like…"

Her voice trailed off when Peggy held up her hand before speaking. "The time will come, if it's a good deal, and we can ask then. But right now, we're not the Little Sisters of the Poor, you know. We're still going to have plenty of bills to pay."

Julie put her hands on her hips, "That's why I don't understand not asking Kelly. Wouldn't the rent be helpful?"

"Of course it would, but I don't think we know Kelly well enough to know if it would work out with us, to say nothing of Genevieve."

"I guess. It just seems so ideal," said Julie.

"I just don't think we know enough to call it ideal," insisted Peggy.

"Okay, let's just drop it."

"Good idea," agreed Peggy.

That evening, after everyone had eaten leftovers and several pieces of pie, Peggy found herself alone in the kitchen with Genevieve.

"You know, Genevieve," began Peggy, "Julie and I are extremely grateful for your wonderful gifts to us. We are wondering if you would like to come and live here, in the apartment over the garage?"

"Oh, my goodness," said Genevieve, grasping her heart and slumping onto an available kitchen stool. "That is the kindest thing anyone has ever asked me. Are you sure it wouldn't be too much of a bother? Do you think I can contribute my share? Are you absolutely sure this is something you want to do? Does Julie agree?"

Peggy laughed, and then assured Genevieve that the offer was genuine. She, Julie, and the kids all wanted her there. She surely could contribute and they would love to have her near. The tears began to flow down the cheeks of the older woman. She got up, hugged Peggy, and told her that she would love to be a part of their family, if they would have her. "I just love the kids, you know!"

"And they love you," said Peggy, smiling. "They will be delighted to hear the news."

As evening closed in, another round of leftovers was consumed, with extra emphasis this time on dessert. Most of the pies disappeared.

As the women prepared to leave, Genevieve whispered something in Peggy's ear, and then everyone was hugging as the holiday came to an end.

After the door closed, Peggy and Julie were alone. The kids were upstairs, playing video games or talking on the phone. Julie asked Peggy about Genevieve's message.

"She asked if we had given any thought to having Kelly share the garage apartment with her."

"What did you say?" asked Julie excitedly.

"I told her it might be a good idea, but maybe we should wait until we all know Kelly better," replied Peggy.

"It is a great idea! Don't you think so?"

"I do," said Peggy, "although all of this is happening so fast that it's like a residential tornado."

Julie laughed. The two women chatted as they did a final cleanup in the kitchen and dining room. It had been the best of days.

CHAPTER 43

While the mood 300 miles to the north was also festive, it had been a workday, too, for Al and Charlie. They tried to pull together final details for the trip and rehearsed their lines for the interrogation before the new week began. Once the week began, things would shift into high gear. On Thanksgiving morning, the two lawmen went over final details once more, laying out everything in a timeline that would start on Sunday with simultaneous calls to Kelly Hammermeister and Julie Sonoma.

As the two parted to head home for Thanksgiving celebrations with their families, Charlie said what everyone close to the cases was thinking,

"Do you really believe that we are actually near the end of the mysteries surrounding this goddamn maddening series of deaths? It seems hard to believe that we might actually put things to rest. I just pray that next week produces what we need to close this case once and for all."

Later that evening, appetites sated and that warm afterglow settling in, Al sat with his family in his comfortable, south La Crosse home. He was lost in thought. While the holiday buzz swirled around him, he was going over the plans for Sunday and beyond in his mind.

What would the women be like? Would one stand out as a suspect? Would they know immediately? Would they be able to get into the head of the killer? What could have led to this senseless string of killings that grew each year?

***

The Thanksgiving celebration was not so festive at the Berzinski home. Charlene and Charlie stayed well clear of each other. Charlie grumbled while he cooked, clanging and clattering pots and pans to keep everyone else on edge. When he wasn't grumbling, he, too, was lost in thought about the journey ahead.

Charlie was silent as the group consumed the meal. Although he prepared it without much care and concern, he figured it might have been the best meal he ever cooked, since he managed to make enough food that he could get a second helping, even with all the hungry mouths to feed.

When it was time for the dishes, the members of the merry and talkative group scattered like thistle seeds in the wind. Charlie was left to clean up by himself. Even Charlene didn't come into the kitchen. She spent time with her family, making sure they left with multiple containers, filled to the brim with all of the leftovers.

Good riddance, thought Charlie, as they prepared to leave. He didn't bother to say his goodbyes, preferring dirty dish water to shaking hands with Charlene's miserable relatives.

The dishes finished, he confronted Charlene in the living room. They argued heatedly but without violence. Charlie made it clear that if there were not serious changes, he was leaving. Charlene, with just as much force, said she'd rather have him permanently gone than married to his job.

Charlie told her that he was willing to oblige her. He suggested she file for divorce, assuring her that he would honor every wish she had to make sure he was clear of her permanently.

It was not a pretty conversation. Finally, sick of talking in circles, Charlie grabbed his coat, barked goodbyes to the kids, got into the car and, grumbling to himself, headed for Westby.

"Goddamn bitch," said Charlie to the steering wheel. "She's just like you, thinks she controls everything. Well, I'll show her. I think I've been a fucking good provider and all I have to show for it are a witchy, bitchy harridan and three whiny kids. They'll see just how much they miss me and the things my paycheck bought. I'll show that sleazy bitch," said Charlie to the turn signal. "She's shiftier than you are."

Turning his attention to the radio, he snapped it on and shouted above the noise. "Don't you give me one ounce of bullshit, either." The radio quickly replied, demonstrating its position by spewing forth Patsy Cline's "I'm Sorry."

"The hell you are!" stormed Charlie. "You're just as unrepentant as that bitch in south La Crosse." He rode the rest of the way in silence.

Friday was a holiday. Both Charlie and Al wandered into their respective offices late in the morning. On the off chance that Al was working, Charlie dialed his number at 11:30. Al answered the call and then Charlie spoke.

"Hmm, I see you couldn't stay away, either. Wanna get some lunch?"

"How about comin' over here?" responded Al. "Jo sent so damn many leftovers, I couldn't eat them in a week. I'd be grateful for the help."

"Be right over. It'll be nice to have some turkey. Only got a couple little pieces yesterday."

Uh oh, thought Al, *bad day at Charlie's. Damn*, he thought, *I'd hoped it would work out better. Maybe he and Charlene are better off apart. Better not campaign for any sort of reconciliation strategy.* As he was thinking about what he would say to his friend, Charlie walked in, smiling, removed his jacket, sat down, and demanded the promised food.

"Where the hell's the food?"

"Over there," said Al, pointing to the small table at the rear of his office.

"Let me get some food and then we'll talk," offered Charlie, who seemed to be in a great mood.

"Geez, after your turkey comment, I thought you'd be in a bad mood," replied Al, "but you seem in great spirits."

"Damn right. That bitch is gonna divorce me, and I couldn't be happier. Can't wait."

"Wow, must have been a great Thanksgiving."

"It was so goddamn typical that I couldn't wait to get out of there, Al. But I made damn sure I had the conversation you suggested. Char was ready to fight, but when she heard she could have whatever she wants, she was all for it."

The lawmen talked through lunch. Al decided his gruff buddy had made up his mind and thought it might be best for both of the Berzinskis after all. After lunch, the two men went over their notes thoroughly and discussed strategy again, tweaking earlier plans only slightly. They grabbed a beer at midafternoon and departed, deciding to reconvene at 2 p.m. on Sunday. Al headed home and Charlie took off for Westby, thinking about the short ribs Mary said she would make for dinner.

Saturday flew by at the Rouse house. And Charlie had the best non-work Saturday in a long time. He did a number of honey-do chores for Mary and she treated him like a king: bacon, eggs, waffles, and toast for breakfast. Lunch was a terrific hot roast pork sandwich, and she promised him a ribeye for dinner.

"Mary, you are terrific," said Charlie to her at lunch. "You cook as well as my mother did and you treat me like a king. I just might stay forever."

She studied him for a while and smiled. "You know, Charlie, you're a great guy. If you were just a few years older, I might hit on you myself. Unfortunately, you're young enough to be my son, if I had one."

"Mary, if you hit on me, I doubt I could resist. If I were you, I wouldn't talk like that. It's been so long since I've been in bed with a lady that I just might be compelled to wrestle you into bed!"

"Charlie, you better get back to the garden," said Mary. "You stay any longer and I might be out of my panties and into the tusslin'!"

"I think that'd be fun," said Charlie, laughing. "But I better get the chores done first. Then you'll be really thankful, right?"

"We'll see," said Mary, gently pushing him out the door. "We'll see."

Charlie hit the garden while Mary turned to her kitchen, thinking how much fun a roll in the sack would be with the big, burly lawman.

It didn't happen that night. When Charlie came in, he showered and watched college football.

Mary busied herself in the kitchen and later fed Charlie and her six other guests a feast fit for a king; it was a good night with lots of laughter.

***

Sunday dawned dark and dreary. The sky spit snowflakes as if it was ridding itself of a bad taste, giving warning that the worst was yet to come. Charlie had breakfast, lounged around until noon and then headed for his office.

"Be back early for dinner," teased Mary as he prepared to leave. "Don't work too hard this afternoon. No guests tonight; we'll be alone. Roast duck for dinner. Maybe I'll show you a few old girl's tricks."

Charlie left laughing.

In La Crosse, Al, JoAnne, and the kids went to St. Paul's Lutheran Church for service. As they left the house, the temperature was rising, clouds were moving in, and the forecast for the season's first major snowfall seemed more realistic.

When Al and Charlie met at Al's office at 2 on Sunday afternoon, the snow was falling heavily. The first few minutes were spent debating whether or not these conditions would postpone their trip south.

"Channel 8 said Chicago was the epicenter," reported Al. "They said up to 13 inches. No travel into the city is advised."

"That matches 19," replied Charlie. "I caught the noon news just before leaving. If anything, the Channel 19 report was even worse than the one you heard."

"So, what do we do?" asked Al. "Do we call now, make the appointments, and take a chance, or do we wait a day for things to clear?" Al thought for a minute before answering his own question.

"How about we call the airport? Maybe the folks at the weather office can give us a better read."

"Good idea," said his partner, reaching for the phone and aggressively punching buttons from memory. After a number of nods, several um-hums, a few negative shakes of the head, and an emphatic "whoa," the conversation ended.

"Well?" asked Al.

"It's supposed to end just after midnight," reported Charlie. "Temperatures will continue to rise to near freezing overnight tonight, but the wind will pick up tomorrow and blow out of the northeast at more than 20 miles an hour. The bureau chief said he thinks we will make it to Chicago if we leave by late morning."

"We could set the interviews for early evening," suggested Al.

"I think interviewing them away from their offices would be good," mused Charlie. "If they're not in familiar territory, they're more likely to slip up and say something they didn't want to."

"Good point," said Al. "We know both Sonoma and Hammermeister are with the Kahn Clinic. That should make things easier."

"It should," said Charlie slowly, "but you never know, right?"

"Right…but in some ways it makes things easier, I think."

"Their working together is interesting, makes it seem like there has to be a connection,"" offered Al.

"Sure does," followed Charlie. "Why don't we do what we first talked about and arrive unannounced? That'd solve everything. If we get delayed by weather, no sweat. No time for them to plan, either."

Al stared at Charlie for several seconds. "Yup, surprising them is the best strategy. We can split up and hit them at the same time."

"That'd be best. That wraps up the details, right? Mary has a duck planned for dinner. I wouldn't mind a nap," said Charlie.

"Don't forget, the Packers are playing the Vikings," reminded Al. "How can you think about a nap when those two teams are playing? Have you no respect? The green and gold need all the support we can muster. I'm all in favor of knocking off, but not to take a damn nap. I'd like to watch what promises to be a damn good football game. So alright, let's get the hell out of here."

"How about we meet at Ma's at 8 tomorrow? We'll have a big breakfast, hit the offices to grab our things, and then head for the Windy. We'll get there about midafternoon. Sound good?" asked Charlie.

"Great idea. We'll take your vehicle. The SUV is a lot better than the cramped quarters of that bug of mine," said Al.

"That'll work," agreed Charlie. "We can go over the questions again on the way, but I think we have that part nailed. Hit 'em hard right from the start, shake 'em up, and keep 'em talking."

CHAPTER 44

Peggy and Julie had just fed the boys that Sunday evening. With Lauren at a girlfriend's house and Jake and Brody playing basketball in the drive, the two friends sat together on the sofa in Peggy's living room, discussing the future. With Christmas coming, the two mutually agreed that they should aim to be in their new house before the holiday.

"It would be great to celebrate the holiday there, wouldn't it?" mused Peggy.

"Absolutely!" exclaimed Julie. She turned pensive.

"A penny for your thoughts," said Peggy.

"Oh, nothing really. I was just thinking about Genevieve. She's been so good to us. It seems like we should be doing something nice for her."

"Sounds like you have something in mind," said Peggy. "Have you been thinking about this for a while?"

"Not really," admitted Julie. "But she's been so good to us…and… and…"

"And what? If you have an idea, spit it out."

"I don't have it all planned," began Julie. "But, what if we completely redecorated the garage apartment? We could get that lift you talked about. We could furnish it with things we know that she loves."

Peggy listened intently before speaking. "Redoing the garage is a great idea; so is the lift. It might be a long time before she needs it though. She's one spry lady! Having her near, she'll still have a piece of the house. Don't forget that we'd be repaying her each month for her kindness, since she won't have to pay rent."

"Can you believe the laboratory?" asked Julie. "That's incredible. The fact that it's hiding in the garage is unbelievable!"

The entire property was magnificent, even dressed dully in its pre-winter garb. Nonetheless, the dried oak leaves that now covered the ground offered a brownish gold carpet, crackling underfoot when stepped on. All the nooks and crannies offered surprises, from fully furnished dollhouses to games of all sorts. It was a wonderland.

"Oh, my yes," agreed Peggy.

The two women talked and talked about the treasures they had seen the day before. As they talked, they forgot all about the time. The clock ticked toward midnight. "Wanna stay over? You might as well. I'm sure the boys are in bed by now," said Peggy.

"I have nothing ready for work," protested Julie.

"Let's just swing past your place, and you can pick up what you need for the next couple of days. Tomorrow night, we'll stay at the house, I suppose," replied Peggy.

"Yes, the house," agreed Julie. "Sure, take me home so I can pick up things for Brody and me."

A half hour later, the two women were snuggled in bed together.

"Don't take this the wrong way, Peggy," said Julie, "but beyond a kiss or two, I think I'm ready for sleep."

"Me, too," mumbled Peggy, snuggling her mouth into Julie's neck. "See you tomorrow."

CHAPTER 45

Fortified by one of Ma's famous breakfasts, Charlie and Al headed southeast on I-90 at about 11 a.m. on Monday. The highway still showed evidence of Sunday's storm. Snowpack covered the surface wherever the road was sheltered from the wind. It made driving difficult, and Charlie was especially cautious as they drove toward Chicago and the meetings, they hoped, would shed light on and maybe solve the mystery of these drownings.

"I'm hopin' that by walkin' in at quitting time, we'll catch 'em by surprise. Might result in things that'll be helpful. It would be great if we can collect DNA swabs. That could put this thing to rest," said Al.

"It sure could," agreed Charlie. He thought for a while. "Bet they will be crafty. These are two professional women living in large-town America. I don't think we're gonna benefit from 'country-bumpkin' syndrome. I bet they'll be smarter'n hell, educated, and crafty. Gettin' anything is gonna be difficult," said Charlie.

It was just after 4:30 in the afternoon when Charlie pulled the SUV into the parking lot of the Kahn Clinic, a beautiful building with modern architecture that featured concrete, stone and glass in interesting patterns.

Shoulder to shoulder, they walked through the wide front door. Stopping at the information desk in the spacious and comfortable lobby, the two lawmen pulled out their badges, asking where they might find Julie Sonoma and Kelly Hammermeister.

The attractive blonde receptionist smiled. "They both work in ear, nose and throat." She pointed to their offices. "Take this hallway to the first intersection and turn right. You'll find ENT reception at the next intersection. Paula is the receptionist. She can show you to Julie and Kelly's offices."

Thanking her, the two men headed down the hall. It had been agreed earlier that Al would interview Julie Sonoma. Charlie would talk to Kelly Hammermeister.

Following the directions, two minutes later they were standing in front of a desk where a name plate read *Paula Harris*. Paula was an older woman with snow white hair, a twinkle in her blue eyes, and glasses that made her look like Mrs. Santa Claus.

"Hello, gentlemen, can I help you?" asked Paula, rising.

Al and Charlie introduced themselves, showed Paula their badges, and told her they were investigating a case in La Crosse, Wisconsin that led them to Julie Sonoma and Kelly Hammermeister. They would like to talk to them.

"Oh my goodness," said Paula, a worried look crossing her face. "I do hope they aren't in trouble. Julie is an absolute dear, and Kelly seems cut from the same cloth. Kelly just started a couple of weeks ago, so I've hardly had time to get to know her. Would you like me to call them? I'm sure both are working on end-of-the-day records."

"Please don't bother them," said Al. "Just tell us where their offices are. We'll just walk in and introduce ourselves."

After assuring Paula this was simply routine, the men headed to the offices.

As Al reached the door marked *Julie Sonoma*, it was closed. Charlie continued down the hall.

Knocking gently, Al heard a soft voice speak.

"Come in," said the soft voice.

Opening the door, he was unprepared for the sight. Julie Sonoma was spectacularly beautiful, a brunette with radiant skin that seemed to glow. As she rose from her chair, Al noticed that she was about five foot eight or more with a figure that was just as spectacular as her face. He knew she reminded him of someone, but he couldn't think who.

"Hi, Julie?" said Al. "I'm Allan Rouse, a detective with the La Crosse Police Department."

As they shook hands, Al realized just how soft her hand was, how gentle her touch.

"I'm here," said Al, almost stammering in response to her beauty, "hoping to ask you a few questions about a case I'm working on."

"I can't imagine how I can help you, detective," said Julie, finally letting go of his hand. "But, I'll be happy to try." Her voice seemed calm enough, but Al sensed a pronounced nervousness, too.

"I hate to bother you," began Al as Julie sat back and waved him to a chair. "My partner and I are looking into a series of drownings up in La Crosse. As we put things together, we found out that you were close to the first victim. As we continued to look, we found that your colleague Kelly Hammermeister had been married to another victim. We decided to drive down on the slight chance you might be able to help us."

Silence settled in. Julie looked puzzled. The look suggested she was mystified by his visit. That wouldn't normally be the case if she was involved. Mesmerized by her deep brown eyes, he was content to wait it out.

"Detective Rouse, your visit brings up horrible memories of my boyfriend's death. His death is something that I have been trying desperately to understand for more than 15 years. Every time I reach into the past, I break down. I guess I'm just warning you that tears might flow at any time."

"Don't worry about that," said Al in a soft, gentle voice. "I am sorry to come here, surprise you, and ask you about a painful time. I don't like this, but new developments make us think we might have something."

Tears welled up in her eyes. The first drop of water trickled down her left cheek, making her look vulnerable. In spite of his official role, Al's heart went out to her. He suddenly saw himself as a bad guy. He didn't like it.

They talked for the next half hour. Julie remained tearful but steadfast. Al had a tough time seeing her in the role of perpetrator. She was just too sincere, too straight forward.

"Julie," he said finally, "I hate to ask you this, but would you mind if I collected a DNA swab? It's a painless exercise. I just rub a swab around your mouth."

The look on her face was shattering--so painful, so questioning--that his heart seemed to stop.

"Does that...does that mean," she stammered, "that you think I somehow had something to do with Shawn's death?" The sobs began deep in her chest, and tears began to gush from her eyes.

Al immediately sprang to her side, grabbed his handkerchief, offered it to her, and spoke soothing words, trying to help her regain her composure. He found himself not liking at all the reaction he had caused.

Many minutes later, her sobs subsided, the tears receded to a steady trickle, and she was again able to talk.

"Julie, I don't for a minute think you had anything to do with Shawn's death or any other," began Al, "but we found some questionable materials on several of the victims. We're reaching out in an attempt to try and bring closure to these deaths. The main goal here is to eliminate you from the investigation."

They talked a little more.

"Detective, I have nothing to hide. I wish you hadn't surprised me and didn't call to set up an appointment. The suggestion that I might have been involved is ludicrous, but if the swab is something I have to do to assure you I had no involvement, let's get it over with."

The swab completed, Al apologized, again, and the talk continued. Al and Julie now maintained professional distance, but they also talked about friendly issues, including family, health, job, and life satisfaction.

As the discussion wound down, Al was sorry to see it end. He liked the woman; he liked everything about her. In spite of his happy marriage, it was hard to look at her and not have fantasies.

He rose, apologized once more, thanked her, and told her he had enjoyed meeting her. She seemed sincere when she told him that even though he had opened old wounds, she had enjoyed meeting him. *Did she really mean it?*

Down the hall, Charlie was ending an equally pleasing discussion with Kelly Hammermeister. He, too, had found her credible. He also believed that if she had played a role in any of the drownings, he would be stunned. When he raised the question of the DNA swab, she understood immediately and offered no objections.

"Please, Deputy Berzkinski, go right ahead and do the test," said Kelly. "If there is any suggestion that I somehow have had something to do with the drownings in La Crosse, I want to do anything I can to convince you that I was not involved."

Charlie quickly removed the vial from his pocket and ran the swab of the stopper-like device around her mouth.

"I am genuinely sorry, Kelly. This is just one of those things we have to do. We want to make sure we have taken every step that might provide information."

"Thank you, Deputy Berzinski. That's appreciated. If someone murdered my husband, I want that person caught! I want an end to these tragedies."

The conversation continued for the next 45 minutes. A wide range of topics were covered, and, even though Charlie, much against his feelings, tried every trick he knew to get his interviewee to slip up, she did not. All of her answers were immediate, articulate, and convincing.

As they talked, Charlie became more and more aware of Kelly's beauty. Her blonde hair was nearly platinum. It didn't look to him like it had been colored. Her facial features were severe. *Patrician*, he thought. But, there was a softness in her deep blue eyes that was mesmerizing.

Under any other circumstance, Charlie might have flirted unabashedly. As it was, he struggled to keep his entrancement hidden and maintain his professionalism.

When he had asked his final question, he thanked her for her cooperation and prepared to leave.

"Deputy Berzinski, would it be fair for me to ask you a few questions?" asked Kelly, pleasantly.

"That's not in the script," began Charlie. He then realized how much fun he was having. "Sure, why not?"

"I just have things that make me curious."

"Go ahead. Let's have it."

"Well, what led you to me? Are you talking to everyone who was connected to a victim?"

"No," admitted Charlie. "Let's just say there were things that made us want to talk to you and Julie Sonoma."

"Julie? You're also talking to Julie? Whatever for?"

"Well, crap," said Charlie, realizing he had gone too far but now was stuck, "we found some clues that suggested a person with medical knowledge. As we searched the information, you and Ms. Sonoma caught our attention. The surprise grew when we found you worked at the same place. It seemed…maybe too coincidental. I'm only telling you because you have passed every one of my tests."

"It's shocking that you're talking to Julie. We're becoming good friends. I only just learned her boyfriend drowned. I was amazed."

"Kelly—and please, call me Charlie—Julie's boyfriend was the first drowning, we think. His death started it all. That's why we wanted to talk to her."

"Makes sense, I guess. But the thought that Julie is involved doesn't add up. She's wonderful. Everyone likes her. She's been great to me. I just love her."

Charlie smiled. "I haven't met her. But if you say so, I'm a believer."

"Deputy Berzinski," teased Kelly, "I do believe you're flirting with me."

Charlie, his face reddening, was anxious to move on. "Do you have any other questions for me?"

"Are you flirting with me?" replied a persistent Kelly.

"Shhh…goddamnit…oh, fuck, excuse me!" stammered Charlie. "Oh, goddamn…oh, shit…"

By this time, Kelly was laughing out loud. "Deputy, you're a nice man with kind of a rough mouth, I now believe. If you are flirting with me, I'm okay. It's flattering."

"I let my words get away from me sometimes. Flirting? No, but you're very beautiful, you know!"

"Oh, shush, listen to you. Beautiful? Hardly. Cute, maybe. But I'm nothing special."

"Beg to differ with you. You're beautiful." Charlie's face was reddening again. "You're downright gorgeous!"

"Stop it!" said Kelly, laughing. "You're gonna give me a big head. Best get back to business. What kind of clue led you to me?"

"That one's sensitive. Let me just say we found evidence that provided DNA."

"That sounds ominous," said Kelly, contemplatively. "I suppose you're not going to say what kind of evidence?"

"Nope. Off limits," emphasized Charlie.

"Charlie, it's spooky to be interviewed. You're thinking murder, aren't you?"

"I suppose so," agreed Charlie, nodding. "That's enough. I think we'd better stop. I could talk all day. But then I'd get in trouble."

"I want you to know I enjoyed the last hour. You're a nice man. You're easy to talk to. You made me comfortable and relaxed. I could talk to you for a long time, too. But I'd probably just make you angry!"

"I doubt that!" exclaimed Charlie, smiling. "The last hour was great. You're a great young woman."

"Well, then, having enjoyed the time will be our little secret," replied Kelly, now flirting herself. "I wouldn't mind seeing you again! I hope it happens!"

More than a little awed, Charlie eased from his chair, smiled, and shook Kelly's hand.

"C'mon," Mr. Charlie," she chided. "We know each other better than that." She hugged him firmly.

"We…llll…Kelly…how 'bout…you call me…Charlie," stammered Charlie.

"Charlie it is," agreed Kelly and then took his hand. It seemed to him that she squeezed it a couple of times and held it just a little longer than normal.

CHAPTER 46

Charlie walked toward Julie Sonoma's office, wondering what had just happened. He felt like a high schooler getting ready to ask a girl he didn't know very well to the prom. His heart was reacting interestingly, but his conscience was also hard at work, reminding him that he was a married man of 14 years and the father of an 11-year-old girl and a nine-year-old son. *Screw it*, he thought. *Charlene is nothing short of a bitch. She doesn't like me, either. And we're calling it quits, besides.*

Charlie whispered his inner voice, *that's quite a young lady you just met. Beautiful and fascinating too. I think she likes you.*

Head down, thinking intently about Kelly Hammermeister, Charlie almost ran headlong into Al.

"Whoa," said Al with a smile. "Based on the look on your face, that must have been some interview."

"It was goddamn interesting, Al," admitted Charlie, "Kelly Hammermeister is one beautiful woman, nice, too. But I'm hungry, let's get out of here and find some place to eat."

"Jesus, Charlie," chided Al, "you're only interested in food and another word that begins with 'f.'"

"Ease up, Al!" shot Charlie. "I haven't had a piece of ass in forever, so don't be talking to me about 'another F word.' As for eatin', yes, goddamnit, I like to eat. So could we please find somewhere to chow down?"

As they left the clinic and walked toward the parking lot, Al tapped his companion on the shoulder and pointed across the street. "How about Italian?"

The blinking red neon sign read *Luigi's. Great food like mama used to make.*

"Hell, yes," said Charlie. "I'm hungry enough to eat the ass out of a skunk. I bet Luigi's has somethin' bet

"I won't take that bet," responded Al. "From here, it smells damn good."

Charlie and Al had just been seated in a booth in the dining room and ordered a glass of wine when Charlie, looking across the dining room, saw Kelly Hammermeister walk up to the hostess desk with two equally beautiful companions, both of whom seemed a little bit older.

"Don't look," said Charlie quietly, "but my interview just arrived for dinner. Wow, she's with two beautiful gals. They grow 'em gorgeous down here!"

"Is one a brunette with short hair and a charming nose that tilts upward?"

"Yup," noted Charlie. "The other has the greatest auburn hair I have ever seen. Wow, what a trio! I think they've turned every head in the place."

"I'm betting the brunette is Julie Sonoma," said Al. "No idea about the third."

"Well, you're gonna know," whispered Charlie. "Kelly's seen me. They're headed this way with the hostess."

"Well, well," said Charlie, rising to his feet as the four women arrived at the table. "This is a surprise. Kelly, my associate, Detective Allan Rouse of the La Crosse Police Department."

"Hello, detective," said Kelly, shaking his hand. "Let me introduce my friends. This is Julie Sonoma," said Kelly, pointing to the brunette.

"Julie and I have met," said Al, smiling." Charlie shook Julie's hand. Kelly continued. "And this is Peggy Russell."

Both men shook hands with Peggy, and then stood back to contemplate their three new acquaintances.

"When I saw you," said Kelly, nodding toward Charlie, "I suggested you might enjoy some company. I'm not sure how familiar you are with Arlington Heights. I'm a newbie, too, but Julie and Peggy are vets. They can tell you anything you want to know about the area."

She looked from Charlie to Al. "But, maybe I was too presumptuous."

"No way!" said Charlie quickly.

The hostess pointed to a round table next to the booth Charlie and Al occupied. Al stepped in. "We're flattered by the invitation, but we'll stay here. After all, we've just met and we're here on a case," said Al.

"Oh, so we're suspects?" asked Kelly, her eyes twinkling.

"Everyone is a suspect when investigations are underway," replied Al, "but I don't think we've heard anything today that would put you deeply into that category."

"I was teasing," said Kelly, "but we don't often meet people from near home and."

"We'd like to accept your invitation," said Al, "but it seems better for us to stay here."

The hostess seated the three women at a table nearby. As Al and Charlie again sat down, Charlie was staring daggers at Al. "What the hell was that about!" whispered Charlie, loudly. "You just turned down a warm invitation from three beautiful women and made us seem like stuck-up assholes!"

"Charlie, calm down," said Al. "It's just best to keep our professional distance from women who could be suspects."

"I get that," agreed Charlie, "but I don't see how enjoying dinner with three beautiful women sabotages our case." Charlie thought some more for a moment. "But, I guess you're right. Thanks, Al."

Dinner over, the officers got up to leave. They stopped at the women's table to say goodnight. They chatted for a few minutes. "We don't have a place to stay. Any recommendations?" asked Charlie.

"Any thoughts about what you might like?" asked Julie.

"Any place that's clean and has two rooms with beds would do just fine," said Al. Charlie nodded.

"There is a Holiday Express just a few blocks from here," said Peggy. "Would that work?"

"Perfect," said Al. "Can we walk?"

"You could, but why would you do that on a night as cold as this?" asked Peggy, who chuckled. "Worried about a DUI?"

"Absolutely not," replied Al, his face reddening, "but we've had a long day…a tough drive. A walk would do us good."

Directions received, Al and Charlie departed. They decided to drive anyway, retrieved their car, and headed for the motel.

"Remember, Charlie, we have had a few glasses of wine, so take it easy, okay?"

"Absolutely, Al. I'll be as cautious as a teenager taking his driving exam."

CHAPTER 47

As the two lawmen departed, Peggy frowned. "What do you suppose brought those two to Arlington Heights?"

"No mystery about that," responded Julie. "They wanted to talk to me. Peggy, I guess I never really told you, but the only man I've ever loved—Brody's dad—was, far as I know, the first in this string of youth drowning deaths in La Crosse. It was a terrible time for me. I had just figured out I was pregnant when I found out my boyfriend, Shawn, =Shawn Sorensen, was dead. I never had a chance to tell him."

"He went out with friends on a Friday night when I had to work. The next time I saw him, he was in a coffin. It was awful, Peggy…just awful."

Tears now rolling down her cheeks, Peggy dabbed at her eyes with a Kleenex. She looked at her friend and grabbed her hand. "Oh, Julie, I knew about the drowning, but I didn't know it was the first of several. Julie, I am so sorry…so, so sorry," said Peggy. Sitting quietly, Kelly spoke up softly. "And they came to see me, too. My husband, Tom, was the eighth drowning victim. I never talk about it, either," admitted Kelly.

"Oh, my god!" said Peggy. "Both of you have lost men to drowning in La Crosse. That's eerie! I am so sorry."

"I know you are, but there's nothing anyone can do to ease the pain. It's still sharp. Every time I hear about a drowning, it's like exposing a nerve. I will never get over it. Brody is a spitting image of his dad. Same eyes, same hair, same build, and nearly the same voice. He is a constant reminder of the love that I never really got to know."

"I know how Julie feels," agreed Kelly. "My husband wasn't a good guy, but when you live with someone, sleep with him every night, and then, suddenly, he is gone and never coming back…well, it's…it's kind of indescribable. He was a terrible husband, but I loved him enough to marry him. I don't think I'm going to do that again…marry, that is."

"There are all sorts of things going through my mind," said Peggy, looking from Julie to Kelly. "Have I taken advantage of you? Is our relationship something I have forced?"

Seeing the mystified look on Kelly's face, Peggy spoke softly. "Julie and I comfort each other physically, if you know what I mean. It's something you'd probably figure out sooner or later."

Julie looked at Kelly, a worried look on her face. "Everyone has needs, I guess. Even though I didn't know I had them, I did. Peggy's helped me greatly and having someone wonderful to share tender moments with is a blessing."

"I have grown very fond of you. I have known for a long time that my feelings for women are more pronounced than they ever were for men. Even when I was married to Lauren and Jake's dad, I knew that. But until you, I never acted on the feeling," admitted Peggy.

Kelly broke in on the conversation. "I'm envious. I have physical needs too, and they are becoming more regular all the time. I have tried several vibrators. They give me orgasms but they don't create warm feelings."

"What Peggy and I have found are warm feelings," admitted Julie. "My feelings for her are very different than my feelings were for Shawn, but they also are very real. It's just not the same. One thing I know is if I lost you, I would be devastated."

"You're not going to lose me," said Peggy. "I'll work to understand how you feel. As long as we can be together and share the closeness, I'll be satisfied."

"You do make me envious. I don't have any desire for women. But a man would be nice. Not on a permanent basis. But every now and then," said Kelly after listening to Peggy and Julie.

An awkward pause enveloped the table. Peggy broke the silence. "So why do you think Allan and Charlie came to see you?"

"They probably think I know something that might be helpful to them," suggested Julie. "I doubt I've seen the last of them. Al is a really nice guy. Actually, I wouldn't mind seeing more of him!"

"They probably think I know something, too," offered Kelly. "I was swabbed. Were you, Julie? I'm sure they think it's way too coincidental to have two people close to two of the drowning victims working at the same place. You're right, Julie, I'm sure we haven't seen the last of them."

"Like you, I actually hope we haven't," continued Kelly with a chuckle. "I like Charlie…he's handsome in a big teddy bear sort of way. I'll admit I hit on him pretty hard. But I think he liked me, too."

"I was swabbed," offered Julie reflectively. She turned to Kelly. "He's married, too, isn't he? "I liked Allan, too. It's the first time I've felt like that since I noticed Shawn in the first class we took together. In any event, I doubt we've seen the last of them. I think they may be back often."

"Why would that be?" asked Peggy.

"Think about it, Peg. Two women close to two drowning victims in the same place working at the same clinic? Wouldn't you be suspicious? I'm guessin' they found something that led them to me and Kelly," said Julie. "The swabs they did? That means they have a DNA sample they're trying to match, I would guess."

"Well, I doubt they are going to find anything here," said Kelly. "But I'm glad they came to see us. I just had the first great conversation I've had with men since Matt died. I'd love to see more of them." Peggy looked from Julie to Kelly, a mystified look on her face. "You two are something. You just met these guys and already you have them in your bedrooms."

"Maybe," said Kelly, laughing. "Charlie has a great butt; did you notice?"

"No, but I did notice that Allan has the most adorable green eyes. They are almost hypnotizing. In fact, if they're sticking around, maybe we should ask them over for dinner," offered Kelly.

"I'm not sure that's a great idea," said Peggy. "They're cops, you guys, you just met them, and they're married. What sense does it make to invite them over for dinner?"

"It's just that we rarely meet anyone from around home. It would be nice to get to know them better. I know they're married, but no one is suggesting a tryst here. I just thought it would be good to…"

As her voice trailed off, Julie picked up the conversation. "I'd like to talk to them more, too, but not just to chit-chat. I'd like to see if we can learn more about why they really *are* here."

"I don't think you'd get anything out of them," said Peggy. "Al is a professional and I'd say he keeps his partner in tow most of the time."

"Well, still, I think it's a good idea," said Julie, "and I just happen to have Allan's cell number. He gave it to me in case I thought of something more about the case. Couldn't we just have them over for a nice dinner?"

"I suppose we could," said Peggy, her tone indicating she might be changing her mind. "If you guys think it's okay to invite a couple of law officers who are married to dinner, who am I to disagree? I can't imagine why they would agree, though. I guess if you're determined, go ahead and call. Then we can get out of here." She paused for a moment. "Do you think we should order something for the kids to eat? That way we won't have to cook. Why don't I do that while you two call your boyfriends?"

"Peggy!" said Julie firmly, "they are not our boyfriends. We were just going to offer a friendly dinner. If that's not a good idea, as you seem to think, let's just forget it."

"Oh, c'mon," replied Peggy, "I was only teasing. Go ahead and call them. And when you talk to Allan, ask him if he and Charlie have a cute friend who is about my age. I don't think I'm interested in a man, but who knows…"

"Maybe Peggy's right," said Julie, looking at Kelly. "Maybe it's not such a good idea."

"So you don't care about me," chided Peggy. "Just teasing, but if you want to invite them, do it."

When the waitress brought out the takeout food order, the three women quickly left, statements about "see you tomorrow" echoing around the empty neighborhood. As Kelly walked toward her car, she looked back. "Julie, call them. See what Al says."

CHAPTER 48

"Great gals, don't you think?" asked Charlie, as he and Al walked away from Luigi's toward their car before heading to the motel.

"They are nice," agreed Al. "It's hard to believe that Julie would have anything to do with the drownings…she just doesn't seem the type."

"Neither does Kelly," said Charlie. "Perhaps, our opinion is colored by the fact that both are so goddamn beautiful. They even have a third friend who is just as beautiful, maybe even more beautiful. I sure wouldn't mind seeing more of that Kelly…or Peggy…or Julie, for that matter. Probably best I don't, though, because it might cost me my not-so-happy home. Do I care? Hell, no! And wouldn't it be nice to introduce Rick to Peggy? I bet they'd hit it off great. She might even get him to the altar."

"That's just what…" began Al when his cell phone rang. Looking at the screen, he frowned. "It's Julie. Wonder what she wants? Did we leave something behind at the restaurant?"

"Rouse, what's up?" answered Al. He listened and nodded several times.

"Tell you what; let me talk to Charlie. We really don't have a plan for tomorrow. I don't know if we will be around, either. We might head home."

The conversation finished, he faced his partner. "Julie, Kelly and Peggy are inviting us to dinner tomorrow night."

"Great!" exclaimed Charlie, a sly grin spreading across his face.

"You're incorrigible! Get your mind above your belt and please focus," said Al. "I'm just not sure it's a good idea, Charlie. It might influence how we handle this case, and that definitely would not be a good idea."

"I'm crushed," chided Charlie. "How could you possibly accuse me of a philandering eye? But, Al, couldn't a quiet dinner contribute to our knowledge?"

"I didn't accuse you of having a philandering eye. I accused you of having two philandering eyes and a dick that sometimes doesn't listen to what your brain is telling it. But you make a reasonable point about acquiring additional information."

"Maybe we can tell them yes, but also say that it's not a thing we normally do? We could tell them that talk about the case will be off limits," suggested Al.

"Well" began his partner, "I am susceptible to blonde hair and blue eyes. In fact, I hope to dream about Kelly tonight. The hotter the dream, the better. And don't give me any crap about how pure yours are. I saw how you looked at Julie!"

Al rolled his eyes.

Charlie continued. "Uh huh, and tell me you aren't going to be thinking about a stunning brunette with an upturned nose and sparkling brown eyes?"

A few seconds went by. Al looked down, kicked the concrete, and looked up again. "Yah, it's pretty darn hard to forget anyone as attractive as Julie…or Kelly…or Peggy for that matter. But I doubt dinner is a good idea."

"C'mon, Al, lighten up. We're big boys. We can take care of ourselves."

After they chatted about the invitation for a few more minutes, Al weakened. "Okay, Charlie, I can see I am not going to talk you out of this," said Al. "It's against my better judgment, but I'll call to say we'll come."

"Julie, Al. We'd love to come. Charlie says he needs lots of rest, so we're going to hit the sack, sleep in, write our reports, have dinner with you folks and then head home on Wednesday."

He listened. "Nah, we eat anything. In fact, Charlie eats everything… and I mean everything. I'll try to keep him in check. Where will we be going? No, just an address will do, our car has a GPS."

He took a pad from his pocket and put the phone to his ear, talking as he wrote. "6807 North Kennicott, pull up the drive and park in front of the garage at the back of the house. Got it. Okay, we'll see you about 6:30. Is there anything we can bring? Wine. Okay, white or red? Red it will be. See you tomorrow."

"Whoopee!" exclaimed Charlie.

"Whoa, boy…get a grip!"

"I don't care!" exclaimed Charlie. "C'mon, buddy, let's find that motel. I got a dream that's waitin'."

"Don't suppose," mused Al, "that we could convince Rick to join us? We'd be doing him a pretty big favor."

"I'd like to invite him," agreed Charlie. "But I'm sure he would refuse a long drive alone. Maybe he'll come if we tell him who's waiting for him here. How 'bout that?"

Tuesday dragged past for Charlie and Al. After taking advantage of the Holiday Inn Express's free hot breakfast, they spent a few hours typing notes, and then decided they'd earned a nap. Because of their dinner date, they were going to be spending another night at the motel, which was a good thing because both of them were still tired, in spite of having slept for nine hours. Charlie had been disappointed to report when he awoke that Kelly had not appeared in any dream.

After their nap, they agreed to look for a liquor store to buy some wine. Al also thought they should pick up a box of chocolates to bring as well.

The two awoke at about 3 p.m., showered and shaved, and headed out to buy wine and gifts.

"Do you realize how crazy this is?" asked Al when they found their car, got in and he started it. "We're acting like two high school juniors on prom night and the subjects of our affection are the only two suspects we have in a high-profile serial killer case. Does this make any damn sense?"

"Yup, pretty fuckin' crazy," agreed Charlie, grinning. "But it ain't against the law to arrange interviews with suspects!"

"Oh, so that's what this is, right? An interview? You've been mooning around for a day now. I don't remember that being the case in other investigations we've worked on."

"Aw, shucks, Al, give me a goddamn break. Kelly is a beautiful lady... and there's no reason for her to be a suspect. But you? Now that's different! I mean, playing footsie with our prime suspect *is* fuckin' different. Hell, it's a lot different!"

"Shut up, will you? I don't want to talk about drownings anymore."

"Well, if I'm not mistaken, you're the guy who brought it up. Now suddenly it's an off-limits topic. A little goddamn sensitive, aren't you, buddy?"

"I'm having a bit of trouble with this whole thing," admitted Al. "It's highly unusual to be having dinner with your prime suspects. It's even crazier to be approaching dinner with the same feelings I used to have when dating a girl for the fourth or fifth time and wondering if I could round second on the way to third."

"Hmmm," chided Charlie, a wide grin spreading across his face, "at least you're admitting you're feeling like I do. If that isn't progress, it's sure as hell a sign that misery loves company."

"Can it, will you?" muttered Al. "Look for a liquor store!"

"Yes, sir!" snapped Charlie, saluting and then looking out the window, grinning.

CHAPTER 49

Two quick stops later, Al carefully guided the Suburban up the wide driveway that wound up a hill through a well-manicured lawn. He parked in front of the large garage, as instructed, noticing lights in the upstairs window.

"Wonder what the hell that is?" asked Charlie as he struggled to get out of the car, carefully guarding a sack, which contained four bottles of wine, a dozen roses wrapped in cellophane, and a large box of chocolates. "And hey, how about giving me a goddamn hand? I can't carry all of this myself. I don't want the goddamn chocolates all over the driveway, you lazy asshole!"

Al grabbed the wine and the men turned to walk up the sidewalk. Just then the lawn lights and porch light went on and Kelly opened the screen door.

"Talk about punctuality! You guys are right on time. It's exactly 6:30. Did you have a good day?"

"A good day?" barked Al. "I had to spend it with this guy!"

Kelly laughed softly and replied. "Aww, Al, but Charlie is so cute. He's just like a big teddy bear. And look, he comes bearing gifts: roses and a surprise box, too. How could anyone that thoughtful not be great to spend a day with?"

She turned to Charlie. "If Al doesn't want to be around you, I'm happy to step in. Are the roses for me?"

Charlie's face glowed red. Even in the dark, he looked like a full-faced Rudolph.

"Well, um, yes they are," said Charlie, handing her the bouquet. "But this is for all of you." He handed her the box. As Kelly turned to go back into the house, he faced his partner and whispered. "See, smart ass, I told you she liked me."

Following Kelly inside, the men entered the kitchen where Julie and Peggy were busy preparing food that smelled so good it made Al's mouth water and Charlie's stomach growl audibly.

"Listen to me. I'm not sure what you're makin', but it sure has my stomach growling," said Charlie with a grin.

"Charlie…Al…I'd like you to meet Genevieve Wangen," said Kelly as an elegant, silver-haired lady arose from a chair at the table and walked toward them, smiling broadly.

Extending her hands, she grasped Charlie's with her left and Al's with her right. "You must be Charles," said Genevieve, nodding to the left. She nodded to her right. "And that would make you Allan."

"That's us, ma'am. Very pleased to meet you," said Al, glancing at his partner with a look of total surprise.

"We sure are," chimed in Charlie. "Any friend of theirs," said Charlie, pointing at Kelly, Peggy, and Julie, "has to be a great person. We've heard that about you, too. How you helped Julie and Peggy move to this great house. We are pleased to meet you!"

"Oh, young man," replied Genevieve, "these girls are just what I have been looking for. The house became too much for me to handle, even with lots of help. I finally had to admit that. I looked and looked for people who would care for it like my Henry and I did. Then I found Julie and Peggy. Now I'm living right next door in the carriage house. I'm so happy they like the place."

"It's beautiful," said Al, looking around the comfortable kitchen.

"You really haven't seen anything, Al," began Julie. "How about I give the two of you a little tour? Peggy and Kelly can finish dinner. We'll be ready to eat when we're finished if we don't take too long. Don't forget to open the wine and let it breathe a little," urged Julie, looking back over her shoulder.

"Go ahead and monopolize our guests. We'll just do all the work while you play," chided Kelly.

A hurt look crossed Julie's r face. "I was just trying to be hospitable, Kelly. If you want to lead the tour, I'll be happy to help Peggy," offered Julie.

"Actually, I'd like that," said Kelly, shocking the other women. "I want to spend every moment I can with Charlie. I think he's the best."

"No fighting, children," admonished Peggy, jokingly. "How about both of you go? Go! I'd like the kitchen to myself, if you don't mind. I'm sure Genevieve will help if I need help. Go!"

"Well, okay then," teased Julie. "We'll be back in 10 minutes. We're all hungry!"

Julie gave Peggy a wide smile, removed her apron and joined the threesome.

The group began to move through the large, sturdy house, the mood light-hearted and conversational. Julie made a great tour guide and her manner, which made it obvious she was unaware of her great beauty and presence, was pleasant. She made the tour efficient but thorough, first exploring the downstairs, then the second floor and its six bedrooms and baths, and finally working in a peek into the walk-in attic on the third floor.

"After dinner," said Julie as they descended the stairs, "we'll have Genevieve show you her apartment and her laboratory. You won't believe it. She has a chemistry degree. She used it in health care to compound formulas. She made things doctors wanted but couldn't get in pharmacies."

"Now, don't look like lawmen, you two. Genevieve has a pharmacist's license that our clinic pays for to this day. It makes her available to give our docs advice on meds. Before you ask, yes, it's legal!"

"Here we are, back," said Julie, leading them into the dining room where the table was set, steaming food in place and the wine breathing. Both the red and white were in decanters, but the white was beside the table, residing in a magnificent silver ice bucket with its own stand.

"Wow," said Al, "this is something."

"Please don't think we're affluent," said Peggy. "Genevieve and her husband lived a good life. We're pleased to benefit from her generosity."

"Oh, my dears, I looked for a long, long time to find the two of you. It's just so nice to have two such responsible people looking after the house. And I get to help! My Henry would be so happy. He was a good provider. He made sure I would enjoy a comfortable lifestyle until I die. Wasn't that nice?"

"Very nice, ma'am," responded Al. "But I can see why he would do that for a woman like you."

"Oh my," said Genevieve, blushing. "You are a real gentleman. My Henry was a real gentleman, too. He always made sure I was happy. I miss him greatly."

She dabbed at her eyes as Peggy picked up the conversation. "We are committed to making you happy, too."

"Yes dear," said Genevieve with a smile. Kelly finally ended the pre-dinner conversation. "Let's eat before the food cools off."

They sat with Kelly and Charlie on one side, and Julie and Al on the other. Genevieve and Peggy were at the ends and Peggy sat nearest the kitchen. Genevieve insisted on saying the prayer before the meal.

That done, wine was poured and the food served. Charlie said the pot roast was the best he had ever tasted. It seemed only seconds had passed when he heaped his plate for seconds with meat, mashed potatoes and gravy, carrots and asparagus. Al was a bit more circumspect, trying to maintain a modicum of professionalism but he, too, found the food excellent.

The meal over, Peggy suggested that she and Kelly clean up the dishes while Julie and Genevieve showed their guests the carriage house. They found the upstairs apartment to be comfortable and spacious, with seemingly every convenience known to man.

"It's perfect, isn't it?" asked Julie.

"Really nice," said Al.

While the apartment was beautiful, when Genevieve unveiled the door to her laboratory, Al and Charlie were blown away. The lab was more modern than anything they had seen. Every piece of equipment imaginable was housed here. Even though the space was compact, the cupboards were expansive and filled with chemicals, all of them neatly labeled.

"I fiddle here, boys," reported Genevieve, giggling slightly. "I have made some outrageous compounds. Some have failed abysmally, but some have been powerful. I use a lot of Etomidate and Midazolam. Those two drugs are extraordinary. You can do almost anything with them. Either of them mixes well with other drugs. Each provides relief from any kind of pain. They will also knock out a horse if administered in the right place in the right amount."

Al quickly followed up. "Right place?"

"Well, with humans, you can create almost immediate unconsciousness, which is important to surgeons—if you inject through the ear canal. With horses or cattle, it's in a nostril. Small animals are best injected in the hind quarters."

"Interesting," chorused Al and Charlie, glancing at each other.

The tour ended, the six friends assembled back in the dining room for a dessert that was also great. It combined chocolate, cherries, vanilla ice cream, and raspberry topping. Charlie, of course, had two portions. He might have had a third, but Al stepped in.

Shortly thereafter, the two men excused themselves, lamenting that they would be leaving for La Crosse early in the morning.

"Well, I sincerely hope that you didn't find what you were looking for here," said Julie, tightly gripping Al's arm.

"We always find something," replied Al, lightheartedly. "Most of the time, it's just being able to eliminate some piece of evidence or some potential suspect."

Julie turned his body to face hers, hugged him passionately, and delivered an appropriate kiss, just brushing her lips past his in a move no one noticed. She whispered in his ear. "I hope I haven't seen the last of you, Al. Please, come again!"

"Same here," said Al, his conscience echoing warning bells loud enough, he thought, to be heard.

Kelly, meanwhile, was embracing Charlie, lingering a bit too long in his arms. It was an embrace the other four people tried to ignore. After friendly hugs to Peggy and Genevieve, Al and Charlie got back into the car and returned to the motel.

CHAPTER 50

"Nice, huh?" commented Charlie as Al drove down the drive, then accelerated into the lonely street.

"Yeah, and did you see that laboratory?"

"That's what I'm talking about. I was blown away by the lab, but even more stunned by what Genevieve had to say. Do you think it's possible that…"

"An 80-something woman could be a cold-blooded killer Al interrupted his partner, finishing the thought for him.

"Yeah, could it be?" repeated Charlie.

"Well, she sure seemed on target," speculated Al. "She knew about the drugs, the ear canal, and seems to have run extensive research on sedatives and anesthetics. What more is there?"

"I don't know, but could an 80-something lady be our killer?" asked Charlie.

"Well, if we go back 15 years, it would put her in her 60s. Given how spry and fit she is I'd say it's possible she could have done the early ones. But now? Maybe, I suppose, but it just doesn't seem possible, does it?"

"There's the issue of the younger women," said Charlie, reminding himself and his partner of the reason they came to Arlington Heights.

"You think they might have teamed up?" asked Al. "Maybe. But they just don't seem the killer type to me. I know Julie and Kelly have reasons to be upset, maybe even upset enough to kill, but they just don't seem the type."

"No, they don't. But we've been involved with cases where the criminal was the most unlikely of those investigated. Remember the Hartley case? We cracked that one 26 years after the kidnapping. The perp was the nicest goddamn little old man I'd ever met…until I found all the women's underwear in his basement."

"That was spooky," agreed Al. "Yes, we've had some bizarre cases, but if those women are killers, I'll be a monkey's uncle."

Charlie peered at him intently, causing Al to glance at him. "What? Oh, you're insinuating that my looks qualify me to be a primate's relative?"

"Well, buddy, if the monkey suit fits, maybe…?"

Charlie turned and looked out the window, laughing as Al muttered and concentrated on his driving.

There was a long gap of silence. "I may look like a monkey, but I'm smarter than you are. I didn't see you getting a DNA sample from Peggy and Genevieve."

He patted his pocket and Charlie stared at him. "You actually found time to collect samples?"   .

"I did," said Al, "and samples of Etomidate and Midazolam, too. I don't know if drugs have signatures or markers, but I thought it couldn't hurt to grab some just in case. I always carry vials and swabs. You just never know."

"Then we should know more tomorrow," said Charlie. "I sure as hell hope the results don't point at any of the women. It would be fuckin' heartbreaking to arrest 'em."

"That mind set will get you in trouble," replied Al, "especially if it teams up with your plumbing. The combination would be sexual!"

"But, God, Al, aren't they fuckin' beautiful?"

"They sure are, but I worry about being too close. Julie's lips actually touched mine as we said goodbye. I had to restrain myself. I could just as well have turned, kissed her and set off something more."

"Sparks. A goddamn good term," said Charlie. "Kelly's sensational. She pressed herself against me and I almost broke out of my pants."

They drove on, both contemplating the events of the day.

***

Up early the next morning, Al and Charlie had a big breakfast at the motel, then loaded the SUV.

"Careful," cautioned Al, as Charlie prepared to put the duffel bag containing the samples and vials into the car.

"I am, I am, goddamnit!" He puttered around for about five minutes, then asked Al to take a look.

"I made sure the damn bag's surrounded by soft sides. It's cushioned and wedged in tight. It ain't gonna move."

"Looks good," declared Al.

The suitcases went into the backseat, and the two men headed for I-90 and the trip north. Charlie was driving. Al lounged in the passenger seat with his head back and eyes closed.

"You know, Charlie, I've been thinkin' more and more about the lab and Genevieve. She sure as heck could have whipped up the drug."

"She sure as hell could have," agreed Charlie. "Didn't it sound like Peggy, Julie, and Kelly just met the old lady?"

"That's what it seemed like," agreed Al. "Shit, we have more questions than answers."

"It's true. We better go deliver the samples, and the sooner, the better."

The trip passed quietly. Conversation explored the crime, potential solutions, whether the Packers would win the Central Division, and if the Badgers would again be great in basketball. And, of course, the beautiful women they had met.

"At least we can bet on the goddamn Badgers," said Charlie. "Bo Ryan is the best. He always produces, even when the Badgers are supposed to be down. Have you seen his new camping commercial? It's goddamn hilarious!"

"Mike McCarthy is pretty darn good, too. I expect the Packers to make a run if Rodgers stays healthy," replied Al.

"Well, they're in a goddamn good spot," agreed Charlie. "And Bo says the Badgers are way down. That means they'll probably win the Big 10."

A stop at Monk's in the Wisconsin Dells for one of the best burgers in the state fortified them for the rest of the trip.

Back in the car, Al took the wheel. The Suburban headed north. They sped through Bangor, then West Salem. When the outskirts of Onalaska came into view, Charlie became curious. "Are we taking the samples to Rick?"

"On the way," said Al, turning onto Highway 16 for the trip downtown. "You know, Charlie, if we find any reason to return to Illinois, I think *we should* ask Rick to come along. I bet he and Peggy would really hit it off, don't you?"

"I do…yes, I do. But while you were saying that, I was wondering," continued Charlie, "if we have to send the samples to the goddamn DCI?"

The Division of Criminal Investigation was a component of the state's Justice Department and it had a lousy reputation. It was known for sketchy service, endless waits, and sloppy work. Officers went out of their way to avoid it.

"I've been thinking about that," admitted Al. "I don't think we can ignore 'em, but we can make sure we get a fast job. We should use both Rick and DCI. I'd like to go directly to Gundersen, if you can spare the time."

"Go for it. I want to know when we'll hear something."

Ten minutes later, the lawmen walked into Rick's lab. After hellos, Al set the duffle on the counter. He unzipped it and placed the vials and samples, neatly organized, beside the bag.

As Al began describing the contents of the samples, the door opened and Pat walked in.

"I heard you were here," said Pat. "What do we have?"

"Oh, hi, Pat," greeted Rick. "Al was just explaining the samples."

She greeted Al and Charlie as old friends. As Al turned back to his work, the door opened again and Sarah Giles walked in.

"This is getting to be like old home week," said Rick, smiling. "Let's call George Lee and see if he wants to join the party. We can do all of this together."

He dialed the phone, spoke for a minute and hung up. "George will be right here."

It wasn't a minute before the door opened. Dr. Lee entered, smiling at the group gathered around the counter.

Al, with help from Charlie, told them about the trip, the women they had met, explained the samples they had collected, and ended by explaining Genevieve Wangen's laboratory.

"You wouldn't believe the place! It has the best of everything. Every piece of equipment you could imagine. And, near as I could tell, a pretty thorough inventory of drugs and compounding materials," commented Charlie.

"It's something, that's for sure," agreed Al. "Mrs. Wangen is in her 80s. She's a spry, very fit 80-year-old, but I doubt she's strong enough to wrestle a guy into the river. I doubt she weighs much more than 110 pounds. But maybe…"

"Let's take a look. If Sarah's willing to help me, we could have a pretty thorough report by this time tomorrow," predicted Rick.

Sarah agreed. "Rick, how about you take the DNA samples? I'll analyze the drugs."

"Works for me, but I hope Pat will be willing to collaborate," said Rick, nodding at Pat.

"Absolutely, I'm available full-time."

"Don't forget me! I know some things about sedatives and anesthetics. That might be helpful to Sarah," offered Dr. Lee.

Rick looked at his colleagues, then at Al and Charlie. "We have the best team in La Crosse, that's for sure. I'm pretty certain if there's something to be found, we'll find it."

"Go for it," said Al. "Charlie, not much we can do. What do you say we spend a little time at our offices, then head home?"

"I won't be goin' home," said Charlie, "but, great. Let the experts work without us poking our noses in here and there and looking over their shoulders. Besides, I'm ready to take a look at the mountains of crap that I bet hit my desk while we were gone. That done, I'll head for Westby and more home cookin'. Oops, almost forgot. What about Hooper and Whigg?"

"Oh, God, you're right," said Al. "We'd better bring 'em up to date."

With that, the two officers were out the door. The doctors separated the samples. Sarah and George Lee left for Sarah's lab, while Rick and Pat settled in to work where they were.

***

The next day dawned clear and crisp. As Al got out of his car at Ma's, he could see his breath. Charlie's truck pulled up beside him. Charlie jumped out and slapped him on the back. "I feel like an expectant dad whose wife is in labor and headed for the delivery room."

"Delivery room!" said Al, laughing. "You can tell how old your kids are. There aren't delivery rooms any more. They are called birthing suites now. Dads and moms stay together."

"Oh, yeah, I guess I knew that," acknowledged Charlie. "But, you know what I mean. I mean I'm so excited I can hardly sit still."

"Yeah, but if the tests provide answers, our friends will be involved. But, look on the bright side. We will have cracked one of the biggest serial cases in history. If there's nothing there, then we're back at square one. We have a pretty good idea these drownings weren't accidents, so if the tests show nothing, we're back looking for a needle in a haystack," evaluated Al.

Charlie looked at his partner, nodded his head, and sighed. "Well, we are just going to have to wait. But we sure as hell don't have to wait to get Ma's cakes. Let's go."

Inside the tiny eatery, it was the typical chaos. Ma was trading jibes with her customers while working the counter and doing the cooking. Her trusty waitress, Evelyn, was waiting tables. Since there was no room at the counter, Charlie and Al grabbed a table. Evie was there instantly.

"My favorite cops," said Evie, offering a wide smile. "What'll it be?"

"Evie," began Charlie.

"Hell, Charlie, I know what you want: four eggs over easy, six strips of bacon, three pieces of toast, a tall stack of pancakes, and a waffle on the side, right?"

"Yup, 'course you can throw yourself in so I get a little exercise to work this off," said Charlie, gripping his stomach.

"Now, Charlie, you behave yourself," cautioned Evie. "Besides, you couldn't handle me. I need a real man."

"Aw, goddamn, Evie," lamented Charlie. "You sure know how to hurt a guy."

"Charlie, at your age, you should know better'n to hit on an old hen like me. Besides, I don't want to be responsible for you having a heart attack. The breakfasts you eat are as near poison as it comes."

"Aw, cut me some slack," said Charlie. "I just want my little breakfast and I want to eat it in peace and quiet."

"Okay, fair enough!" Evie smiled.

"Evie, I want the special: the eggs scrambled and wheat toast. Add two strips of bacon, will you, please?" asked Al.

"Sure, Al. At least there's one gentleman in this place."

Evie spun on her low heels and stomped toward the counter, yelling as she went. "Ma, Charlie wants the cholesterol special: the four eggs over easy and the waffle on the side." She disappeared into the kitchen.

As the two waited, they chatted about next steps, thinking out loud about what they would do if the tests were positive or negative. Forty minutes later, having eaten, they left Ma's, promising, as they separated, to let each other know the minute one or the other heard anything.

That something came at 3:30 that same afternoon. A phone call came from Rick to Al, suggesting that he and Charlie get to the lab ASAP.

"I assume that means we have something?" asked Al.

"I want both of you here when we tell you what we found," said Rick.

CHAPTER 51

At 4:10, Charlie came huffing into the Gundersen Clinic. Al was waiting for him.

"I didn't want you to accuse me of hearing first," said Al. "But now that I see what you look like and hear you puffing, it's probably a good thing I waited. I'll probably have to do CPR in the next five minutes."

"Mouth-to-mouth? You? Forget it! I'll be just fine," promised Charlie, bending over to catch his breath.

Anxious but slowed by Charlie's overexertion, the two men walked slowly toward the lab. As they pushed open the wooden doorway, they were greeted by Rick, who was wearing a smile big and bright enough to make his stainless steel world shine.

"We have matches!" burst out Rick, unable to constrain himself. "One perfect match! And another that's also perfect, but interesting."

"So, goddamnit, tell us," wheezed Charlie, his voice rising to almost a croak.

"Easy, easy, both of you," cautioned Rick, "let's not get carried away. I want you to hear every word and I want to deliver the messages slowly and carefully."

"Got it," replied Charlie, pulling out his notepad.

Rick began acting as a consummate professional. "The trace we found on the victims' hairs, that is, produced a perfect match to all three hair samples. This is interesting, because the samples were of different colors and different lengths. It's also unusual, because the samples seemed to be of natural color, at least to the unaided eye."

"We also found, as you know, puncture marks on all four of the bodies that were exhumed. The puncture marks proved to be from a needle and the tissue samples examined indicated the punctures were likely made by ultra-fine needles. That would be the ideal instrument for a shot into the auditory canal. Our tests showed that Etomidate was used on two of the four exhumed bodies. Midazolam was also found—but in three bodies, including the two with Etomidate. The fourth body contained a trace of Propofol, powerful and normally used in veterinary practices on large animals."

"The clear match, as the result of hairs found on two of the three bodies, was from a female, a match for Mrs. Genevieve Wangen. We matched the two hair specimens. At first, we thought we were dealing with a blonde, but, as it turned out, the color is gray, near platinum. That gives it a blonde cast. When we matched that to the specimens you brought back, we got a match to Mrs. Wangen. But there's still a mystery. We have a dark hair specimen as well, but that isn't a perfect match to any of the people sampled. But, whoever it is, is a relation of Ms. Sonoma. The short explanation is that mitochondrial DNA is inherited through the maternal line. This means that all sons and daughters inherit their mother's mitochondrial DNA. This heritage enables researchers to trace lineage far back. We believe the hair to have come from a male, likely either an immediate ancestor of or an immediate descendant of Ms. Sonoma. Since we believe the hair to be from a young person, we think Mrs. Sonoma's son should be tested."

"So if I'm following," repeated Al, "we have a solid match and a kind-of match?"

"I wouldn't say 'kind-of.' What I would say is that we have two people involved with the killings. One appears to be Mrs. Wangen. The other appears to be a relative of Ms. Sonoma," explained Rick.

"Mrs. Wangen! Well, I'll be damned. Never in a thousand years would I have believed her involved. First of all, how the hell could someone as old as her and with her build overpower a young man? It just doesn't work," said Al.

Sitting quietly until now, Pat spoke. "Could she have had help, say, Ms. Sonoma's son?"

"Never say never, I suppose. I didn't get the idea that Genevieve and the Sonomas knew each other until now," replied Al. "I just don't see Genevieve as a killer. We know she has prepared drugs. Most of them were anesthetics. She's just a bit of a thing. She wouldn't even make two bites for Charlie."

Rick suggested working in the conference room office. The group made a quick stop at the cafe for coffee, and they were soon huddled, making plans.

CHAPTER 52

That same evening in Arlington Heights, Julie, Peggy, Kelly, Genevieve, Lauren, Jake and Brody were settling down at the table for dinner.

Kelly had done the cooking, and the odors coming from the oven had everyone's mouths watering.

"I made lots," said Kelly. "There are two twice-baked potatoes for each of you, more barbecued ribs than we can eat, corn on the cob, baked beans, and, for dessert, there is pumpkin pie. It's still the Thanksgiving season, I figured."

"Speaking of Thanksgiving, Genevieve, will you lead us in prayer?" asked Julie.

"Of course, dear. Let's fold our hands and bow our heads. Dear Lord, you have been uncommonly generous this Thanksgiving season. We have eaten abundantly, but more importantly than that, we are all new friends, becoming fast friends. I am grateful for the presence of all of you, especially you, Brody, because of all you have done for me. Lauren and Jake are learning, too, and to have three marvelous young ladies in my life, Lord, is a prayer answered."

"So thank you, Lord, for all you have done for us this season. Bless us O Lord and these thy gifts, which we are about to receive from thy bounty, through Christ our Lord, amen. In the name of the Father and the Son and the Holy Spirit."

"Amen," chorused everyone. Julie turned to Brody. "Young man, just what have you been doing for Genevieve? You really seem to be special friends. I'm very happy, Genevieve, that he is being helpful to you, but that is an absolutely new behavior."

"C'mon, mom, I help you all the time," said Brody, mournfully. "If you gave me half as much credit as Gen, I'd probably do even more."

"Gen? Her name is Genevieve, Brody, and I'd rather you call her Mrs. Wangen," scolded Julie.

"Oh, dear, please don't discipline him. Brody and I have become such good friends. He's been over to Westminster several times and I asked him to call me Gen. If there is any fault, it's mine."

Julie looked from Brody to Genevieve. "Over to Westminster…that's interesting. Young man, why didn't you tell me you had been visiting Mrs. Wangen? I mean Genevieve…or Gen, I guess. I suppose the informality is okay, Genevieve, but I try to teach Brody good manners and respect. That means addressing elders properly."

"But, dear, we have become such good friends," said Genevieve, defending Brody. "I would hate for us to be on such formal terms."

"You do seem to have become good friends," said Julie, her face breaking into a smile, "but just what have you been doing together?"

"We talk. Our talks make it seem as if I have known your son for a long time," said Genevieve, wistfully. "He reminds me so much of my son when he was Brody's age. It's almost like having a family—a real family—again. We play video games. Brody has shown me how to play; I love the games."

"Now that's a blessing," admitted Julie. "I hate those darn games, so if Brody has someone to play with when Jake is busy, I'm relieved."

Dinner continued with the ordinary chatter and the exchange of not-so-friendly retorts between Lauren and Jake. Genevieve interrupted the incessant conversation at the table. "Have we heard anything from those nice boys…what were their names…Al and Charles?"

"Not a word, but why would we?" asked Julie. "They seemed satisfied with the information they gathered. I didn't expect we'd hear from them or see them again, for that matter."

"That's too bad. They seemed like such nice boys. You and Peggy seemed to hit it off well with them. I am so glad to have this new family, but you and Peggy seem lonely. I imagine it must be lonely without men in your lives. I miss my Henry terribly."

As Julie was preparing to reply, her cell phone rang. She picked it up, answered, and smiled. "Al, speak of the devil. We were just talking about you. Genevieve just asked if we'd heard from you. I told her I didn't expect to, so this is a surprise."

Once she got off the phone, she broke the news. "Allan and Charlie are returning to the Chicago area. They want to pay us back for the dinner we made. They want to take us all out to dinner. They're coming next

Tuesday and they are bringing along this Dr. Olson they mentioned when they were last here."

The entire group broke out in wide smiles.

"Isn't that wonderful!" exclaimed Genevieve, clapping her hands.

But Brody quickly broke in, asking the question that was on his mother's mind. "Do you think they found something? I sure hope not; that would be a bummer."

"Young man, I rather suspect that Al and Charles want to see your mother and Kelly again. It seems like they are bringing a friend, too, so Peggy will not be lonely. Isn't that nice?" added Genevieve.

"I sure hope so, Gen…oops, Genevieve," replied Brody.

"That's much better, young man, but the word isn't sure, it's surely."

"Mom, do you ever ease up? How about some slack?"

Brody looked at his empty plate, then at Lauren and Jake. "How about we play video games for a while?"

"Good idea," agreed Jake, quickly. They ran off to the other room, while Lauren waited at the table, clearly wanting to be part of the grownup talk.

CHAPTER 53

"Okay, that's in play," said Al, turning back to his four friends. "Now, we have to really plan how we are going to approach the visit, right down to who will do and say what. I don't want this puppy getting away from us when we are this close."

For the next two hours, they planned out every detail of the upcoming visit. Pat looked at her watch and exclaimed. "My goodness, it's almost 9:30. I'm famished."

"How about we head for Kate's?" asked Charlie. "I'm hungry and I know darn well that there will be nothing waiting for me at home except a cold shoulder. That just ain't gonna cut it tonight."

"Are you gonna buy?" asked Al.

"Are you goddamn kidding? on a deputy's pay? I thought maybe the La Crosse Police Department would offer, since Rick, Pat, Sarah and I cracked the case for you."

"In your dreams," retorted Al.

***

Later, the remnants of a generous and excellent Italian meal centered around homemade pasta crowding the table, Pat said what they all were thinking. Raising her glass of Chianti, she toasted the group. "Here's to a successful end to this mystery, and to the friendships that have been forged in pursuit of the truth."

Cheers echoed around the table. Everyone turned to Charlie when he slapped his forehead.

"Oh, crap, we haven't said a word to Hooper or Whigg!"

"Let it go, partner," replied Al. "We'll catch them first thing in the morning and they'll be none the wiser. We've all earned a good night's sleep, including Hooper and Whigg. Let 'em slumber peacefully."

With that, the group parted ways. Al, Charlie and Rick agreed to meet Monday morning to catch up on any further test results and make final plans.

A few minutes later when Al arrived home, JoAnne greeted her husband warmly. "You look positively bushed! I am so glad that you got a good dinner. I had card club tonight and the only thing I had in the house was a can of spaghetti. I'm sure Kate's was better."

"It sure was," agreed Al, "but we skipped dessert. I thought I might have that here."

JoAnne appeared startled. "Dessert! Do you think that I have had... oh, *that* kind of dessert. That kind I can handle."

"I've been thinking about your luscious boobs all afternoon."

"Allan Rouse, you are incorrigible. But I love that you love them."

***

Meanwhile, at Charlie's house, the greeting was not nearly as warm.

"I'm home!" yelled Charlie as he walked through the back door. He mumbled softly, "but only for a minute."

"I suppose I'm supposed to turn cartwheels!" snapped Charlene. "Get your stuff and get out."

"Goddamnit, Charlene, give it a break!" bellowed Charlie. "I just came by to pick up some clothes. Just go back to the TV, or whatever the hell you were doing. I'll be out of here in a flash."

"Lock the door behind you; I'm goin' to bed," said Charlene, snippily.

"Goddamnit, Charlene, I do my goddamn best," replied Charlie. "But nothing I do is good enough."

"You're right; it's not. Why don't you just get yer stuff and get the hell out!" The door slammed and Charlie was left alone, climbing the stairs, shaking his head, and anxious to do exactly as she said.

Same old, same old, he thought. *It just never changes. This is the last straw.*

As he pulled things out of the closet and got ready to carry them to the car, Charlie thought about Kelly, wondering if she would be as impossible to live with as his wife. *Well, one thing is for sure, Kelly sure as hell is a lot better looking. It would be a joy to sit across the table from her. She even smiles sometimes.* Even this cheery realization made him sad for a moment.

CHAPTER 54

Dishes done, Kelly got ready to leave and Genevieve retired to the apartment above the garage. Peggy and Julie crashed on the sofa. Peggy, gazing at her friend and lover, sensed something was wrong.

"What is it, Julie?" asked Peggy. "You look like death warmed over."

"I've been meaning to tell you something," said Julie, "but it's a long, long story. Perhaps it should wait."

"Are you kidding? The way you look? You'd better get it out."

"Okay, I guess," said Julie, sliding across the couch. "But you're gonna have to hold me close."

"Gladly," said Peggy, hugging her.

"You know…" began Julie, starting to sniffle. "You know that Shawn drowned in La Crosse. He went out with a group of friends on a night when I had to work. He and his friends got wasted. No one noticed when Shawn went to the bathroom. Worse yet, no one noticed that he never came back."

"It was a mindless, stupid act. It never should've happened. When he came out of the bathroom, so the theory goes, he walked out the door and into the river."

"I'll never forget the sound of the knock the next day or the look on his best friend's face. 'Shawn's gone,' he had said. By the look on his face, I knew it was forever."

"I screamed, sank to the floor, and the next thing I remember was waking up the next day with my folks sitting by my bed. I began to scream again, pleaded with my mom and dad to tell me that it was only a dream. It wasn't. Shawn was dead. That day my world died, too."

Julie was sobbing now. Peggy hugged her tightly, whispered in her ear and told her everything would be all right.

Finally, Julie got the sobs under control and began to talk again.

"It wasn't until after the funeral that I missed my first period. I attributed it to my body being screwed up because of my grief over his death. When another month went by and there was no period, I began to think the unthinkable that the one of the few times we made love had resulted in a pregnancy. A trip to the doctor confirmed it. My world crashed again."

"I thought about killing myself, about having an abortion, about running away and never coming back, but, then, with the help of my mom, I made a decision to keep the baby. Both my folks were great, and when Brody was born, I knew I made the right decision. He was beautiful. He looked like a miniature version of Shawn. I am so glad I have him. Each day he reminds me of his dad and the wonderful man he was."

"I knew you had a lover," said Peggy. "And I knew he drowned. I also suspected—from your words and actions—that there was something more to the story. But I didn't know the circumstances. That's tragic. But it's a long time ago. Are you sure you aren't carrying the burden a little too long?"

"That's not what I wanted to tell you. That's just the background. The reason I feel so badly is much, much worse."

"That's hard to believe," said Peggy, soothingly. "What could be so bad?"

"Peggy, I was furious…with life…furious with Shawn's friends. I couldn't put it behind me. I got into a really, really bad place, Peggy…a horrible place. Now I'm a serial killer."

Peggy's face suddenly had a horrified look. "You? I'm confused. What are you saying? Tell me more."

"You didn't know me then. If you had, you wouldn't recognize me today. I was so miserable. I just wanted to get even with everyone for what the world did to me! Much as it seems like a dream, I did it! The first killing was the worst. Then it got easier and easier."

Peggy thought for a while, and then looked with tenderness at her best friend and lover. "I don't believe it. You have some sort of traumatic stress problem. You could never be a killer. Not in a thousand years."

"Peggy, the last killing was just a few weeks ago, the weekend I left Brody with you to go to La Crosse."

"Julie, I'm not sure what you're talking about. I have had Brody stay over lots of times, but I didn't have him during a weekend."

"I am just so fuzzy about things. I know I've done some terrible things, terrible! Memories of the earlier killings are much clearer. After Shawn's death, I had to get revenge. I had to! On the first anniversary—with Brody just a few months old—I did the first one."

"I put…my…training to work…put together really potent drugs. It's really hazy, Peggy, but I went to downtown La Crosse. I waited for a drunken student outside one of the trashiest bars. As soon as it got dark, I saw several. There was one who reminded me of Shawn's roommate. I grabbed him, jabbed him, guided him to the river and pushed him in."

"I remember it being easy; exhilarating, even. I grabbed him around the neck. I whispered to him. The poor sucker thought I was coming on to him. I gave him a push. I went home, rocked Brody to sleep, went to bed and slept like a baby. When I read about it the next week, I realized it wasn't a dream."

"That was the first one. But there were more. I always did it in the fall. But not on the same date. I didn't want to make it too obvious, though it's not like the police ever caught on—at least until Al and Charlie came around. Now I'm scared. It seems like a dream. But, Peggy, I did it. Now they're coming back! They're going to arrest me. I can't bear to leave Brody. Peggy, you have to promise to keep him…to take care of him! Please, promise!"

"Of course, of course," said Peggy, soothingly. Julie quieted but had also shut down at the same time. She couldn't speak. She stared blankly into space. Peggy was rocking her gently, singing softly to her, almost like she would to a baby. Julie began to snore lightly.

Peggy considered what she had heard. *Was Julie—this lovely lady, extraordinary mother, competent nurse—really a murderer? Was she in some sort of deep state of depression that caused her to hallucinate about being a serial killer?* The notion of Julie as a murderer was simply incomprehensible. There had to be something more to this story.

CHAPTER 55

Back in La Crosse, Al was also thinking of Julie. He was anxious to see her again, of course, but he was also grateful that clues didn't point to her as the killer. He was worried, though, about her son as an accomplice.

As JoAnne slept, he laid there in the dark with his eyes open, trying to play out in his mind how the trip to Arlington Heights might turn out. *If Brody Sonoma was involved, as the signs suggested, how would Julie react?*

He realized something about himself as well. As he lay there, the thoughts about Julie that tumbled around in his brain were not normal thoughts. They were not the kind of thoughts a happily married officer for 22 years should think about a female friend of his, a woman that was not his wife. Rick's conscience nagged him every second about these thoughts. The harder Rick tried to erase these thoughts, the more they tumbled around in his brain. Haunting thoughts of the beautiful brunette with the sad eyes and winning smile would not leave him. Al realized he had experienced these thoughts for another woman a very long time ago. He realized, guiltily, that he had these thoughts when he first met his wife. Her name was JoAnne Kelley then. While dating, they had lost their virginity for the first time, together, in their junior year of high school. No other woman, for the last 22 years, had brought these feelings back for Al until he met Julie Sonoma.

They were married when Al graduated from the criminal justice program at the University of Wisconsin in Madison. JoAnne stayed home, attended Viterbo College for two years and then transferred to Western Wisconsin Technical Institute to obtain a med tech degree.

They had now been happily married for 22 years with two children they adored. They were seemingly destined for a long life together. But now their love story—and his equilibrium—had been disturbed by a woman in Illinois. He wondered if he wanted it to be. The answer to this question worried him. He turned on his side and tried to sleep.

Charlie, meanwhile, was tossing and turning in an enormous and lonely bed. As he twisted, his thoughts raced. He realized that neither he nor his wife had been happy for a long time. *Tonight's little explosion*, he thought, *was the opening salvo in the final days of their marriage.*

He, too, was haunted by images of a beautiful Illinois woman. *Kelly seemed perfect. She was beautiful, kind, considerate, and fun to be around. In fact, he had to admit that he eagerly looked forward to next week's trip.*

He surely wasn't happy at home, but neither did he like being alone. The Westby B&B was a great facility. Mary was a wonderful cook, and, God knows, she had come onto him like a Mack truck. He thought that he might have responded if he hadn't met Kelly. When Kelly let him know how much she liked him, all thoughts of Mary vanished.

As he tossed, he wondered about Al's feelings toward Julie. Did Al fantasize about her as well? He knew Al was happily married. Yet, Charlie saw how Al looked at Julie. Al seemed more than a little mesmerized by the dark-eyed brunette. Charlie considered that Al may have even more on his mind regarding Julie. As for the case, he guessed that Al was worrying about what connection Julie's son might have to the La Crosse murders.

What would the next week bring? By this time next week, would the case be solved? Would the accused killer or killers be behind bars? What about himself? Would his seemingly destined relationship with Kelly actually happen?

There was also Rick to consider. Rick was a great guy and one of La Crosse's most eligible bachelors. Charlie knew that Rick dated extensively. He had been connected romantically to at least seven or eight prominent area women, but none of them had been able to get him to the altar.

Peggy is a phenomenally good-looking lady, thought Charlie. *Based on Rick's preferences, Peggy could be exactly his type. Wouldn't it be hilarious*, he thought to himself, *if he, Al, and Rick were all on the verge of romances in Arlington Heights, Illinois?* He chuckled to himself as he thought of the three of them triple-dating in Charlie's SUV.

By the time Charlie finally dozed off, the sun was coming up. A half hour later, he would be up and, after a big breakfast at his beloved Westby B&B, heading to work.

CHAPTER 56

Peggy awoke the next morning in the same place she had fallen asleep the previous night: Julie was in her arms. As she disentangled herself, she realized that her neck felt like a moving escalator. Muscle spasms coursed up and down her spine.

Free from her comfortable spot in Peggy's arms, Julie stretched, yawned, looked at her friend, and began to tear up.

"C'mon now," said Peggy softly, sitting down and putting her arms around Julie again.

"Please, tell me you don't hate me! Please tell me you're still my friend," said Julie, sobbing.

"Oh, sweetheart, there's no worry about whether I love you or not—I do, with all my heart."

Brightening, Julie smiled. "Peggy, you always make me happy. Thanks for believing in me."

"Of course I believe in you. What I don't believe is that you had anything to do with those deaths. I think you were so traumatized that somehow you began to believe you were responsible. I have heard of things like that."

"I wish it were hallucinations. But it's not, Peggy, it's not. I did it. I remember doing it. And for a while it even made me feel good. Now I just feel terrible."

"It's going to be alright," reassured Peggy. "I promise."

As Peggy smiled at Julie, tears trickled down the brunette's face. She managed a smile, though, and felt better than she had in weeks. It was as if a great weight had been lifted. Peggy felt better, too, because the woman she loved appeared to finally be free of her great secret.

Peggy had a plan to help Julie already. At work, she planned to visit Dr. Ezrah Toritz, head of the behavioral health unit at the Kahn Clinic. She wanted to pose some hypothetical questions to him. She wanted to see if she could get a handle on the best way to get Julie the help that she obviously needed.

As Peggy was planning her strategy, suddenly, Julie was animated, bubbly, and especially beautiful. Her eyes sparkled and a smile lit up her face, warming the room with its intensity. She moved to Peggy, embraced her, and kissed her long and lovingly.

"Peggy, I really love you; I think I'm finally coming to grips with this lesbian love thing. I realize that I am very definitely in love with you."

"And I'm in love with you," whispered Peggy.

After what seemed like minutes, the two women finally separated. "How about we shower, get ready for work, and then stop for a bite to eat on our way?"

"Sounds like a great idea," agreed Julie.

Soon clouds of steam billowed from the shower as the two women, totally captivated by each other, used the soap and water in expert ways to create a great morning experience.

"My," said Julie, as she gently wiped Peggy's breasts, "this is a wonderful way to begin the morning. I sure hope it isn't the last time our day starts this way."

"It won't be," promised Peggy, returning the favor with vigorous swipes of the towel that traveled from Julie's stomach to a place north of her knees.

***

Soon, Peggy steered her Escape out of the North Kennicott driveway. A short stop later for bagels and coffee, the drive continued toward the clinic.

"I hope I'm not touching a raw nerve," began Peggy, glancing at Julie, "but we should give some thought to next week's visit. I've been thinking about it. Wouldn't it be great to have them back at the house? We can order a catered dinner. Let the guys pay, if they are intent on buying. I just think it would be nice to enjoy their company there rather than going to a restaurant for most of their visit."

"It might," began Julie hesitantly, "allow some hints about the reason for the visit. I would like to think it's friendship…but I just know it's more. I'm sure it's me."

Peggy sensed Julie's descent into another dark mood. She quickly grasped Julie's hand. "Now, Julie, let's not be expecting trouble for this visit before we know what's going on. I'm looking forward to meeting Rick. I thought you'd like to see Al, too. I guess it's funny to be saying, but Charlie and Al really are nice guys. And strange as it seems, I also miss the touch of a man from time to time. Forgive me?"

"Absolutely…and I do like Al and Charlie, but focusing on friendship is hard when you know what I know. I'd love to see Al…but I don't want to make a trip to La Crosse in handcuffs."

Peggy laughed. Her friend gave her a puzzled look. "I was just thinking that handcuffs might be fun. Sorry, Julie, I'm kidding!"

Peggy turned the car into the Kahn Clinic employee lot. "At break, why don't you call Al and tell him the plan? If he protests, tell him that we can get the food sent in. He and Charlie can pay."

"Oh, don't forget their friend…what's his name…Rick?"

"Yes, Rick," answered Peggy. "I have this Dr. Kildare image in my mind. What if he turns out to look like Ichabod Crane?"

Julie and Peggy broke out in laughter from this hilarious comment. Peggy was pleased her comment made Julie laugh. The things that made Julie laugh were very few these days.

"If he looks like Ichabod, I'm going to be heartbroken," admitted Peggy. "I could also use a man in my life."

CHAPTER 57

Al had just booted up his computer and begun checking his email when his phone rang.

"Hi, Al greeted the friendly voice. Al instantly recognized Rick's deep voice.

"Rick," responded Al in a joking manner, "what makes you call so bright and early?"

"It's about this Peggy…Russell, is it?" began Rick. "Alright, so you guys say she's beautiful, charming. It's pretty hard for me to believe that. I like you guys, but you're a couple of jokers. You only get serious when you two are chasing bad guys. You wouldn't be setting me up for a cruel prank, would you?"

"Not at all," assured Al in a serious tone. "Peggy is everything we told you. She's wonderful. I'm guessing she'll take your breath away. You'll be speechless."

"Speechless? That'll be a new one. I'm rarely at a loss for words. Anyway, she sounds perfect. You better not be putting me on. If you aren't, she might be just what the doctor ordered. Pun intended!"

"You're gonna be mesmerized. Maybe, though, you can stay alert enough to help," replied Al.

"You can count on me. I'm a doc. We are, as a group, serious, discerning, intelligent, observant, unerring in…"

"And ego-maniacal," interrupted Al, laughing and ending Rick's comeback.

"And ego-maniacal," echoed Rick in such a way that Al could imagine the grin on his friend's face as he said it.

The two friends chatted on for a bit. Suddenly, Al's phone beeped, signaling an incoming call.

"I've got another call, Rick, talk to you later."

Hitting the disconnect button for the call with Rick, he quickly answered the incoming call. "Rouse. How may I help you?"

"Al, it's Julie," said the woman, her voice sending a shiver through his body and putting a smile on his face.

"Now, how can I help my stunningly beautiful friend from Illinois?" asked Al, an easy but teasing tone in his voice.

"Allan Rouse, shame on you! Is a happily married man supposed to be dazzling a friend with false compliments?"

"As a matter of fact, yes. And, for the record, every word was true, even understated."

"You sure know how to flatter a girl. Is that how you schmooze all your suspects?" asked Julie.

"Suspect? Who said anything about a suspect?" asked Al. "We're just coming to Illinois to take you out to dinner to repay your hospitality. We also want to introduce your friend Peggy to a good friend of ours. Rick is a great guy. We told you about Rick, didn't we?"

"You did," assured Julie, "but does he really fly and walk on water?"

"Aw, we weren't that flattering," replied Al. "Whatever you do, don't say that to him. It will go straight to his head. You know doctors. But Rick is a regular guy. He's nice as can be and down to earth."

"Great," said Julie.

"It'll be a fun dinner. About as serious as it will get is a chat with Mrs. Wangen. We'd like to tap into her knowledge, if you think that's okay," asked Rick.

"I'm sure she'd be happy to talk," replied Julie, a bit more reassured. "She will be there. That's why I'm calling."

"You're calling to tell me Mrs. Wangen will be there?"

"No, no, we have a thought about dinner. We're wondering if you'd come back here to the house?"

Al quickly protested.

"No way are we gonna do that! We're taking you out! Our treat!"

"We just thought it might be more comfortable at our house," explained Julie. "We also knew you'd be stubborn about it so we could have food catered. You can pay."

"Better," yielded Al. "We'll go with your plan. You order food. We'll pay. We'll also handle serving *and* cleanup. Deal?"

"Deal! Anything special?"

"Rick's a typical doc. Pain in the ass. Order red meat sparingly. Go heavy on the chicken, fish, and seafood."

"That'll work. We have this great seafood restaurant. I think it does catering. How about shrimp, scallops, rice, veggies, and something light for dessert, key lime pie, maybe?"

"Sounds perfect. Make the arrangements. We'll be there after you get home. You plan the time; we're staying at our favorite home away from home, the Holiday Inn Express."

"All right; exciting!" exclaimed Julie. "We'll make the plans. See you Tuesday. Can't wait!"

The call ended. Al relaxed in his chair, thinking about Julie, her friends, his friends, and the situation—awkward, but hopefully less awkward than he feared. What really consumed Al's thoughts were Julie's parting words. *Did she really mean that she couldn't wait to see him again? Was it just the way she ends a conversation?* He sincerely hoped it was the former reason. He called Charlie and Rick to tell them the news. The three friends agreed to meet Monday for breakfast to plan their strategy for the visit. They would also have lunch together the same day to talk about the dinner and the trip.

After the calls ended, Al tackled the stack of papers in front of him, thinking it was time for him to plunge in and get it done.

***

It was a busy weekend for everyone. By mid-afternoon on Friday, Al had cleared his desk and stopped by to brief Chief Whigg, bringing him up to date on the investigation and the plan to visit the women again. His supervisor voiced his approval. "Great police work, Al. You're in charge of this one. Play it the way you want. Just be careful," advised Whigg.

"We will, Chief, we will," assured Al with more conviction than he felt. He did feel more satisfied than he had for a long time.

Almost the same conversation was occurring a couple blocks south, as Charlie was briefing Sheriff Hooper. "We think we may have it locked up next week," reported Charlie. "We might return with a suspect or two."

"That'd be wonderful," replied Hooper. "Remember, Charlie, we want to announce any developments in this case alongside Whigg and Al."

"I figured that, sheriff," agreed Charlie. "We'll make sure credit is placed where it belongs. Lots of people included. We can't forget Rick, Pat, Dr. Lee and Sarah at Gundersen."

As he turned to leave, the sheriff offered some advice.

"Remember, Charlie, don't let this friendship thing get in the way of your police work!"

"Won't happen, sheriff. Won't happen," promised Charlie.

CHAPTER 58

The weekend passed quickly. When Al, Rick, and Charlie met Monday morning at 6:30 at Ma's, each of them brimmed with ideas.

"We are going to have to play it really, really goddamn cool," said Charlie. "We don't want to frighten Genevieve off before we get the stuff we want. Any ideas?"

"I don't think the old girl is going to be hard to crack," said Al. "I think Genevieve is going to admit whatever role she played, but I think she will only do it when she's alone with us. I have a hunch there's something she knows."

"I suggest we try to isolate her in her lab with just us lawmen. Once we have her talking, we move into what we know. We should take a light touch—ease into it so we don't frighten her off. I've been brainstorming some ways to approach her. Why don't I read them out loud and explain them?"

Charlie nodded his head. Al began to read, adding comments as he went along.

Gen, you seem to know a lot about DNA. "We'll turn her answers into additional questions from there."

Since you know that, you'll understand when we tell you we found things that have us confused.

"She'll respond, I'm guessing, with something like, 'Confusing?' "

You'll take the next statement, Charlie.

"Then you say, *Gen, we found hairs on one of the victims that was a positive match.* After that comment, you will switch gears. *Let's forget that for a minute. We really want to talk to you about how the murders were done.*

You know, it just doesn't make sense that fifteen young men would walk out of a bar, no matter how drunk, and into the river. Even if they did, the water nearest some bars was only a few inches deep. That doesn't make sense.

"We will let'er think about that; we don't say a word. If she says something like, 'What do you think happened?' I'll jump in with a response."

Gen, they had to be drugged. When we figured that out, we thought about drugs that might cause that kind of reaction. My guess is she'll now be listening intently. We'll wait… and if she doesn't speak, you can continue on."

Then we got a big break. One of the Gundersen docs found a puncture wound in the latest victim's ear. They think it was made by a needle. Then the docs found traces of Etomidate. There was more, too. A few hours later, they found Etomidate had been mixed with Midazolam. The docs thought that combination would be just what a killer needed to lead her victims to death.

"And that," said Charlie, would be goddamn certain to be followed by, 'Why do you say her?'"

"We have a comeback for that.

That's because we found a few hairs on two of the bodies that came from a female.

"By then, we should have her hooked. It should be simple to reel 'er in, don't you think?"

"Fuckin' yes!" agreed Charlie. "If she's involved, we're gonna know it."

The two lawmen talked for another 30 minutes, while Rick listened intently. Never shy about eating, as Al talked, Charlie found time to push down four eggs, bacon, sausage, toast, and pancakes.

"You know, Charlie," said Rick, smiling. "From now on, it looks like we're gonna have more of these talks…just so you can eat your breakfast. You're slowin' down in your old age."

"Ease up, man" said Charlie, catching none of Rick's humor. "I had a pretty goddamn tough weekend."

"What's up? You seem down. You should be at the top of your game… ready to charge!" replied Al.

"It's Charlene," said Charlie. "She's really on a tear. I stayed in Westby all weekend. She wants me out, Al. Hell, I want out! I'm goddamn sick of it all."

"Oh, Charlie," began Al, but Charlie held up his hand to stop him.

"Actually, Al, I want out more'n she wants me out. She's been impossible for more than a year. I've slept alone more than I have slept with her. Sex is nonexistent. I've had it, goddamnit! Once we get this case over with, I'm going to get the paperwork started. It's gonna be hard, the kids'n all, but they don't like to see us fightin' all the goddamn time either, so at least they won't have to put up with it anymore."

Charlie paused for breath. Al let the silence linger for a moment. "I s'pose a certain blonde in Arlington Heights might cushion the fall?"

"Too much to hope for," responded Charlie, quickly. "But Kelly has been a pretty nice weekend fantasy. It will be good to see her."

"I understand," agreed Al. "For me, it's a bigger problem. I'm happily married. JoAnne is everything a man could ask for. She's a great cook, wonderful mother, solid homemaker, and great in the sack. She loves sex—initiates it more than I do. And it's never the same; it's always exciting."

"Stop!" demanded Charlie, "You're makin' me sick. Your home life is too perfect."

"I know, I know. JoAnne's a dream. But I can't stop thinking about Julie. I'm as anxious to see her as you are to see Kelly."

"Life sure is fuckin' complicated, ain't it? On one hand, things are great. On the other, they suck. Go figure," lamented Charlie. He pushed himself away from the table and stood up to signal he was done. "At least, we seem to be making progress on the case, right?"

"Yes. And you've been a major player," said Al, praising his crestfallen friend. "Why don't we head to work, take care of the pile of paperwork that is sure to be sitting on our desks, and then I'll pick you both up for lunch at about 11:30. Good?"

"Perfect," said Charlie, opening the door and setting the little bell hanging above it into a barrage of tinkling noises. "We might see you tomorrow, Ma," called out Charlie over his shoulder. "We're going to need real food; lots of work to do."

As the door closed almost silently but with a slight bump, all the three men heard laughter. They suspected that they had missed a pretty sharp retort from Ma.

CHAPTER 59

It was 9:00 a.m. and Peggy had been up for an hour, making a to-do list. She was on her second cup of coffee when a bleary-eyed Julie came into the kitchen.

"Is there coffee?" mumbled Julie, slumping into a chair at the table.

"I'll get it for you, honey," said Peggy, springing to her feet and heading to the cupboard to fetch a cup, filling it with strong, black coffee.

Fortified by coffee, Julie came slowly to life, eventually sitting up straight, smiling at her friend, and acknowledging a good weekend.

"We got a lot done, didn't we?"

"That we did," replied Peggy. "In fact, I think there's only one thing left to do."

"What's that?"

"Well, I've been thinking about Kelly's feelings for Charlie. I have a hunch that you may feel the same way about Al. I'm wondering if we should have a talk about how we're going to approach tomorrow. I don't want to be the wet blanket."

"What does that mean…?" asked Julie.

"Well, if I like this Rick and he puts a move on me, I don't want to do anything that is going to upset you," replied Peggy.

"I've been thinking about that, too. Al is wonderful; he's attractive. I guess you could say I have some feelings. But he's married."

"So is Charlie," reminded Peggy. "I don't think Kelly cares. In fact, she says that marriage is not happy. She thinks he'd jump at a friendly relationship with a female."

"What makes her think that?"

"She told me it's not what he's said as much as how he looks and acts. He does look at her like that; I've seen it."

"Well, you have a lot more experience than I do," said Julie, "but I think the opposite is true of Al. I think he's kind of attracted to me, but I also believe he has a very happy marriage…a wife he loves. I don't think he's gonna make a pass. I might welcome one, though; just to find out what it's like."

"If there is a pass, act on your feelings, okay? Don't hold back because of me."

"But Peggy, I love you. I don't want to make you upset. Are you sure you won't be upset? If you will be upset, please tell me. I don't want to hurt your feelings."

"Well said. My feelings towards you are at least as strong as yours towards me, but I agree with you," said Peggy. "At the same time, I don't think either one of us would do something to anger the other."

"Girlfriend, I think it's time to hit the shower or we're gonna be late to work," urged Julie. "How about joining me in the shower?"

"Um, I'd love to. That little glimpse of you through your nightgown has me excited."

Thirty minutes later, showered and glowing, the two friends talked as they dressed.

"I think we should hold a little meeting with Gen, Kelly and the kids tonight," said Peggy, "to make sure everyone knows the program. I want to be sure there are no awkward moments."

"If I didn't know you better," said Julie, grinning, "I'd think you anticipate some sort of physical experience."

"Maybe you're right," agreed Peggy.

"We'd better get a move on!" exclaimed Julie, looking at her watch. "We're gonna be late!"

"Right behind you," said Peggy as Julie headed out the door to the garage. "Let's take your car."

Later that day with the workday over and dinner served, Julie, Peggy, Genevieve and Kelly gathered around the table in the main house for Julie's spaghetti and meatballs, a tossed salad with about eight kinds of vegetables chopped finely and well mixed by Peggy, and crusty French bread contributed by Kelly. She had stopped at Andre's Bakery on her way out of work.

Talk was animated as the four women began to eat after a dinner prayer.

"I wonder," said Peggy. "Are these guys just coming back because they want to see you again?" She looked from Kelly to Julie.

"I sure hope so," said Kelly, a tinge of blush covering her face.

Julie wasn't so sure. "I'd like to think that, but I suspect they have something more to talk to me about. I'm worried, to be honest."

Julie turned to face her best friend. Peggy's face morphed from a pleasant look to an assuring one in an instant. Peggy had visited the behavioral medicine doctor at Kahn. The visit confirmed her thoughts: traumatic things can do funny things to the brain. She was sure Julie was hallucinating. She also thought a little male attention would be good for her and bring her back.

"Now, no expecting trouble without any evidence to support it," said Peggy.

Sitting quietly while eating her dinner, Genevieve suddenly looked up. "I don't think there is anything for you to worry about, Julie. I have a feeling. I think you should relax. Have a good time with that very nice boy, Al!"

"Boy?" asked Julie, a smile cracking her face. "Gen, he's a man…and a very attractive one at that!"

"That he is," agreed her older friend. "If I were you, I'd take advantage of any time you can spend with him. Let him know you like him. A woman your age needs the close friendship of a man. I know. My Henry was the best. He took care of my every need. Let me tell you, when I was your age, I had needs at least twice a day. My Henry never let me down…never!"

All the women were blushing except Gen. As Gen thought about her admission, she clarified things. "Just because I'm a dried-up old prune now, doesn't mean I was always like this."

"Gen!" said Peggy, howling with laughter. "That picture never crossed my mind."

"Well, I once was one racy lady. I was hell on wheels. Lost my virginity at age 16 and never looked back. As I think of it now, I can't believe I didn't get pregnant. We'd even sneak outside school for a little lovemaking during lunch hour. Almost got caught once by that handsome math teacher. His name was Greg Green; what a looker."

"During lunch hour?" asked Kelly. "You were screwing around during lunch hour when you were in school?"

"Well, not exactly screwing around," admitted Gen. "My boyfriend had the best fingers. He could get me purring in a couple of seconds and screaming in less than a minute. I was always ready. So was he. Whenever we found the time and a place, we made use of them."

"Now this is a new one," commented Julie. "You're a stately, cultured, well-mannered woman. Who knew you were such a sex bomb when you were in high school? What's wrong with this picture?"

"I'll tell you what's wrong with it," said Gen. "You never had it right to begin with. I can tell all of you right now, that if either Charlie or Al proposed a roll in the sack, old as I am, I'd beat them to the bed. Having to use your hand all the time is just not the same as having a good man taking care of your needs."

Julie, Peggy, and Kelly looked at each other in shock and giggled.

Gen closed her eyes, as if viewing images from the past in her mind. Kelly, Julie, and Peggy laughed softly, not wishing to interrupt the old woman's memories.

"Oh, ladies, I hope you have a love as sweet as mine and Henry's. It was the best. Even after what seems a long, long time since he died, the thought of making love to Henry causes me to tingle."

"I think we'd all love to experience that kind of love," said Kelly, expressing the feelings of the three young women.

CHAPTER 60

The next day, the sun had begun its nightly descent when the Suburban drove into Arlington Heights. It was one of those blustery, late November days, the wind brisk and the temperature plummeting by the minute promising more than just cold, windy weather.

"Feels like snow," said Al.

"Now, how the hell could you know that?" asked Charlie. "You haven't been out of the car since Madison when we stopped for a whiz. That was two hours ago."

"Boys, boys, how about both of you ease up? I can't wait to see these women we are visiting, so how about you knock off the bickering and we try to be in a good mood for dinner?" suggested Rick.

"Agreed," said Al. "Charlie, let's stop first at the motel, check in, freshen up and get ready to go. Let's see, it's about 4:15, so we have more than an hour to kill before our hosts are home. Tell you what, I'll buy us a drink in the bar while we wait."

"Goddamn, I'll vote for that!" exclaimed Charlie, stepping down on the accelerator. Both Rick and Al jerked forward a bit as the car leaped forward.

"Charlie, what the devil are you doing?" asked Rick sharply. "I can't imagine any Arlington Heights officer or an Illinois State Trooper is going to be much taken by the La Crosse Sheriff logo spread across each side of this vehicle. It wouldn't look good if we arrive home to a headline in the *Tribune* detailing the arrest of one of La Crosse County's finest in Illinois."

"Not to worry boys, I have friends all over this goddamn planet," said Charlie, smiling. "There won't be any tickets for Charlie in Arlington Heights tonight."

"You're awfully damn confident. If I were you, I wouldn't be so certain," cautioned Al.

"Okay, okay, you win. I guess I'm just a little high at the thought of seeing Kelly again. Hey, Rick, did I tell you, she likes my goddamn butt? Ain't that a kicker?"

"You've only told me about a hundred times in the last two hours. To be honest, I checked it out when we stopped in Madison. I think it's a pretty ordinary butt. Given what I saw, I'd be cautious about how much you broadcast the fact that Kelly likes your butt. I think it would reflect poorly on her taste."

"You guys are too goddamn much!" snapped Charlie. "I don't really give a damn what either one of you think. You wouldn't tell the truth, anyway. Besides, you're just jealous!"

"Dream on, big guy, dream on," said Al. "Hey Charlie, that's it on the right. You were about to drive right by the place. What the heck…"

"Just excited…just a little goddamn excited," admitted Charlie. "I'm anxious to see that blonde."

An hour and a half later, freshened and reinvigorated, the three La Crosse residents were back in the Suburban. Al was driving now.

"It's a beauty, Rick," promised Charlie. "The goddamn house is enormous and comfortable, too. The occupants, I must say, are the best part."

CHAPTER 61

"They're here!" yelled Peggy, looking out the window and over the driveway as the Suburban turned into the lot and proceeded up the hill.

"I'm so nervous," admitted Julie. "I'm just about to burst at the seams!"

"Now, dear, there's nothing to worry about," said Genevieve, patting Julie gently on the shoulder. "This is just a social call. You, my dear, are mesmerizing."

Genevieve looked Julie up and down, noticing how the scarlet dress and black high heels showed off Julie's best features.

"So are you two," said Genevieve, looking at Peggy and Kelly.

Peggy was wearing a short, black dress that fitted her gorgeously. Kelly wore a short, royal blue skirt and a lovely white blouse.

"My, all of you are so beautiful," complimented Genevieve. "If I was a young man, I'd be working mighty hard to get one of you out of your clothes and into my bed."

"Gen!" said Peggy, smiling. "Is sex all that you think about?"

"At my age and not having Henry around anymore, it's just about the only thing I enjoy thinking about," replied Genevieve. "Now, you three run along to the door and greet your guests. I'll see if the children are ready to join us."

No sooner had the doorbell rang than Julie opened it. Her eyes immediately found Al's. The warm smile betrayed her happiness of his arrival.

"Hi, Al," greeted Julie as he came across the threshold and leaned forward to hug her. As his cheek brushed hers, she looked disappointed.

"Is that the best you can do when you see an old friend?"

Before he could move or reply, she bent his head to hers and kissed him deeply, her tongue flicking across his lips.

"Mm, much better," said Julie, stepping back. "Al, that's how you are supposed to greet a friend."

"Hi, Charlie," said Julie, hugging the deputy sheriff. She paused for a moment. "You must be Rick. My goodness, is every gentleman from La Crosse as good looking as the three of you? If they are, it's not the way I remember it."

She accepted a light hug from Rick and took a large bouquet from Al, several bottles of wine from Charlie, and chocolates from Rick. She then moved to the side so Peggy and Kelly could greet the guests.

Kelly gave Charlie quite a kiss. Julie saw them, smiled and then broke it up with a joking comment.

"Hey, you guys—Peggy and Kelly—could you take a breath and help me out here? My arms are full of gifts."

"I've never seen such a large bouquet. Did the shop have any flowers left?" wondered Peggy.

Kelly chimed in. "The liquor store must have suffered a serious dent in its wine inventory. This must have a dozen bottles in it."

"This box appears to be chocolates," said Julie, nodding at the box in her hands. "Aren't these handsome men the best, girls? I think they're telling us dinner better be good."

"Oh, oh, speaking of dinner, Julie, I'd better call the caterer to let them know our guests have arrived," said Peggy.

Julie nodded and looked at the guests. "Yes, call them now. I'll help the guys open some wine. Kelly, could you make sure Genevieve knows we are getting ready to eat? Could you also check on the kids?"

"Right away," replied Kelly.

Quickly, the group opened and poured the fabulous wine. Just as everyone was settling back in the living room, Genevieve swept into the room, looking more like a queen than a widow.

"Goodness, Genevieve!" exclaimed Charlie. "I came to visit Kelly, but I just may have to ditch that idea in favor of spending the evening with you."

"Oh, you darling young man," said Genevieve, preening because of the compliment. "I think that's a great idea. You know, I bet I could show you some moves you haven't experienced before. Would you like a tune-up before dinner?"

"Gen!" said Kelly firmly, "we told you hitting on our guests was off limits!"

"Your guests? My, how possessive we get after a telephone conversation or two and two casual dinners," teased Genevieve.

As the adults talked, Kelly returned with Jake and Lauren right behind her. "Brody will be right down," said Kelly. Brody walked in right after Kelly finished that sentence.

"Hi, Mr. Rouse and Mr. Berzinski, it's good to see you again." He turned to Rick. "We haven't met. I'm Brody."

"I'm Rick. Pleased to meet you. Who are these two good-looking folks?"

"I'm Lauren Russell, Peggy's daughter. This is Jake, my younger brother."

"Only 18 months younger," said Jake indignantly.

"Lauren, Jake, and Brody, this is Dr. Olson. He is a medical doctor from La Crosse," corrected Julie.

"How about we settle on Rick," said the La Crosse doctor. "No formalities tonight. I was told this would be a casual, friendly dinner."

The doorbell rang. Peggy and Julie hurried into the kitchen to greet the caterers.

"C'mon in folks," said Julie to the man and the woman at the back door. "You can bring things in this way; the kitchen is right here." She gestured behind her and the two chefs nodded.

The young woman spoke. Her name was Marie.

"We hear this is a special evening. We have created something especially for you. Why don't you two rejoin your guests? We'll take care of the dinner. We should be ready to serve appetizers in about 20 minutes; the salads about 20 minutes after that, and the main course will be ready when we have cleared away the salad dishes. Sound good?"

"Sounds great; I'll bet it'll be good," said Julie, beaming. "If it's half as good as the food you serve in the restaurant, we'll be in heaven."

***

Soon wine and conversation were flowing freely in the living room, all seven adults and the three children participating in jokes and idle chit-chat. A jovial mood took over and led to good-spirited comments and retorts. Everyone got in at least one good dig, but Genevieve beat out everyone else. By the end of the evening, she had the three men wrapped around her fingers, praised her three younger friends with great compliments in front of their admirers, and advised the three children on interacting with authority figures.

"Now, Lauren," began Genevieve, "you know that Mr. Rouse and Mr. Berzinski are law officers. Rick is a doctor. So, if you are going to woo anyone, concentrate on Dr. Olson. He's got the bucks."

"Gen!" shouted a red-faced Peggy. "What kind of a way to treat our new guest is that? He'll think we are all shameless hussies."

"Young lady," responded Genevieve, "I want you to know that I am a shameless hussy. And I am damn proud of it."

"Gen," teased Lauren, "what is a shameless hussy? Why are you proud of being one?"

"A sham…"

"Oh, for God's sake, Gen, Lauren knows full well what a shameless hussy is. Don't humor her by responding," said Peggy.

"Well, I don't know what a shameless hussy is," said Jake. "How about tellin' me?"

"Jake," began Rick, "a shameless hussy is someone who makes young boys tingle and old men like me wish they were young and tingling."

"Now that," teased Brody, "is a tactful statement if I ever heard one. Jake, a shameless hussy is someone who gets men, young and old, in the sack and shows them a good time."

"Brody Sonoma!" exclaimed Julie. "That's enough! Stop this right now, all of you!"

"Relax, Julie," said Rick with a smile. "After all, it's my fault. I egged Jake on. Brody just saw a need to set the record straight."

Julie nodded, obviously ill at ease. An uncomfortable silence settled in.

"Hey, what is this, a goddamn wake?" cracked Charlie. "Let's have some wine…get the happy back. Want some, Jake?"

"Some of the red, Mr. Berzinski, please," said Jake, playing along and chuckling as he covered his mouth with his hand to stifle laughter.

"Jake Russell, no wine for you!" yelped Peggy. "Now all of you: stop it! You all know better."

"Yes, mom," said Jake, breaking into laughter, "but you and Julie are so fun to tease. You're always so uptight. How about lightening up and havin' some fun."

"I'm always for fun," said Genevieve. "So let's have some!"

The party was just hitting its peak, the wine erasing any awkwardness, when Marie entered, pushing a serving cart.

"Appetizers are served," announced the chef. When Marie had the attention of her guests, she explained the luxurious spread.

"Tonight, we are serving Moon Shoal Oysters from Barnstable, Massachusetts. They are known as the Bugatti of oysters. Another shellfish being served as an appetizer is diver scallops from Maine, supplied by the best seafood buyer in New York City. We have prepared them in ocean water seasoned with seaweed. We have two types of bread: a ciabatta baguette and a Pugliese Petite Boule artisan bread supplied by Pierre Trudeau in nearby Cicero. We are serving the baguette with basil-seasoned butter. The Pugliese is spread with a homemade pate. There are three cheeses on the tray: a Belleweather Farms Crème Fraiche, from California; a Humboldt Fog, a white, creamy goat's milk cheese with a thin layer and coat of vegetable ash from California as well; and an Uplands Cheese Company Pleasant Ridge Reserve extra-aged cheese. The Uplands cheese is the 2010 American Cheese Society winner for best in show, as well as a 2011 American Cheese Society winner. It is an Alpine-style cheese made in Wisconsin. Meat selections on the cart include a steak tartare, as well as creamed ham and turkey spreads. There is also a selection of olives, dried fruits and nuts. Please help yourselves."

"I'm on it!" shouted Brody, blocking Jake to keep him from getting to the serving cart first.

"Boys, boys!" shouted Peggy. "Just where are your manners? Our guests will think we have raised you as ragamuffins."

"Sorry," said Brody, obviously hurt by Peggy's reprimand. Jake was also contrite.

"Gentlemen," said Peggy, sweeping her hand toward the cart, "please lead us."

Thirty minutes later, appetites stimulated by the generous selection of appetizers and another glass of wine, the guests were summoned to the dining room by the male chef.

CHAPTER 62

Light conversation continued as the group moved to the dining room. The dining room table sparkled with fine china, crystal, and polished silver flatware. Chef Mark Andre welcomed them to the dining room and directed them to their places. Julie sat next to Al, Charlie sat beside Kelly, and Rick and Peggy were together at one end of the table. Genevieve and Brody occupied the opposite end of the table. Lauren and Jake sat across from each other, next to Peggy and Julie.

Chef Mark stepped forward, wiped his hands on his apron, positioned his chef's hat and asked for their wine preference. He had a 2009 Black Estate Chardonnay from Waipara, New Zealand or a 2010 Bruno Giacosa Roero Arneis from Piedmont, Italy. Sensing that Brody was about to speak up and order wine, Andre quickly offered another selection. "For the children, we have a choice of sparkling water or diet Coca-Cola."

Drinks served, the chef walked into the dining room to tell them the dinner menu. They would be eating giant rock lobster tails from Maine; broiled, pan-seared scallops cooked with butter and oregano; and seared Ahi tuna. The sides would be mashed parsnip and potato infused with butter, and a small bundle of bacon-wrapped asparagus.

"Man!" exclaimed Charlie, "this stuff is fit for a king. Chef Mark, do you travel?"

"For a man of your appetite, Charlie, I would be foolish to say no."

His guests were still laughing as the two chefs began to serve the main course. The plates set; the room grew quiet as everyone concentrated on the food. In fewer than 15 minutes, the plates were bare. Charlie and Brody had consumed an extra helping of each item.

"Chef Mark, you have done an awesome job. In fact, you forgot only one thing," assessed Charlie.

A disappointed look crossed the chef's face. His response was almost inaudible. "And what, Mr. Charlie, did I miss, pray tell?"

"You forgot," said Charlie in a stage whisper, "to tell us where the gas room is. The food was terrific, but I fear belches and worse might be worthy of a private place. Just in case such a place is required!"

Chef Mark smiled. "But Mr. Charlie, we did think of that. The great outdoors is fewer than 20 steps away, either via the front door or the back door. Please feel free to excuse yourself whenever it is required."

As the chef turned to depart, gales of laughter broke out again.

"And," said Rick, now fully under the wine's influence, "Charlie, don't return until all traces have vanished."

"I'd like to go right now," said Charlie. He looked around and called out toward the kitchen. "Is there anything for dessert?"

Chef Marie came into the dining room, smiling, and wiped her hands on her apron. "You didn't really think we would forget dessert?"

"Well, no, of course not," stammered Charlie, "but Kelly and I are thinking about leaving to get away from this group of critics. I sure as heck didn't want to take off until I find out what's for dessert."

"Charlie!" yelled Al.

"Trust me, Charlie, you don't want to leave. Chef Mark has prepared his internationally known Shangri la Cake. It's a wonderfully light, strawberry infused batter with light cherry filling and chiffon Brule frosting. It is to die for."

"You've sold me," said Charlie, settling back into his chair as if awaiting a prize. Soon the cake had been served and, just a wink later, the plates were as empty as before. Everyone looked uncomfortable with the rich and enormous amount of food they had eaten. Charlie rolled his eyes, patted his stomach, and announced his intentions.

"I, for one, need the private space that Chef Mark referenced. Excuse me, please, while I relieve myself of some stomach bubbles."

As Charlie walked out of the room, Al looked at Rick.

"Leave it to Charlie to walk out just when the real fun begins," said Al.

"Just what are you talking about, Al?" asked Julie, looking inquisitive.

"Well, Julie, it's nothing really, but as long as we were coming down for dinner, we thought we would mix a little business with pleasure. Charlie and I have told Rick so much about Genevieve's laboratory and her work with anesthetics that he made us promise to try and get her to show it to him. Genevieve, might you consider another tour, this time for Rick and me…and maybe Charlie, too?"

"I would love to show you three young men around," said Genevieve, looking at her three young female friends with a wide grin.

Julie, Peggy, and Kelly stood, saying that they and the children would help the chefs to clear the table and pick things up.

"That's just great!" exclaimed Genevieve.

Peggy and Julie quickly agreed to chaperone the kids, who needed to get ready for bed after helping with the dishes. Kelly decided her presence was needed in the kitchen, where the chefs and their two helpers had begun the clean-up. They said they needed some advice on the leftovers and Kelly agreed to provide it.

Genevieve led the three men out through the front door, around the path to the drive and then toward the carriage house, as she called it. Four large doors dominated the front of the building. There was a pedestrian doorway at each side of the garage.

"That door," said Genevieve, pointing to the door at the left, "leads upstairs to the three-bedroom apartment. That's where I live. This door over here leads into the main part of the carriage house and then to the laboratory."

As she walked them toward the door, she spoke.

"I am so glad we have this time alone. Truth is, it *is* a real pleasure to be alone with three young men. But I rather suspect that you have questions for me. It's just as well we keep it between the four of us, don't you agree?"

"Sure," said Al, looking at Charlie and Rick who both nodded in assent.

"Well, let's get started," said Genevieve, chuckling as she reached into her pocket, produced a key and unlocked the door. "Just let me get the lights, then you can follow me."

The lights came on. Al, Rick, and Charlie followed Genevieve, who walked beside a marvelously restored old car. The car's make and model escaped them.

She noticed the puzzled looks. "Don't feel bad; I asked my Henry over and over what kind of car it was. For your information, it's a 1929 Bentley…something they call a 4½-liter blower, whatever that means."

She suddenly twittered behind her hand. "My Henry understood that I had my needs, and pleasured me almost every day. But when he got to tinkering with this damn car, I actually had to beg from time to time."

The three men looked at each other, trying hard not to laugh.

"Oh, for goodness sake, go ahead and laugh, young men. I know you think it's funny. In the first years of our life together, we spent more time in the sack then we did anywhere else. But, unfortunately, I suspect that you did not come here to talk about my sex life."

"Here we are," said Genevieve, standing back and sweeping her arm forward, gesturing for the men to enter.

When the wall moved, Rick walked into the lab, his mouth dropping open as he entered. "My goodness, Genevieve, this is better than the one I use every day."

"Oh my, yes, it has everything…absolutely everything. When my Henry did something, he did it to perfection. My Henry was an engineer and treated everything like an engineering exercise. He had blueprints—a multitude of elaborate designs—before building began. But when it did, it was like a crusade for him until he had it done. This lab took him less than a week to put together. Of course, he had a floor plan, all drawn to scale, with every piece of furniture located in its specific spot. Then, when he began to put it together, it was just like a jigsaw puzzle."

"By the way, when my Henry finished, the lab had every medicinal chemical known to man in its cupboards and a supply of pharmaceutical books the equal of any university library in the country. The books are a little outdated now, but more than adequate for the things I do."

"So, Genevieve," began Charlie, "we would like to talk to you about the chemical traces we found on a couple of the La Crosse drowning victims and some of the DNA results that we found on some of the bodies."

"Oh young man, let's cut the Nervous Nellie crap. All four of us know that you're here because you found some evidence that has led you to me. And I certainly didn't make it hard for you to find me. So how about we make a deal? You make me a couple of promises and I will tell you anything you want to know."

"It depends upon the promises, but we can sure hear what you'd like from us," said Al, more firmness than he had intended hardening his tone.

"I am going to tell you some things you don't know, and I am going to confirm some things you think you know," explained Genevieve. "Some of this information I don't want to tell Julie, Peggy, and Kelly—at least not now."

"We can't commit to anything until we know what it is," said Al, "but we're ready to listen."

"Okay, here's one, for starters. I'm responsible for those drownings—every one of them except the first one. I'm perfectly prepared to pay for my crimes…happy to pay, in fact. To be honest, I wish Wisconsin had the death penalty. That would be better yet. I've been anxious to join my Henry for the last 16 years."

She glanced at Al and sensed his nervousness. "Go ahead and read me my rights, Mr. Al, if that's what is making you nervous. I'm not going to fight anything or protest anything, but I'm sure you want to do this by the book. After all, how many serial killers does a La Crosse cop catch in a career?"

Al pulled out his shield, turned it over and quickly read Genevieve her rights.

CHAPTER 63

"Okay, here's what I want to keep quiet: I'm Julie's aunt. I'm the much older sister of her mother. I was 20 years older, born to Julie's grandmother illegitimately and given over for adoption soon after birth. I have always known who my parents were. I was raised near them. I was grateful that they made sure I had a good life. But I was disappointed that they never told Julie's mother, Marjorie, that she had an older sister."

"I think that made me even more determined to protect my niece. When she lost her boyfriend to drowning, she was so sad and so bitter. I decided that I would avenge her pain. So I began to visit La Crosse each year to—let's say, *assist*—in a drowning. I guess you know that I used a mixture of Etomidate and Midazolam to create a certain hypnotic pliability in my victims, so I could walk them to the river and help them in without them fighting back."

"When you were here the first time, I knew you had put it together. I'd like to leave with a little of my dignity still intact. Would you help me with that?"

"It depends upon what you want, Genevieve. There are some things we won't be able to commit to, but we'll work with you," said Al.

"I'd like to spend tonight here in the apartment," said Genevieve. "That's all I really want. Tomorrow, after the women have gone to work, you can pick me up and take me back to La Crosse."

"Oh, man, Genevieve, that's impossible," began Al. "We simply can't leave you alone. It's just not possible."

"What do I have to do to convince you?" asked Genevieve, almost pleading. "It's really important. I want to leave with my dignity intact, and I can't do that if you haul me out of here in handcuffs tonight."

"How about giving us a minute?" suggested Charlie. "Maybe we can figure something out."

The three men moved to the corner and began a spirited discussion, led by Charlie. He was appealing for understanding.

"C'mon, Charlie, be realistic!" snapped Al. "Think about what it would be like if something happened…if she took her own life, or walked away! Then what?"

"I know, I know," agreed Charlie, "but she's such a nice old lady. She'll keep her word."

"Are you nuts?" said Al, almost screaming and then suddenly realizing how loud he had gotten. He reduced his voice to a whisper. "But Charlie, this 'nice old lady' just admitted to 14 killings. How many nice old ladies do you know who have killed 14 people?"

"Okay, okay," said Charlie, caving. "You're right. I just wish there was some goddamn way to help her."

Rick had been listening intently. "I have an idea. I'll bet I can find drugs in this lab that I could use to create a 10-hour knockout punch. What if I did that? Maybe we can get Genevieve to enter into a little ruse with us so we can preserve her dignity—at least for tonight. I will walk her upstairs. We'll say she felt faint, and that I came along to make sure she was all right. After she's in bed, I will go in to check on her and give her a shot. She'll be out for 10 hours; I will guarantee you that, if I can find the drugs I want. That way she'll get her way, preserve her dignity. We can say we'll come back and check on her after the girls leave for work, before we take off for home. I'll bet she'd even let us handcuff her to the bed. Whadda ya say?"

"I'm not so sure," said Al. "I'm still worried about something happening. We'd wind up looking like idiots."

"Al, goddamnit, how about seeing this from Genevieve's point of view? Why don't you cut the old gal a little slack?" asked Charlie.

"I don't like the thought of leaving her alone…just don't like it!" said Al.

Genevieve had been sitting quietly on a stool by the counter. The men turned toward her.

"Did you figure anything out?"

"We have an idea," began Rick, "but we need to see if you'll go along with it."

He explained the plan to her. She thought for a minute. "Sounds good. Let's do it!"

"Not so fast. I haven't agreed to anything," said Al.

"And why not, young man?" asked Genevieve. "I'll give you my word."

"Excuse me, Genevieve, but I'm not in the practice of putting much stock in the word of confessed murderers," said Al.

"Why won't you believe me? Didn't I just tell you what I've done? I won't be a problem; I just won't."

"I believe you, Gen, but this goddamn by-the-booker is just bein' stubborn," said Charlie.

"Well, what will it take?" asked the old lady. "Do you want to sit by my bed all night, Al?"

"Now there's an idea," said Rick. "How about we tell the women that Genevieve got very ill while showing us around. I'll offer to stay with her during the night to make sure she's all right. Will that work?"

"I hate to put you on the spot," said Al. "Maybe I should stay."

Charlie's face grew redder by the second.

"Goddamnit, Al, are you nuts? If you stay, it'll look just like what it is: a crime scene. We're sayin' she's sick. It's a helluva lot more explainable if Rick stays if he's willing. I say let him do it."

Al thought for a while, then nodded his head and reluctantly agreed. "I guess it'll work…if Rick's willing."

"Seems like it would solve everything," said Rick.

Rick then turned to Genevieve. "Why don't you help me find some of that Propofol, Midazolam, and Etomidate? I'll make you a cocktail that will guarantee you 10 hours of pleasant dreams."

Twenty minutes later, the foursome returned to the main house, joining Julie, Peggy, and Kelly for a bedtime glass of wine. The three couples disappeared to their own mysterious places, leaving Genevieve alone and smiling to herself in the living room.

After a half hour alone, Genevieve began to gasp.

"Help! Please, help," cried Genevieve.

Rick and Peggy rushed into the room. Rick knelt by the old woman to take her pulse. Al and Julie came into the room soon thereafter.

"Al, could you go out into the car and get my black medical bag?"

After conducting as thorough of an examination as the circumstances would allow, Rick announced that he thought it was an anxiety attack. He said it was more on the severe end of the scale.

"I think if I help her up to her room and, Peggy, if you help her into bed, I'll watch over her tonight. That way we'll all feel better. Al, Charlie, do you mind getting my stuff out of the hotel room in the morning? Maybe I can shower here before we head home?"

"Sure, whatever you want," said Al quickly. Charlie nodded in agreement.

Rick took his bag and helped Genevieve to her feet. With him on one side and Peggy on the other, they began to walk Genevieve toward the apartment and her bed.

After they had gotten her into bed, Rick gave her the shot and complimented her on a great acting job. He was rewarded with a smile from his patient. Rick sat in the rocker beside her bed until she fell asleep. After a while, Peggy came in and pulled a chair close to his. They talked quietly while the patient began to snore softly.

At 5:30 the next morning, Rick checked on Genevieve. She was still sleeping soundly. Not long after Peggy and Julie had left for work, Al and Charlie showed up, carrying Rick's suitcase.

"Just set it over there," suggested Rick. "I'll help Genevieve out of bed and you can sit with her while I shower."

Charlie made a pot of coffee in the kitchenette of the apartment. The two law officers and Genevieve sat at the table drinking coffee. No one had much to say. When Rick joined them, fresh from a shower, Genevieve excused herself to get ready for the trip.

Rick's cell phone rang soon after the old lady departed.

"Hi. Glad you called. Genevieve just woke up a few minutes ago. She seems to feel much better this morning."

"Rick, thank you so much for your help! Genevieve means so much to us that we just couldn't bear to have something happen to her. I also want you to know I was pleased we had those few minutes alone. I hope that I see more of you, Rick."

"I feel the same way, Peggy, and I can assure you that I do plan to see more of you." They chatted for a few more minute before Rick ended the conversation. "Al and Charlie got here a few minutes ago. We're having coffee while waiting for Genevieve to finish her shower. I want to be sure she's fine before we go."

"We'll get home from work as soon as we can to make sure Genevieve is all right. Do you think I should come home at noon to check?" asked Peggy.

"I'm sure she's going to be fine," said Rick. "No need to come home. You might give her a call, though. Thanks for everything, Peggy, I had a great time."

At 9, Genevieve emerged from the bedroom, carrying an envelope. "I wrote a little note to Julie, Peggy, and Kelly. I imagine they are going to be pretty shocked when they read it. They'll probably hate me!"

"They are going to be surprised, that's for sure," agreed Al. "Shocked, probably. But I doubt they'll hate you. It'll probably take them a while to get over the shock, but my guess is they'll understand you were only trying to help."

Genevieve went back into the bedroom to get her suitcase. Rick stood at the counter, sipping on his coffee.

"What's the matter with you?" asked Charlie.

"I'm worried to be honest," responded Rick.

"Me too," said Al. "You know, guys, we went way out on a limb for her. What if she hands us up? We'll look like keystone cops!"

Charlie grew sober. "Yea, that'd be a bitch! We'd be in a world of hurt!"

"We sure would," said Al.

"Look, I think she was very happy that we helped her out," assessed Rick. "I think if you tell her to forget last night's little accommodation, she'll do it."

Charlie and Al nodded their assent.

"Let's go," commanded Rick.

Charlie and Al gathered Genevieve's bags and loaded them into the SUV. That finished, Rick and Genevieve emerged from the carriage house. Al helped the old woman into the back seat. Charlie got in the other side and handcuffed himself to her. Al got into the driver's seat with Rick into the front passenger seat and they set off for La Crosse.

Ten minutes later, Al steered the vehicle down the on-ramp to I-90. The 300-mile journey had begun.

"Well, young men," said the old woman. "This should be another adventure!"

"Al was a little nervous about you skipping out, Genevieve," cautioned Rick.

"I knew he would be. Good for him to stew a little, but I always keep my word," chided the old woman, tapping the back of the front seat with her toe.

"Sorry for the three bags, but I thought I'd better bring some things with me. Don't imagine I'll be back. I hate to leave this place that my Henry built. But I need to pay for my crimes. So, young men, let's get going."

Twenty minutes later, the Suburban was on cruise control and heading north. Genevieve was in the back seat with Charlie. She was handcuffed, but didn't complain. In spite of the restraints, she carried on a pleasant conversation, explaining exactly what she had done and why.

"I watched Julie for years. She never knew I was watching. I knew how severely she had been affected by Mr. Sorensen's death. While Brody is a blessing, he was a constant reminder of what Julie had lost. She was a mess; I felt awful. When I caused the first drowning intentionally, it was in an effort to help her understand that she was not the only victim. It happened to others, too. After all, the victims had families. I didn't plan on more than one or two. But after the first couple, it became a passion. It made me feel good. Isn't that terrible? I wonder if I would have stopped if you hadn't come along. But I knew my time was up when I heard you had found the puncture marks. And then you showed up here."

"Do you remember the second murder, Genevieve?" asked Al.

"I remember every one, Al."

"Tell me about the second one, will you?" asked Al.

"Well, as I recall, he was a tall, dark-haired young man. I'm not very good with names. I waited for him outside an east side bar, Chub's or Chubbie's, something like that. It was so easy. He provided no resistance… just walked with me to the river, where I pushed him in, waved goodbye, and disappeared."

"How old are you, Genevieve?" asked Al.

"I will be 80 years old in a month and ten days," reported Genevieve emphatically.

"Well on some things you have an amazing memory, Genevieve," began Al, "but you don't seem to have much of a memory for the young men you killed. Tad Schwartz was the second. He was a football player at the University of Wisconsin-La Crosse. He was only five foot six, although he was definitely wide. In fact, there were no dark-haired young men among the first three, omitting Julie's boyfriend as the first. Jerry Przytarski was a freshman at Viterbo. He was the third victim. He was blonde and had a crewcut. Tedd Duncan, the fourth, was a UWL sophomore. While he might have been dark-haired, his hair was dyed platinum…almost white. How do you explain your lack of memory?"

"Oh my, Al," said Genevieve with a twitter, "regardless of how sharp you think I am, I'm an old, old lady. Surely, you don't expect me to remember in flawless detail every one of the young men I have killed, do you?"

Charlie joined the conversation.

"Gen, it's hard to believe you would forget the first couple victims. I can understand them blurring after a while, but the first couple? Not likely."

"Well, it is what it is, Charlie," said Genevieve, her voice taking on an angry tone. "I do the best I can. If that's not good enough, you'll just have to live with it."

Conversation grew sparse as the SUV sped northward, crossing the border into Wisconsin just a few minutes after noon.

"Into Wisconsin," noted Rick. "Nearer home, sweet home!"

"And a jail cell," said Genevieve flatly.

"Genevieve," said Al. "There's one little mystery we haven't cleared up. On one of the more recent bodies, we found some hairs that seem to be Brody's. Why would that be?"

"Oh, m'gosh, I don't know," confessed Genevieve. She thought for a while. "Sometimes when Julie and Brody were gone, I'd get into their apartment…just to smell them and get closer to them. Do you know what I mean?"

"Not really," said Charlie. "That seems goddamn spooky to me."

"Well, I didn't see it as spooky! They're my relatives; I wanted to be closer! I even picked up a couple of Brody's shirts, just to have something of his with me."

"So he never helped you with any of the killings?" asked Al.

Genevieve's response was instant and heated.

"Are you crazy? Involve that dear young boy in my revenge? Of course not." She sensed Al's doubt.

"Absolutely not! I may be old but I'm not crazy. I'd never ask him to do something like killing."

"I guess you've explained the hair, Genevieve, but it seems a bit odd," replied Al. "Better think about some of the things you might have overlooked."

"I might have overlooked lots of things, young man! But I did not overlook this. Brody was not involved!"

"Okay, Gen, I believe you," said Charlie soothingly. "Al's head is a little harder than mine. His head takes a lot goddamn longer to get something through it."

"Forget it," said Al. "I'm satisfied." His tone, however, suggested that he wasn't.

The next 50 miles passed in silence with everyone lost in thought. Charlie broke the silence.

"How about stopping for gas and lunch at that truck stop north of the Sun Prairie turnoff, the one after Madison? They have great hot roast beef sandwiches: two pieces of bread, mashed potatoes made from real potatoes, thick-sliced roast beef and all of it swimming in tasty gravy. What do you think?"

"I think, Charlie," said Rick, laughing, "that you are an amazing medical specimen. You eat all the wrong things, and you eat them in huge quantity. You zip through your physical exams with ease. How do you do that? What you eat would kill a normal man in less than five years."

"Genes, my friend, goddamn genes," said Charlie, smiling. "I come from sturdy Polish stock. That's my story and I'm stickin' to it."

"I get weary just hearing you describe the things you eat," said Rick, sighing.

For the next hour, the car moved along smoothly. There was little traffic. They made good time, nearing Madison at about 1:15. Fifteen minutes later, they took exit 135B to Sun Prairie and pulled into the truck stop a few seconds later.

Al parked the SUV at the gas pumps. Before anyone exited the car, there was a discussion about how they would handle the stop.

"Al, you head on in, order and eat. After I fill the truck, I'll find a parking place and when you are finished and back, Rick and I will come in to eat," suggested Charlie. "Gen, how do you want to handle eating? Do you want to go in with Al? It will have to be in handcuffs, of course."

Genevieve closed her eyes. She seemed to be deep in thought, although a smile grew across her face.

"I'm thinking about an old woman in handcuffs walking into a restaurant with a handsome young man," said Gen, opening her eyes. "That might be a fun experience. What do you say, Al? Should we give it a try?"

"If that's what you'd like, we'll give it a try," agreed Al. He opened the door on her side as Charlie unlocked the cuffs. Quickly, Genevieve was handcuffed to Al and the two walked around the vehicle and into the restaurant. While the odd couple drew some stares, the truckers took a look then returned to their food. They had seen similar things.

A half hour later after eating sandwiches, Al and his prisoner were returning to the car, while Charlie and Rick departed to eat.

CHAPTER 64

Al opened the door for Genevieve and helped her into the truck. He handcuffed her to the seat brace, closed the door and sat in the front passenger seat. Charlie would drive the last leg.

Suddenly, Genevieve grimaced and attempted to rub her left hand. She couldn't quite make it.

"Al, could you uncuff my right arm long enough to allow me to rub my left hand? I have a bad cramp and I just can't seem to touch my hands together."

"Sure," agreed Al, sensing no danger. Instead of exiting the truck, he turned in his seat and, resting on his knees, unlocked the cuffs. Genevieve rubbed her wrists to restore the circulation. She began to massage her left hand with her right. When she paused briefly, Al didn't see her twist the ring on her index finger. The next thing he felt was a sharp pain in his neck.

"Ouch!" yelped Al, grabbing for his neck. Before he could touch the spot, he began to slump forward over the seat. He was out cold.

"Oh, young man," said Genevieve to her unconscious companion. "I might be old, but I am still lethal. You won't die from the injection but you're gonna sleep for a few hours. When you wake up, I plan to be long gone. You caught your killer, but she still has things to do!"

Slipping from the back seat, she turned to pull at Al's body until he was splayed out on the back seat.

"Sleep well, young man," said Genevieve, twittering to herself. "In different times, we could have made beautiful music together. But now I must be on my way."

Closing the door, she looked across the massive expanse of concrete littered by trucks. They were everywhere, but she was looking for a specific one or at least one with three specific features: it had to be pointed south, its motor had to be running, and there had to be a way to get into the trailer. She glanced furtively around the lot, then saw what she was looking for.

A few moments later, having found a running truck with a sleeping compartment, she approached it cautiously. She couldn't believe it, but the sleeping section was at the front of the trailer rather than part of the tractor. It was even unlocked. Using nimbleness gained from her strenuous workouts, she was quickly inside the compartment and even more pleased at what she found. It was obvious the compartment had not been used as a sleeper for some time. While there was a spring attached to brackets on the wall, there was no mattress. The floor was littered with things, marking the compartment as simply a storage place.

Perfect, she thought. She found some paper to cover the rusty spring. She also put two old furniture blankets on top of the paper, and then covered that with her coat. She decided that if the compartment grew chilly, she would turn one of the blankets into a cover. Genevieve took off her suit jacket and folded it into a pillow. Looking around, she discovered that she could lock the door from the inside. Thinking that might spare her from being discovered immediately, she turned the clasp. It was unlikely, given the condition of everything, that the driver would have a key.

Soon she heard footsteps alongside the truck. The door opened, someone climbed into the cab and closed the door. No one entered the passenger side of the truck. The gears moved. The truck lurched gently and then began to move slowly.

"Goodbye, boys," said Genevieve silently to herself. She smiled and decided a nap would be good. The medication's effects from the previous evening had not yet completely worn off. Soon the whir of the wheels and the whistle of the wind flowing over the trailer lulled her to sleep as the truck rolled down I-90 toward Chicago.

Charlie and Rick came out of the restaurant. The first thing they noticed was a sleeping Al.

"Look at that, will you?" said Charlie, "Al has lunch and the first goddamn thing you know, he's taking a nap."

"Charlie, he wouldn't be sleeping on the job like this," chided Rick.

"Goddamn, you're right!" shouted Charlie, running to the car, opening the front door and shaking Al. When there was no reaction, he shook harder and harder.

"Goddamnit, Al, wake up! For Christ's sake! Wake up!"

"Better let me have a look," said Rick, sensing that something more than weariness might have affected his friend.

Grasping Rick's arm and feeling for a pulse, he sighed in relief.

"He's alive, thank God. His pulse seems normal." He pulled up Al's left eyelid and examined the pupil. "I think he's been drugged. His pupil would indicate the kind of catatonic state that an anesthetic would produce. I'm guessing if we did a blood test, we would find a mixture of Etomidate and Propofol. I suspect, given the fact that the drug was probably administered by injection during the last hour, Al is likely to be out for the next few hours. So, what do we do now?"

"Well, she couldn't have gone far," speculated Charlie. "A woman her age on foot in unfamiliar territory has gotta be in the area."

"Unless she hopped a ride?" suggested Rick.

"Now, who the hell would do that, Rick?" asked Charlie. "I can't imagine a goddamn trucker givin' a ride to an 80-year-old woman without asking a helluva lot of questions."

"Suppose you're right," agreed Rick. "We should start looking. Every minute we waste is another minute she's moving on."

"First, I have to call the Dane County sheriff and the Sun Prairie police. We're gonna need their help covering the area. We're lucky in one sense; there isn't much around here for a couple of miles. A lady as old as Genevieve has to be hiding nearby."

Twenty minutes later, the truck stop parking lot was teeming with squads. The sleek silver SUVs from Dane County with *SHERIFF* emblazoned on their sides in black letters with a white strip had arrived. Sun Prairie's black cars with bold blue stripes and *POLICE* inscribed in a white box arrived last.

Deputies and policemen gathered together. Charlie told them what he knew; starting with the fact that Genevieve had confessed to 14 La Crosse drowning deaths and was being taken from Illinois to La Crosse to be charged.

"She's almost 80," noted Charlie. "She looks it, too. But she has a spryness that's deceptive. Moving the last eight victims from a bar to the river gives you an idea of her capabilities. Don't underestimate her and don't take any chances. She's not armed. She didn't take Al's gun. She might have more drugs. If she does, she goddamn well knows how to use them."

"She's wearing a black, long-sleeved dress with blue accents on the chest. She also had a blue blazer. Jewelry was prominent but tasteful for a classy woman: a necklace with large black and blue stones and a matching bracelet. She's on foot. Her shoes weren't built for walking." He looked toward the area adjacent to the truck stop.

"The crops are out. I doubt she'd take the field. But these woods," mused Charlie, spreading his arm toward trees that came within a few yards of the concrete parking lot, "are likely where she went."

"Let's get some of you scattered around the woods; they're not too big or too dense. The rest of us can line up and do a thorough canvass of the area. We should be able to do it in two sweeps. It seems likely she went east. Let's do that section first. If we don't find her, we'll sweep the area to the north. If you walk the first leg, you'll stand the second—if we have to do a second. Everyone ready?"

One Sun Prairie officer standing at the rear of the group raised his hand.

"Has someone talked to the truckers to make certain she isn't hiding out in one of these rigs?"

"That was done," said Charlie, "while we were waiting for you to get here. Cabs, trailers, and storage compartments were inspected. There wasn't a trace."

Swiftly, the lawmen divided into two teams, half heading out in their squads to stand watch at the edge of the woods. It was agreed that three cars would be stationed outside the north area of woods, to make sure she couldn't slip out that way.

Intentionally, all the cars used sirens. The tactic was designed to get their quarry to go to ground in the woods, where they were sure to stumble across her hiding place.

Buoyed by thoughts of a quick and successful search, the lawmen left behind to make the first walk through the woods moved toward their beginning positions in small groups, chatting animatedly as they went. It was the last day of November, and it was brisk but sunny with a light wind blowing from the west.

When the groups were in place, a whistle blew. The group started moving in sync toward the trees a few hundred yards ahead. They were glad that the last hay cutting of the season had left the area between them and the trees cut short. No one could hide in the growth that was left, browned now by the wind and temperatures as winter settled over the area. The cut grass made walking easier. They thought they were close.

Back at the Suburban, a City of Madison CSI unit combed through the vehicle, looking for clues as to how the old lady escaped. Though they moved cautiously, there was little thought given to the notion that the escapee had help. The randomness of the stop and the in-transit decision about where the stop would be made pointed to a solo effort, although a ride from an unknowing trucker was a possibility. Charlie and Rick thought that chance was remote.

Inside the truck stop in a currently unused back dining room, Rick watched over Al. The officer was slumbering on a gurney. The doctor had begun an intravenous drip that would wake the detective slowly and gently.

Three hours later, the spring in their step was gone from the lawmen. The sun was now dipping beneath the horizon. The group had made two full passes through the woods. With the exception of some interesting items left behind by amorous adventurers, a few squirrels, and two skunks that caused a temporary halt until they were gone, the group had found nothing.

Now they were tired, soaked in sweat, crabby, and disgusted. As they moved to a table set up by the folks at the truck stop and stocked with coffee and pastries, the disappointment was palpable. They were quiet. Whatever discussions that did occur happened in hushed tones.

Charlie huddled with the Dane County Sheriff and Sun Prairie Chief of Police. The three officers were just as disappointed as their colleagues. The concern showed in their faces.

"I am very sorry," said Charlie. "I was certain she would have headed for the woods. Where else could she go? What trucker would pick up an old lady dressed like she was on her way to church? What kind of story would convince a trucker to give her a lift?"

"Money, maybe? Based on what you said, it doesn't sound premeditated," suggested the chief. "I doubt she could have set something up in the few minutes she had. You said you put her to sleep last night with a strong sedative and were with her until she passed out. Based on the likely time she woke up, she might have had, what, 20 minutes, in which to think of something?"

"That's about right," agreed Charlie. "We were in her apartment when she showered and dressed. She wasn't near a phone of any kind."

As Charlie got ready to talk more about the situation, a hand touched his shoulder. Turning, he saw a haggard Al with Rick. Rick's hands were on Al's shoulders as he walked behind him.

"Al!" exclaimed Charlie, breaking to a smile. "Are you okay?"

Rick looked nervous. "I gave Al permission to come out here because he was so damn unruly in the restaurant. I couldn't keep him on the gurney.

And, Charlie, you are now my back-up. He doesn't get to do anything except listen and offer opinions. Got it?"

"Got it!" replied Charlie. He looked at Al. "You'd better behave because I have a gun!"

"You're not very frightening, Charlie," muttered Al in a weak voice. "And at this point, I don't think I'm up to giving anyone trouble."

"Well, you must have given Rick a bad time. He's not very happy."

"He's a fussy old woman. Don't do this! Don't do that! I think 'don't' is the only word he knows," said Al.

"Al, he's just looking out for you," chided Charlie. "He's a good guy. You really oughta listen to him."

"Look who's making that suggestion! When have you ever listened to anyone, Charlie?"

"Listen you guys; knock it off, will you? This bickering, even if goodhearted, is not good for Al," said Rick. He noticed the grin on Charlie's face.

"And don't you dare come up with some smart-ass remark, Charlie!"

"Awww, me, Rick…how could…"

"Because you know damn well it's true. That's why I can," admonished Rick. "Now get back to work so we can find Genevieve and get home."

Turning back to the group, Charlie heard the Dane County Sheriff speak.

"I don't think finding her is going to be easy, to be honest. She's gone. I'm pretty sure she's not here. If she wasn't in the woods, and she's not inside the truck stop, she must've caught a ride out. We shouldn't dismiss the notion that she could have stowed away."

"Or," said Al, looking around, "maybe we should also be searching these silent rigs?"

"We did that while you were sleeping, Al," said Charlie. "But if she hitched a ride, how do we deal with that? If she caught a ride from a driver, he'd probably have known that there was something fishy. Maybe she paid him. We didn't search 'er because she was so cooperative."

"We made some bad mistakes," admitted Al. "By the way, did you call La Crosse to let them know what's up?"

Smacking his forehead, Charlie looked stunned.

"Goddamn! No, I didn't. I was so busy thinking about catching her and the search. I didn't give it a thought."

"I don't think we've done anything to communicate the news," said the sheriff. The chief nodded in agreement.

An hour later, a thorough second search had been conducted of every tractor and trailer. Nothing was found.

"I guess we've done all we can here," said a crestfallen Charlie. "Thanks a bunch for your help."

Charlie took Al's arm. Both of them expressed their thanks for the help.

"I think it's time to face the music. Let's call from the car," said Al.

"Good idea." Charlie's response was nearly silent.

CHAPTER 65

"This ain't gonna be pretty," commented Charlie as he sat in the driver's seat. Rick opened the door and helped Al into the place where Genevieve was seated just before she escaped. He got into the passenger seat next to Charlie.

"No, it isn't," agreed Al, slurring his words just a bit and speaking slowly, "but we'd better get it over with. An issue this big may already be circulating. If we don't let anyone in La Crosse know, they're gonna be hoppin' mad. You'd better dial either Whigg or Hooper and ask 'em to connect the other. It'll be easier to talk to both at once."

Charlie punched the numbers. The Bluetooth connection was made and soon all three could hear the phone ringing.

"La Crosse County Sheriff's Department!" boomed a female voice across the speaker.

"Hi, Sherry, it's Charlie. Is Dwight at his desk? Good. Put him on the line?"

"Hi, Charlie. We thought we'd have seen you by now. Where the heck are you?" asked the sheriff as he came on the line.

"We're just outside Sun Prairie, boss. We've got bad news. Could you connect the chief? We think we should explain to both of you at the same time."

It was obvious the sheriff wanted to know more, but he agreed to Charlie's request.

"Gi'me a second. I'll see if I can get Brent."

The line went silent for a minute. Charlie, Al, and Rick were left to their thoughts. The two lawmen were trying to figure out what they were going to say to their bosses.

"Okay, Charlie, I've got Brent on. Go ahead."

"I'm going to do the talking," said Charlie, with Al and Rick nodding. "Al has had a pretty trying day."

Suddenly, both Hooper and Whigg were talking at once.

"Sheriff, chief, this is Rick. How about letting Charlie explain? Then we'll answer questions."

When the La Crosse voices quieted, Charlie began a recap of the day's events.

"We left Arlington Heights at about 9 this morning. It was a normal drive. Genevieve—Mrs. Wangen—was talkative. She led us to believe she expected to get caught. She said she was actually relieved. We had her cuffed. Al rode in the backseat with her. Rick and I were in front."

"Near Madison, we needed gas. I was hungry. We decided to stop at the truck stop outside Sun Prairie. When we got there, I filled the truck. We pulled into a parking spot. We decided Al and Genevieve would eat. After Al and Genevieve finished, Rick and I'd eat. Al and Genevieve would wait in the truck."

"Jesus, Charlie, get to it!" urged the sheriff. "What the hell's going on?"

"After Rick and I ate, we came out. Al and Genevieve were nowhere to be seen. We looked in and saw Al on the back seat. At first, we thought he was takin' a nap. We suddenly realized the prisoner was gone. Rick looked after Al. I had a quick look around. When I didn't see the prisoner, I called Dane County's Sheriff and the Sun Prairie Police Department for help. S'pose I shoulda called you, but there was no goddamn time to think."

"There were lots of trucks scattered around—you know how damn busy it is But it seemed likely she had headed for the woods…about a 100 yards from where we parked. There was grass between the lot and the woods. The grass was cut; no one could hide there."

"We got great help. The sheriff and police were here in a flash. There must've been 50 of 'em. A couple of them helped Rick get Al into the truck stop. Madison CSI showed up to work on the car. The sheriff and chief helped me organize a search."

"We were sure a woman as old and well-dressed as Genevieve would've been conspicuous tryin' to hitch a ride. Guess we were wrong! We scoured that goddamn woods four times, back and forth. A few used condoms. A few squirrels. Two skunks, both of them now dead. No Genevieve. Not even a piece of cloth…or a hanky…nothing."

"We called it off about 10 minutes ago. We then realized we'd forgotten to call. We feel terrible."

"We'll deal with that later," responded Hooper. "Anything else?"

"Not a goddamn thing!" admitted Charlie.

"And Al? What's his condition?" asked Whigg.

"I'm fine, chief."

"He's not fine," said Rick, jumping in. "I think he was injected with the same drugs Genevieve used on her victims. We're lucky she's skilled. A little too much of the drug—likely a mix of Etomidate and Propofol—and Al would be history. But she knows what she's doing. I think she had no intention of killing him. I think she wanted to put him out long enough to escape."

As Rick finished, there was silence. When no one had said anything for almost a minute, Charlie asked the bosses a question.

"Whadda you want us to do? We could hang around here. But based on the search, we think she took off in a truck or car, prob'ly a goddamn truck. I'm guessin' she stowed away. Rick says Al needs further treatment and can travel. When we get home, Rick's gonna admit him and rinse his system."

"I guess," began Whigg slowly, "there isn't much that you can do there. Without an idea of where she went, we've nowhere to go. Can't stop every semi on I-90. C'mon home so Al can get what he needs here."

"Agreed," chimed in Hooper. "Wrap up whatever you have to do and head home. This is a kick in the nuts, Charlie and Al. There's no way you should have left her with a single man. You know that, both of you. What the hell were you thinking?"

"Sheriff, we all feel like hell. We know we screwed up and we're willing to turn in our badges, if that's what you want. She was so damn cooperative that she just lulled us, I guess," lamented Charlie.

Whigg broke in.

"She's an old lady. Sounds like, with the exception of the single guard, you played it straight up! Prob'ly relaxed a little too much, though. But anyone might've done that, given the circumstances. The main thing now is for you boys to get on home. Get Al to the hospital. When he's ready, we'll get together for the debrief. But for now, what has been done?"

"Sun Prairie and Madison have put out an all-points bulletin directed at truckers, asking them to be on the lookout. I think we have done all we can to get the news out," said Charlie. "We feel like crap. We know we let you down."

"What we need now is for both you boys to get back here, get some rest and then get back on the search," said Hooper. "If I were there, I'd be kicking your ass, Charlie. But that wouldn't do much good now that she's gone. Let's concentrate on getting her back in custody! No sense in crying over spilt milk. What's happened has happened!"

"Absolutely," agreed Whigg. "We'll catch 'er. My guess is when we do, it'll be because of you boys and your knowledge."

The conversation ended. Charlie looked at Al and grimaced.

"Goddamn, did they really say that? Somehow they aren't blaming us, or at least we aren't in the doghouse in a major way."

"They're pissed, that's for sure," said Al in a lazy voice from the back. "And they should be. What good would reaming our asses do? What's done is done. I'll get mine later from the chief, but right now he's thinkin' about getting her back."

"C'mon, Al, ease up on yourself. Wasn't your goddamn fault. Wonder where she had those goddamn drugs."

"She was twisting her ring. Wonder if that was it?" suggested Al.

"It's not hard to believe that she'd have some drugs stashed away," mused Rick. "You did everything right. We just continued a pattern that begun 14 years ago. We underestimated the old gal, as I'm guessing people have for years. Much as I despise her for what she's done, I'm kind of amazed. She's one calculating old lady. She admits to killing 14 men. We should have been a hell of a more vigilant!"

"God, yes," agreed Al, leaning over. "You're gonna have to handle the drivin.' I'm not up to much except sleepin'."

"How about," suggested Charlie, "you get your ass back into the seat? Stretch out and take a nap. There's a quilt and pillow in back. I'll grab that. We'll make you as snug as a bug in a rug."

Al comfortably encased in his wooly cocoon and nearly asleep, Charlie guided the Suburban out of the truck stop and back onto I-90, heading north.

CHAPTER 66

While Charlie, Rick, and Al were finishing things up in Sun Prairie, Genevieve slept soundly as the trailer passed through Merrillville, Indiana, and turned from I-90 East onto I-65 South. She had fought to stay awake as her unknowing chauffeur moved her ever farther away from Sun Prairie, Arlington Heights, and her former home on North Kennicott. The whir of the tires had been too much to withstand in her sleepy state. As the big rig rattled its way down the freeway, she closed her eyes and was soon sound asleep. Although she snored gently, her driver had no idea that she was there. The sounds of the truck masked any sounds coming from the cabin in the front of the trailer.

Not long after the La Crosse trio began the journey back home to La Crosse two hours after the escape, Peggy and Julie arrived home. Driving into the garage, Peggy looked at her companion.

"I don't know about you, but I definitely need a glass of wine. How about we have one? Then we can talk about dinner."

"Sounds great! I'm not even going to go upstairs," said Julie. "We can call Genevieve, in case she wants to come over."

The two women headed up to the house. Once inside the warm, cozy home and their coats shed, Peggy went straight for the wine. Julie walked upstairs to check on the children. Peggy called Genevieve. She let it ring until the answering machine clicked in.

Three hours later, having consumed several glasses of wine and a barbecued chicken dinner prepared by Julie, Peggy decided to check on Genevieve. She wearily climbed the steps to the apartment. When she tried earlier, she assumed that the older lady was out with friends. Genevieve did that frequently. Peggy was surprised, though, when she opened the door to the apartment and found it shrouded in darkness.

Typically, if Genevieve was going to be out late, she always left a light on. Peggy, exhausted by the stress of a busy day at work and the wine, didn't see the envelope on the counter next to the fridge.

Peggy decided to leave the light on for her elderly friend, and then stumbled downstairs. Twenty minutes later, after removing her makeup and changing into her nightshirt, she tumbled into bed. Sleep came immediately.

Long before Peggy awakened in the morning, on a freeway 180 miles south, Genevieve was shaken awake by new sounds. The truck had slowed. It was obvious that the driver was backing up. Although she heard the roar of the motor, she also heard another sound: the squeaks associated with someone turning a crank. *I wonder*, she thought to herself, *if the driver is dropping the trailer? If he is, where is he dropping it? Nothing I can do about it*, she thought. *I'll just wait it out.*

Three hours later, she had not heard a sound. She figured it was probably safe by now. Genevieve moved cautiously from the bed area, crept to the door, and gently turned the lock. Pushing gingerly on the door, she opened it just a crack. She saw nothing. Everything was shrouded in inky blackness.

Hearing and seeing nothing, she pushed the door open. She could see nothing past 10 feet away from the truck. *This may be good*, she thought, *because if I can't see anything, I can't be seen—especially in my black dress.* Growing more confident, she sat on the edge of the compartment, legs dangling. In order to enter the compartment, one had to step on the wheel hub and then the top of the tire before crawling into the sleeping area. Now there was no tire or wheel hub. The tractor was gone.

The woman was not fazed by this stroke of bad luck. Now, it was time to do a quick search around the compartment. While the search turned up a number of grimy, oily rags, there was also a working flashlight. She smiled to herself. Feeling much more confident, she moved back the door to the compartment and jumped down. Now came the tricky part: She had to figure out where to go next.

She made her way toward a very dim light. The surrounding area appeared to be a freight yard for a trucking company. Suddenly, a small, low wattage bulb appeared beneath a meager tin shade. She looked down at her clothes. They were much the worse for wear. *How could she continue her escape looking like such a mess?*

It was time to put first things first. Noticing a loading dock off to her left, she moved toward it, stopping behind a trailer to make sure there was no night watchman. After watching carefully for an hour, she turned the flashlight on, shielding it from the dock area. She looked down at her watch. *3:05 a.m.* Plenty of time to kill.

Genevieve decided the dock offered the best possible shelter, so she walked there. Using the flashlight carefully, she noticed three stacks of boxes. They were positioned in such a way that someone could squeeze behind the second stack and be shielded from view by the other containers.

She squeezed her way behind the boxes, pulled over a container, and sat on it. Realizing she could arrange her shelter into an area with a backrest, she pulled the box over, made a few minor adjustments in its position, and settled down to wait for dawn.

***

In Arlington Heights, Julie rested in Peggy's arms. She was thinking about Al and wondering why he, Charlie, and Rick had come to Illinois again. *Was it just to see us? The only thing that vaguely resembled business was the tour of Genevieve's laboratory.* She surely wasn't disappointed that Al had returned. She definitely had enjoyed the 30-minute rendezvous following dinner. Although Al was cautious, they had both agreed that they loved seeing each other again, as crazy as it sounded. They also found themselves attracted to each other. Just before he left for the lab tour, he kissed her like she hadn't been kissed since Shawn. Her toes tingled and her body quivered. It took only one kiss!

It seemed that Peggy had a great time with Rick, too. He was, of course, reserved, as Peggy had reported, but the conversation seemed destined to lead to something more.

"He's wonderful…good looking, intelligent, interesting, and, I think, interested," remarked Peggy before going to sleep. "I just wish La Crosse wasn't so far away. I'd like to see more of him."

As the women talked, Peggy reached down and kissed Julie. Julie's fingers reached down to a hairy place that was already moist. It didn't take long before Peggy was squirming.

For at least 20 minutes, the two women used tongues and fingers to pleasure each other, bringing each other close and then backing off. The fifth time was the charm. Julie gasped.

"Peggy, I just can't wait any longer!"

Peggy let herself go too, reaching orgasm shortly after Julie.

"Oh, my god," whispered Peggy, breathing hard, "that was wonderful!"

Julie, her breath coming in short gasps, finally managed to speak. Oh, Peggy!"

She snuggled into the crook of Peggy's arm and kissed her tenderly before rolling over. Even though she was totally fatigued, sleep just wouldn't come. Julie heard the clock chime every hour. At four, she finally gave up, rolled out of bed, and headed for the shower. As she soaked under the hot spray, scrubbing her body briskly, she thought about how much she missed a man. It was such a surprising thought. Even though she was very inexperienced, Julie remembered fondly the few times she and Shawn had made love: the magic of it, and the incredible feelings. It was sensational.

These thoughts made her feel restless. She grabbed the hand-held shower and directed the spray to the most effective place. It wasn't as intense as the feelings with Peggy, but it was just right for the morning—a soft, gentle release that left her satisfied with a pleasant tingle. *That will get me through the day nicely.*

After toweling off, she slipped into her underwear, applied her makeup, put on a robe, and walked down the steps to the kitchen to put the coffee on. Ten minutes later, her Keurig dispensed a great-smelling cup of hazelnut coffee. The Danish pastry, fresh from the microwave, added whiffs of raspberry to the air.

She retrieved the *Chicago Tribune* from the back steps and settled down to spend some time alone, satisfied and happy.

As she was diving into the paper, Peggy walked in, rubbing her hair against a towel to dry it. "Mm, that smells great," said Peggy. "I need a cup to wake up."

"The Keurig's on; I left it for you," responded Julie. "There's a Danish or two in the cupboard. Help yourself."

"I wonder about Genevieve," said Peggy. "It's not like her to miss dinner and breakfast. You haven't seen her, have you?"

"Nope, not a sighting," said Julie.

Peggy, looking worried, set her cup on the counter and put down the plate holding a Danish.

"I think before I heat this up, I'll take another look." Peggy walked off, left the kitchen, and headed toward the carriage house.

Just as Julie was turning to the neighborhood section of the paper, there was a sudden, frantic banging on the backdoor. Peggy's shouts were incomprehensible.

"Coming!" shouted Julie, heading onto the back porch.

Peggy wrenched the door open. She looked like she'd seen a ghost.

"What is it Peggy; what's wrong?" asked Julie.

"It's Genevieve," began Peggy, sobbing. "Julie, she left this for us. She's been arrested and is on the way to La Crosse with Charlie, Al, and Rick. Here, you read it; I'm too upset to concentrate."

Julie took the paper, opened it and began to read.

Dearest Julie, Peggy and Kelly,

What I have to tell you is going to shock you, but I am asking in advance that you read this letter thoroughly and think about it before reacting.

I figured when Al, Charlie, and Rick scheduled a trip back so soon that they planned on questioning me about the drownings in La Crosse. I have been expecting such a visit for several years. You see, I am responsible for those drownings, and, although I knew when I killed my first victim that it wasn't right, I just couldn't stop. But let me tell you why.

Julie, dear, you are my niece. Your mother and I are sisters. I am much older than she is. Our mother and father had me while they were still in high school. In those days, having children before marriage and before graduating from high school was nearly a mortal sin. Since neither of my parents was capable of raising a baby, still children themselves, I was sent to live with a sister of my father in eastern Wisconsin. Your mother and I saw each other once—at a family reunion. Neither of us knew then that we were sisters. We only knew we were relatives. It was later that my "mother"—or the only person I ever knew as "mother"—told me that she was really my aunt. I also knew that she had raised me and loved me as her own. When she told me the whole story, I knew I wanted to know more about my family, but I also knew that I didn't want to create a situation that would be awkward or, worse, problematic. So I grew up with my real family at a distance. I then moved to western Wisconsin. I lived near enough to Alma, in Bay City, to make numerous trips downriver to "spy" on you, Julie, and your family. I learned everything I could about all of you, but I fell in love with you, Julie, because you were a very good girl, faithful to your parents and your values.

When you moved to La Crosse to go to college, I moved too. I began to work at the Cass Street pharmacy. I watched you from afar, completely moved by your devotion to your classes and your work. I rejoiced when you met Shawn. I thought true love would be a gift to you, one that would make your life complete. I grieved with you when Shawn drowned, and, of course, I was there. Your grief triggered the revenge killings. In my love for you, I wanted to make up, in some way, somehow, for the loss you had suffered. I watched as you grieved. I felt your pain and knew that you hungered for revenge. I was also there when that emotion boiled over and you became such a bitter person. I had to help you. So, I began taking one life each autumn to try to avenge the love that you lost. I rejoiced when I could tell that you were happy when each death occurred.

When I met and married my Henry and we moved to Illinois, I still made a trip back to La Crosse each year to continue my vengeance. As I did that, I knew with each death that I was closer to being caught. And after my Henry died, I really didn't care what happened to me. I felt as I think you felt when you lost Shawn.

I'm sure that you, by now, are confused, because you believed I had lived here for ages, raising several kids and caring for Henry. In truth, I lived here only for seven years. I was Henry's second wife, and the children he had by his first marriage became my children, although they were gone and much too grown up and busy to care much about me or Henry. In fact, they probably resented me living in their late mother's home. But I was very happy with my Henry. Our love was deep and true, and when he left me, it was much too soon.

I am writing this letter to explain, in part, why I wanted you to have this house. Now that I will likely never see it again, it will make me happy, wherever I spend my last days, to know that you are comfortable here.

It is my hope that all of you will forgive me for what I have done. Julie, in many ways, I did these things to help you out. Although you may not fully understand now, please know that as your aunt, I felt a special kinship to you and a special need to help out.

I suspect all of you will be horrified at the notion that an old woman could do these nasty things. Please, don't think of me as an old woman. Please think of me as someone who wanted to help—particularly Julie, but also Peggy and Kelly, too.

I only wish that I had more time to spend with you. I want you to know that you made an old woman happy in the few days we have known each other. Where I am going, I will have lots of time to think about what I have done. I hope this house makes you happy, and that you will live here many years. I hope when you have to leave it, that you will remember what I have done for you and help someone else.

If you can forgive an old lady, I hope that someday we might see each other again; although I imagine that will be at whatever prison they put me in to live out my final days.

Well, I suspect Al, Charlie and Rick will want to leave soon. I shall look forward to spending a few hours with them. I am sure that I can handle whatever comes after that.

What wonderful memories you have given me to remember you by.

With fondest best wishes and sincere love,

Genevieve

Her hands trembling, Julie slumped into the chair by the table. She bent her head and, after a few seconds, began sobbing softly.

"I know how you must feel, Julie," said Peggy, soothingly, "but it's apparent that she loved you very much."

"Who loved who?" asked Lauren as she walked into the room.

"Genevieve left us a letter," said Peggy softly, retrieving the piece of paper and handing it to Lauren. "It explains a number of things and reveals some astounding things about the old woman, too."

Lauren took the sheet and began to study it intently. With Julie still crying, Peggy watched the changing expressions on Lauren's face.

When she was finished, she sat down next to Julie and put her head in her hands.

Finally, after minutes of silence, Peggy spoke.

"I hate to break this up, but we have jobs to get to. We are going in, aren't we?"

"I just don't know if I can," said Julie. "But what will I do if I stay here? All I would see are ghosts…of Shawn…of the other victims…of Genevieve. I just don't know what to do."

"Tell you what, come with me. We can talk with Dr. Swenson. He's a great psychologist. I'll bet he will know exactly what to do. I'll be back in a bit," said Peggy.

When Peggy returned, she had news. She had reached Dr. Swenson, and he would be happy to talk to Julie when she got in.

"I also called Kelly," said Peggy. "She's going to cover for you until we know what Dr. Swenson suggests. I doubt they are going to expect you to work, but I don't know that for sure."

When her friend had left the room, Julie became lost in thought. Obviously, Genevieve had taken steps to make sure she was discovered as the La Crosse serial killer. *How had she known? What would cause someone she had never met to give her this kind of gift? It was a true gift. Is that how she should treat it? What should she do? What could she do?*

CHAPTER 67

As the sun began to rise, spreading its light across the truck lot and the dock area, Genevieve stirred in her hiding place. Looking at her watch, she saw that it was 6:16. *Time to get moving.* Standing up, she smoothed her clothing and then her hair, making sure she had left nothing behind. When she was satisfied, she moved the boxes back where she found them. After a final look around, everything was in order. Genevieve walked down the steps and out of the yard.

As she looked right and left, she saw lights to her right, but a long way off in the distance. *No problem, the walk will do me good. I just pray I find a place with a washroom so I can clean up a bit.*

Nearly an hour later, she found what she was looking for. *Pak-A-Sak.* The sign's lights were continuously blinking: *The Place to Go For All Your Convenience Needs. Snacks, Beverages, Gas, Oil.*

Perfect, just what I need. I can slip in there, use the restroom, freshen up, and buy some things to eat. Her stomach felt hollow. Genevieve realized she had only consumed half a bagel and a light lunch, and that was the day before, the day she escaped.

Cautiously, she approached the store, smoothed her hair and dress again and walked in. A bell tinkled. The young man behind the counter greeted her as she entered. Given the clerk's appearance, sleepy and disinterested, Genevieve doubted if he'd pay her any attention.

She asked for directions to the restroom. The clerk lazily raised his arm and pointed to the rear of the store.

"It's all the way back and to your right. You'll see the signs."

When she walked into the restroom, she was grateful to see that the Pak-A-Sak store was definitely set up for truckers. The room was spotless. Large sinks gleamed in the light. She washed as extensively as she was able and fixed her hair the best she could. She knew what she had to do and was anxious to do it.

With that in mind, she approached the clerk, picking up food items as she went. She deposited them at the counter.

"One more thing, dear," asked Genevieve. "Where's the coffee?"

"If you want a cup, it's right over there," said the clerk, pointing. "Since you've paid me already, if you drink it black it's on the house. If you use cream, the owners say I have to charge."

"I'll be drinking it black, dear," replied Genevieve. "You're very kind. Thank you!"

Genevieve poured her coffee from a large coffee pot, picked up her bag of snacks, and went outside to sit on a nearby picnic table to eat her breakfast. A bag of powdered doughnuts and two snowballs made her feel better. The coffee really hit the spot. By now, it was a few minutes before 8. She stepped back into the store and asked the clerk to either call her a cab or give her a number to call.

"I'll have one here in a minute," said the clerk. True to the clerk's promise, a black and white taxi pulled up in just a couple of minutes. The driver, a friendly looking black man, hopped out of the cab to open the door for Genevieve.

"Where to today?" asked the cab driver.

"Young man, I would like to buy a car. Not a new car. But I do want a good used car from a reliable dealer. Do you know anyone like that?"

"I do," said the cabbie. "I buy all my cars from a Tom Wood dealership here, and there is one just a few miles from here. I'll have you there in a minute."

The driver pulled the cab into the dealership in about five minutes. Genevieve counted out the $5.65 fare, but changed her mind. She pulled out a ten and gave it to him.

"Thank you very much, young man, you've been very helpful. I expect to buy a car here, so there's no need to hang around," said Genevieve.

"Thank you, ma'am, and good luck," replied the cabbie. The cab turned and sped out of the lot.

Genevieve walked into the dealership and saw several cars that she liked. Henry always told her that the key to buying a car was to get a make and model that had a reputation for being good. She thought that she'd look for a Chrysler to honor Henry.

"Good morning, mam," said a salesman. "How can I help you this morning?"

"Young man, I'm from Illinois," explained Genevieve, "and I've come here to buy a good used car."

"Any particular make or model?" asked the salesman.

"I'd really like a Chrysler product," said Genevieve. "My late husband worked for Chrysler for years and years before he retired. He passed away just two years ago."

"You're in luck. I have a great 2014 Dodge Charger. It's a two door, but it's a great car and I can make you a really good deal."

The salesman walked her into the lot and down a line of cars until he came to a jet black Charger.

"It looks great! What's the price?" asked Genevieve.

"I could put you in this vehicle for $16,500, and we'll do the financing ourselves. How does that sound?"

"Actually, I'm paying cash," said Genevieve. "Will that make any difference?"

"Well…I can probably get the sales manager to knock off $500 for cash."

"How quickly can I have all the details done so I can get on my way?"

"I think we could wrap up the paperwork in about two hours. The biggest deal will be the license plates. Are you going to get Illinois plates?"

"No, I think I'll wait until I get to Texas. Can I do that?"

"We can put a 'license-ordered' tag on the car. That will be good for two months, I think."

"That will be great; plenty of time," responded Genevieve.

Two hours later, Genevieve steered the freshly washed Charger out of the lot and headed for Dallas. After driving out of the lot, she programmed her GPS to take her to Dallas via the backroads, where she thought she would be less conspicuous. By early afternoon, she had turned off I-70 at Terre Haute and was traveling down Highway 36 toward Evansville. She decided that if any road was boring, she'd find another. If she didn't know where she was, neither would anyone else.

Genevieve knew the authorities would have put out an all-points bulletin. They would find out about the auto purchase eventually, so she planned to dump the Charger in Evansville. *I'll find a seedy dealership, and buy something reasonable and nondescript.* She would drive that car a few hundred miles and trade it again. While that was happening, she would make a decision on where she'd end her trip.

CHAPTER 68

In La Crosse, the scene at police headquarters was chaotic. Sheriff Hooper, Chief Whigg, Charlie, Al, and Rick were locked in a conference room, maps spread on the table as they talked animatedly about what to do.

"Well, one thing is certain," said the chief. "We can't keep this under wraps. We need the help of police forces from here to the Gulf, Atlantic and Pacific. We need the public to be watchful, too. We're going to have to hold a news conference."

He noticed the sour look on his detective's face.

"Al, it's not your fault. How could you know the old lady would have a concealed sedative? You guys played it right. Sometimes things done right can go wrong."

"I just feel as if I let everyone down," said Al. "I'm supposed to be smart enough to know not to turn my back on a suspect, no matter how old or how docile."

"It is not your fault," replied Charlie's. "If either Rick or I had been in your position, the same thing would have happened. Let's let go of the guilt and get on with trying to find the old girl."

As the five people stared at the map, Charlie slapped his forehead.

"What?" asked Hooper.

"We need to call Peggy, Julie, and Kelly!" said Charlie, nearly shouting. "We should have done that a long, long time ago."

"You're right, absolutely right," agreed Al. He turned to Rick. "Have you still got Peggy's cell number?"

"I do," said Rick, checking his phone for the number. He handed the cell to Charlie.

Fifteen minutes later, Charlie was disappointed. It had been great to talk to Peggy, but she and her friends swore that they knew nothing about Genevieve's whereabouts. Peggy read the letter to him out loud. Charlie, by then, had the group in La Crosse on the speaker phone, so everyone could hear and be heard. Peggy had her speaker phone on too.

"We were shocked when we read the letter this morning," said Peggy.

"Shocked? That's an understatement," quipped Julie. "There's no one in the world who would believe someone as kindly as Genevieve could be a serial killer. To be honest, I still can't think of her in that way; it's just not possible."

"She has been so very nice and accommodating," chimed in Peggy. "Do you guys really believe she's the killer? Doesn't it seem strange that someone of her age and size could wrestle guys into the river?"

"Ms. Russell, this is Brent Whigg, the La Crosse Police Chief. I agree with you; it seems very unusual, but unusual things happen all the time in our world. We have our questions, certainly, and had we gotten her back here, we would have begun a thorough vetting process. It would have included a polygraph test, better known as a lie detector. So we do have questions, but until we have her, we won't be able to come to any conclusions."

"Please, please call me Peggy. This seems so formal; it's kinda spooky."

"Peggy, this is Sheriff Dwight Hooper. While we agree with the chief, all we really have to go on is what Mrs. Wangen told Deputy Berzinski, Detective Rouse, and Doctor Olson. They insist that they found her confession credible. So we have questions, but the deputy and detective are trained law enforcement officers."

"That's not to say we always get it right," broke in Al. "But the chief and sheriff are correct; we usually do get it right. Hard as it is to consider Genevieve a serial killer, stranger things have happened. We have doubts, sure, but until we have her back in custody, there isn't one thing we can do about it. That's why if you know anything, no matter how small or seemingly unimportant or unrelated, please let us know. It may be very helpful."

"Would you send us copy of the letter?" asked Charlie. "The original would be better...for fingerprints and such. If you have any photos of Genevieve, would you scan them and send them along?"

"Peggy and I have some pictures, but giving them to you would feel like we'd be accusing Gen of being guilty," said Julie.

"Julie, you do want us to find her, don't you? Even if she's not guilty, it would be nice to know she's okay, wouldn't it?" asked Al.

"I…guess…so," replied Julie. "I guess when you put it that way; it seems like the right thing to do. I can fax them to you. Is that okay?"

"That would be perfect," replied Al.

"I can't do it until I get to work. Is that soon enough?"

"Just fine," replied Al.

"This still makes me feel disloyal to Genevieve. It just does!"

"But Julie," said Sheriff Hooper, cutting in, "you do want us to catch the killer, don't you?"

The statement hung in the air until Peggy's voice came across the speaker.

"Of course we want the killer caught. We just don't think its Genevieve. She's just a very nice, very kind elderly lady."

"How do you explain the escape?" asked the chief. "Doesn't it seem odd that someone who had confessed, took advantage of an opportunity, drugged a police officer and escaped?"

"Yes," agreed Kelly. The voices of the other women could be heard in the background. "But the notion of Gen as a killer just seems odd."

"Until we have her back," broke in Al, "we won't be able to get answers to the questions all of us have, Kelly. Please help us; the photos are the key. Julie, we're gonna have a unit from the Illinois Bureau of Investigation over there shortly to go through the apartment. Please be helpful and let them in. They will have a warrant, allowing the search."

"Of course, if I have to let them in, I will," said Peggy.

"That will be helpful," commented Charlie. "They know that we want them to be as unobtrusive as possible, but you can keep an eye on them. It probably will be best to stay there during the search. I'm sure they will be there for quite a while. If you need something from the apartment, wait until they are there, okay?"

"I guess so," said Peggy.

The officers hung up the phone and got back to work. Julie and Peggy drove to work, where the day passed with agonizing slowness. Julie spent most of the day with the psychologist, who tried to help her work through what had just happened. She didn't say a word about her perceived role in the killings.

The workday finally finished, the two women drove home together. Peggy began dinner, suggesting Julie take a nap before eating. After getting things out for dinner and checking on Julie, Peggy decided to go to the apartment to wait for the crime lab folks. Just as she prepared to leave, Brody and Jake came into the kitchen.

Jake was hungry. "What's for supper, Mom, and when are we eating?"

"Jake, …Brody" began Peggy, "we'll think about dinner in a minute! But right now, please sit down. I have something to tell you."

As Peggy was finding a seat at the table, Julie walked into the kitchen.

"Is Lauren upstairs? She already knows, but I'd like to have her here," said Julie. Brody said that she was upstairs. Peggy suggested Brody get her, so they could talk to all of them at the same time.

Soon all three children were sitting around the kitchen table with Julie and Peggy.

"We have some very bad news," began Peggy. "And you are going to have trouble understanding it. We talked to Al, Charlie, and Rick. They called to tell us that they had arrested Genevieve in the drowning deaths of a number of young men in La Crosse."

As Peggy explained what they had been told, Julie began to sob. The looks on the faces of Brody, Jake, and Lauren showed more and more confusion and sorrow. When Peggy finished, Lauren looked up and said what was on all their minds.

"I don't believe it! Genevieve is wonderful! She loves us and I love her, too. There's no way she'd do this…no way! I've been thinking about it all day…since you let me read the letter this morning. I just don't believe she did it!"

"We agree," said Peggy, "but until they find her and have a chance to question her, there isn't going to be any change in how they think. And right now, they think she's guilty."

"But, mom, that's crazy," said Jake, "Genevieve is the kindest, nicest person I know."

"Yes, she is, Jake," said Peggy, soothingly. "But we have to help the police get her back so that can be proved, okay?"

"I s'pose," said Jake.

A moment later, Brody commented on the status of dinner.

"Mom, I'm really hungry."

"We'll eat in a little while," said Julie. "First, I have to fax a letter from Genevieve to Al and Charlie. We have to scan some photos and send those, too. Peggy is going over to meet some Illinois cops. They are going to search the apartment and lab. As soon as that's done, we'll have dinner. Okay?"

"I guess," said Brody. "What are we havin'?"

"How about burgers and fries?" asked Peggy.

The kids nodded.

"Good, then I'll get going right now while Julie is taking care of the things our police friends need. We're also waiting for Kelly. We asked her to join us. She's a good friend. We told her what's going on."

CHAPTER 69

"All right, fellas, let's get the news conference planned and get out of here," grunted the chief.

The other three men nodded. Whigg went to the white board and picked up a marker.

"Okay, help me out here," said Whigg. He began writing out the plan.

Background—Sheriff Hooper
DNA Information—Rick
Arrest—Al
Trip Home—Charlie
The Escape—Al
Next Steps—Chief Whigg
How You Can Help—Sheriff Hooper
Questions—Chief Whigg to delegate

"How does that look?" asked Whigg.

"I think that about covers it," said Hooper.

"Is this how we want to divide this up?" asked Al.

"I think we have to find some background to provide context," said Hooper. "Chief, I think you should handle that piece."

The lawmen, plus Rick, worked diligently for the next half hour. One by one, they delegated the responsibilities.

Once they decided all the assignments, Whigg talked to the public information officer to get the word out to the media: news conference at 8 a.m. the next day. When that was done, the group worked for another 45 minutes, doing a kind of mock rehearsal and critiquing each other as they went.

It was after 8 p.m. when Al, Charlie, and Rick left together. The chief and sheriff stayed behind to talk some more

Al was down; that much was obvious.

"C'mon, Al, get your dobber up," urged Charlie. "You didn't do anything wrong. Nobody blames you, either. You gotta shake it off, goddamnit! We need you on this. If all you do is mope around, you're gonna be for shit."

Rick looked at Al.

"Al, it isn't your fault. Charlie's right, you've gotta shake it off. We need you…"

"To be honest, I feel like shit. It has nothing to do with the drugs. It's the horrible knowledge that I let all of you down. I did it! I am responsible for a serial killer being on the loose. How do you think that makes me feel?"

"Goddamnit, Al, it ain't your fault! Let's just get on with getting' her back," said Charlie. "We're all going to feel better when that happens."

"That's easy to say, Charlie. But you're not me!" retorted Al.

"Geez, guys," said Rick, "you sound like kids. This is no one's fault. Genevieve's a little old lady. Why would we suspect that she'd have drugs hidden somewhere? Charlie, you head home for some rest. I'm takin' Al back to the hospital for the night. I want more drip through his system before we face the media tomorrow. No arguments, Al. I'm the boss here."

"Do you have any idea how badly I want to sleep in my own bed?" pleaded Al.

"Yes, I know," said Rick. "You're just like thousands of people I've treated. No one wants to stay in a hospital. I understand. But that's where you're going to spend the night."

"Okay, let's get it over with. Take me. I'm dead tired," conceded Al. "I can call JoAnne, can't I…to tell her what's happened and where I am?"

"Absolutely," agreed Rick, "and if she wants to join you, I can set you up with one of our new suites."

Al thought about that for a while.

"On second thought, I think I'll wait for the morning. If I call her now and she comes over, she'll fuss around all night and I won't get any sleep."

"I think that's a good choice," agreed Rick.

Rick and Al got into Rick's sports car and headed away. Charlie sat in his SUV for a minute, thinking. He finally started the engine, drove slowly out of the lot, and headed down Highway 14-61 to Westby.

CHAPTER 70

It had been dark for an hour but Genevieve wasn't tired. Exhilarated by the escape from her captors, hitching a ride to Indianapolis, buying a car and heading south, she had ridden the adrenaline rush for seven hours on her way south.

After starting out toward Texas, she changed her mind as she maneuvered her way around Indianapolis on the beltway; the car's GPS set to take her toward Dallas. She thought that she would be harder to find if she changed the program. As she reached the interchange with I-65, she decided to take I-65 south. She didn't know, of course, that she had been on this freeway a day earlier for several hours, as the trucker drove his rig south. Now she drove on winding roads for four hours, and then stopped for gas and food.

She traded cars at Elizabethtown, Kentucky. She swapped the Dodge Charger for a 2009 Chrysler Sebring. It was a nondescript, gray, four-door model. It was clean, had 68,000 miles on it, and a full tank of gas. She drove it as far as Nashville before changing cars again. This time, she bought a Jeep Cherokee from what appeared to be a questionable sales lot on the outskirts of town.

Five hours later, having crossed into Alabama and darkness closing in, she decided a night of rest would be good. After she cleared the Huntsville area, she looked for a place to stop, pulling off the freeway at Hartselle and following the signs to the Express Inn. It was a pleasant looking place. The building had white stucco entrances that opened onto the sidewalk in front of the units. *This is good because I can be near the car.*

She checked in and made her way to the room. It was pleasant: two double beds, neatly made, and a kitchen unit. She decided to go out and get a few things to tide her over, since she clearly was not dressed in a manner that would afford a comfortable meal at a restaurant. She found a Big A convenience store just down the road. She bought some snacks and two TV dinners. She also purchased a small box of hazelnut-flavored Green Mountain Coffee K-cups for the room's Keurig maker.

She returned to the motel, put the steak dinner in the microwave, brewed a cup of coffee and, while that was happening, fully undressed after making certain the blinds were completely drawn. Taking the cup of coffee with her, she went into the spacious bathroom, washed all of her clothes in the sink and hung them on the quaint gas drying machine mounted to the wall. She took a long shower, making the water as hot as her skin could stand, in an attempt to wash away the grime from a two-day journey.

I sure thwarted those nice young men from La Crosse, she thought to herself as she toweled off and then wrapped one of the large bath towels around her to retrieve her dinner from the microwave. Before sitting down at the small table, she turned on the flat screen TV and changed the channel to CNN. *If I make the news, I will find it here first.*

She ate her dinner slowly, enjoyed the coffee, and was relieved when she saw a number of what she thought as more minor stories on the news channel. There was nothing on the escaped serial killer in Wisconsin. *I wonder what's up with that?* She would have expected it to be a lead news story by now. After thinking about it for a while, she decided it was good news. It gave her another day to put some distance between her and La Crosse.

Her dinner consumed, she turned off the TV and crawled into bed naked for the first time since Henry had been alive. *My, what a sex life we had.*, She let sleep wash over her, hoping she might enjoy Henry once more in her dreams. She was far too exhausted to dream.

CHAPTER 71

In Arlington Heights, Peggy and Kelly finished cleaning the dinner dishes while Julie supervised getting the kids off to bed. Announcing that she was utterly exhausted, Kelly excused herself and headed for a spare bedroom upstairs. Peggy and Julie snuggled on the living room couch.

"I just can't figure out what Genevieve is up to," began Julie, cuddling closer to Peggy. "We both know she didn't commit those acts, so why did she tell the police and us that she did? It's very bizarre."

"Julie, if you really murdered those men then, yes, it is bizarre. I really think that you hallucinated. The details and timing that you remember from committing the crimes are all wrong. Genevieve makes sense as the murderer, except for her age. Think about it. She has a much better knowledge of drugs. She has been compounding sedatives for years. You have done some compounding, but I don't think you have the kind of knowledge to put the right combination together and deliver the right doses that killed those men. Do you really think you could have done that?"

"Peggy, I *did* it! I remember doing it. Why can't you believe that? Genevieve had no real motive. I just wonder what all of this is really about. What's making her do this?"

"I think she did it and you're hallucinating!" said Peggy with firmness in her tone. She was weary of these conversations with Julie. Peggy truly believed that Julie's mind, somehow, became confused after Shawn's death. "I know you think you were there. Julie, when I've asked you about the specifics, your answers have been vague at best and completely off track at worst. Somehow I think things got all messed up in your head and you have been blaming yourself without cause."

"I am not, Peggy! I don't know how many times I can tell you that I murdered those people."

"Okay, fine. Just for a moment, let's suppose that you really did it. If you killed all those men, and if Genevieve really is your aunt, as she says, then it makes sense. She wants to protect you because you're family. You have a son to raise. Genevieve does not have children. I can see why she would want to protect her niece. Julie, if you really did kill those men, think about it this way: what a marvelous gift this is for Brody, you, and us. Genevieve was so generous in giving us this house. It makes sense that she'd admit to the killings. After all, she has lived a good life. At her age, most of it is past. In prison, she will be okay. No one is going to bother her and my guess is that the guards will give her special treatment. She has wealth, we know that. There is nothing she needs. So what about this doesn't make sense to you?"

Julie wasn't convinced. "Who would spend the rest of their life in jail for crimes that someone else committed?"

"I don't know anyone; that's true. I just don't believe that you did these killings, Julie. I truly don't think you have it in you. How about this? Genevieve is telling the truth. Maybe your subconscious merged with some facts that really aren't facts, but hallucinations or bad dreams instead. Even if they're true, if Genevieve is your aunt, she is old and childless. It does make some sense that she'd give you this incredible gift."

"It may sound logical to you, Peggy. But it's not. Can I really let her take the blame and the fall for my crimes? I'm not sure I can…in fact, I doubt I can."

"Julie, let's just give it a rest, okay? Let's go to bed. You may feel differently about this in the morning."

Peggy got up from the couch. She turned off the lights, took Julie by the hand, and led her upstairs. Julie followed as if in a trance, her eyes filled with tears that occasionally dribbled down her cheeks. Peggy took Julie's head in her hands and kissed away the tears.

"C'mon on, I'll help you get ready for bed. I'll stay with you until you're asleep," said Peggy gently.

A few minutes later, Peggy helped Julie remove her make-up. She washed Julie's face gently, helped her out of her clothing and into her nightgown. She took her hand, led her to the bed, helped her under the covers, and then climbed in on the opposite side. Peggy embraced her friend, whispering to her for 15 minutes. When Julie's breathing grew steady and deep, Peggy slipped out of the bed, checked on Lauren, Jake, and Brody, and went to her own room. She prayed that Julie would begin to understand that either Genevieve was guilty, as she had admitted, or, if Julie was telling the truth, was giving her the gift of freedom.

Peggy quickly fell asleep, haunted by thoughts of Julie turning her back on Genevieve's gift. Even though she didn't tell Julie, she was terribly conflicted as well. However, she truly believed her friend was hallucinating. Even so, how could she help Julie? What sort of psychiatric help would get Julie to believe, if true, that she never killed any of those men? *Please, Lord*, she silently prayed, *help Julie. Please help me to help her*. Peggy began to recite the Lord's Prayer but fell asleep before she could finish it.

CHAPTER 72

It was before 7 when Al and Charlie arrived at Ma's to fuel up for a busy day. The topic of discussion: the upcoming news conference, just two hours away.

Charlie exercised constraint this time. He ordered his customary four eggs, toast and pancakes, but passed on the usual waffle.

"Starving yourself now, partner?" asked Al. "I'm the guy who's on the fence for letting the killer escape. No one is going to give you a bad time."

"Cut it out! Damnit Al, you know that we all share the blame for the escape. If we had done it according to the book, Rick and I wouldn't have left you alone with Genevieve."

"C'mon, Charlie! Do I really look like someone who should need help keeping an old lady in handcuffs from escaping?"

"No, you don't, but facts are facts. If we had done it by the goddamn book, Genevieve would likely be in custody. We wouldn't be getting ready for a news conference. Oh, and speaking of news conferences, what are you going to say?"

"I'm gonna tell the truth. What else is there?"

"I mean, what facts are you gonna cover?"

"I plan to tell 'em about our trip to Illinois and that we took Genevieve to the laboratory in the garage, where she admitted to the killings."

"You're not gonna tell 'em everything about the trip, are you?"

"Charlie, are you nuts? Of course, I'm gonna tell 'em that before the lab tour, we stole a few minutes for some make-out time with the women we had met on an earlier trip. These women were our earlier murder suspects. Gimme a little credit, will you? I'm not ready to have someone investigating *my* homicide."

"Just needed to ask, partner, just needed to ask," replied Charlie. "I couldn't care less. My marriage is on life support, but I worry about you and JoAnne."

"Right now, I'm tryin' not to think about anything but the conference. I assume you'll cover the trip from Arlington Heights to Sun Prairie. I'll pick it up at that point and talk about what I remember of the escape. We'll let the chief and sheriff handle the rest of it. Okay?"

"Yup, fine. Oh, look what's here."

Their food had finally arrived. Evie was balancing four plates on one arm and carrying Al's breakfast in her right hand.

"Here we are," stated Evie. "Eggs over easy, bacon and toast for Al. We got eggs over hard—four of 'em—with bacon and sausage, hash browns, and pancakes for Charlie. Honest to God, Charlie, I don't know how you survive these meals. There's enough cholesterol in that breakfast to kill an elephant."

"Cut it out!" growled Charlie. "I'm just a growin' boy. Growin' boys need their food, damn it, Evie."

"Don't you be cussin' at me, Charlie. Yes, you're a growin' boy! You're growin' wide rather'n tall," quipped Evie, laughing as she walked away.

"You'd better pick up the pace, Charlie. We have to get to the station to make sure everything is set up right."

"Uh huh," mumbled Charlie, his mouth full of food. "Be d'n in a mi'ut."

"Chew and eat; chew and eat," said Al, brightening as his friend moved through his food much like a wood chipper moves through a pile of brush. *Come to think of it*, he thought, *Charlie even looks kind of like a wood chipper.*

CHAPTER 73

As Charlie and Al ate, Genevieve started to stir after a dreamless night. She liked the feeling of the crisp sheets on her naked body. The sheets brought back memories of Henry. She'd awakened many times to the light touch of Henry's hand on her hip. It was a restless hand, too, that always crept southward until he found the perfect spot. *Oh my, if I don't stop this, I am going to be guilty of social crimes, too. It had been such fun; such great fun!*

Rolling over, sitting up, and putting her feet on the cold floor quickly erased all notions of friskiness from her mind. She walked, still naked, to the bathroom, relieved herself, and turned on the shower. Before she had fallen asleep the previous night, the seed of a plan began to form in her mind. She'd the presence of mind to convert her cash accounts into cashier's checks right after she found out about the second visit from the La Crosse men. She knew that she'd have to redeem some of them for money before the news broke or they would quickly lead the police to her.

Genevieve decided to visit the public library, if there was one in the area. There'd be a computer there for research to see if her idea would work.

After paying her motel bill and directions to the library in her head, she arrived at the library promptly at 9 when the doors opened. Thirty minutes later, she had what she wanted. Genevieve made a call to a land broker in Hayden, Alabama, just over 50 miles away. She soon had an appointment for 4 in the afternoon. She got into the car, drove back to I-65 and turned south. An hour and a half later, she arrived in Birmingham, looking for Regions Bank at 1901 Fifth Avenue N. Her library search had revealed that Regions was the largest bank in Birmingham. *That would be her best bet at anonymity.*

At the bank, she cashed five of her cashier's checks for a total of $100,000. She took the 990 hundred dollar bills and put them in a purse that went right into her handbag. The remaining $1,000, broken into varying denominations, went into another compartment in the purse.

Back in the car, she drove to North Birmingham to find a bail bondsman. Soon she found one, the sign tacked to a ramshackle brick building on a street filled with young loiterers. She parked outside, went in, and quickly got the information she needed.

An hour and a half later, she was now Rosalie Burton of Cleveland, Ohio. She had a new driver's license, Social Security card, and two other forms of photo ID's. She could simply disappear and start a new life.

At 5 p.m. she was the owner of a rustic 51-acre plot t in the Hayden area of the Alabama National Forest. The plot t included a two-bedroom cottage in good condition, so she was told, and had all the comforts of home. It came furnished and ready for move in. After closing and paying for the property with more cashier's checks, which made the land broker incredibly happy, she drove to her new property, parked the car behind the house and went inside to inspect the purchase.

She found it exactly as she hoped, complete with sheets and towels, dishes and small appliances that included a coffee maker, blender, and mixer. There was a 27-inch television set hooked to a rooftop antenna. The broker told her she'd be able to receive signals from the Fox and NBC affiliates in Birmingham and, depending upon the conditions, maybe the CBS affiliate, too. Although Birmingham was fewer than 25 miles away as the crow flies, the mountain ranges that bordered her property made reception spotty.

Perfectly okay, she thought. She wanted privacy and assumed she'd found it. If she had covered her tracks effectively, maybe she could live out the rest of her life in comfort.

CHAPTER 74

While Genevieve was settling into her hideaway, Al and Charlie were enjoying a beer at Schmidty's Bar and Restaurant on State Road, hoping they were discreet enough to enjoy some privacy. The three La Crosse TV stations had been replaying segments of the news conference all day, and their reporters were scurrying around the city looking for sound bites to spice up their reports. Already WLAX, the ABC affiliate, was promoting a special that would air at 8 p.m. on Friday. Word around town was that ABC and CBS network news teams were on their way to La Crosse.

Al and Charlie had left police headquarters at 3 p.m. The morning news conference had been held at about 8. After three straight hours of grilling, they were both exhausted. While Rick, Chief Whigg, and Sheriff Hooper had handled their parts of the conference excellently, with the exception of a few extra minutes with Rick following the conclusion of the formal conference, Al and Charlie had been on the spot for an unrelenting series of questions from reporters.

The formal part of the conference went well. The chief handled the background in his customary soft, easygoing nature. He made sure Al, Charlie, and Rick received plenty of compliments during his explanation in an effort to lessen coverage of the escape.

Rick had done a thorough job of the identification process, carefully covering the discovery of the puncture wound and giving full credit to Dr. Patricia Grebin for noticing the wound. He also praised Sarah Gile for the research that led to identification of the sedatives used to make the drowning victims compliant and helpful in committing their own deaths. Rick's explanation provided a thorough description of the drugs used and the reactions they caused. He led reporters through the steps to the discovery of DNA evidence. He also gave reporters a verbal picture of the laboratory built for Genevieve Wangen by her husband Henry. Photos of the lab were also available to reporters. They were snapped up hastily.

As Al described Genevieve's arrest, including her confession in the laboratory, he seemed ill at ease under the bright lights. Nonetheless, he had done a competent job of taking reporters through the steps that brought Genevieve into custody. When he turned it over to Charlie, his friend's manner injected some sorely needed humor into the conference. He talked about sedating Genevieve for the night in Arlington Heights, collecting her for the trip north the next morning, and the uneventful drive from Illinois to the truck stop.

"There was no hint that the articulate, prim-and-proper, and anxious-to-confess old lady had anything up her sleeve, let alone those drugs," commented Charlie.

When Al talked about the escape, the room went completely silent. In fact, it got so quiet you could hear his footsteps.

"I brought Genevieve back to the car after we had eaten," explained Al. "Charlie and Rick were there when I handcuffed Genevieve and put her in the backseat."

"We briefly chatted for a while. I turned on the radio to listen to some music. I had a big lunch and felt kind of drowsy. The next thing I knew, I was waking up on a gurney in the truck stop."

"And Genevieve was gone, right?" shouted a reporter.

"Yes, Genevieve was gone. It must've happened within 15 minutes of Charlie and Rick going into the restaurant. I really don't remember anything, although Rick's investigation proved that I was injected with a sedative—likely the same sedative that Genevieve used on most of her victims. That makes sense because the victims drowned; they didn't die from injected drugs."

"How do you feel now?" asked a female reporter.

"Obviously, ma'am, I'm embarrassed. I feel terrible," began Al when another reporter broke in.

"What would you do differently?"

"Recognizing that hindsight is always 20/20, I would not have been so relaxed. If I'd been more alert, I would've seen what she was doing. Maybe I could've stopped it. But I didn't get that chance. Now we're looking for her. We need your help."

After several more questions, Chief Whigg stepped back in.

"We will answer more questions later, but right now I'd like to take you through our next steps and solicit your help, okay?"

When no one objected, the chief began to speak.

"Thanks to the young women who lived with Genevieve in Arlington Heights, we have obtained a photo of the suspect. We are hoping you will use it and distribute it widely. Make it available to your networks and your other publications. And, Harry, we're hoping you and your colleagues over at the *La Crosse Tribune* will also make it available to the Associated Press. It will be the key to catching her."

"At this point, we have no real idea where she is. We searched the woods around the truck stop thoroughly; we thought she'd be there. She wasn't. It seems likely she caught a ride in a vehicle that had stopped at the truck stop, but we don't know what kind of vehicle. None of the truckers, who left the truck stop that afternoon, is aware of a passenger. To be honest, she could be anywhere. But we are hoping she will make mistakes that will lead us to her. With your help, we might get a break. Thank you."

Sheriff Hooper stepped in, providing everyone with a thorough description of the subject as well as an update on what she was wearing when she escaped.

"We are reasonably confident," reported Hooper, "that she did not have a change of clothes with her, because the small suitcases she had packed and brought with her remained in the vehicle after the escape. She could have purchased some clothes. We have no idea if she had cash with her and, if so, how much."

An hour filled with Q&A passed quickly, after which the broadcast journalists scattered to meet deadlines and record sound bites for breaking news reports. The print media journalists hung around and continued questioning.

Soon, the story became national news. Everyone with a television set heard about the capture of the elderly serial killer and her escape. It was certain to be the story of the year in the La Crosse area and it would be right up there on the national list, too.

As the two lawmen enjoyed a beer off the beaten track, tucked into a back booth in Schmidty's bar room, they began to formulate a plan.

"I think we need to go back to Chicago," began Charlie. "Spend some more time with Peggy, Julie, and Kelly. We really haven't talked to them about their opinions of Genevieve and her capability to carry out the killings. For all we know, she might have had help."

"I think you're right, Charlie."

Monday was a beautiful day with not a cloud in the sky. The temperature was brisk, but it was still warm for January. Charlie's Suburban headed south. Al was in the front seat with Charlie. Rick was in the back, having taken the week off to make the trip.

Charlie thought about Kelly as he drove. He was excited and couldn't wait to see her. Rick was also excited. He had enjoyed Peggy's company and was anxious to see her again. Al was more cautious, but Julie's good looks dominated his thoughts. It had been a bad month. First, he felt responsible for Genevieve's escape, no matter what the chief and his friends said. He felt even worse that he was having an emotional and physical affair with the dark-haired beauty. This meant that he was cheating on JoAnne, who had been his love in high school and turned into a wonderful wife.

***

Four days later, following lunch with the three women in Arlington Heights, the Chevy truck was again on I-90, this time heading north after a disappointing week for the case but an exciting one for the three couples. The visit made Al feel even more conflicted.

They had spent each night with Julie, Peggy, and Kelly. After the La Crosse trio spent Monday night at the Holiday Inn Express, at Julie's insistence, Al, Charlie, and Rick took over the apartment over the carriage house. The men drew straws for the bedrooms and hide-a-bed in the living room off the kitchen. Rick and Charlie won the bedrooms and Al wound up in the living room.

From then on, it was all about their personal relationships. The pace, to say the least, was feverish.

After a nice dinner out on Tuesday evening, all three couples went their separate ways when they got home. Rick and Peggy went to the apartment, Kelly and Charlie occupied the family room, and Al and Julie took over the living room. Kelly was now occupying a bedroom in the main house. She, at the invitation of Peggy and Julie, planned to move into the carriage house after the men left.

Peggy and Rick talked for a while, then lapsed into an easygoing romantic session. Deep kisses and tender fondling followed. If it hadn't been for Al's return two hours later, it's likely they would have wound up in bed. Each felt a bit cheated about this

Charlie and Kelly were past all of this. Each of them was partially undressed when Al called out that he was leaving.

"I'll be along in a minute, pal," answered Charlie.

Al and Julie had been more subdued. Although they kissed several times and held each other tightly through the evening, they spent most of the time talking.

Julie, Al sensed, had things to tell him, but even though he tried every trick he knew to get her to open up, she remained resolutely silent, except for saying how she felt about him. The mere mention of Al's name animated her speech and features.

"I need to tell you, Al, that you are the nicest male human being I have met in 13 years. I love to be with you and I love to have you snuggling me. I have only felt that way about one other man."

"I'm flattered," said Al tenderly. "But I'm feeling guilty. I have a wonderful woman at home, and here I am wishing I could spend more time with you."

"I can understand that," answered Julie. "How about we make the most of the time we have together, whatever that is? That will help us know if this is real or not."

Charlie and Rick were having no trouble with this at all. Peggy was all over Rick the first time they were alone in the apartment. Soon they were nude and making love with the excitement of teenagers. They were good together, incredibly good.

I hope this lasts forever, thought Rick to himself. He had been looking fruitlessly for this kind of romance since finishing his residency in St. Louis. Maybe this was it. Peggy's thoughts were nearly identical. Since completing college and finding her job at Kahn, she never went without dates. But she never found a man to whom she would make a long-term commitment. She had slept with a few of her dates, but only for sex, never because of love. This, she sensed, was different…very different.

Before Friday arrived, all three couples had made love. Although Al felt guilty and Julie knew it, both of them were unable to stop. The sex was incredible, mindboggling, and toe-tingling. Several times she nearly told him her secret, but stopped, unwilling to end the magic.

Charlie and Kelly were headed for a long-term relationship, already talking about what they would do when Charlie's divorce, a foregone conclusion, was final. The biggest issue right now was where they would live. Kelly adamantly insisted that it should be Arlington Heights, where there was no baggage for either of them. Charlie didn't know if he could leave La Crosse. He worried about being separated from his kids.

Rick and Peggy were falling in love. They were made for each other. The love they shared in their three days together was the best either of them had ever experienced. They, too, talked about making their relationship more permanent. Peggy knew that she would move, if he asked her. After all, as a nurse, she was eminently employable in today's health care market.

And so, as the Suburban began its trek back to La Crosse, each of its occupants was quiet, lost in thought. Nothing that they had learned in Arlington Heights offered any clue to Genevieve's whereabouts. The two lawmen were certain Julie, Peggy, and Kelly were being truthful regarding the mystery of Genevieve's disappearance. But Al also knew there was something that Julie hadn't shared with him. He could tell something was bothering her—he was an investigator after all. Al didn't know where their relationship was headed, but he also knew that he was serious about Julie. He thought this was love.

Back in La Crosse by midafternoon, they dropped Rick off at Gundersen. Al and Charlie met with Chief Whigg and Sheriff Hooper at the La Crosse County Law Enforcement Center.

They told their bosses they had learned nothing useful. As far as Julie, Peggy, and Kelly were concerned, Genevieve's whereabouts was a mystery; she had vanished without a trace.

Chief Whigg revealed that there was one lead and it was going to take Al and Charlie to Birmingham, Alabama. It was in Birmingham, the chief said, that Genevieve Wangen had, almost a month earlier, cashed a number of cashier's checks made payable to her. The amount was a staggering $2.4 million. Aside from the checks, there had not been another mention of Mrs. Wangen, or any clues to her whereabouts.

Al and Charlie would be flying to Birmingham on Monday, where they would meet with employees of Regions Bank. The bank employees had met with Genevieve and turned the cashier's checks into a fortune in cash.

Buoyed by a new lead, the two lawmen headed home to prepare for the next step in the investigation.

CHAPTER 75

In Arlington Heights, Julie and Peggy helped Kelly move her things to the apartment above the carriage house. It wasn't much of a job. Kelly had been living in a furnished apartment, so the only things they had to move were her clothes and a few personal belongings. After helping her settle in, Peggy asked Kelly to come for dinner. Peggy and Julie headed back to the main house, where cleaning chores awaited them.

The kids were out, so the two women decided to make a game out of cleaning. They would reward each other with special prizes after each chore. Kisses, snuggles, feels and more were on the prize list. The chores were prioritized; the more difficult and demanding tasks earned the biggest rewards.

It was a good afternoon. Peggy put two chickens in the oven to roast about 3 p.m. Chores completed soon thereafter and each of the women breathless from the rewards, at about 4 o'clock they settled into the living room sofa. Julie snuggled into Peggy's arms, put her head on Peggy's shoulder, and began to talk.

"Peggy, I'm trying to sort out everything I did. I'm trying to understand why I did those horrible things. I just can't put it together. There are so many gaps. Do you think I blotted out the most horrible things?"

Peggy listened for a bit. Julie finally paused for breath.

"You mean *if* you did those things? Don't you think that's a valid question, Julie?"

"No, it's not a valid question!" responded Julie immediately, fierceness in her voice. "I know I killed those men! I just can't remember the details. It's maddening."

"You know, Julie, I'm concerned about your memory loss. Aren't you?"

"Sure. It's horrible to know you did something and not remember how you did it."

"There's something very funny about that, Julie. You're too young to suffer from memory loss. I think you need to see a doctor. Maybe someone at the clinic…"

"Absolutely not! Don't even think it! There's no way I could open up to anyone at work. Except you, of course. I trust you."

"Julie, patient-doctor privilege is a strong ethic in the medical profession, even required by law. If not at Kahn, then where? I think you need to get help for your own peace of mind."

"God, Peggy, how could I confess these awful things to a stranger? I don't think I could. What if I wind up in prison? What would happen to Brody?"

"You know that if anything happens to you, I will raise Brody. I will do it as if he is my own son. I expect you would do the same for me, wouldn't you?" asked Peggy.

"Sure! Absolutely! No question about it!" responded Julie.

Julie buried her head in her hands and began to sob.

"I have a confession," began Peggy, just loud enough to be heard by Julie. "I talked to Dr. Toritz at the clinic about your symptoms."

"You what?" Julie was nearly hysterical now. "How could you? Peggy, you're supposed to be my friend. How could you do that?"

"Shut up and listen for a minute!" spat out Peggy. "He doesn't know who I was talking about. I asked using hypotheticals."

Julie calmed a bit.

"He told me what I was talking about isn't common, but it does happen. It's called something like Traumatic Cerebrovascular Accident. It happens in cases where severe anxiety triggers a stroke-like condition," said Peggy.

"Are you saying I had a stroke?" asked Julie. "A stroke makes no sense."

"Well, it doesn't make sense that you don't remember the details of 14 murders either. I think the least you should do is see a doctor."

Silence settled in. Julie spoke in a very small voice.

Will you go with me?"

"Of course I will; I will do whatever you want," said Peggy soothingly.

"But I don't even know where to go or where to start."

"How about I talk to Dr. Toritz? I'll tell him the person doesn't want to come to Kahn. I'll ask what he would recommend."

"I think that would work," said Julie hesitantly. "Let me think about it. I'll let you know tomorrow, okay?"

"Great. Now let's rest for a while before dinner."

Dinner was a fun affair. The children chattered incessantly. Kelly, being relatively young, playfully argued with the kids and they loved it. It was obvious that Kelly's move into the carriage house was something the kids were going to love. Julie was quiet, noted Peggy, but she seemed in a more upbeat mood.

After dinner they watched *The Blind Side*. There was popcorn and soda during the film. When it was over, everyone was tired, even the boys. It was just a little after 10 when Peggy turned off the downstairs lights and headed upstairs.

When she opened the door to her bedroom, she was surprised to find Julie already there.

"I don't want to be alone," confessed Julie. "I need you near me."

"Sure, no problem. I'm gonna take a quick shower and I'll be in."

"Please hurry," urged Julie. "Please…"

Fifteen minutes later when Peggy came back, Julie was asleep and snoring gently. She crept into bed and turned toward her friend but didn't touch her. She listened to Julie's breathing steadily for a while, and then also fell asleep.

The next day, Julie was quiet as she and Peggy made lunches for the kids, steered them off to school, showered, and got ready for work.

As they walked from the parking lot to the clinic, Julie spoke.

"Are you going to talk to Dr. Toritz today?"

"I plan to," responded Peggy. "I'll let you know what I find out."

When Julie joined Peggy for lunch, her friend had some news.

"I had my little chat with Dr. Toritz. He recommended a female psychiatrist at Uptown Psychiatry. I have all the information. Do you want to call, or should I?"

"Could you call?" asked Julie, her eyes filling with tears. "And make sure you schedule a time that both of us can make. Wednesday afternoons are best for me."

"That'll work for me, too," said Peggy. "I'll call this afternoon."

***

Two weeks later, Julie and Peggy arrived at Uptown Psychiatry to see Dr. Ananya Agnihotri. Julie felt comfortable with her immediately.

While Peggy attended the first session, her presence was unnecessary. Dr. Agnihotri was charming, friendly, personable, and reassuring.

On her third appointment, Julie confessed the crimes she believed she had committed to Dr. Agnihotri. While the doctor made no promises about silence, after quizzing Julie extensively and noting the wide gaps in her memory, she came to believe that extensive and gentle treatments would be needed to determine if Julie really had done those crimes.

Thus began a long-term journey to help Julie figure out her own mind. She saw the doctor every two weeks. As the months rolled past, progress was made, but it wasn't sufficient for the doctor to determine if Julie's memories were real or not.

CHAPTER 76

The same morning that Peggy called Dr. Agnihotri to make Julie's first appointment, Al and Charlie boarded a Delta jet at the La Crosse Airport. They were bound for Birmingham and seated together in exit row eight, seats C and D. It was a short hop to Minneapolis, where they caught a flight to Atlanta and then changed planes again, landing in Birmingham at 4:24 p.m., right on time.

The Birmingham Police Chief had offered to send a car, but Al and Charlie opted for a rental, thinking it would give them more independence. They booked a room at the Embassy Suites. They'd be bunking in the same room. Saving money was important, the sheriff told Charlie.

At 9 a.m. on Tuesday morning, February 14, 2012, the two La Crosse lawmen walked into the Birmingham Police Department and asked the male receptionist to see Chief A.C. Charles.

The chief was a big man with a wide smile and a firm handshake. It was obvious from the drawl that he was Birmingham born and bred.

The chief brought them into his office, a comfortable suite in a corner of the building overlooking downtown.

"Great view," said Al, looking out the window before taking the offered seat.

"I like it, because I can always find action by looking out the window," said Chief Charles. "Sometimes, though, it can be distracting."

As they talked about the view and the pleasant weather in Birmingham compared to the 12-below temperatures that gripped La Crosse, a tall, slender, handsome man, looking about 45, walked in.

"Meet Detective Ralph Walters," said Chief Charles, introducing Charlie and Al. "Ralph followed up on the few leads we had after we traced your suspect to Regions Bank here. The trail quickly dried up, but

Ralph can tell you all about that. You can work with him while you're here. Ralph's been on the force for more than 30 years. He knows every nook and cranny in Birmingham for sure, and maybe in Alabama, too."

"That's an exaggeration," said Detective Walters, smiling. "But I've been around a long time. I'll help in every way I can. I'm not sure there's much I can do, though. Genevieve Wangen arrived here on January 16 and disappeared the same day. She's apparently a crafty cookie. Except for what she looks like, nobody could tell us anything more. I searched every place and talked to everyone I know who might know something. To me, it's obvious she had help. I couldn't find that person. Her trail has gone cold."

"It looks to us like she made Birmingham the place of her disappearance," agreed Al, "and from every lead we've followed and what you've said, she did a good job of it."

"You're right. We were on her not one hour after she visited Regions, but she was gone without a trace," said Detective Walters. "I spent some time on it off and on for a couple of weeks, but nothing I tried turned up anything."

The three lawmen talked until noon. Al felt they had not left a stone overturned. While the Birmingham detective tried his best to be helpful, Genevieve had vanished, pure and simple.

They treated Detective Walters to lunch, thanked him, and visited the folks at Regions Bank. President T.L. Evans surprised them. Expecting a man, they found instead a good-looking, dark-haired woman.

"Call me Terri. I like to surprise people like you. I saw it in your faces. You were expecting a man, weren't you?"

When Al and Charlie sheepishly nodded, Terri smiled. "Can I get you anything before we get started—coffee, water…soda?"

Al settled for coffee and Charlie asked for a Pepsi.

"This is Coke country," said Terri. "Pepsi is a bad word down here in Dixie. I'll forget you said it." She also had coffee. When the beverages were delivered, Charlie got a coke and Terri began to fill them in.

"Mrs. Wangen showed up at our main bank here. She spoke to a teller and asked for someone with whom she might talk about converting cashier's checks to cash. When the teller found out the amount, she called me. I helped Mrs. Wangen in our office. With that kind of money involved, I naturally hoped that we might begin a banking relationship. She was pretty adamant that wouldn't happen. She was looking for property. When she found it, she wanted to be ready to snap it up. She said that she always paid cash. I tried to direct her to our real estate division for help but she didn't want any of that. She just wanted the money. We had the $2.4 million, but it took our cash resources down to near nothing."

"Ma'am," began Al, "did she say anything else that might offer a clue as to where she was going?"

"She said nothing that I remember. I got the idea that she was looking around here, but I don't think she said that. I guess I just thought that why else would she come in here for $2.4 million?"

"I agree," said Al, following up. "But there wasn't any hint of where she might be headed? No request for information?"

"Not a thing," said Terri, flashing her brown eyes. "She was all business. She just wanted the money and to be gone."

Al and Charlie spent another 15 minutes probing the bank executive's memory but found not one helpful piece of information.

As they walked out of the bank, Charlie spoke.

"Now what the hell do we do? Do we even know where to look? This is one fuckin' mess, if you ask me."

Al looked at his friend and laughed.

"You've got it, pal. It is one fuckin' mess. But I've got an idea. How about we find a nice place for dinner—I'll treat? I'll tell you what I have in mind."

"Now yer talkin'," replied Charlie. "I'm ready to eat." He looked at his watch. "It's been 4 1/2 hours since lunch. I'm goddamn hungry."

"Yer always hungry, Charlie."

They went back to the hotel, freshened up, and then asked the concierge for a suggestion. "Hot and Hot Fish Shop," replied the concierge. "When yer here, ya gotta do it; it's great!"

Great it was. Charlie was like a kid in a candy store. He finally settled on three pork dishes and two shellfish plates. Al watched in awe as his friend put away more food than he could believe.

"Ya, know, Al, a little dessert would be nice. But this is a kinda classy place. I've really gotta fart, so I think we oughta leave."

"Whatever you say, partner," said Al, laughing. He paid the bill with a personal credit card because he wasn't certain how he would explain a $600 bill to the chief. *Actually*, he thought, *I'm not sure how I'm gonna explain it to JoAnne, either. Oh well, I'll work it out later.*

Outside the restaurant, Charlie's expulsion was so loud that Al checked the windows on the sides of nearby buildings. "Geez, Charlie, that's the biggest fart I've ever heard. How do you do that?"

"Well when you work like a horse and eat like a horse," explained Charlie, "ya fart like a horse. That's what my old man always said and I believe 'im."

Even though their hotel was east of the restaurant, Al began to walk west. "Hey, Al, yer goin' the wrong way," said Charlie, grabbing him by the arm.

"I know that, Charlie," said Al, "but the wind is blowing out of the west. If you think I want to be downwind of that recent explosion, you're nuts. I'm gonna find a cab up here. And if you've got any other gas stored up, I suggest you get rid of it before getting in the cab. If not, you'll be in the cab alone. I'm pretty sure the cabbie'll bail with me."

"Goddamnit, Al, knock it off!" shouted Charlie.

"Okay, okay. Let's forget it," suggested Al.

They slept well that night and for the next two. They ate well every night. Even though Al had them call every realtor in the Birmingham phone book, they failed to turn up even one promising lead.

By Thursday night, Al was totally discouraged. "It's a dry hole, pal. Time to get home. We'll just have to hope she screws up one of these days."

"She will," replied Charlie. "I'm goddamn sure she will!"

EPILOGUE

November 2014.

In La Crosse, Wisconsin; Arlington Heights, Illinois; and Hayden, Alabama, people were thinking about the series of drownings that took place in La Crosse from 1997 through 2011. For fourteen years, one young man had drowned each year after drinking heavily in downtown bars and ultimately walking to and disappearing into the Mississippi River.

On this day in La Crosse, Peggy Russell and Rick Olson were celebrating their first anniversary. Hopelessly in love with each other, neither Peggy nor Rick bothered to think about the deaths that brought them together nearly three years earlier.

Charlie, now divorced, was aggressively courting Kelly Hammermeister. The couple was planning their marriage, although no decision had yet been made about their place of residence. Both knew that detail would have to be decided soon. The only things they had decided so far were that Al, Rick, Julie and Kelly would be in the wedding. The ceremony would take place in Arlington Heights.

Al, still the chief of detectives in La Crosse, was haunted by the drowning deaths that had ended following the confession and disappearance of the alleged serial killer. He was also haunted by the hidden love that he shared with Julie Sonoma. Right at that moment, she was in Arlington Heights, thinking about the drownings that had begun with her first love, Shawn Sorensen. She and Al saw each other as frequently as their busy lives would allow. Julie was now in charge of all nurses at the Kahn Clinic and raising a standout high school athlete. She and Brody continued to live in the house on North Kennicott. Julie purchased Peggy's share of the property.

Brody Sorensen was the spitting image of his father, reminding his mother daily of her first love. The love that had sent her, she believed, on a killing spree that lasted for fourteen years. *Someday,* Julie thought, *perhaps she and Al would be together permanently.* She knew that would be a problem. She was comfortable with their clandestine relationship. They saw each other infrequently, but each time they did, she wondered what he would do if she told him the truth about the unbelievable gift from Genevieve. Meanwhile, she still kept appointments with Dr. Agnihotri, who believed they were making progress. The doctor obviously believed that some sort of mental event had messed up Julie's brain, causing her to think she did things that she hadn't.

In Hayden, Alabama, Rosalie Burton was, on this uncommonly warm day just before Thanksgiving, at the local post office, picking up a box. It contained, she knew, a variety of sedatives and opiates that she would compound, on request, in the recently completed laboratory in her comfortable cabin in the woods.

Funny, she thought, *that the gift she had given her niece led to a new identity and a new career.* Known as the Black Widow, she made killing potions for seedy figures. No one knew that the kindly, elderly Sunday school teacher's pastime was turning out deadly concoctions. Genevieve thought about this as she rocked in the chair on the porch of her cabin later that night. *Al was a very nice boy. Too bad I had to deceive him like I did. I wonder if we will meet again?*

They would. Likely soon.

ABOUT THE AUTHOR

Gary Evans had three careers until retiring and turning to his first passion: writing. *Death by Drowning* is his first work of fiction. A series of young male drownings in a town near his home on the banks of the Mississippi in Winona, MN, piqued his interest as a mystery writer. Evans spent 30 years in Midwest newsrooms as an award-winning writer, editor and publisher. He spent 12 years as Vice President at Winona State University. He ended his career as the President and CEO of Hiawatha Broadband Communication, one of the nation's first alternative entrant telecommunications firms, after 15 years. Married to Ellen, they have two grown children, Gregory and Natalie.